Johnson
2724
F. Ave.

BREAKING OUT

BREAKING OUT

DEREK MAITLAND

ST. MARTIN'S PRESS · NEW YORK

Library of Congress Cataloging in Publication Data

Maitland, Derek, 1943-
    Breaking out.

    I. Title.
PZ4.M229Br   1979   [PR6063.A353]   823'.9'14   78-19423
ISBN 0-312-09523-6

one

Noel Chisholm's transfer from Emu Plains prison farm to Parramatta Jail was an event bizarre in nature, profound in consequence and a total balls-up on the part of the driver and two prison service escorts charged with the simple task of getting him there.

Instead of their prison van nosing its way right up to the towering steel gates of the jail—a landmark of somewhat dubious historical value in the heart of Sydney's western suburbs—it managed to locate the quiet side street approaching the penitentiary and then appeared to have second thoughts about the matter. It careened up the gutter and onto a grass verge on the left side of the street, then broadsided back onto the roadway and lurched right across the pebble-studded asphalt to mount another wide grassy strip on the other side. And there it came to rest, with its steaming bonnet only three inches away from the mottled trunk of a eucalyptus tree and a lawn sprinkler spinning furiously under its chassis.

And it was there, a hundred yards from the jail's tall honey-coloured stone walls, that Chisholm elected to take leave of his escorts—grinding the gearshift back and forth to find neutral and switching the windscreen wipers on in a bid to kill the ignition. When several other attempts to quell the shuddering, overheated engine had failed, he did what he considered any other man inexperienced with prison vehicles would have done—he rammed the bloody thing into forward gear and took his foot off the clutch. And the engine's death-spasm jolted the van's front fender right against the trunk of the tree.

Safely anchored, Chisholm relaxed at the wheel and allowed his senses to merge as one with the suburban tranquillity around him, a stillness broken only by the swish and slap of the lawn sprinkler's fierce jets hosing the underside of the vehicle. He breathed deeply the precious air of freedom. He watched the jail, waiting for cries, sirens and gunshots to erupt from guardposts that sat atop each end of the front wall, their louvred windows and black tar-papered roofs belly-dancing in heat waves that shimmied off the sun-baked stone.

"We're here," he announced.

"Whassat? Where? Who? Oh . . . holy hell!"

Jennings, chief of the two-man uniformed escort party slumped together on the seat alongside Chisholm, had awakened from his coma, jerking up into a stiff-backed posture, blinking his horribly bloodshot eyes and sucking his teeth. He yawned, stretched himself and then groaned again with pain.

"Christ, I tell yer what, Nole—my mouth tastes like the inside of a bloody incinerator and my head feels like it fell off somewhere along the bloody way."

"We all fell off somewhere along the way," Chisholm murmured, gazing blearily at a parade of red-bricked bungalows, neatly trimmed lawns, frangipani blossoms, long-legged and thick-plumaged eucalypts and the gossamer comets leaping from the sprinklers—the whole tableau arranged with such sedate menace that he feared a trap, a last vilifying howl of lawn mowers if he should dare make a gauntlet-running dash from the bullwagon to the three-to-five stretch awaiting him in the jail.

"Well, at least we got here in one piece," Jennings yawned, and he began jabbing his elbow into the ribs of his uniformed companion, Roberts, who was huddled against the passenger door and apparently dead to the world. "I must be the greatest mug alive, Nole, letting you con me again like this. Especially after the last trouble you dragged me into." He gave up punching his partner and anxiously checked the man's pulse. "If I remember rightly, we left Emu Plains with you handcuffed and locked up in the back. Nothing can go wrong this time, I told myself. I've got Roberts here and the driver with me for added security . . ." His jaw suddenly dropped as an awful thought struck him. "Nole! *Where's the driver?*"

"He's in the back. I felt it best to lock him up for his own safety—and ours," Chisholm explained, studying miniature rainbows that hung in the sprinkler mists. "I'm afraid he became physically irresponsible and emotionally deranged back along the Great Western Highway, near the turnoff to Doonside. Ran a red light with speed, intent and foul language and nearly collected a fully loaded semi."

Jennings let his breath out with a whistle. "It's no bloody wonder. He's a Jehovah's Witness. He doesn't normally drink."

"You mean he doesn't drink normally," Chisholm observed. "He took only two swigs of the stuff and transformed immediately from a friendly, self-effacing young Christian into a screaming, belligerent lunatic. It takes me at least six belts to achieve that, and I don't even believe in God."

Jennings had given up trying to arouse his unconscious partner. He was now resurrecting his own person, buttoning his blue shirt and re-knotting his tie, prodding at what looked like brown acid stains on his jacket. He gently eased his peaked uniform cap from Chisholm's head and began brushing it clean with his sleeve.

"Jesus, Nole," he said, closely examining the cap's Department of Corrective Services silver insignia—making sure Chisholm hadn't swiped it or something. "It's a blessing to get you off our bloody hands. But I reckon we're going to miss you."

"I never really was one for pastoral life," Chisholm mused, watching the jail. "Contrary to popular belief, you don't commune with nature out there in the wilderness, nor do you walk tall in the sun. You're too busy scanning the ground at your feet for snakes, funnel-web spiders and cow's shit. Or fighting floods, bushfires and blowflies. Besides, I feel lost and insecure without fixed and definitive boundaries around me. I need an island, not a boundless horizon and a barbed-wire fence."

"If you hadn't driven through that barbed-wire fence you wouldn't be where you are now."

"Correction. Let's not skirt the issue with simplicities. No-one gets three to five years in a maximum-security jail for driving through a barbed-wire fence. If that were the case, half Australia's rural population would be in the clink."

"OK, Nole. If you hadn't driven through the prison mess hall, the recreation block, the equipment shed and the superintendent's outside shithouse—before you wiped out the barbed-wire fence—you wouldn't be where you are now."

"That's closer to the truth." Chisholm poked a long bony finger at the prison officer's second shirt button. "Never be afraid to face the facts. They won't hurt unless they sense fear. And the fact of the matter is, if I hadn't been driving the prison's combined harvester I wouldn't be where I am now anyway—I'd never have survived the first bloody impact." Chisholm reached down and hauled a bottle of foul brown liquid out from under the seat.

"I don't know about that, Nole," Jennings sighed. "All I know is that if I hadn't been too pissed to scratch myself I'd have probably been aboard the bloody harvester with you. And then we'd both be on our way to Parramatta Jail. And I wouldn't have been smashed out of my skull in the first place if you hadn't conned me into drinking that bloody poison."

"Poison?" Chisholm brandished the bottle at him. "This isn't poison, dear fellow. It's a noble stimulant that satisfies two of the average Australian male's most cherished excitements—gambling and competitive sports. One shot of this and the race is on, the surgical alcohol sprinting through the system intent on opening up a bloody great hole in your guts, and the Ovaltine and milk fighting to get there first to throw a protective lining on the stomach-wall. The stakes are the highest, as in Russian roulette. Except that I suspect that death by bullet would be far more tolerable than the prolonged agony guaranteed by this shit. Anyway . . . ." Chisholm uncorked the bottle, and powerful fumes smelling not unlike the exhaust of a taxiing jet airplane filled the cabin. Roberts, the second escort officer, suddenly snapped out of his death-like stupor, lifted his head and began retching violently out of the passenger window.

"Let's have one more for the road," Chisholm suggested. "I've still got another hundred yards of outside world to negotiate."

Jennings fended the evil brew away. "No. No. No more of that, Nole. You conned me twice already. I wanna live long enough to enjoy my bloody retirement."

"As you wish," Chisholm sniffed. "Probably the best thing for you in the long run. Quit while you've still got a few brain-cells intact. You'll probably need them to cope with your blocked prostate and years of rampant excitement watching the passion-fruit vine grow on your back patio."

"No. I mean it, Nole. No more!"

"Come on, you piker! One last little trip down insanity alley. To behold the true colours of the mind."

"No! Aw, Christ . . . OK, one last shot, and then we'd better see about getting you safely behind bars."

Chisholm took the first swig, followed by his chief escort, leaving the stricken Roberts to heave his heart up out of the window. Chisholm held his breath, then ground his teeth violently, then let out an anguished gasp and pounded his clenched fists on the steering wheel. Jennings went purple in the face, tore frantically at his tightly knotted tie, fighting for air, then lifted his feet and proceeded to kick savagely at the dashboard.

"*JEEEE*-ZUSSSS CHRIST, NOLE!" he gasped. "This stuff doesn't exactly improve with age, does it?"

"It gets worse," Chisholm reflected, tears springing to his eyes as his mind debated whether his system could cope with the last few fingers of rotten bilge lying in the bottom of the bottle. He prudently handed it back to his still-twitching companion.

"You may find some use for it back on the farm," he said. "May I suggest you consider its merits next time you want to burn off a paddock for ploughing. But for Christ's sake keep a fire appliance handy." He struggled around on the seat, pushed the door open and tumbled out onto the sprinkler-sodden grass verge. Spray from the metal dervish under the van momentarily lashed him. Grabbing at the connecting plastic hose, he fought it into a tightly bent condition, then knotted it, thereby strangling its flow. He then elevated himself to a standing position and slammed the door of the van.

"Well," he said, hanging to the frame of the open window, "the time has come to go forth in search of new pastures. I would dearly love to have made a go of farming, but it was not to be. I did, however, learn two things—how to drive a combined harvester, and how strong the mutual bond is that exists between man and the lemon tree. As Khalil Gibran might have put it: *Their roots delight in your free giving.* I might add that the acid does wonders for their growth, and they in turn provide something to hang on to while you're taking a pee."

Jennings said: "I'd better escort you right to the door, Nole."

"No, don't bother. I can find my own way. Besides, I'll have enough trouble explaining my arrival without you tagging along pissed as a newt."

Jennings hauled himself up behind the steering wheel. He reached out and shook Chisholm's hand.

"Look after yourself, old mate. And God be with you."

Chisholm smiled. "God has been with me since the day I was born. The bastard won't lay off." Again he pointed the bony forefinger. "As I've told you before, put your faith in racehorses or one-armed bandits but *never* into matters spiritual or immortal. There's no bloody hope for any of us."

two

WITH THAT, NOEL CHISHOLM TOOK HIS LEAVE, slipping and skating on the wet grass but otherwise maintaining forward perambulation through a pall of prim middle-class vindictiveness that he imagined hanging over the quiet street. Behind-the-curtain stuff. Little old ladies peering through the slits in their venetian blinds, too gutless to come out and fight. They sent their poodles instead, one of which sped across a lawn, deftly dodging the outer reaches of a sprinkler's spray, and yapped hysterically at Chisholm's heels.

"Up your gumboots," he muttered, mindful that one does not provoke yapping poodles by spinning around and attempting to convert them over the nearest rooftop, lest the little buggers bite.

Chisholm was a fairly tall man, just under six feet when in a standing position. He was gnarled of wrist and both flushed and wrinkled of face, which was not surprising considering the misspent nature of his life. Yet while he was definitely well-weathered, he bore no outward signs of decay. Indeed, it could be said that he was almost athletically slim of build and strong of shoulder; and that, combined with his sandy, ill-disciplined hair, his slightly boyish features and his fine fingers, belied all initial impressions of him—particularly that of his age, which was no less than fifty-eight years, thirty-five of which had been spent permanently and illustriously plastered.

He had piercing, still-youthful blue eyes that seemed to adopt independent bearings in moments of extreme inebriation, that twinkled and moistened in moments of humour, that cast hypnotic spells upon the weak and unwary and blazed dangerously only when outrages of the most atrocious kind touched upon his deepest, most sensitive moral core—which he referred to as his inbuilt shit-detector. Signals from this detector galvanised him into a bare-knuckled fighting stance of such quaint and uncompromising Marquis of Queensbury style that opponents were inclined to laugh rudely and view him as a bloody pushover—until the world blackened before them and they doubled up in agony, massaging their balls. It should be noted, however, that the shit-detector became operational only in instances of heinous insult or injustice. The rest of the time, Chisholm had a tendency to brawl just for the hell of it.

Those same blue eyes, when reading or supervising the act of writing, became owlish and professorial behind the lenses of a pair of spectacles which he carried in a plastic pouch in the breast pocket of his shirt—removing them in moments preceding physical combat with a care and ceremony so rivetting that he could usually plant a surprise punch or two on the average bloke before having to observe the conventional ritual of squaring off and calling each other shit-filled drongos or piss-weak inveterate wankers. He had a mischievous smile bordering on the wicked—depending upon his particular mood at the time. He also carried with him a dashing elegance that showed in the wardrobe he had chosen for this day of transfer to Parramatta Jail. Shunning the tatty Emu Plains uniform of rough shirt and dungarees, he had selected instead a white sports shirt, fire-engine red V-necke-' pullover, fawn-coloured herringbone slacks, soft alligator-hide slip-on shoes and a deep brown neckscarf, knotted carelessly but arranged in the manner of a cravat. Under his arm he carried a paper bag in which were wrapped his most precious personal belongings.

Chisholm reached an intersection facing the main gates of the jail. This he crossed without incident, the poodle having by now broken off contact and returned to base. In one of the enormous steel gates, the left-hand one, there was a door with a small observation grille set into it. Chisholm halted, turned and studied freedom for the last time, blew a raspberry at it, then swung back to address the door. He announced his presence by pouding his fist on the steel-plate.

"Shop!" he yelled.

Had this been any other day, the face that loomed up against the other side of the grille would have been that of a rostered main-gate duty officer from a guardpost and reception room just inside the wall. But on this day, with the scheduled delivery from Emu Plains almost three hours overdue, and no word having been received on its whereabouts, the dark, bushy-browed eyes that stared menacingly through the opening, and the beefy, florid face that accompanied them, belonged to none other than the legendary Bull Sanderson, the jail's deputy superintendent and chief warder.

Here was a man whose very name was enough to strike awe and trepidation into the hearts of criminals and malcontents throughout the walled empire of the New South Wales Department of Corrective Services; a man whose reputation outside Parramatta Jail had been compounded once and for all in the immortal outburst of one particular pitiful wreck of a human being who screeched: "Bull Sanderson? I wouldn't piss in that bastard's ear if his brains were on fire!" The fact that this shriek came not from a common criminal, but a broken fellow prison officer, only made Bull Sanderson's stature burgeon in the imagination from a mere misanthrope to the awful spectre that Chisholm was confronted with now—that of a murderous man-killing Brahma bull staring purposefully through a picket fence.

"Ah, innkeeper," Chisholm chimed. "I believe this to be my place of lodging for the next three to five years. With time off for good behaviour, I hesitate to predict how long I'll be here. So let's say five years to be on the safe side."

Sanderson blinked. Then his hostile gaze dropped from Chisholm's rakish hair and slightly crossed eyes to the V-line of his flaming red sweater. He quite naturally assumed that he was being pestered by a well-dressed but inebriated public nuisance.

"Piss off," he growled, "or I'll ring the bloody cops."

Chisholm sighed somewhat heavily. "We seem to have got this whole matter arse-about, arriving at cross-purposes in retrospect of opening on a fucked-up note. Allow me to introduce myself. I am Flying Officer Noel Maurice Chisholm, RAAF, VSOP. With bar. If you care to check your list you'll find that an advanced booking was made several weeks ago."

"*Chisholm?*" The door was wrenched open before Bull Sanderson's surprised bark had but died away on the torpid afternoon air. "What the bloody hell are you doing here without an escort? Where's the bullwagon? How did you get here?"

"By approved means, I can assure you. It's just that the lads were weary after such a long drive and were anxious to get another crop of spuds in before the sun went down. Being accommodating and sympathetic by nature, I offered to walk the last hundred yards. I can appreciate now that they were probably more than happy I didn't ask them to bring me right to the door."

For Chisholm had by now studied the deputy superintendent of Parramatta Jail. And in full frontal, tightly framed in the open doorway, Bull Sanderson looked even more terrifying than his reputation allowed—a towering six and a half foot living caricature of Desperate

Dan or Big Bad John, both of whom would have turned tail and shat if they'd crossed his path. Sanderson gave the impression of being an entire hunk of Australia masquerading in a human form that began at the level of two huge, highly polished, steel-capped regulation prison officer's black boots and developed vertically in the shape of massive legs of iron-hard *jarrah* that would have found a mo;^ natural setting in the giant rain-forests of Western Australia, a torso as thick as a tallow factory's boiler, arms that looked capable of tearing up the entire trans-Australia railway, brawny hands the size of Holden hub-plates, a neck that looked like a section of piling material swiped from a high-rise construction site, a square-hewn jaw that looked about as easy to dent as Ayer's Rock, with the crowning remainder of his appearance even more bizarre. For, with the rest of his big crew-cut head chiselled into a craggy yet neat geometry, he was strangely handsome—if you chose to ignore the brooding suspicion that glowered from his dark, heavy-browed eyes. On the whole, he looked like someone definitely *not* to be regarded lightly, nor otherwise fucked about with.

Even Noel Chisholm was momentarily nonplussed, buttoning his lip for five minutes while Sanderson led him into the reception room next to the guardpost and officially checked him in as a resident of Parramatta Jail. This first formality completed, Sanderson demanded and was immediately granted a squizz at the contents of Chisholm's paper bag.

"You got bad feet or something?" he asked, peering into the bag.

"They're my fighting boots," Chisholm explained.

"Rubber-soled running shoes?"

"A valuable asset in certain situations. That I grant you," Chisholm conceded. "Otherwise, unlike leather soles, they afford complete and totally adhesive traction in circumstances where there's gravel or dust underfoot or the floor is a slippery sheet of spilled beer or the other bastard's blood."

"Interesting," Sanderson murmured, handing the parcel back. "Fancy yourself a fighter, do you?"

Chisholm's eyes guilelessly held the prison chief's dark challenging glare. "I just this moment decided upon retirement," he said. "A regrettable decision, but one that has been on my mind for some time now. Since I entered this jail, to be exact. I shall miss the thrill and excitement, of course, but no doubt find some sort of solace in regular Bible study."

Bull Sanderson grinned. Which is to say his granite features were devastated by a slow-motion explosion not unlike a gelignite blast on an outcrop of Pilbara iron ore. Wrinkles softened the chiselled face, especially around the eyes, in which bemused lights danced like lightning in a dark thunderhead. When he smiled, he became a different man altogether. The trouble is, he rarely had anything to smile about.

"Somehow," he said, "you don't strike me as a bloke cut out for Bible-bashing." Still grinning, he clamped a huge paw on Chisholm's shoulder and guided him toward the door. "The only God-botherers we get in here are the lunatics or the coves who've got no more bloody fight left in them. Oh, and of course"—Sanderson coughed somewhat apologetically—"our superintendent, the Reverend Mr Hunt. But even the Reverend's been giving the good Lord a tea-break or two lately."

"No doubt allowing Him more time to piss on me," Chisholm observed. "However, I should like to meet the dear Reverend."

"We're on our way to see him right now."

"Excellent. His name, right throughout the penal system, has become synonymous with virtue, justice and the principle of allowing a frank and open expression of grievances before the gas guns and rubber hoses are brought in. I believe he is also of the Presbyterian persuasion, which gives us a great deal in common."

They were stepping outside into a harsh, almost blinding glare that the high afternoon sun exploded off the sand-coloured walls and the salt-flat surface of a bare concrete courtyard that lay before them. The courtyard was bounded by a tall, steel-framed, cyclone-wire fence, beyond which lay the facade and entrance of the jail's single-storey administration block—an incongruously charming colonial relic of thick stone walls and slate roof.

Bull Sanderson cocked a suspicious, quizzical look at Chisholm. "You? A Presbyterian?"

"My father was resident minister of our chapter in Lithgow, the town where I was born," Chisholm explained. "Throughout my formative years we had a great family act going—he exhorting the faithful from the pulpit and me striving to hit high C in the front row of the choir. My mother, a loving and devoted schoolteacher, played the harmonium, of course. We also had a little spotted dog named Patch, who used to sit up and beg while I took the collection plate around. One day, as I was passing the plate between the pews, one of our most devoted brethren, a well-to-do grocer named Tucker—or was it Fucker?—placed a single florin on the silver tray and helped himself to a ten-bob note. He stared at me, a slight grin playing around his fat mouth. I stared at him, so stunned that I knew not what to do. Then tears sprang into my eyes . . . When, in later years, my parents died—passing away peacefully within months of each other—I'm happy to say that they remained totally unaware of how sadly they had equipped me for life's true realities."

They had reached the wire fence, and Sanderson, pulling a large ring of keys from his uniform, was bending to unlock a steel-framed gate. He paused and glanced up at Chisholm.

"And that's why you're now a dangerous trouble-making piss-pot, right?"

Chisholm smiled wryly. "You forgot to add incorrigible."

"I didn't have to," Sanderson growled. He pushed the gate open and then turned to confront Chisholm, tilting his peaked cap forward so that its visor shielded his eyes from the sun's glare. He spread his huge hands on his hips. "You know what? You smell like a bloody petrochemical plant," he rasped. "Don't think I haven't already had a good look at your file. Don't think I don't know about the catastrophe you caused up on the farm. And don't for one bloody minute think I don't know something else went haywire on the way here from Emu Plains. There'll be a little inquiry into that later."

"I would like to make it clear right now," Chisholm retorted, "that Jennings and the other escorts were in no way responsible for events that may have taken place on the way here. They acquitted themselves with exemplary courage and devotion to duty. Indeed, if they are guilty of anything it is *compassion*—responding as they did to my anguished, claustrophobic screams in the back of the bullwag-on. Of course, that's where they made their fatal mistake. But when all is said and done, they accomplished their mission. They got me here."

"Yeah, well that's one point which might go in their favour," Sanderson admitted grimly. "And now that you're here, maybe this is as good a time as any for you and me to get a few things straight between us—before we go see Reverend Hunt. First, when it comes to discipline, I'm the boss-cocky of this jail, and I can either be an absolute bastard or I can leave a bloke free to make some kind of en-durable life for himself in here. It depends entirely on the bloke."

Sanderson paused, and his huge officious bulk relaxed as a more

11

intimate tone softened his voice. "Look," he said. "You're not exactly the average type we get in here. You're fifty-eight, well-educated, you've got a pearly tongue and a lot of cheek to go with it, and from what I've seen of your file you've been knocking around overseas for half your life. You've also got an unfortunate bloody capacity for creating turmoil. Now, I don't fancy having to pull the usual warder-con bit on you—it'd be undignified for both of us. At the same time, I don't want you to go thinking you've got carte bloody blanche to tear this place to the ground. I run a good secure jail here, and I want it to stay that way. So, what I'm offering you is an *understanding*, a sort of gentleman's agreement. You don't give me trouble, I don't give you trouble. Is it a deal?"

Chisholm's answer was a proferred hand, which neatly diverted Sanderson's attention from his smile.

"You can count on me," he pledged.

And they shook on it.

"Now that we're friends, why stand on so much formality?" Chisholm suggested magnanimously. "Call me Noel."

"That's very nice of you, Nole." Sanderson grinned. "You can call me Mr Sanderson."

three

AS NOEL CHISHOLM WAS ESCORTED INTO THE administration block, there to be greeted by (Rev) Hunt, little did he know that a welcome of a far stranger nature was being prepared elsewhere in the jail.

Outside the offices, beyond the mess hall, recreation block, chapel and sick-bay, there lay a vast heat-blistered asphalt quadrangle that stretched to a series of tall barn-like cell blocks. On the left-hand side of this combination parade ground, exercise yard and prison riot facility, another steel-framed wire fence acted as a partition and checkpoint for a smaller open court known as The Pen.

This wired-off compound played an important role in the lives of the jail's three hundred and fifty desperate inmates, all but a tiny few of whom shared, besides their transgressions, a common crawling, itching frustration—the likes of which can only be articulated in terms of an extreme spiritual and physical craving for a fuck and a good fight. Or a good fight and a fuck. Or vice versa. Or any other number of the limited combinations of this two-headed, tail-chasing obsession.

The Pen, however, was no place for fucking, though no doubt a bizarre fantasy of this ilk was, on this day, at this particular moment, creeping soft-soled like a suburban peeper through the dark tortured landscape of Henry Trembler's depraved intellect. Henry often had occasion to nudge himself up against the wire around The Pen, his thick-lensed spectacles flashing semaphore signals from the sun as they scanned a daily flesh-market of glistening, muscle-bound and absolutely gorgeous frustrates working off their steam on the handball courts, weights, exercise bikes, punch-bag, trapezes and a set of parallel bars. Henry was not rated as possibly the world's greatest living sex offender for nothing. Nor was he serving a simple life sentence. As the skinny, middle-aged, balding and despicably obscene little bastard often openly boasted: "I am here for the duration of Her Majesty's pleasure. But I can assure you, the pleasure is entirely mine."

On this day of Chisholm's arrival, Henry Trembler had it made. Not only was he inside the wire of The Pen, he was also surrounded by and otherwise within immediate bodily contact of most of the prison population, the closest of whom were jostling about in a bid to keep well clear of the dirty little snake's reach while the majority directed their noisy, heckling attention at something that acted as a vital earthing point for the constant static of crowded, confined prison life—a portable boxing ring.

This facility was erected whenever any personality clashes developed into open grudges. Its value was such that very few men in the jail could remember it ever being dismantled—so regularly was there occasion to stage the sombre, almost majestic ritual in which Bull Sanderson would escort the protagonists to The Pen, plant armed guards around it to control the spectators, check that the two fighters were firmly gloved and safe in their leather-bound head protectors, call in Lyle Walker to referee the bout and then turn away to take an intense interest in the sky, the outer prison walls and their armed guardposts, the beauty of nature, the ugly nature of men's ways—confident that with Lyle Walker in the ring with them the worst the two meatheads could do would be to knock each other out.

The two men now getting ready in the ring were Kevin Murphy and Harry Pearce. They represented a tradition somewhat broken, in that it wasn't until Bull Sanderson had disappeared in the direction of the administration block, his attention taken up with the problem of the missing Chisholm, that they suddenly started hurling insults and punches at each other.

"You two going to fight, or is this going to be a kiss-an'-make-up deal?"

The question, directed by referee Lyle Walker, reflected a growing angry edge to the clamour of the surrounding crowd, as Pearce did knee-bends in one corner and Murphy bounced about in the other, limbering up in his gloves and headgear and making hideous expressions with his white mouthguard.

"This is a fight all right," Murphy retorted savagely. "I'll murder the bastard."

"You couldn't murder a bloody pavlova cake," Harry Pearce sneered, sending Murphy into a frenzy of shadow-punches that knocked the shit out of the padded cornerpost.

The crowd's impatience rose to a furious, swindled howl. Walker quickly restrained the violent Murphy with one hand and checked his gloves and the soles of his feet with the other.

"Come on. Let's get this show on the road, or we'll have the whole mob in here punching it out."

He leapt into the centre of the ring, gesturing at Murphy and Pearce to follow him, then raised his hands to quiet the bitter roar of the crowd.

"SHADDUP!" he yelled, and the noise of the multitude immediately became but a whisper. "All right, you two," he said to Murphy and Pearce. "No kicking, biting or gouging, stand back when your man goes down, fight like gentlemen and keep your language clean—or I'll be tempted to join in and murder the pair of you."

A former welter-weight professional boxer, with hands registered as deadly weapons, Lyle Walker was not kidding. Having beaten two men to death in a catastrophic bar-brawl, he was also expressly barred from using the ring himself, or so much as touching a pair of gloves. Like an alcoholic fighting the urge to drink, he saw his only salvation in a steadfast day-to-day pledge to keep his fists, and his erratic homicidal tendencies, under tight control. Instead of belting heads, he bashed bibles, and sorely did he bother God in moments of temptation and despair, which usually beset him worst when he was refereeing fights in the ring.

He turned to Murphy. "OK, you ready?"

"Ready," Murphy snarled.

He turned to Pearce. "You ready?"

"Let's get on with it," Pearce growled.

"OK—let us pray."

As the two fighters stood with heads bowed and gloves crossed in front of them, Lyle raised his tightly closed eyes to the burning sun.

"Oh Lord," he prayed, "let Thy divine goodness and mercy shine upon these two fallen angels and please—I *beseech* Thee—make sure they don't fight dirty that I might be tempted to intervene in the name of the Father and of the Son and of the Holy Ghost amen."

"Amen," Pearce and Murphy echoed.

"OK. Get stuck into it."

Lyle Walker bounded back toward the ropes. Pearce and Murphy warily circled each other, Pearce moving slowly, marking his man, while Murphy danced about on the balls of his feet. Pearce threw a probing left jab that Murphy neatly countered with his gloves. Pearce jabbed again, and as Murphy's gloves blocked it he dove underneath them with his right, aiming for Murphy's solar plexus. Murphy hunched slightly, curving his belly around the punch, then threw a right that missed Pearce's head by two inches and glanced harmlessly off his right shoulder. They then barreled into a tight clinch, and Harry Pearce hissed into Murphy's ear: "How long do we have to keep up this bloody charade?"

"You know how long," Murphy panted. "Until the new bloke comes out of the admin block."

"Break!" Lyle Walker barked, slapping Pearce's shoulder, and the two men sprang away from each other and danced around again, making a great show of sweat and harmless swipes. Within seconds, amid loud mockery from the crowd, they were back in another tight bear hug against a cornerpost.

"There must be another way of doing this," Pearce gasped.

"Yeah, we could sit watching him for months. Or we could just walk right up to him and say hey mate, we're planning a jailbreak—how'd you like to be in it?"

"Come on, break it up!" Walker bawled again, and they broke up to dance another ducking, weaving ballet. Pearce caught Murphy up against the ropes, and he got in under his guard to pummel his stomach with lightning-swift soft blows.

"Hey, watch it," Murphy winced. "That hurts."

"I still think this is developing into one of your more notable fuck-ups," Pearce hissed.

"Look, he just about tore Emu Plains to the bloody ground, didn't he? He sounds like a real mean and dangerous bastard."

Murphy swung a tight left jab at Pearce's ear, missed completely and allowed himself to be flung backwards against a corner and practically smothered by Pearce's sweating body.

"But that still means," he hissed, "that he's got to be *tested*."

By this time, the mean and dangerous Chisholm was engaged in combat of a far loftier level with (Rev) Clement C. Hunt, superintendent of the jail, who was more popularly referred to by both prisoners and warders as Old Clemency. His nickname wasn't just a play upon words, nor was it an antonym for a man of monstrous demeanour: If that had been the case, Bull Sanderson would have been known by many in the prison service as Sandy instead of "fucking Sanderson."

No, it was a fundamental and undeniable fact that (Rev) Hunt, a man called upon to confine and punish three hundred and fifty of Australia's most irredeemable felons, was a Christian man in both name and deed. He was also no bleeding-heart fool, as he made clear to Noel Chisholm, checking through the newcomer's illuminating prison file.

"It would appear to me, Mr Chisholm, that we would do well to keep you under close observation," he observed softly, the tone of his speech very close to standard English—the twanging vowels of his native accent refined by an educational background that spelled private school followed by seminary. His sun-washed, myopic grey eyes glanced over the rim of his spectacles at the elegant Chisholm, who was seated directly across the neat, well-ordered paraphernalia of his glass-topped office desk, his precious paper package balanced on his crossed knees. "I think I need hardly impress upon you," (Rev) Hunt continued, "the fact that this is a maximum-security penitentiary and, as such, is designed for the expressed purpose of resisting destruction. It also has an innate capacity to resist violence with violence—an unfortunate matter of fact, but one for which there appears to be little alternative."

Chisholm accepted the implication with good humour. "A delicate matter elucidated with finesse," he smiled. "However, you can rest assured that I have absolutely no designs upon the structure of this institution—unless there happens to be a Sherman tank handy. And even then I would shrink from aggressive acts against what is, indeed, an important cultural monument—the oldest penitentiary in Australia. As a proud and native-born Australian, I believe we should preserve our heritage, particularly our jails, so that in a millennium from now, when this vast continental time-capsule is finally opened, future men will be able to see where the world once dumped all its bad bastards."

(Rev) Hunt's sensitive gaze studied Chisholm for a couple of seconds, then sought out Bull Sanderson, who was sitting as straight as a ramrod on a chair against the wall. Sanderson raised his eyes to the ceiling. (Rev) Hunt turned his attention again to Chisholm's file.

"You have just elucidated a point which, quite frankly, confuses me," he confessed. "Somehow I find it difficult to reconcile this vivid and disturbing indictment of your character with the fact that you are obviously a man of superior intelligence and considerable education, and, if the details of your religious upbringing, war record and previous penal history are accurately stated herein, you possess qualities which should be manifested in a solid moral conviction." (Rev) Hunt clasped his hands together on the sheaf of departmental papers in front of him and looked Chisholm straight in the eye. "To put the issue quite bluntly: What went wrong?"

"To reply in the succinct, nothing less than my entire faith," Chisholm explained. "And this was such that I should have been pronounced holy, indeed canonized, for my conscientious objection to World War Two, inclusive of all fronts and theatres. Instead of that I did eighteen months in Long Bay, with periods of solitary confinement in which my war effort largely involved defensive manoeuvres against the warders. When I eventually emerged, hastening to join the Royal Australian Air Force, the ranks of the anti-Christ had gained a new recruit and the academic world had lost an imminent giant—destined, as many said I was, to become perhaps the youngest dean in the history of Sydney University. I was only twenty-three at the time, yet among other things I could recite the entire Charge of the Light Brigade backwards—a feat which might well have saved a number of lives at Balaclava, had I been there at the time. However, I no doubt would have objected to that little shindig too."

Again (Rev) Hunt's eyes sought Bull Sanderson's support. Sanderson coughed and studied the caps of his boots.

"But as your record shows, Mr Chisholm, you subsequently fought with distinction as a fighter-pilot against the Japanese. Was that not a re-affirmation of faith?"

"Hardly, dear Reverend. God and I quickly came to the conclusion that there was little I could possibly contribute to the fight against the Japanese. In fact, I might well have prolonged it right into the fifties. As it was, I was more gainfully employed in a discipline squadron, flying transports between Darwin and Broome, for indiscretions aggravated by drink of a high alcoholic content which the balance of my mind was disturbed."

"Ah. No doubt the strain of combat."

"Not quite." For once, Noel Chisholm's bold manner collapsed. His fingers fiddled with the paper parcel on his lap. He observed things on the floor. "I saw something in the Pacific," he said. "Something that I have no wish to resurrect now. Suffice to say that from that moment on, my life was redundant, all my naive hopes and dreams shattered. I realised there was no bloody hope for any of us."

In a short embarrassed silence that followed, (Rev) Hunt's hands fidgeted with the pile of papers as he sought more clues to this strange and complicated man.

"I note here that after the war you left Australia and subsequently spent the next thirty years in other parts of the world. Were you perhaps running away from this thing that you had seen?"

"No, I was running away from Australia. It was a question of basic survival. I realised that, mentally, I was deteriorating into a state of extreme and critical withdrawal—an educated, cultured, English-speaking Anglo-Saxon stuck on the rim of a sun-baked, insular desert island down at the absolute arse-end of the world. I might add that I faced certain physical dangers too."

"I don't quite understand."

"It is not an easy concept to articulate," Chisholm said. "Perhaps it is best to analyse it in its simplest form. At barbeques, for instance, whilst the men gathered round the beer-keg engaged in base jocularity and the women perched together at a discreet distance discussing babies and hysterectomies, I had a compelling habit of engaging the ladies in attempted intercourse while the men drew lots to decide who was going to thump me first for interfering with the sheilas. At dinner parties I displayed the same penchant for liberal and indiscriminate use of the word *fuck* in mixed company—a habit that led to the same male threats of a punch in the bloody mouth."

"I see." (Rev) Hunt's fingers combed through the sparse licks of greying, salt-and-pepper hair that criss-crossed the pate of his thin, high-browed head. To be perfectly candid, his features and physique would not have looked out of place in the baggy shorts, khaki blouse and wide-brimmed hat of a Boy Scout leader. "Am I free to deduce from all this," he asked, "that you fled what has been commonly referred to over the years as our *cultural desert*, not to say our peculiar social codes and customs?"

"You are," Chisholm allowed.

"Then why, after thirty years abroad, did you come back?"

Chisholm again searched the floor, as though for answers.

"Perhaps because, despite my violent feelings about this strange wilderness, I am still an *Australian*, and that's a hard thing to ignore, especially when you've used up the rest of the world behaving like one the way I did. Perhaps I came back to find out why I am an Australian. Or *how*. Or what legacy of inbred insanity caused me, for instance, to be trampled year after year in the traditional running of the bulls at Pamplona—just to prove that an Aussie's not afraid of a ton of maddened and swiftly perambulating horn-ed beast. I can still recall with clarity the first time I braved the moment of truth. It was early one morning, when I was having considerable difficulty trying to quiet my shakes enough to read the breakfast menu in a cantina. I finally ordered a raw egg, topped up with three double brandies and milk. I was so beset with the ague that I suffered nightmares negotiating the first draught 'twixt table and lips, and spilt most of the foul liquid over my duds anyway. The second glassful I managed to partially consume, and the third soared to my lips with flourish and went down without touching the bloody sides. The *patron* and other customers went wild with applause.

"After holding my guts down for a few minutes I paid the bill

19

and my respects all round and fell out into the narrow street—where half the population of Pamplona seemed to be running somewhere. I thought, quite reasonably, that it was a public foot-race, something to do with a religious festival, and decided to show them that no national in the world can out-run a bloody Australian. I remember that I crouched down on one knee in the regulation starting position, lifted my bum for a lightning take-off—and that's when a snorting raging black bugger as big as a brick shithouse stampeded right over me.

"The next year I went back to take another crack, and got steam-rolled again. And from then on it became a sort of annual tradition, the constant anticipation of which only served to worsen my drinking problem."

(Rev) Hunt was staring openly at Chisholm, his jaw hanging and his wide eyes like saucers balancing on the upper rim of his spectacles. Sanderson, across the room, shifted in his chair and erupted into another fit of coughing.

"But I digress," Chisholm conceded, when all in the room was silent again. "There are, of course, other reasons why I came home. One was the idiocy with which I responded to Gough Whitlam's call to all intelligent, accomplished but confirmed expatriates to return and help build a new enlightened society after twenty-three unbroken years of slumbering conservative rule. I hurried home, with others, anxious to claim my rightful place in the sovereign, mid-Pacific utopia that this nation was finally to become. Needless to say, my first bar-beque convinced me that nothing was about to change, nor would it probably ever.

"Mindful of the need for prudence, I was congregating with the males around the keg and we were all eyeing a brood of female squawkpersons massed like nesting parakeets at the other end of the patio. 'Jeez, Nole,' said one male acquaintance, a stockbroker clad in the new renaissance attire of tailored shorts, long knee-length hose and cream-coloured, silver-buckled shoes. 'I wouldn't mind taking a stiff prod at that little blonde sheila with the big tits.' Warming to the situation, I immediately opined that I would not be adverse to feeding a few inches to the tall but attractively framed bird with the de-lightful set of knockers next to her. 'What kind of a dirty bastard are you?' he expostulated belligerently. 'That's my sister!'

" 'Does that,' I politely inquired, 'automatically exempt her from the natural and emotionally rewarding bodily function of a good fuck?'

" 'You filthy obscene cunt!' he hollered, and we fell to fighting, which all the other emancipated and similarly attired drinkers joined in immediately—all similarly intent on beating and kicking the shit out of me."

With deliberation and dignity, (Rev) Hunt removed his spectacles and placed them on the desk. He then rubbed his eyes and gently massaged the bridge of his nose. Then he placed the glasses back on and studied Chisholm's file.

"I note here," he said, "that your occupation is listed as *playwright.*"

"Ah," said Chisholm. "I was wondering when we would transcend the mundane and get to higher matters."

"I hope you won't think this rude, but I don't think I've ever had the honour of reading any of your plays or seeing one performed."

Chisholm accepted the implied ignominity with a wave of the hand. "Don't be embarrassed, my dear fellow," he said. "I've not yet had the distinction of writing one."

"I see," said (Rev) Hunt.

four

OUTSIDE IN THE BLAZING SUN, HARRY PEARCE and Kevin Murphy were by now sweating so furiously that when Pearce manoeuvred his opponent into yet another tight embrace on the ropes, Murphy literally slid out of his grasp like greased rubber. And yet another derisive howl went up from the angry crowd around the ring as Murphy then unleashed a vicious haymaker at Pearce's head, missed by a mile and very nearly fell flat on his face. Pearce guided him to the nearest cornerpost and propped him up with one gloved hand while the other tattooed his heaving chest and belly with soft punches.

"This is the last time I get involved in any of your hair-brained bloody schemes," Pearce vowed, gasping into the leather padding over Murphy's left ear. "*Eight rounds*—and we still haven't seen hide or bloody hair of the new bloke!"

Murphy swung another punch at Pearce's head. Halfway through the swing, all strength seemed to desert him, and the blow collapsed into a limp and desperate grapple at Pearce's neck for balance and support. Another obscene roar of mockery and insult erupted around them, during which Murphy attempted to stiffen up his opponent's flagging spirits.

"Hold on a couple more minutes," he croaked, blinking on sweat that trickled freely into his eyes. "Willie Crewe's down there in the crowd. It's all starting to happen."

Willie Crewe had indeed arrived on the scene, his black, tightly curled hair poking up through a thicket of crew-cuts and sun-speckled semi-bald domes with the majesty of a young fir in a stand of scraggy paper-barks. His enigmatic, almost blank blue-green eyes swung lazily back and forth from the tired combat taking place in the ring to the yelling, fiercely gesticulating throng around him. His expression was indulgent, almost contemptuous, as though he were coolly surveying wards of some omnipotent power that he possessed. Behind the faint amusement that showed in a slight curl to his thin lips, his thought processes ignited and flared in an erratic Morse code that signalled something of the subtle essence of his emotions. *Punch, kick, shit, bastards, hate, blood, stab, turds, watch your back*, the signals warned, pointing at once to the motivating crux of Willie Crewe's power. Also, of all the men in The Pen, he was the only one standing with ease and apparent nonchalance within Henry Trembler's filthy reach—which said a great deal about the sort of company he was in the habit of keeping.

"Ah, Willie," Henry Trembler murmured, his tongue whipping across his evil chops with the swift flicker of a lizard's lick. "I came here to enjoy the a la carte and found myself in the middle of a veritable smorgasbord. I can't say as I'm disappointed. Nothing quite stimulates those old tired and jaded depravities as the sight and smell of sweaty male flesh."

"I was going to say," Willie replied absently, his psychopathic gaze searching the crowd for one Timothy Botham, a young post-adolescent newcomer to the prison. "You're a bit outside your bloody element here, aren't you, Henry?"

"I'll admit I'm more of a hayshed man," Henry confessed—a skinny fox ogling the surrounding chook-run. "I get nervous in open country. There's no cover. Especially for obscene and therefore strictly furtive behaviour. I remember when I first played doctors and nurses as a child. I was concealed in tall paspalum grass in the middle of a large paddock, fiddling inside the skirt and panties of my little playmate from next door—checking her pulse, as I explained it—and totally unaware that through the principle of elevation and trajectory of sight her mother was watching the whole show from the upstairs bedroom window of their two-storey house. I never forgot the lessons learned that day. Nor the pain that followed my shock exposure."

"Where's Botham?" Willie Crewe demanded—new spasms of emotion now flashing and beeping in his crippled mind.

"Over the other side of the ring. Probably keeping well out of your way," Henry explained. "I've told you before, Willie—while he's protected by Harry Pearce you'll never get to him. Get rid of Pearce, and he's all yours."

"I'll get Pearce," Willie grunted, his fists flexing like cat's paws at his side. Then, as thoughts of Harry Pearce inflamed other more immediate and pressing pains, he asked: "Where the hell's that new bloke? He should be out here by now. I don't like being kept waiting. It gets me hot under the bloody collar."

"I must say that I'm both stunned and bloody delighted by that which you've just told me," Noel Chisholm was at that moment saying as his introductory meeting with (Rev) Hunt approached its close. "Had I known that conditions in this jail were so enlightened, I would have arranged my transfer from Emu Plains with greater expediency."

(Rev) Hunt allowed a tiny shiver of pain to upset the fragile tranquillity of his eyes. "There is little that one could term enlightened about the (Rev) Clement C. Hunt Arts and Crafts Society," he explained gently. "Though it may seem to be a giant stride in civilised thinking, not to say an important breakthrough in penal reform, to allow prison inmates to paint, write poetry and books, make sculptures, mould pottery and otherwise foster and develop their hitherto suppressed creative and artistic talents, in reality it is a last-ditch attempt to keep the lid on our jails. Rehabilitation has been tried and abandoned. Dignity has been proferred, and slung back in our faces. Artistic endeavour has now been instituted on the hopeful premise that when men are consumed by their creative drives they have that much less time in which to plan escapes."

(Rev) Hunt paused to shuffle Chisholm's papers into a neat pile, then to close the file. Looking up again he allowed a tight, somewhat sardonic smile to lighten the heaviness of his expression.

"It is ironic," he said, "that while culture and the arts are screaming out for funds and recognition amid imprisoned minds at large throughout this nation, imprisoned men are being lavished with paint-pots and potter's wheels and every conceivable persuasion to give expression to their abstract and higher selves. Membership in the (Rev) Clement C. Hunt Arts and Crafts Society is not only suggested, it is compulsory—the only alternative open to those who shun it being solitary confinement with only the Holy Bible for companionship. I am not anyone's fool, Mr Chisholm, yet there are times when I like to reflect with some hope and less trepidation on the fact that not one man in this jail—not one man in the open jail, that is—has yet shown anything inferior to an obsessive desire to allow his creative urges free rein."

"Nor shall I," Noel Chisholm pledged. "I have an abject fear of solitary confinement—such a revulsion, in fact, that I have been known to break out in a violent panic in airplane toilets, causing distress for both passengers and crew. No doubt the subconscious roots of this trauma lie in my experiences in Long Bay, along with horrors imprinted during childhood by venomous red-backed spiders poised for the first flash of innocent white arse in our claustrophobic outside dunny. However, I not only completely endorse the pursuit of the arts, I shall also lend study to its wider application. No doubt visions have already crossed your mind of a national arts and crafts society in which the same objective is sought, the same compulsory membership applies and penalties are similarly severe. It could be one way of greening the cultural desert."

"It could also compound the problem enormously," (Rev) Hunt sighed, "by filling our jails to overflowing."

He rose to his feet, a movement that Bull Sanderson interpreted as the termination of the meeting—getting up from his own chair and standing at attention at Chisholm's back.

"I have enjoyed and gained much from our little chat, Mr

Chisholm," (Rev) Hunt declared grimly. "I sincerely hope that our association remains a mutually pleasant one. Mr Sanderson will now escort you to cell-block C, where you have been allocated quarters. You will find them comfortable and conducive to both spiritual reflection and to the theatrical masterpiece that I assume you will apply your particular talents to over the next"—he checked himself with another tight smile—"I was going to say five years. But of course, we won't have the pleasure of your company that long, will we, Mr. Chisholm?"

"Alas, no," Chisholm replied, getting up to leave, "for I am dying."

(Rev) Hunt's smile froze upon his face. "Dying?"

"We are all dying," Chisholm declared.

"Ah. Yes, of course."

Chisholm halted at the door and turned. "Some of us, unfortunately, much sooner than others," he added, leaving another startled expression in his wake as he followed Bull Sanderson out of the room. As Sanderson led him along a central corridor pointing them toward the rear of the administration block, he glanced sideways at the great master of theatrical works and let out a soft snort of amusement.

"I'd hate to have to pick a winner out of that little skirmish," he said. "You belted him pretty hard in the last round, but I reckon he took the overall match on points."

"He also had a bloody great prison, with ancillery forces, backing him up," Chisholm observed.

"Right. And keep that in mind, Nole."

At the end of the corridor they negotiated a locked and heavily barred gate that opened out onto harsh sunlight and another tall wire-mesh security fence—this one containing yet another locked checkpoint controlled from a guardpost set just to the left of it. Beyond lay the vast glare of the main quadrangle and the lofty cell blocks.

As the guard fumbled with his keys, Sanderson said: "I'll give you a couple more points to keep in mind, Nole. If you want some bloody peace in this clink, keep to yourself. If you want trouble, get in with Harry Pearce and Kev Murphy and you'll end up knee-deep in shit every day. Pearce is all right, but Murphy's one of the biggest fuck-ups I've ever set eyes on."

The gate clanged behind them as they passed through it. All at once, as though the wire fence had been a sound barrier, a roar of male anger and vilification reached their ears, and Sanderson gazed across at the crowd of cons jostling and waving around the ring in The Pen.

"What's going on over there?" he asked the checkpoint guard.

"A fight, Mr Sanderson. Murphy and Pearce."

"Murphy and Pearce? Why wasn't I informed about this?"

"You were busy. We've got men posted around it. There's no danger. Nothing's up."

"Everything's up when Pearce and Murphy suddenly stage a bloody donnybrook," Sanderson growled. "Pearce is a bloody killer, and Murphy couldn't punch his way out of a wet paper bag. That's why they're as thick as thieves together."

"Well," said the guard, "Murphy's not doing too badly from what I've seen. They've gone twelve rounds and he's still on his feet."

That wasn't entirely correct, as Murphy himself would have testified—sprawled as he was over the ropes with his gloves hanging uselessly at his sides, his eyes glazed with sweat and exhaustion and his chest and belly heaving violently in a struggle to gulp oxygen into his stricken system. Harry Pearce wasn't much better off, either. He was on his hands and knees in the middle of the ring fighting to muster enough energy to clamber up on his feet, haul himself across to the ropes and plant one right in the middle of Murphy's stupid mug.

"I'll maim you for this, Murph," he croaked, his threat a mere whisper amid a cacophony of vile abuse broadcast by the surrounding crowd.

Lyle Walker bent and tapped his trembling shoulders.

"You going to get up and finish this mockery, Pearce? Or do I start counting you out?"

"You must be bloody joking!" Harry gasped, quickly heaving himself up from the canvas. "Counted out on account of *that* dingbat? I'd be the laughing stock of the bloody jail."

"Watch that language!"

Amid a fresh outbreak of coarse banter and the slinging of various crudities, Pearce staggered over to Murphy, pulled his right glove back for a stunning wallop, then paused in mid-swing and followed Murphy's averted gaze down into the crowd. There, on the fringe of the mob, was Bull Sanderson and a weird-looking cove in a flaming red pullover who, if he hadn't just popped in to say cheery-pip, could well be the terrible scourge of Emu Plains. Or could he? Harry studied the fire-apple sweater and accompanying cravat.

"You sure that's the bloke?"

"It must be," said Murphy. "Yeah, look—he's got his clobber wrapped up in a paper bag."

"It could be his lunch."

"At four in the bloody afternoon?"

With a loud gasp of relief, Harry collapsed, falling against Murphy. "Thank Christ for that."

"Yeah. We can call it quits now."

"Oh no you can't," said Lyle Walker, grabbing the two heavily sweating combatants, tugging them apart by the wrists and holding them at arm's length. "What's going on here?" he demanded.

"What do you mean, Lyle?"

"I mean that after twelve rounds I'm wondering if you two came in here to fight or get funny with each other. You haven't laid a decent punch on each other yet. And what's all that whispering about?"

"We've been ironing out our differences," Pearce explained. "We don't wanna fight any more."

"You should've thought of that before you came in the ring. You know the rules—both of you."

"What's going on up there?" the voice of Bull Sanderson boomed from the crowd at the foot of the ring. "You two going to fight, or do I have to come in there and deal with yers myself?"

"Shit," Harry sighed.

"Watch that mouth of yours, Pearce," Lyle warned him. "You both know the rules. Nobody leaves the ring till one of you's down for the count."

"Christ," said Murphy.

Lyle Walker said: "Right, Murphy. Just for that you can be the one who goes down."

"Like buggery."

"It's either that," said Lyle, "or I start getting peeved and irritated. And you know what that could lead to—*God help us all!* Now, what's it going to be?"

"Walker!" Sanderson bellowed. "Get those two bastards moving, or I'm coming in there!"

Murphy turned on Harry Pearce with a contemptuous sneer. "Some fucking fighter you are . . . You couldn't punch shit out of a bloody garbage bag, yer dead c—"

Next thing, Murphy was flat on his back at Pearce's feet, well and truly out for the count. And Lyle Walker, regarding Harry with a mixture of respect and excitement in his eyes, said: "You're a real king-hit merchant, aren't you, Pearce? He didn't even see that coming."

"He didn't want to. It would've scared him shitless," said Harry, untying his gloves and bending down to begin shaking and slapping Murphy back to consciousness—just as he'd once done with Willie Crewe, sweet Willie, the former King's Cross strong-arm thug and hired killer, now a lifer handling the dual responsibilities of prison cook and SP bookie. As his background suggested, Willie Crewe was quite a nasty piece of work. And prison had done nothing to improve him. Torn from the streets, he had simply transplanted himself— ruling most of the jail with his deadly fists and violent psychopathic nature and taking it upon himself to conduct a little initiation ceremony for all new arrivals; punching the daylights out of them in the ring.

If he beat them, and he invariably did, they succumbed to his evil authority and joined a large scared and sheepish flock of subjects that jumped at his slightest whim or approach. Only five men in the entire clink had come out on top of Willie Crewe, and two of them, Bull Sanderson and Lyle Walker, had won by default, on account of nobody—even Willie Crewe—being stupid enough to challenge them. Two others, Kevin Murphy and the young Timothy Botham, had escaped Willie's clutches because of the protection of one man, Harry Pearce, and Harry had dealt with Willie seven years before, encountering him shortly after his release into the open prison from the solitary confinement facility, known as the Blockhouse, where he had spent three months for his own protection before being introduced to the prison community.

Just why Harry had done three months' protective solitary was something that really didn't seep through Willie's confused, psychotic reasoning until it was too late. Only then did he reflect upon the fact that Harry had been in no real need of protection at all—that he happened to be a wide cut above most ordinary crims, even violent gangland killers. In fact, he belonged to a most dreadful category of criminal. Probably the most dreadful of all, if you care to ponder briefly upon the horrifying image of sparkling, razor-sharp steel and terrible bludgeoning motions. Harry Pearce was an *axe murderer*. Apart from that, he wasn't such a bad sort of bloke, and he was good with his dukes, too.

Had Willie considered this, he might well have shrunk from in-itiating his ritual pre-fight challenge, which usually took the form of a sophisticated invitation not unlike the way he deliberately ladled Har-ry's lunchtime stew down the front of Harry's clean and crisp prison fatigues on the tucker-line in the mess hall. Harry accepted and re-turned the challenge with equal elegance. "You looking for a thump in the head—you dead-shit?" he snarled, and within fifteen minutes they were in the boxing ring squaring off at each other with a huge, strangely hushed audience packed around the ropes.

For twenty minutes, Harry took one hell of a beating from Willie Crewe, a lean and thin-lipped man whose spare shoulders and biceps disguised the trained, killer instincts of a hired thug and contract man. Harry used his fists to block whatever he could of the younger man's crippling punches, but not once attempted to lay one of his own on the punk. Five times he went down on the canvas, his nose broken and spraying blood, his face a mass of cuts and blackening welts, his lips torn and two teeth loosened at the roots. The fifth time he went down, he stayed down, flat on his back—his belly and rib-cage heaving with exhaustion.

The audience gave a satisfied cheer, part of which was a tribute to Harry's staying power, and Crewe turned away with a smug grin and sauntered to the ropes. Harry slowly hauled himself up onto his knees, then to his feet, and as Crewe stuck a leg through the ropes to leave the ring, he said very clearly: "You're still a bloody dead-shit."

Willie Crewe climbed back into the ring and approached Harry with the confident swagger of a man about to enjoy himself a bit.

"And you're a real bugger for punishment, aren't you, Pearce?" he grinned, slackening his guard as he pulled back for a final upper-cut at Harry's wrecked face.

And that's when Harry knocked him cold with a punch that Crewe never had a chance in a bloody lifetime to see coming, and the crowd outside the ring saw only as the faint blur of an accomplished king-hitter.

five

To GIVE WILLIE HIS DUE, HE'D BEEN magnificent in defeat and undeterred by humiliation. Not once, in the seven years since that fight, had he allowed reason and common sense to cool his smouldering, seething hatred for Harry Pearce, or his avowed aim to get even with the bastard once and for all. Nor had he hung up his gloves. He continued to initiate the new arrivals—beating the shit out of every single one of them and thereby denying them a place in Pearce's tiny elite—just as he was now about to test and initiate the newest newcomer of all, Noel Chisholm.

Willie had been hugging close to Henry Trembler on the edge of the crowd, malevolently eyeing the elegant Chisholm, while Pearce and Murphy worked themselves into their final sweaty paralysis up in the ring. By the time Bull Sanderson rushed away to the ringside to sort out the absurd spectacle, Willie had developed a deep and abiding hatred for Chisholm—particularly for that flaming red pullover and poofta-ish chocolate-brown neckscarf of his. And when Harry Pearce knocked Murphy cold like that, so searing was the blend of emotions that boiled up inside Willie that he could see no relief from the pain unless he tore Chisholm limb from limb.

"OK, Henry—get ready to pick up the bloody bits," he told Henry Trembler, brushing him aside in his haste to get to Chisholm before Bull Sanderson had a chance to twig that there was a new fight in the offing. With a sneering grin on his face and his fists flexing spasmodically at his hips, Willie approached the mysterious man from Emu Plains and set in motion his traditional pre-fight ritual.

"Hey, shit-for-brains. I don't like the look of your ugly stupid mug. Or that poofta gear you're wearing. What you got in that bag—your nightie? You know what you can do with that big red honker you've got stuck in the middle of your face? Go ram it up a dead bullock's bum!"

At the first sound of Willie's taunts, the crowd around them turned away from the ring and pressed in on this new source of excitement, measuring the tall and silent Chisholm against the tall and infuriated Willie Crewe, whose psychotic rage had by now become so uncontainable that tears actually sprang into his eyes as the scorn continued to pour from his twisted mouth.

"You know what you remind me of? A turd done up in a bloody Christmas stocking. I reckon if someone squeezed your ugly bloody head you'd crap your pants. You wanna call me a liar? You wanna make something of it? You go ahead, feller—I can do you like a dog's dinner with one hand tied behind me bloody back. Fucking oath I can. I happen to *hate* piss-weak bastards like you!"

Like faces at a tennis match, the combined gaze of the crowd switched to Chisholm, leaving Willie's shocking expletives to fade in the late-afternoon heat. Chisholm was carefully reaching up inside the front of his sweater. His hand emerged with a plastic pouch, out of which he produced his black-rimmed, executive-style spectacles. These he placed on his nose; then he peered closely at Willie as though examining something quite fascinating and peculiar through a microscope. Such was the tension by now that you could have heard a pin drop amid the surrounding pack of cons as they waited breathlessly for Chisholm's opening retort.

Chisholm gazed studiously into Willie's hate-filled face.

"Would you hit a man with glasses on?" he asked.

Willie blinked. Then got angrier.

"You bet your fucking life I would," he raged, his fists twitching and grabbing again as he barely restrained himself from leaping at Chisholm and banishing him altogether from his tortured world.

Chisholm sighed heavily. "I suspected as much," he said sadly, still studying Willie's savage features. "You see, without the aid of spectacles I couldn't be entirely sure whether I was being confused with someone else or whether I was simply dealing with something that had slithered out from under a rock. I realise now that I was wrong on both counts. Only a total bloody lunatic would stand there screaming obscenities and shaking like that with his fly undone and the tip of his old feller poking out."

Willie's reply was an involuntary one. And it was his undoing. With an instinctive "What? Where?" he let his gaze drop for a split-second, and Chisholm walloped him right on the jaw with a punch that had the catapulting impact of a horizontal pile-driver—slamming Willie right back into the crowd, where a few unfortunates fell underneath him as he sprawled outstretched to the ground.

The cry went up. "Fight! FIGHT!"

Chisholm was grimacing painfully and sucking his knuckles. "Now look what you made me do!" he yelled at the threshing melee of Willie and other men. "I'll never play 'Chopsticks' again!"

Willie managed to disengage himself from the undergrowth of waving limbs and was up and crouching, coiled for a spring at Chisholm's throat. As he threw himself at Chisholm he ran smack into a ton of bricks, and Bull Sanderson halted him in mid-flight, holding him back with a huge forearm and hammy hand.

"What's going on here!" Sanderson bawled.

"He king-hit me!" Willie screeched. "The dirty bastard thumped me when I wasn't looking. I demand fucking satisfaction!"

Still holding Willie at bay, Sanderson addressed Noel Chisholm. "I should've warned you about Willie," he said. "He's got this funny idea in his head that he runs this bloody jail. Do you wanna have a go at him now, or wait until you're settled in and nicely comfortable?"

Chisholm bent and picked his paper parcel up from the hot asphalt. "Never put off until tomorrow that which can be done today," he said. "I'll do Willie now, and then settle in."

Another excited cry went up, and the crowd turned to mass once again around the boxing ring.

"Boy, I'm gonna beat the living Christ out of you, feller," Willie spat, turning with the crowd and marching furiously toward the ropes.

"Watch him, Nole," Sanderson said. "He's a nutcase, but he's got a dreadful pair of bloody fists. And he doesn't know when to stop."

"I've got my fighting boots," said Chisholm. "And they don't know when to stop either."

With the crowd surging around the ring, Harry Pearce was helping haul the groggy Murphy through the ropes. Murphy saw Willie Crewe leap up through the ropes on the other side of the canvas and caught a glimpse of Chisholm pushing his way through the mob to the ringside, and a broad smile broke out on his pale, still shaken features.

"It's on, Harry. Now we see just what that bloke's made of!"

Harry was still slightly ill-humoured. "What if it turns out he's made of bloody paper?"

"Then he doesn't get to break out with us, does he? Jesus, Harry—stop worrying, will you? Just take care of the physical stuff and leave the bloody thinking to me."

"That's what you told me before we went went twelve bloody rounds in this bloody heat," Harry replied savagely. "You got some smart ideas, Murph, I'm not denying that. But Christ, you certainly go about them the hard way."

"Harry, nobody's come up with an easy way of breaking out of jail. If they had, we wouldn't be in here now, trying to get out. Would we?"

Harry simply shook his head, mulling that one over, as he and Murph melted into the tightly packed throng around the ringside and watched Willie Crewe dance and strut in the ring, waiting for Chisholm to come and get his head bashed in. With the help of willing hands, including a darting surreptitious goose up the nether regions from that dirty little creep Henry Trembler, Chisholm was rocketed up through the ropes and left to confront Willie on the grubby canvas. Chisholm stood in one corner, still wearing his spectacles and nursing his paper bag, while Lyle Walker jumped up into the right carrying gloves, head protectors and mouthguards.

"No gloves," said Chisholm.

Willie Crewe looked confused, then broke into a leering grin. "No gloves?"

"They get in the way," Chisholm explained.

"Jesus," said the excited Willie, "you're really in for a hiding, mate. You realise that?"

"No gloves!" Lyle Walker announced loudly, and the crowd erupted into a shrill pandemonium of whoops and whistles.

"No gloves!" Kevin Murphy yelled at Pearce. "I told you that bloke was a hard bastard! This is going to be a little bloody ripper!"

Up in the ring, Lyle Walker had brought the two protagonists together and was reciting his usual riot act. "No biting, kicking or punching below the belt—OK?"

"Come on," Willie gnashed impatiently, his fists already raised and feet dancing a light jig as he advanced on Chisholm. "Get those fucking glasses off an' let's go!"

"As you wish," said Chisholm, and he thrust his paper parcel at Willie. "Hold this a second, will you?"

Willie reached, faltered and then sprang backwards.

"You think I'm that dumb? You think I came down in the last bloody shower?"

"We'll see," said Chisholm, and he turned to Lyle Walker, handing him the package. Walker naturally accepted it, and when the parcel was firmly in his hands Chisholm did an incredible thing. With rocket speed he let fly with his left fist and belted the referee right in the side of the head—and Lyle Walker, hitherto undisputed champion of the entire jail, looked curiously at him for a second, then crashed to the canvas like a pole-axed steer. As the crowd bellowed with amazement, Willie Crewe stood gaping at Walker's crumpled, unconscious form just long enough for Chisholm to deliver his coup de grace, and a second later Willie felt as though a bomb had exploded between his legs, as though someone had taken a gun and shot him.

The roar of the crowd and all other sounds of the world seemed to turn in on him, rushing like water down a big black hole; and all things visible became twisted and distorted before his eyes, like reflections in a warped mirror, before a cloudburst of black stars gave way to a crimson film and the sheer, unimaginable agony of the boot in the balls overcame him and sent him screaming to the canvas.

Noel Chisholm casually retrieved his fighting boots and then turned to face the shrieking crowd and forest of fists that waved in gales of horror and anger around the ring. And as he calmly removed his spectacles and began returning them to the protective custody of their plastic pouch, Kevin Murphy spun on Harry Pearce down below the ropes and yelled:

"That was about the dirtiest bloody act of a king-hitting ratbag bastard that I've ever seen!"

"Yeah," Harry agreed. "It was absolutely bloody shameful."

"Looks like we've got our man, eh?"

"I reckon he'll do," said Harry.

six

As NIGHT SETTLED, SINKING TO ITS NEST like a sleepy beast, so did the silence of eventide draw close and snuggle over it—a silence that Harry Pearce welcomed. Like a cool breeze on sunburnt skin, it brought him tingling relief from the day-long clamour of the jail, the clang of steel upon steel, the intermittent shriek and toll of sirens and bells, the constant bellow of coarse male voices and the measured, insistent tread of metal-studded boots on concrete and heavy iron catwalks.

Alone in his cell on the upper floor of cell-block C, Harry waited until the silence and solitude had completely encapsuled him, then took up a sculptor's chisel and a shiny new wooden mallet. Turning to a tiny workbench that was set neatly into an alcove of his whitewashed, arched and ludicrously Spanish-style quarters, he hovered lovingly over the warm buttergold hue and sharp, unviolated symmetry of a two-foot cube of naked sandstone. For one sweet moment it was as though he was back amid the haphazardry of joists and pulleys and marble slabs of his old workplace alongside Rookwood Cemetery, the main resting place for souls departing the metropolitan area of Sydney. In the stillness, with tools poised, with his emotions tingling, he listened to his heart. And it whispered:

"In loving memory."

Then he heard something else—the mournful, tinny agony of Timothy Botham's mouth-organ. Tonight, Botham was playing "Danny Boy," just as he had played it night after night for two whole bloody months or more. And as on all previous nights, he was playing it very badly—torturing the tune and the instrument so mercilessly that Harry Pearce felt like rushing down to his cell on the ground level, tearing the poor bloody thing from Botham's lips and stomping on it to put it out of its misery.

Instead, Harry threw his tools down on the bench, strode angrily to the guardrail at the edge of a catwalk outside the open doorway of his cell and yelled into the cavernous, softly lighted interior of the cell block:

"Anyone who plays a bloody mouth-organ in a prison is definitely bloody sick!"

And back came Botham's post-adolescent donkey bray, pealing up from his own place of agony among the lower cells: "It's not a mouth-organ. It's a harmonica!"

"I don't care if it's a bloody regimental brass band!" Harry raged. "Quit it!"

"Hey, Harry," another voice called out, "give us a go, will you? I'm trying to work." It was Kevin Murphy, straining on tiptoe on top of an empty fruitcase to add a particularly intricate touch of Prussian blue to the iris of a dog's eye in a mural he was painting on the wall alongside Timothy Botham's cell.

"I'm trying to work too!" Harry retorted. "And I can't do a stroke of it while he's making that racket with that bloody mouth-organ of his!"

"It's not a mouth-organ," Botham whinnied.

"I don't care what it is!" Harry roared. "You blow the bloody thing once more and I'll come down there and flatten it! And you!"

With the threat echoing around the walls of the tall, cathedral-like block, Harry marched back into his cell for a second attempt at work. He would create a masterpiece, he vowed, as he again held the chisel and mallet over the sandstone. He would draw deeply upon the twin wells of his skill as a stonemason and his natural creative rage to produce a work of art, the likes of which had not yet been seen in the short but flourishing history of the (Rev) Clement C. Hunt Arts and Crafts Society. More than that, Harry promised as he held his breath and delicately positioned the chisel for his first truly artistic blow, it would be a *monument*.

And that's when Kevin Murphy walked in. And said: "Just about to start work, are you?"

Harry said nothing. Instead he very slowly lowered the chisel and mallet and leaned forward until his forehead was resting lightly on the cool, virgin stone.

"Jeez," said Murphy, "I don't know how you sculptors do it—you know, turning a lump of bloody rock into a thing of beauty. I mean, if I make a mistake I can just paint over it. But how d'you know your first wallop's not going to smash the whole thing to smithereens?"

Harry raised his head from the stone and shot Murphy a murderous look. "Haven't you got something else to do? Like go pester some other poor bastard who's trying to get a bit of work done in peace?"

"Oh, am I disturbing you?"

"No," Harry sighed. "I sit here night after night with my tools in my hand waiting patiently for someone to barge in and bugger everything up."

"Actually," said Murphy, "I thought I'd drop in before I go and front the new bloke, Chisholm, and like start feeling him out on the old whatsit."

Harry said: "You make that sound very rude, Murph. What whatsit?"

"You know. The thingummyjig. The how'dyamacallit."

Harry sat down on his bench, next to the stone, and, in a suffering manner, raised his eyes to the ceiling. "I'm not sure I know what you're talking about, Murph."

Murphy shook his head with exasperation. "Jesus, Harry—sometimes you make me wonder . . . Gimme a bit of paper and a pencil."

"What for?"

"Just gimme a bit of paper and a bloody pencil."

Harry rummaged through books, magazines and various working implements littering his bench. He found a bit of paper and a bloody pencil. He handed them to Murphy. Then, as Murphy licked the pencil-lead, he sighed again and said: "All right, Murph. I know what you mean. Why can't you just come out and say it, instead of going through all this bloody rigmarole?"

Murphy angrily tossed the paper and pencil back onto the bench. "This is no joking matter, Harry! There are ears flapping all over the bloody place. Let one little whisper drop and we'll have everybody and his bloody dog broadcasting it all over the jail."

"How do you know this Chisholm bloke'll want to be in it?"

"He tried to break out of Emu Plains, didn't he? He's tough, and he's dangerous. You saw the way he belted Christ out of Walker and Crewe."

"Yeah," Harry said. "And I also remember belting Christ out of you, too, Murph. And do you know what I was thinking when I did it? I was thinking, Murph's done it again—another complete cock-up."

"What're you talking about?"

"Hasn't it occurred to you, Murph, that Willie Crewe would've started a fight with Chisholm whether or not you and I went twelve bloody rounds in that stinking bloody heat to set it up? It's Willie's way of doing things. He always has a go at the new blokes."

Murphy smiled condescendingly. He wasn't chairman of the Prisoner's Action Committee of Parramatta Jail for nothing. A bloke in his position, with his sort of responsibility, had to think of everything.

"Yeah," he said, "but we had no way of telling *when* he'd get around to punching Chisholm out, did we? He might've had a go at him tomorrow. Or maybe next week. Or maybe six weeks from now. And we can't afford to wait six weeks, can we? Old Clemency's arts and crafts exhibition is all set to go off four weeks from now. And that's when we've got to be ready to go too. And if we don't pull it off on that exact date, we'll have to wait a whole year for another bloody opportunity. And there might not be another bloody opportunity. Old Clemency might drop dead like the bloke he replaced, or he might be transferred, or he might—"

"OK, OK," Harry interjected. "I get the picture."

"You see what I mean, don't you? You don't just say OK, let's thingummyjig off out of here. A whatsit like this takes careful planning, meticulous attention to all details. Split-second timing. *Nothing* must go wrong. Hundreds of little elements have to be taken into account. The Minister—will he stay here long enough for us to grab him? Or will he fly in by helicopter, say hullo and bugger off straight back out of here? Will we have enough explosives? Christ, Harry—you overlook one little factor and the whole scheme goes to the shithouse."

"OK," said Harry. "So where does Chisholm fit into all this?"

"I haven't got that bit worked out yet," Murphy confessed with a frown. "I'll have to sound him out first—see what he's got to offer. Maybe he can handle all the killing." He took a quick look around Harry's cell, checking that everything was secure, then turned to leave.

"Right. I'm on my way."

Harry said: "Haven't you forgotten something?"

"What?"

Harry pointed at the bench. "Hadn't you better burn that bit of paper?"

"Oh Christ. Yeah."

Harry watched blandly as Murphy grabbed the scrap of paper from the table, produced a cigarette lighter from his fatigues, then set fire to it.

"Good thinking, Harry. You can never be too sure. If this fell into the wrong hands it could screw everything."

"Yeah," said Harry. "Especially when it's got nothing written on it. That'd really get everyone thinking."

When Murphy had gone, Harry stood for a few moments studying the untouched block of sandstone with an intensity that slowly, ever so gradually, reawakened the vision and sweet mood with which he'd first approached his work. When he again saw clearly the artistic triumph that it was to be, he picked up his mallet and chisel, made a last-minute check of the grain of the block, then carefully positioned the cold steel tip for his first cut.

And that's when Timothy Botham wandered in. And nonchalantly blew a short sharp scale on his harmonica.

Harry hurled his chisel at the bench and, brandishing the mallet, advanced on Botham with the black rage of a flash thunderstorm.

"Gimme that thing!" he bellowed.

"What, Harry?" Botham quavered, his heavy-lashed, nut-brown eyes wide with fear as he quickly slipped the silver-plated nuisance behind his back.

"That mouth-organ!"

"Harmonica."

"GIMME IT!"

Botham reluctantly handed it to Harry, and Harry took it to the bench, laid it flat on its side and then savagely pounded it with the mallet. Such was the fury with which he attacked it that he didn't stop until it had been reduced to an unrecognisable sliver of scrap metal about an eighth of an inch thick. Then he turned and glared threateningly at Botham's horror-stricken features.

"You're lucky, mate," he growled. "You don't know how bloody lucky you are."

"Yeah," Botham croaked, glancing from Harry's angry, glittering glare to the wreckage on the bench. "I was gonna take up the cello. But they're too big to like carry around with you all the time. But it's easy with a harmonica, see, because it fits neatly into your pocket."

And he produced another one from his fatigues.

seven

Kevin Murphy's first close encounter with the infamous man from Emu Plains began in an atmosphere of confusion, deteriorated into a state of dumbfounded shock and culminated in near-disaster. Confusion arose when Murphy, even Murphy, quickly twigged that Noel Chisholm was not exactly what you'd call your average everyday run-of-the-mill outlaw. And Murphy quickly latched on to that fact when, having been welcomed into Chisholm's cell, having exchanged the usual pleasantries about the jail's food, accommodation and the going price of a pack of snouts, he got down to the business of feeling Chisholm out by first asking him how he'd ended up in the clink in the first place.

"Drunk and disorderly," Chisholm explained. "With complications."

"Come again?"

"Complications," Chisholm repeated. "At my hearing before the Court of Petty Sessions in Lithgow, I dismissed my solicitor on grounds of professional incompetence, largely because he insisted on me pleading guilty and paying up, and elected to conduct my own defence. All went well until the police prosecutor, no doubt under the misguided impression that he had an open-and-shut case, had the temerity to describe me as an *unemployed itinerant*. I arose and voiced objection immediately, entering a plea of tort of defamation. The magistrate instructed me to belt up and be seated. We engaged in legal argument. 'Your Worship,' I submitted, 'I am well aware that my client stands before this bench as plaintiff in this litigation, that is to say the party of the second part hereinafter referred to as The Mug. However, insomuch and notwithstanding the veracity of the evidence hitherto submitted, my client has instructed me to point out that not only is he in possession of permanent lodgings over the public bar of the Prince of Wales Hotel, he is also the greatest fucking playwright in the world—and the rest of you are a complete pack of cunts!' "

Murphy was already dumbfounded. "Jeez," he breathed. "I bet that went over well."

"It introduced a certain ripple of excitement to an otherwise lethargic hearing," Chisholm admitted. "The magistrate again ordered me to be silent or he would place me in contempt of court. I respectfully submitted that he consider taking a running jump at his good self in spiked boots. Then the police prosecutor took it upon himself to physically restrain me, whereupon I decked him cold with a heavy cut-glass water pitcher. Thereafter, justice turned a blind eye to the proceedings as I conducted a further spirited defence that resulted in three more damaged and sorely aggrieved cops, an outraged magistrate and a list of new charges so grave in nature that I could do little more than advise my client to plead temporary insanity and throw himself upon the mercy of the court. Of course, the only mercy was that I ended up in Emu Plains, and not in permanent solitary in Grafton."

"Grafton?" Despite his shock and confusion over Chisholm's story, Murphy shivered at the very mention of that notorious jail. "Jesus, I wouldn't wish Grafton on my worst enemy," he said. Then he watched with growing fascination as Chisholm rummaged under his cot and emerged with the brown paper parcel that he'd brought with him from the prison farm. Opening the bag, he produced one of his rubber-soled canvas fighting boots.

"Yeah, well," said Murphy, probing again, "so then you nearly destroyed Emu Plains, from what I hear, trying to break out of there. Right?"

Chisholm was now rummaging with his fingers inside the toe-cap of the running shoe. "I wasn't trying to break out of Emu Plains," he said. "The freedom I seek is not earthly, nor is it of the flesh."

Murphy frowned. He couldn't make head or tail of this weird, strange-talking bloke—or the small medicine bottle full of cocoa-coloured liquid that Chisholm had now pulled out of his shoe. Completely bewildered, Murphy ventured closer to the issue that had brought him to Chisholm's cell.

"Well, I tell you what, Nole, I can think of a nice bit of flesh that I'd break out of this place to get to any bloody day of the year." To explain, he pulled a thin leather wallet from his prison blouse and opened it to reveal a heart-shaped framed snapshot of a tall, curvaceous and absolutely stunning redhead in a flimsy two-piece bathing suit.

Chisholm's hands paused at the cap of his medicine bottle as he leaned forward to study the picture. "Who's that?" he inquired. "Raquel Welch in a red wig?"

"My wife, Marcie," Murphy explained proudly. "Isn't she a bloody beaut? You wouldn't think she's had two kids, would you?"

"I wouldn't think she could avoid having kids," Chisholm observed, causing Murphy to flush with even hotter pride.

"That was taken in Surfer's Paradise about three years ago, just before I got done for bank robbery," Murphy said. "Christ," he sighed, carefully watching Chisholm's expression. "Every time I look at that photo I go crazy out of my bloody head to bust right out of this joint."

Chisholm raised his head and looked him straight in the eye. "Don't look at it then," he advised him.

Murphy sighed again. And, confused but undaunted, he tried another tack.

"I'll bet you've got a nice little bit of stuff out there that you'd bust your arse to get to, haven't you, Nole?"

Chisholm smiled, his fingers still playing with the cap of his little bottle. "If you're referring to women of the female sex, Murph, I've got enough of them out there to make penal servitude a bloody blessing in disguise. I have no less than six wives, all of whom I deeply love—all domiciled in as many foreign countries, all legally wedded to me and all sufficiently distant from each other to flaunt and natter their way through life blissfully unaware that they are not strictly in the singular. Of course, if they ever join as a whole, I'll be up to my neck in shit and lawsuits—should they ever manage to track me down."

Murphy was flabbergasted. "*Six wives?* How the hell did you manage to get away with that?"

"In the approved missionary position, I can assure you. There's nothing queer or untoward about me. I married most of them for the children, which is as it should be. Does God not command us: Go ye forth and procreate? It's about the only agreeable bloody thing He ever dreamed up." Chisholm's features strained and reddened as his hands flexed on the cap of his bottle. "Must have seized up," he grunted. "Generally you don't have to remove the top at all. The contents eat their way through. Anyway, to get back to women . . . Like any healthy red-blooded Australian, I have always favoured the direct approach over the trite and time-consuming dalliance of courtship.

It's a practice that worked particularly well with my third wife, the Honourable Lady Cynthia Wilkinson-Hyde, a ravishing young widow of immense wealth and country seat in the craggy coastal wilds of Cornwall. When first I met her, I had been introduced to the household by a young Mayfair fortune hunter of chinless demeanour named Reginald Hyphen-Hyphen. After two years of ardent and heated suit-pressing, young Hyphen-Hyphen had hardly progressed beyond the coy flirtation and an occasional discreet hard-on at the dinner table, and I suspect that he dragged me along for supper to prove that he was not only a man of acceptable social standing but possessed of infinite cultural and intellectual connections as well. Naturally, I turned up pissed, confusing the butler's polite grab at my overcoat as a lunge aimed at ejecting me from the ancestral manor."

Murphy watched, transfixed, as Chisholm finally unscrewed the top of the bottle and lifted the strange draught to his lips. He took a healthy pull on it, then calmly put the cap back on and placed the bottle beside him on the bed. He continued.

"Lady Cynthia turned on an excellent repast. The trout and pheasant testified to the natural abundance of her estate, and the fine wines paid tribute to the extent of her . . ."

Murphy waited politely for Chisholm to press on with his tale. When some time had passed, he attempted to prompt him.

"Her what, Nole?"

"Whose what?" Chisholm queried.

"Lady Cynthia's what."

"Ah," said Chisholm. *"JEEEEE-ZUSSSSS FUCKING CHRIST!!"* This surprise verbal explosion hurled Chisholm sideways on the cot, scaring the wits out of Murphy, who went cold with horror as the man from Emu Plains jerked over onto his stomach and proceeded to cough violently and pound his forehead on the wall.

"Hold on!" Murphy yelled. "I'll get some help!"

"It's all right!" Chisholm gasped. "It's passing!" He struggled around into a sitting position, tears streaming down his face, and punched himself several times over the heart. "God deliver us!" he choked, gulping air like a stricken fish. "Jesus," he breathed, his spasms gradually subsiding. "I could make a bloody fortune out of that stuff as an antidote to cardiac arrest." Wiping tears from his eyes and cheeks, he continued.

"As I was saying, Lady Cynthia had a cellar absolutely chock-a-block with fine wines, several of which were of such celebrated vintage that I confess that I found myself not only falling in love with this rare privileged jewel of English womanhood but with her taste for the little delicacies of life too. I was also developing a contempt for young Hyphen-Hyphen, whose sole contribution to the merry discourse at the table was an occasional horsey laugh, a flutter of the eyes at Her Ladyship and constant reference to the Peerage of Burkes. I myself elevated the conversation to Shakespeare and loosed my first spear directly at the tantalising cleavage of the good lady's exquisite bosom, which the soft glow from several solid silver candlesticks likened unto ripe peaches in a bowl of fresh cream.

" 'Dear Lady,' I murmured throatily, gazing into her lovely eyes.

'When Love speaks, the voice of all the gods
Make heaven drowsy with the harmony.'

"Her eyes moistened, and the rapid rise and fall of her breasts told me that my bolt had gone deep into her heart. Hyphen-Hyphen let out a shrill whinny of excitement and fell off his chair—being pissed as a parrot by this stage. As the servants removed him from the room, more wine was called for, as a result of which Her Ladyship's diamond tiara popped off her head and plummeted like a shooting star into her crepes suzette. And her hair, bursting its carefully coiffured bonds, spread its wings as though it were a mighty bird and its shiny black plumage swept and curled downward over her delicate, milk-white bare shoulders like a raven coddling its young. I gently took her hand, my senses transported to ethereal heights of passion and prose.

" 'Like sheaves of corn,' I whispered ardently,

'He gathers you unto Himself
He threshes you to make you naked
He sifts you to free you from your husk
He *grinds* you to whiteness
He kneads you until you are pliant
And then, He assigns you to His sacred fire
That you may become sacred bread
For God's sacred feast . . .' "

A silence descended upon the tiny cell as Chilholm, his heart a-flame, his soul soaring on sweet sweeping breezes, sat rigid of limb and tight-lipped as though containing an inner turmoil. Murphy stared at him in great wonder, waiting for him to speak.

"Christ, Nole," he breathed, "don't stop now. What happened next?"

Chisholm's far-away eyes turned on him, bewildered, as though returning from a long voyage. He smiled, and did speak.

"Her Ladyship clung desperately to my hand—gathered, threshed, sifted, ground, kneaded and rendered like soft putty in my grasp. In the divine candle-lit stillness, our hearts speaking where words could only fail, I decided it was time to thrust my final dart.

" 'Lady Cynthia,' I murmured, 'do you fuck?'

" 'My dear Mr Chisholm,' she sighed, a tiny sob issuing from her lovely lips and heavy lashes falling demurely over her eyes. 'I thought you'd never ask.' "

eight

UP IN HARRY PEARCE'S CELL, TIMOTHY BOTHAM had put his second silvered shriek-instrument to his cherubic, slightly sullen pink lips to blow another scale. But after glancing at the look in Harry's eyes, he swiftly slipped the accursed thing into the breast pocket of his green prison fatigues.

"It must be pretty tiring, trying to like make something artistic," he observed.

"You've got no bloody idea," Harry muttered, moving away from his workbench and slumping on his steel-frame cot with a heavy sigh. He reached under his pillow for a packet of makings and began rolling a cigarette. "I can do it a lot bloody easier without you and your bloody mouth-organ," he said.

"Harmonica," Botham reminded him, and Harry froze in the act of wetting his rolled gasper, pursed his lips as though to say something, then decided to let the matter slide before he did something imprudent like punching his chisel right through Botham's silly head. He didn't like to think thoughts like that because they reminded him of the axe . . .

"I don't know what you've got against it, Harry. The other blokes don't seem to mind."

Harry's thoughts were skating across a pool that ran deep and dark beneath them. "Mind what?" he asked with a start.

"The har—" Something in Harry's eyes told Botham to belt up before something very terrible happened to him. For once, he belted up. Harry lit his cigarette, pulled deeply on it and blew a jet of smoke at the floor between them. Botham diplomatically stayed beyond arm's reach, near the cell door, his hands thrust into his trouser pockets. He looked as if he was about to whistle. Instead he simply cast his big brown eyes around Harry's cell.

"You've got this place really set up nice, Harry," he observed. "Looks like a real home with those pictures on the wall there, and that worktable and all those books over there."

Harry glanced idly around the cell and said: "Yeah, well I ain't exactly moving anywhere for a while, am I?"

"How long you like got to go, Harry?"

"A lot bloody longer than you, mate," Harry growled, and for a few contemplative moments both of them studied the cell's smart whitewashed walls, the near-absurd colonial architecture of arches curving over the door and alcove, the six-foot steel bunk draped with a loudly striped and tassled Philippine hand-woven blanket—and two Kevin Murphy oil paintings that adorned the walls, one over Harry's bed facing the doorway and the other on the wall across from the workbench.

The painting above Harry's bed was a vertical portrait of Harry himself. Its bottom edge hung only a few inches above Harry's head, and from Timothy Botham's position—he had now slumped swiftly and heavily, like a tired puppy, into a cross-legged position in the middle of the floor—he was looking at an eerie double image in which Harry's face glowered at him from the bed and the portrait regarded him with the same brooding, challenging stare from the wall above him.

To Botham, it was uncanny that a picture could be such a dead-ringer for the subject. In all his school photos, taken each year in a mass pandemonium of guffaws and blushes and protests and flashing bulbs and teachers threatening savage floggings right, left and centre, he had always been bitterly disappointed, year after year, to find that the lens had again failed to duplicate his inherent masculine beauty and had again turned him into a simpering, horsey mama's boy with skin eruptions.

But if Botham could see the exact likeness of the two Harrys before him, he was too young as yet to see Harry Pearce himself. He looked upon Harry with his heart, and saw only what his tender emotions wanted to see—a fatherly warmth and protection in a harsh and dangerous environment. It had taken Kevin Murphy's genius with the brush to say exactly what there was to say about the man. And, on the surface, it was sheer enigma.

Against a neutral sky-blue background, Murphy had painted a face that was neither remarkably long nor noticeably wide, that was just gently rounded with ears that neither jutted out nor hugged close to the skull, a nose that was neither aquiline nor aristocratic nor abnormally flattened and wide-nostriled—though it had been broken in the fight with Willie Crewe—nor upturned nor bulbous. Harry's cheeks were perhaps fuller than they were hollow.

Under his nose Harry wore a reddish moustache that flourished in growth and was turned down slightly at the ends. Even then, if there was anything remarkable about Harry's face at all, the moustache hid it—he had virtually no upper lip; the fleshy part of it had developed inside his mouth, where it tended to pack like a dentist's mouth-wad against his upper teeth and make the moustache protrude further than it should. He did have a knobbly, pugnacious type of chin.

Murphy had filled the space between the lines with features that were brooding, withdrawn, secretive—this impression underlined with heavy jutting eyebrows which overhung eyes that were small, set a little too close together and varied in colour between slate grey and dark marble specked with diamond glints, depending on whether his mood was casually mistrustful or approaching sudden anger.

Harry Pearce was balding, his hairline creeping slowly back from his forehead to the crown, the dry reddish-blond tufts laid in careful spit-licked strands, like buffalo grass cuttings, across the denuded patches. He looked like the sort of man who could drink quietly and rhythmically for hours on end amid the clamour, cigarette smoke and lager fumes of a packed public bar and not once attempt to strike up a conversation. If there was anything remarkable at all about Harry it was his violent, unpredictable temper.

During the two and a half months that Botham had been in Parramatta Jail, he was lucky never to have seen Harry blow his cool. But then, if you asked Botham what he thought of Harry he'd say that Harry was a nice friendly bloke, and "like he's my best cobber in here." This was a role that Harry wasn't exactly ecstatic about, but as he told Kevin Murphy on the rare occasions that they talked about Botham: "Someone's got to look out for the poor little bugger."

Of the two paintings in Harry's cell, Botham liked the other one the best. This one was of great dimension, both in size and subject. It measured six feet wide by four feet deep, covering almost the entire wall, and it had taken Murphy three months to complete. It stirred Timothy, as it did many of the other prisoners, with feelings that were a mixture of calm and confusion.

It was a landscape, conjuring up Murphy's deep love of the rich, half-tamed country on the edge of the wheat belt of the New South Wales central west, somewhere between Lithgow and his birthplace, Orange. With great panorama it featured a floodwave of bald, pea-green, rock-scattered slopes that tumbled gently down from the looming purple-blue haze of the inland foothills of the Blue Mountains. It was harsh, bleak country that Murphy had civilized with a flock of sheep, frozen in various grazing postures, that sprawled from one softly rolling breast of green in the centre of the frame to the rocky cataracts and snagged flood-debris of a creek that wound from left to right, diving into the mysteries of a gully just before it flowed out of the bottom right-hand corner of the canvas.

At that particular corner Murphy had added something that confused most of the prisoners and even angered others. He had added, in stark close-up, working toward the viewer from a low ridge hiding the creek's descent into the gully, a combined harvester. Not an entire combined harvester—just a part of it. In fact, it was just the droop-nosed chaff chute and a section of the seed-separater that was showing, the rest of the machine disappearing right off the canvas. No-one could figure out exactly why Murphy had chosen to do such a thing, least of all Murphy himself. As Henry Trembler, the Queen's lifer, pointed out when Murphy had completed the painting:

"Why bugger up a good picture with something no-one understands?"

"I don't know," Murphy confessed. "I got to the end of it and suddenly had this thing about wheat on my mind. You ever seen the patterns that the wind makes on a big spread of ripened wheat the other side of Bathurst?"

"I wouldn't set foot the other side of Bathurst if my bloody life depended on it," said Henry. "A little matter of sodomy at a Cub Scout jamboree. Naturally it was blown up out of all proportion by the local press. Some of the little buggers actually enjoyed it." Henry slipped his thick bi-focal spectacles on and thrust his skinny, near-bald features up close to the paintwork. "I'll say one thing for you— you did a good job on those sheep."

Murphy grinned. "Coming from an old sheep-dipper like you, I take that as a professional compliment."

Trembler hissed with sardonic mirth. "I tell you what, they're no bloody joke when they start jumping. You've got no choice but to jump with them, unless you want to risk a couple of busted kneecaps."

Timothy Botham peeled his gaze away from the painting and, like a bored puppy, let out a little snuffling sigh. "Perhaps if I played something else . . ."

Again, Harry was jerked out of the deep, dark pool of his thoughts. "What? What are you on about now?"

"Well, maybe it's 'Danny Boy' that gets on your wick. Maybe if I played something else you wouldn't get so uptight about the harmonica."

"Can you play anything else? Like 'Sounds of Silence' or something?"

Botham's brow knitted with thought. "I tell you what. You pick a tune and I'll learn it. It won't take me more than a couple of weeks once I've got the hang of it."

"Forget it," said Harry. "You make enough bloody row with 'Danny Boy'."

Botham frowned, his full, slightly girlish lips pursed as though to kiss his mother's cheek. "I sort-a thought like everyone played a harmonica or guitar or something in jail."

"You been watching too many bloody prison movies, old mate."

Harry checked his wristwatch. An hour yet to go to lights-out and lock-up. He was dying to get back to his precious stone.

"I thought it was a good idea to like help while away the long lonely hours . . ."

"Jesus," Harry breathed. "You start thinking in terms of *hours*, mate, and you'll find yourself with a one-way ticket to the funny farm."

"What else is there to do?"

"Well," said Harry, "what else does a bloke do when he's stuck in a cell with nothing but bloody time on his hands? If he's got any sense he gives his bloody hands something to do."

"I'm no good at paint—" Then Botham realised what Harry was referring to, and he blushed so fiercely that Harry was almost sorry he'd referred to it.

"I'm not that type!" the youth protested hotly.

Harry said: "What do you mean *that type?* Do you think we all took a vow of abstinence when we came in here? Do you think we put our puds in cold storage?"

"No," Botham admitted, still pink with embarrassment. "It's just that I'm like saving myself for someone—you know."

"Who, for Christ's sake?"

Botham took a deep breath and a look of pain flashed across his sweet, innocent features. "The woman I love," he declared.

Harry was about to howl with vile laughter. As it was, his moustache effectively curtained his incredulous grin. "You mean that bloody dragon who got you into this mess?"

"She's not a bloody dragon!" Botham's fists were clenched knuckle-white with fierce indignation. "She's a very fine woman! And she loves me. She told me so."

"She told you so!" Harry allowed himself a little moment of maliciousness. There were moments when he was plain fed up to the teeth with bloody Botham. "When did she tell you that? Just before she phoned for the bloody cops?"

He immediately regretted saying that. Botham's face had gone a sickly white, his brown eyes wide and moist with mortification. Harry sighed and softened his voice. "Look, mate, I know a thing like this is bloody tough for a kid your age. You got a bum rap, and you shouldn't really be in here. But do me a favour, will you? Don't play that bloody mouth-organ. It doesn't help while away the hours, it just makes them even more bloody unendurable. And I've got a lot bloody longer to go than you, mate."

Botham rose petulantly to the challenge. "I'm not in here for a bloody holiday, you know. I got sent down like for burglary!"

"Burglary!" This time Harry did laugh, loudly and rudely. "That's a real heavy sentence, that is—all of one to four with probation after two if you keep your little freckled nose clean. Listen, you silly little prick"—Harry's voice hardened into a harsh snarl—"I've been in here nearly twice that long already—seven bloody years! And I've got another bloody fourteen to go!"

"Well, I didn't kill anyone," Botham murmured.

"You didn't exactly burgle anyone, either," Harry rasped. "You're in here because you went sticking your dick in someone else's bloody sheila!"

Harry could have kicked himself for saying that. It was the one cruel thrust that stuck like a knife in Timothy Botham's heart. Even now, three months after Botham had been escorted into the jail by Bull Sanderson, heads never ceased to shake in amazement, tongues never stopped wagging, over the real story of Timothy's intrepid burglary.

Timothy Botham was a sensitive, kindly lad who'd won pleasing grades each year at school, passed his high school Leaving Certificate and emerged with a natural aptitude for fixing things, be they electric toasters, transistor radios, lawn mowers or Holden cars. Other than that, he was somewhat retarded. He had just turned nineteen years and six months when his boss at the Wetherill Park Four Corners Auto Clinic, a service station on the outer fringe of Sydney's south-western suburbs, sent him along to fix Mrs Muriel Everingham's faulty big end. It wasn't the first time Mrs Everingham's big end had gone wrong. It was a standing joke at the Four Corners Auto Clinic. And Timothy, of course, missed the joke every time his boss leeringly informed him that Mrs Everingham was after someone to fix it for her again.

Eventually it became Timothy's turn to do the fixing, and he went forth on his yellow-tanked Suzuki 125 motorcycle with his tool-box strapped firmly to the back of the pillion, pledged to ensure that the dear lady never had trouble with her big end again.

At Botham's subsequent trial it was never firmly established that he literally went forth a babe-in-arms and ended up in a bear-trap.

Apart from his widowed mother and three elder sisters, Botham had rarely ventured within the fringe of a woman's perfume, let alone got close enough for a squizz or touch of forbidden female things. He wasn't even quite sure why they were female. He had no father to tell him, his old man having started drinking like a fish the moment he and his Australian Infantry Force regiment returned from Alexandria in World War Two and finally staggering off into some unknown oblivion when Timothy was seven years old, leaving the boy at the tender mercy of a warm, loving, man-hating mother and three bullying elder sisters who told him he was now the "man of the house" and proceeded to watch him like a bloody hawk.

Surrounded by females, and having no father against whom to measure his own masculinity, he grew up with a big gap in his development. And as he made his innocent way towards Mrs Everingham's clutches, he could not boast of one solitary furtive, fiddly experience with girls: Throughout his infancy and primary schooling he had regarded them simply as funny high-pitched creatures who spent most of their time screeching and weeping and being sick. In his strictly segregated high school days they were bigger specimens, housed in a complex separated from his classes by a wide no-man's-land of shrubs and a wire fence, who screeched, wept, vomited, waved at the boys and grew acne.

His elder sisters weren't much help. They fought, spat, scratched, connived and spent a lot of their time boxing his ears, and otherwise represented a sort of neurotic wraith of shower steam, pantyhose and hair-curlers, and pink, lace-trimmed, padded nylon brunchcoats that fell apart at the front on rare occasions to reveal pink, lace-trimmed nylon slips.

So it was little wonder that when Botham rang Mrs Everingham's doorbell and finally confronted the dark-haired, full-figured, intrigued lady, he said—without a word of a lie—"I've come to like fix your big end."

Mrs Everingham quickly caught her breath, as though a bucket of ice-cubes had been poured down her remarkably generous bosom. And after looking young Botham up and down, mostly down, she replied: "You'd better come through to the garage and take a look at it."

That was about all that Botham would subsequently recount in the remand cells at the nearby Liverpool Court of Petty Sessions, and upon his arrival at Parramatta Jail. The raw, unexpurgated details came later as his long, lonely hours grew longer and more unbearable. It's enough at this stage to say that after his first visit to Mrs Everingham's home, the trouble with her big end became even more chronic. The poor woman needed all the fixing she could get—her husband being all thumbs and whiskey fumes in such matters and preoccupied with his real estate business and his responsibilities as an alderman representing Wetherill Park on Liverpool City Council. So each week, and sometimes twice a week, Mrs Everingham would telephone the Four Corners Auto Clinic and coyly inform the panting Botham that her big end needed his special touch with the screwdriver again.

This went on for six months, and it was just two days after Botham's twentieth birthday, at the safest hour of the day, about eleven in the morning, the he and Mrs Everingham were resting, spent and sweaty beneath the moist, rumpled sheets of her big double bed, her big end having just performed beautifully, when a car pulled into the driveway right below the bedroom window.

"My God!" Mrs Everingham gasped. "It's my husband!"

The next sixty seconds were a muffled, thumping melee of bare legs and breasts and bums and panic-stricken faces as the two lovers tore frantically into their clothes. Time was fortunately on their side: Both were fully dressed, and Mrs Everingham had shoved Botham roughly out into the hallway, then locked herself in the bedroom, by the time Alderman Everingham's heavy hand rattled the knob of the kitchen fly-screen door.

"You there, Moo?" the tall, florid, overweight man called as he clumped heavily through the kitchen. When he reached the hallway and saw Botham standing there, blushing crimson and still out of breath from the fury of getting dressed, his big mouth fell open and he demanded: "Who the bloody hell are you?"

Botham glanced wildly at the bedroom door, turned to run, then pulled himself together—standing to attention and facing Alderman Everingham with an expression that was both noble and defiant.

"Looks like you caught me red-handed," he said. "I'm a burglar."

And as Alderman Everingham barrelled down the passageway to grab him and tear his young arms and legs off, the bedroom door creaked open and the mussy, sleepy, yawning features of his wife peered out to murmur: "I was taking a nap, dear. I thought I heard voices . . ."

In the ensuing nightmare of police cars, interrogations, threats, cells, his mother's stricken sobs, the formal charges and his first court appearance, Botham stuck staunchly to his story. He had visited Mrs Everingham's home several times to fix her big end, and he thought there might be some money lying around. This seemed to satisfy the magistrate, who, because this was a first offence, remanded Botham for seven days in custody pending reports from his school and a fairly superficial psychiatric report. But it didn't satisfy Botham's fellow prisoners in the remand cells, especially when he began to get a bit scared of the whole situation and confessed to them that he and the dear lady had been having an affair.

"You must be out of your fucking head," they told him. "D'you know you can get six months for first-offence burglary? You're lucky you didn't have a bloody penknife in your pocket."

"Six months is nothing," Botham declared, paling at the thought of it. "It's worth it if it'll like keep her name out of it."

"You're a bloody lunatic! You can't go to jail for screwing some other bastard's wife!"

But Botham's loyalty was indomitable. "She's a fine, like beautiful woman," he declared. "And I will like walk through hell in bare feet to protect her reputation."

It took all of the seven days in remand for the other prisoners to talk some sense into Botham's stupid head. And, thank Christ, they finally convinced him that no bloody sheila, no matter how good she was between the bloody sheets, was worth six months in the bloody clink. So, when Botham was brought forth for sentencing, and the magistrate asked him if he wished to make a statement from the dock, the nervous young man—trying not to look at Mrs Everingham, who was sitting pale-faced at the front of the public gallery, close to her corpulent husband's elbow—said he did have something to say.

"Well, say it," the magistrate said testily.

"I can't say it in front of all these people," Botham pleaded, and out of the corner of his eye he saw Mrs Everingham grip her husband's arm.

"Well, write it down then," the magistrate suggested.

An expectant hush descended upon the courtroom as Botham wrote his short, terse, somewhat unfortunate explanation on a slip of paper, folded it neatly and handed it to the Clerk of Sessions, who placed it in the magistrate's bench. The magistrate slowly and rather dramatically put his reading glasses on and took a long time unfolding the note and poring over the short message. It read:

I am not a burglar. I was having intercourse with Mrs Evering-ham.

Amid a taut, tense silence, the magistrate glanced over at Mrs. Everingham, the good lady by now chalky-white despite her makeup, wearily removed his spectacles and returned them to the breast pocket of his waistcoat. Then he carefully, deliberately, tore the note into tiny pieces.

"In all my twenty years as a magistrate on this bench," he rumbled, his voice almost breaking with emotion, "I have never encountered such a wicked, unprincipled attempt to pervert the course of justice. Not content with your proven, criminal assault on the property and well-being of two of this community's finest and most upstanding citizens, you now have the rank audacity to try to drag the name and reputation of a gracious, highly respected woman and loving wife through the muck of your own contemptuous evil-doings. I am tempted, in a moment of personal anger and revulsion, to bring the full force of the law to bear with new and far graver charges. Nevertheless, I shall cast my personal feelings aside, however much it grieves me, and sentence you, Timothy Albert Botham, to the maximum penalty for breaking and entering with intent to steal—*four years!*"

Four years for unarmed burglary was hardly enough to grant Botham a place of pride in a prison that held some of the most dangerous thugs, thieves, rapists, murderers, kidnappers and arsonists of Australia. Four years for prodding somebody else's wife was an absolutely bloody joke, and it tended to put Botham on the defensive—so much so that one would have sworn he'd held Muriel Everingham at gunpoint day after day, the pin of a hand grenade clenched between his manic, grinning teeth as he raped her brutally and repeatedly—deaf to the horrible entreaties of her trussed-up husband—then fought a two-hour bloody gun battle with the cops before being wounded in both arms and legs and dragged kicking and screaming through a wail of sirens and flash of rotating patrol-car lights to the waiting bullwagon. When this didn't impress anyone, he tended to attack—as he did now in Harry Pearce's cell.

Still smarting from Harry's blast of mockery, he said: "I suppose you're a big-deal crim, Harry, just because you butchered somebody."

"Listen, mate," said Harry, "I'm sorry I put you down. I shouldn't have upset you like that."

"Who did you kill, Harry?"

Harry tensed. His storm-grey eyes began to glitter. "You know very well who I killed—everybody in here does—so don't get bloody smart."

"Wasn't it your wife?"

Harry got up slowly from the bed. He held his clenched fists close to his thighs. "Shut up," he hissed.

"With an axe?"

Shaking now, Harry raised his fists and placed them against his brow. "I told you to shut up, Timothy."

But Timothy stupidly pushed his luck. "You're a real crim, all right. Like you axed your wife to death, then you went and killed your—"

"Shut up! Shut the fuck up!"

Harry had grabbed wildly for his chisel. He held the sharpened steel instrument like a dagger—rushing at Botham; and Botham, suddenly deathly scared, tried to scramble sideways, crab-like, across the floor to escape Harry's blind, murderous wrath. And right at that moment, right when Botham was within an arm's swing of death or disfigurement, Kevin Murphy burst into the cell.

Or rather, he fell in—lurching against both sides of the open doorway, then tripping over his own feet and stumbling against the wall, where, like a marionette cast aside after its performance, he crashed onto his backside on the floor with his arms hanging loosely at his sides and his legs thrust woodenly out in front of him. Harry froze with the chisel poised over Botham's fair head. Botham sprang up from the floor, and he and Harry gaped at Murphy, who sat slumped against the wall with eyes that were strange and glassy and a mouth that worked on words that would not come.

"Murph, what's up?" Harry croaked. "You sick or something?"

Murphy finally made sounds. "Whacko-the-fucking-diddle-lo!" he shouted, staring around him with that glassy expression. "It's on! Chisholm's going with us! Goodbye Parramatta, hullo freedom!"

Harry glanced at Timothy Botham's bewildered face. "That's enough, Murph," he growled. "Put a bloody sock in it."

Botham turned on Harry. "What's on, Harry? What's he talking about?"

"Mind your own business, Timothy. It's got nothing to do with you."

"Holy shit!" Murphy exclaimed, laughing and slapping his thigh. "That bloke's an out-and-out fucking yahoo! He's a one-man bloody riot looking for a place to go ape-shit!"

"Shut up, Murph!" Harry barked. He grabbed Timothy by the shoulder and turned him roughly toward the door. "OK, Timothy— shoot through. Murph and I have got something private to discuss."

But Botham shook him off. "Don't treat me like a kid, Harry! You're gonna break out of here, aren't you?"

"Don't be bloody stupid, Timothy. Only mugs try to break out of here."

"Who're you calling a mug?" Murphy yelled belligerently. "I'm the bloke who planned this whole deal, remember? I'm the one who got it all together. Kept it under bloody wraps. Planned every bloody detail. Not a bloody word to anyone, remember?" Looking up, his eyes gradually focussed enough to spot Timothy Botham. "Oh, hullo, Timothy. You coming too?" And Harry let out a loud groan of exasperation as Murph fell sideways onto his shoulder, then threshed about into a sitting position again. "I tell yer, Harry," he gurgled, "I'm down there listening to that mad flip for an hour or so and wondering if he's all right in the bloody head, and I'm giving the bastard every bloody opening I can think of to get him around to the break, and—"

Again, Harry began pushing Timothy toward the door. "Get lost. I'll talk to you later," he hissed.

"I wanna go too, Harry. You've got to take me with you."

"—and anyhow, I'm just about to give up and call it a day, and Chisholm says thanks for dropping in and all that, and how about one for the bloody road, like . . ."

Harry sighed, let go of Botham's shoulders and, throwing up his hands in despair, ambled over to his workbench, there to lean against it with an air of absolute unconcern as Murphy babbled on. He winced and closed his eyes as Murphy, still slumped against the foot of the wall, suddenly broke down and started weeping.

"Harry," he wailed, "it's been three whole bloody years since I had anything like a sniff of booze. No man should have to go that long. It's bloody criminal!" He snorted and snuffled and wiped his tear-streaked face with the sleeve of his green prison shirt, then abruptly broke into a manic giggle.

Harry looked savagely at Timothy Botham, who was hovering close to the door. "See? He's pissed out of his brain. He doesn't know what he's talking about. Now bugger off, and forget it."

Murphy's giggling switched suddenly to another howl of anguish. "How was I to know the bastard was drinking bloody *pure alcohol?* I took a swig and I thought I was going to bloody die. Chisholm looks at me and he says how d'you feel? I says I can't feel a bloody thing. He says that's strange, most blokes go straight into terminal lunacy on the first swig, and he says try another belt—maybe your brain's had time to build up a resistance. And all the time I'm like trying to tell him *No*—I can't feel anything. I'm numb all over. *Completely bloody paralysed!* But by that time he's forced another shot of the stuff down me . . ." With a horrible moan, Murphy rolled onto his face on the floor. "Christ," he groaned. "I'm gonna be sick."

"Grab his arm, Timothy!" Harry snapped, rushing over to Murphy. Together, they hauled Murphy onto his knees and dragged him across the cell to a toilet bowl set into an open recess behind the wall alongside Harry's bed. As Murphy retched and choked, Harry turned away with his nose twitching on the vile fumes.

"All right, Timothy," he gasped, "I can handle him now. Go to bed."

"I wanna go with you, Harry," Botham insisted. "You know how bad I wanna break out of here."

Harry looked about fit to explode. However, he shot a withering look at Murphy's heaving shoulders, then again took Timothy's arm and moved him toward the cell door.

"OK," he sighed. "If we go, you go."

"You beaut, Harry. When do we go?"

"Christ knows," Harry growled. "You can see what sort of bloody ringleader we've got. Anyhow, we haven't got it all worked out yet."

"You wouldn't bullshit me, would you Harry?"

"No, I wouldn't bullshit you . . ." Harry stopped him at the door, looked hard into his big brown eyes and dropped his voice to a harsh, threatening whisper. "But I tell you one thing, Timothy. You so much as breathe a word about anything—*anything*—that just went on, and—" He gestured at his workbench. "You saw what I did with that bloody mouth-organ, didn't you?"

"Yes," said Timothy.

"Well, I was only playing silly-buggers then—you understand?"

"Yes," said Timothy.

When Botham was gone, Harry dragged Murphy off the loo and onto the bed. Murphy's face was as white as a bedsheet, his eyes like pools of blood in the snow, and he was trembling like a cold, wet dog. Other than that, he had regained some control of his faculties. And he was looking very sorry for himself.

"Sorry, Harry," he said, shivering.

Harry was hardly mollified. "You fucking nong-nong," he rasped. "You buggered everything up again, didn't you? Now we've got Timothy and an out-and-out bloody pisspot knowing we're planning a break. Why don't you just announce it at roll-call tomorrow so the whole bloody jail can talk about it?"

Murphy shuddered and looked as though he was about to throw up again. "Christ, I feel ratshit," he groaned. "Sorry about Botham, Harry. D'you think we can trust him?"

"Looks like we'll have to. Either that, or we forget the whole show. We can forget bloody Chisholm too, by the sound of it."

"No, Harry." Murphy managed to stagger up off the cot and lean rubber-like against Harry's workbench. "That's what I was trying to explain," he said, coughing a bit. "I was down there like trying to test him out, and all the time he was trying to *test me*. That's why he got me pissed. As soon as I could like get my brain working again he says well, I'm sure you didn't come down here just to take a look at insanity alley, did you? And I told him I was chairman of the Prisoner's Action Committee—still treading very carefully, like. So he says what sort of action do you get up to—handing out Red Cross parcels? And I says what sort of bloody action do you think we get up to? And he says search me. And I says what sort of bloody action are you looking for? And he says you're a painter, aren't you? And I says yes. And he says painters use a lot of turps and methylated spirits, don't they? And I says—"

"For shit's sake, Murph!" Harry interjected. "Haven't you got enough bloody brains to see the bloke's nothing but a piss-head?"

"Harry, I'm not a complete dill," Murphy protested. "I could see that we weren't getting anywhere so I started to leave, and I asked him if there was like anything I could do for him. And d'you know what he said?"

"No," Harry sighed, "I don't know what he said."

"He said yeah, you can put me in touch with the bloody escape committee."

Murphy was suddenly overcome by another attack of nausea,

59

with accompanying shivers. He flopped down on Harry's bed again and held his head in his hands until the seizure had passed. Then he looked up at Harry's disbelieving features.

"I know. You could've bowled me over with a bloody feather. I said what, d'you want to break out of here? And d'you know what he said?"

"No," said Harry, "I don't know what he bloody said."

"He said, 'I don't want to break out of here, I want to break out of Australia.' I said, 'I don't understand, Nole.' And he said something about the whole fucking place being a prison of the mind. I said, 'Steady on, old mate—you're stretching the old imagination a bit, aren't you?' And he said, 'Why not? We're all prisoners, aren't we? Why else do we keep coming home?' And then I couldn't make head or tail of what he was talking about after that, on account of being smashed to the eyeballs . . .'"

A distant howl of sirens broke into Murphy's tale, and a bell rang into the lofty gloom of cell-block C.

"Lights-out in five," said Harry. "Come on—you'd better get back to your hole before they start locking up."

As he helped Murphy toward the door, Murphy said: "What do you think, Harry?"

Harry said: "I think we're wasting our time on a nut."

"You may be right," Murphy conceded. "But I still reckon we can't afford to do without him."

"How come?"

"Well, for one thing, he writes plays—and that's just what we need to keep everyone busy during the arts and crafts exhibition, right?"

"Maybe," Harry conceded.

"And another thing—he flies planes."

For the first time that evening, Harry had something positive to say. "That's interesting," he said.

"Yeah," Murphy agreed. "You'd be interested to hear how he flies them, too."

nine

NOEL CHISHOLM NOT ONLY FLEW PLANES, he also had a habit of driving cars through churches. He had also married, among his other wives, a Tahitian beauty and a coffee-brown Moorish girl named Habeeba. On top of that, he had knocked an Australian diplomat flat on his arse in a Spanish bar and pissed on a Maharajah's head in Calcutta. He had also got himself roaring drunk in the cocktail bar of the international terminal at Sydney's Kingsford-Smith Airport when, setting foot on Australian soil for the first time in thirty years, he heard a newscaster open the Australian Broadcasting Commission's lunchtime radio news with the following apochal announcement:

"The Treasurer and Deputy Prime Ministers, Dr Jim Cairns, today stood up and sang 'Waltzing Matilda' in a department store in Shanghai . . ."

The news had cheered Chisholm, for until that moment he had considered himself virtually alone in the world, perhaps the last of the intellectual yahoos—survivor of a great post-war exodus of artists, academics, philosophers, writers, journalists and adventurers who had fled Australia in search of the rest of the world, taking with them the testament of the jolly swagman, an immense capacity for drink, the tendency to stride larger, and louder, than life through foreign places and a deeply religious adherence to the yahoo's sacred code:

> *I can run, jump, fuck, fight,*
> *Wheel a barrow*
> *And ride a bike.*
> *And God help any bastard who looks twice at me.*

It was a code that said much about the sort of Australia that Chisholm and many other expatriates had left behind them, or, in some cases, carried with them—an isolated, insular frontier society with a fierce national pride, an inferiority complex as long as your arm and a cultural development as far behind the times as the distance between London's Big Ben and that mammoth reddish-pink desert boulder near Alice Springs; a place of quarantine which, with its penal heritage as a dumping ground for Great Britain's thieves and rebels, had bred men as strange, tough and individualistic as its peculiar animal life.

Yet they were men torn by conflicting instincts and values—men who thumbed their noses at all forms of authority, yet were prisoners of their own narrow codes; men who disdained the influences of the outside world, yet fought like threshing machines when it came to fighting anyone else's war; men who scorned the Poms, yet looked constantly to Mother England for a mail-order identity; who drank as if it was about to go out of fashion, yet tolerated prohibitive liquor laws that would have caused riots in Paris or Rome; who loved fellow-men and merely fucked women; who wept over Lawson or Banjo Paterson one minute and pounded someone's bloody head in the next; who had a natural instinct to fight for the underdog, unless he happened to be black, brown, yellow or, as he called them, a dago, wop, spick, Nick the Greek or a dirty bloody Arab; who loved the desert and sunburnt sweeping plains, yet clung to the nation's coastal rim; men who were Wild West anachronisms in a world that had already left the real West behind it—who were walking, talking, irreverent identity crises banging on the fly-screen door with a case of chilled beer, a howyergarnmate-orrite?, a joke about the time the lightning struck the shithouse, the latest cricket scores, a profanity of language that collapsed into awkward silence the moment women entered the room and a savage urge to rid the psyche of all conflict by indulging in the one Australian characteristic that guaranteed refuge from all isolation, confusion and yearning—a whacking great almighty piss-up. Followed by a quick chunder or two over the back fence.

Yet there had been a valiant element there, a something untamed and rebellious, before a sanctimonious middle-class reaction to the convict past took hold of the nation, bringing with it the sort of petty restrictions and prejudices that spread with the bloody cancer of red brick-and-tile suburbia, creeping outward from the cities to form big stultifying blobs of coastal cowardice in a nation whose vast heart cried out for the strong and the brave.

There had been the yahoos—the bushrangers, the swaggies, the stockies, the cockies, the larrikins—who knew the bush and roamed it as a dog seeks out every nook and sniffing place of its own backyard, all of them sharing one Australian characteristic: They wouldn't take shit from anyone. Then there were the yahoos who fled—the intellectual and literary rebels, or anyone with any real bloody brains, hounded out of the place by apathy, political reaction, obscenity charges or the long deep sleep of "Pig Iron" Bob Menzies' silly despotic rule; and the artistic dispossessed, who had gone abroad in search of relief from the stark, unremitting landscape of the cultural desert. Then there had been the fuck-ups, the walking wounded like Noel Chisholm, whose reason for flight had encompassed all that the others had left for—along with the added complication of a good old characteristic Australian rebellion against everything that was typically Australian. Which, ironically, only made him more Australian in the long run.

Why had he been such an unorthodox womaniser—in direct antithesis to the general Australian male's regard for women as a quick horizontal handshake, or sneeze in the loins, in between the booze and the lawn bowls championships, why had he married them? Because marriage, to him, was the bow with which child-arrows were shot forth onto the path of life; and children were a pledge of love; and love was in the hearts of all women once you sat down and *talked to them* instead of rolling home pissed as a tick and ripping off a quick poke before shut-eye.

Why had he married the Tahitian girl and the Moorish Habeeba? Because a union like that was tantamount, back home, to marrying an aboriginal or anyone whose skin showed the slightest touch of the old tar-brush. And why had he belted the Australian envoy flat on his dinger in that Spanish bar? Because the lamebrained racist fuckwit had articulated something unspeakable—questioning the prudence of a dinki-di Aussie getting hooked up with a bloody darkie.

Chisholm had encountered the luscious Habeeba in Majorca, up in a highland community known world-wide as The Strip—a watering hole of numerous cheap bars where Chisholm and a wild assortment of international drunks had washed up to drink out their days in style and thrift. Most of Chisholm's colleagues had their names prefixed or suffixed with whatever brand of poison they'd chosen to escort them to their graves, for they were all dying. There was Maurie Martell, Hennessy Harry, Horace Haig, Dolly Dimple, Charlie Three-Thirty-Three and Habeeba, whom Chisholm had labelled in honour of her favourite drink and in defiance of his countrymen's derogatory slang for an aboriginal woman, Gilbey's Gin. Having recently fled the debilitating clutches of Lady Cynthia Wilkinson-Hyde's vast estate, he had already earmarked Habeeba as his fourth wife.

Though a common bond existed among all the drunks on The Strip, Chisholm generally teamed up with Charlie Three-Thirty-Three, the black sheep of a New York Social Register family who was given considerable allowance to get lost and drink himself to death, and engaged in a happy daily routine. This involved Chisholm and Charlie starting each morning at one end of The Strip and drinking their way to the other, while Sergeant Carlos Fernandez, the local Guardia Civil officer, patrolled the street in his uniform and comic black hat, his carbine cradled at his chest, protecting them from danger.

The Strip contained twenty bars, and that was only on one side of the street. There were thirty-two on the other. In between, the street hummed and beeped with heavy tourist traffic. When Chisholm and Charlie had covered the bars on one side, Fernandez would be waiting for them, and, restraining them both from staggering to their deaths, he would drape one over each shoulder, blow his traffic whistle and escort them across the road—with Charlie Three-Thirty-Three carrying his rifle for him.

At each bar they encountered, Chisholm had a rather distinctive way of greeting his fellow drunks. He would stand swaying in the doorway, his hair looking as though winds were playing through it, his eyes practically crossed, and bellow:

"I'm the best fucking playwright in the world—and the rest of you are a complete pack of cunts!"

At each and every bar, heads would turn and mutter salutations, then swivel back to their drinks, for Chisholm was known to all who carried the same mark of death. Except at one bar, one particular day, when Fernandez had helped drag Chisholm and Charlie across the street and onto the sidewalk, prised his carbine gently from Charlie's hands and pushed them into the nearest tavern. Chisholm halted just inside the door, belligerently surveyed the crowded premises and hollered:

"I'm the best fucking playwright in the world—and you're all a pack of cunts!"

And next thing, he was flat on his back on the floor, someone having just jumped up and thumped him right on the nose. And that someone, looming over him, said in an unmistakably familiar accent:

"Listen, feller—I don't care who you think you are. Yer don't use language like that in front of a lady."

Chisholm shook his ringing head and said: "You must be an Australian."

"Too bloody right I am," said the stranger, helping him to his feet.

It turned out that the king-hit artist, a man bedecked in a loud floral shirt, mauve Bermuda shorts and knee-length white hose, was Bert Monkton, third secretary of the Australian Embassy in Madrid. Not only that, but Monkton was so pleased to see another bloke from Down Under that, despite Chisholm's little indelicacy of the tongue, he was anxious to forgo the normal rules of a *shout*, in which each man must buy a round of drinks when it's his turn, and insisted on picking up the whole tab.

A great deal of drinking was done, during which Charlie Three-Thirty-Three passed out under a table and Bert Monkton introduced Chisholm to his lady wife, Maude, a surly, big-boned, uncommunicative sheila who had skin that was sun-dried to a wrinkled, blotchy parchment and who insisted on drinking gin fizzes, topped with a veritable salad of lemon, mint-leaves, lime and orange peel, through a straw. Chisholm took one look at her and felt like challenging her to a fight. However, Monkton swiftly got drunkenly nostalgic and the talk turned to the mind's distant vistas of sunburnt country and sweeping plains.

"I tell you what, Nole, the missus and I have been all over—London, Europe, America, the Middle East, you name it—and I still reckon there's not another country anywhere in the world like Australia."

"You can say that again," Chisholm agreed, wondering if Maude Monkton's facial expression of a constipated cockatoo was permanent or worn just for this particular occasion.

"Yeah, we're the Lucky Country all right, Nole," Bert mused. "We had the right idea right from the start. Keep the buggers out. I mean, look at England these days. All the trouble they're having there. You let one in, you've gotta take every-bloody-body and his dog. Next thing, they're taking the place over like they owned it. Now don't get me wrong—I'm as tolerant and easygoing as the next bloke. I mean, they can't help it if they were born that way. But horses for courses, Nole. Each to his own, I say. I mean, it's like the bloody Eyetalians and Greeks. We had one in our town. Set up a greengrocery right next door to old Bluey Johnson's store. Bluey fixed him. He put a bloody great sign outside his shop saying SHOP HERE BEFORE THE DAY GOES . . ." Bert thought that was so funny he nearly pissed himself with laughter. Chisholm gritted his teeth and concentrated his attention on Maude Monkton, who kept shooting him challenging, hostile looks over the jungle foliage of her *lady's drinks*. Recovering from his hysteria, Bert Monkton bought another round of drinks, leaning heavily against the bar as he got more drunkenly nostalgic.

"No, mate, we're lucky down there. Australia's soon going to be the only decent place in the world to live. Anyhow, three years overseas is long enough for me and Maude. We'll be back in Sydney next year. How long you been away, Nole?"

"Thirty years," Chisholm told him, and Bert whistled with sympathy.

"Jeez, that's pretty tough. And what do you do for a crust, Nole, if you don't mind me stickybeaking?"

"I, my friend, am the world's greatest bloody playwright," Chisholm informed him, and he swung around to yell defiantly at the rest of the bar: "And the rest of you are all a pack of cunts!"

"Ratbags!" Bert bawled. "Dead-shits, the bloody lot of you!" He cocked a guilty eye at his lady wife, Maude. "Excuse my French," he mumbled.

And that's when a pair of slim, delicately tapered coffee-coloured hands crept around Chisholm's neck from behind him and closed gently over his eyes; and Chisholm smelled the musky warmth and heard the close, throaty low whisper of Habeeba. Turning, he swung the luscious, long-legged, mini-skirted creature off the floor and, as Bert Monkton and his wife nearly toppled off their bar-stools with shock, he kissed the dark beauty on her full, flat lips and paid homage to all that had brought her to him.

"Dear lady," he rumbled eloquently, "when thy great Berber ancestor Tariq Ibn Ziyad swept into Spain and crushed all that lay before him under the sword of Islam, he brought with him the blood and fire that my poor old dying limbs feel now through that flimsy piece of material wrapped around your exquisite nether parts. Civilisation has turned full circle, my love: That skirt used to be known as a loin-cloth." And, fully aware of the Monktons' tightly strained politeness, Chisholm introduced the delicious girl by that name by which he commonly and affectionately knew her—"Gilbey's Gin."

And Bert Monkton said: "Jeez, I didn't know we allowed any abos overseas—apart from the tennis players, that is."

And Chisholm said: "She's no aboriginal, my friend. Habeeba is the hybrid of history's bloodiest bedmates, the Arab and the Spaniard. Thank Christ that they came together at a time when man was still throwing rocks at himself."

Habeeba was laughing gaily, her teeth flashing in the smoky gloom of the bar, and Chisholm kissed her again with much drunken reverence. "And one day in the near future," he said, "when I can sober up long enough not to bring shame upon my breed, I'm going to make her my wife and see what a bit of Antipodean can add to her proud strain."

So stunned were the Monktons at this that Maude slopped half her gin fizz over the bar and Bert said: "Jeeeezus Christ! I mean, every man to his own taste, and all that—but I wouldn't have picked you as being the sort of bloke who'd marry a wog!"

And next thing, Bert's body snapped backwards, cannoning into Maude and tipping her arse-over-head off her stool, Bert having been belted right in the mouth by Chisholm's fist, which he now waved furiously at the fallen man as Habeeba clutched at him from behind, fighting to restrain him.

"You see that fist?" Chisholm raged. "It's connected to a thing I have inside me called an inbuilt shit-detector, which activates the moment it gets a whiff of foul-mouthed crap like you!"

Bert Monkton was mouthing oaths from the floor, struggling with Maude, who was trying to haul him to his feet. And Habeeba was clutching tightly at Chisholm's neck and shoulders, holding him back, trying to pacify him with her soft, deep voice.

"No, Senor Chisholm. You must not fight theez man. You are *compadres*. He eez your brawther."

"No brother of mine would ever call anyone a wog. I'd kick his arse from here to breakfast time," Chisholm informed her; and at this, Habeeba stiffened and stepped back from him, and the gorgeous black softness of her lovely lithe body was suddenly transformed into the clawing, spitting, taut crouch of a she-cat. And she let out an unearthly scream:

"A WOG!! I KILL HIM FOR THEEZ!!"

But Chisholm got there before her, stepping forward to plough his fist again into Bert Monkton's flushed, boozy, blood-streaked face just as the man pulled himself up onto his feet—but his good lady Maude stopped Chisholm dead in his tracks with a vicious, lightning-swift kick in the balls that set off such an explosion of agony that Chisholm toppled into a tight forward-roll, clutching at his crotch, and ended up in a foetal position at her feet—one of which she raised again to stomp the living daylights out of him.

And that's when Sergeant Carlos Fernandez rushed into the bar to see what all the commotion was about, and Habeeba—the terrible blood of her ancestors igniting again within her, setting off an absolute cataclysm of violence—snatched the Guardia Civil sergeant's rifle from him, aimed it point-black at the Monktons and, horror upon horrors, OPENED UP ON THEM!

"It eez not loaded," Fernandez sympathetically informed her as the weapon clicked furiously in her hands and Bert Monkton shat himself with fear. Fernandez never carried it loaded for fear of the damage that Charlie Three-Thirty-Three might do if he happened to stumble and fall as they were crossing The Strip. Habeeba went for Maude Monkton, chasing her around the suddenly deserted bar, and Fernandez knelt down on the floor, gazed at Chisholm's pain-wracked face and sighed wearily.

"Senor Chisholm," he said, "why you do theez theengs?"

Chisholm grunted with pain, and gasped: "Because, my friend, I am dying."

"Mother of Christ!" Fernandez breathed, crossing himself quickly. "I am sorry to hear theez."

Chisholm let out another gasping moan. "We are all dying, my friend," he whispered. "I've been dying since the day I saw something in the Pacific. Ever since that day I've elected to remain permanently pissed. And when I'm pissed, I do theez theengs."

As things turned out, Fernandez had to call in a detachment of Guardia Civil reinforcements to restore order when Habeeba went completely berserk with the carbine, swinging it by the barrel and clubbing everyone in sight. Chisholm spent the next fortnight in hospital, after which he paid for the extensive repairs to the wrecked bar with money borrowed from Fernandez, borrowed more money to marry Habeeba, then took her off in search of another island—a voyage of discovery that eventually landed them on the Mediterranean rock known as Malta, where Chisholm immediately made friends with Sergeant Joey Borg, officer in charge of the police station in the tiny fishing village of Kalkara, close to the spot where Dragut died of his wounds in the famous Turkish seige of the Knights of St John, and eventually drove his car through a local church.

Not Dragut. Chisholm.

ten

CHISHOLM'S ATTACK ON THE CHURCH WAS AN ATTACK on a God he didn't believe in. As Chisholm recounted it to Harry Pearce and Kevin Murphy when they visited him in his cell four days after Murphy's initial overtures, bringing with them a gift of methylated spirits which Murphy was allowed to requisition for his artwork:

"It wasn't the church itself that worried me—the Maltese build the bloody things like cathedrals. It says something for Catholicism that the poorest Catholics generally build the biggest churches. No, the toughest part was getting the car up a hundred or so stone steps leading to the main doors without stalling or tearing the arse out of the chassis on the way up."

Murphy asked: "What sort of wheels did you have?"

"A Hillman Imp, blue in colour—a nippy machine with just the right power-weight ratio for the job. I'd had it specially tuned up that morning."

Pearce, being the more suspicious of the two, asked the more obvious question: "Why the bloody hell did you do it?"

"Would you drive a clapped-out banger through a bloody church?"

"No," said Harry. "What I mean is, why did you drive through the bloody church in the first place?"

"Ah." Chisholm paused for a moment, putting his thoughts into order. "Why? Because for much of my life God and I have been locked in savage combat. I, because I refuse to believe in Him. He, because He demands that a power with His capacity to allow such pain, injustice and misery must be loved and worshipped. He commands us to call Him Our Father, but what sort of father could allow his only son to be strung up on a cross, speared with a sword and left to bleed to death? And don't think He did it to save mankind! We're still a bunch of bloody barbarians."

"OK," said Harry, more suspicious than ever. "How could you possibly pull off a crazy bloody stunt like that?"

"I had Joey Borg the policeman on my side," Chisholm explained, pouring methylated spirits into a tin mug and topping it up with orange juice. He took an experimental sip and went a fiery red in the face, clutching at his violently heaving stomach. "Shhhhhiiiiiiiittttt. Not bad," he gasped when his insides had calmed down. "An interesting little brew. The bouquet brings tears to one's eyes. The body suggests a fermentation of dried bullock's shit. The effect upon the brain can only be compared with the impact of a ten-pound hammer on a ripe watermelon. However . . . As I recall, Pal Joey agreed not to arrest me as long as I observed one important condition: that I *not* drive my vehicle through the church of our own village, Kalkara, where his widowed stepmother owned the bar next to the church and his younger stepbrother was the altar-boy there. So I selected a church in the nearby township of Concepcione, which I thought was a fitting and significant name, seeing as I was about to fuck their beliefs altogether. And the Maltese take their beliefs very seriously. It's one of the few places in the world where the inhabitants cross themselves before setting out on a two-mile bus ride. When you see the buses, you realise why. And in these buses, behind the drivers' seats, there are little glass-enclosed tableaux of the Son and Immaculate Mother, their breasts torn apart to reveal blood-swollen, suffering hearts, with gold lettering underneath praying JESUS AND MARY SAVE US ALL. Christ, this stuff is one hundred percent . . ." Chisholm knocked back another belt of the metho cocktail and again fought to hold his insides down. "The church I'd selected was ideal," he gasped when the battle had been won. "It was so big it had a dome that made a mockery of St Paul's. More important, it was situated in the centre of Concepcione's main square, so it had doors on all four sides. At my appointed time, the stroke of noon, with the bells of the church already tolling the mid-day Mass, I strode forth from the little bar where I had been taking refreshment and crossed the hot, baking tarmac to where Pal Joey was making a last-minute check of the Spit's undercarriage. It was a beautiful machine, a Mark Two. Had a four-bladed screw that cut down a lot of the dangerous bloody torque of its predecessors . . ."

Pearce and Murphy were gazing open-mouthed at Chisholm, who had gone completely cross-eyed by now as the meths punched him hard in the brain.

Harry said: "You flew, huh?"

"I flew with John Gorton," Chisholm said. "And I'm glad to say I wasn't with him when he pranged. By that time I'd already been transferred to a discipline squadron anyway."

"Jesus," Harry breathed.

"As I recall, the Spit roared into life at the first touch of the button. I checked the rudder and controls, throttle, altimeter and other sundry instruments, calling them off to Pal Joey, then set the flaps. As the engine howled at the required pitch I waved cheery-pip to Joey and he gave me the thumbs-up for clearance—and with the ribbon of tarmac stretching away before me, with the target towering in the distance, I gunned the Spit toward glory.

"It was the fastest machine I'd ever flown. It seemed like no time at all before I was almost upon the target. The Spit handled beautifully, responding to the gentlest touch. I flew in very low, hardly more than a few feet above the ground, and just when it seemed I was about to plough into the face of the cliff I pulled hard on the stick and booted the machine into a screaming high-speed climb, the Spit bucking and jumping violently as I opened up with my wing-cannon. As I levelled out at the zenith of the climb, the machine hit a patch of bad turbulence, dropping suddenly like a stone and bouncing with a jarring crash off a thermal updraught that felt like solid concrete. My strafing run had taken me right into the enemy's teeth. Hardly any room for manoeuvre. I swung the Spit into a tight starboard evasive turn and all I could see was a swirl of faces revolving sickeningly around me, faces stricken with terror, old crones in black habits and shawls crossing themselves frantically as I twisted and turned to dodge the flak.

"It suddenly dawned on me that my number was up. Nothing could survive such a hellspot. And sure enough, I took a bad hit—

port side, rear cockpit window, right inside the fuselage. A kamikaze priest, fanatic bastard, came straight at me swinging an incense burner like a sling, heading dead into my gunsights. This was my moment of truth: The glory of oblivion, knowing I'd taken him with me, or last-minute evasive action that would leave me free to fight again . . ." Chisholm was by now flying so high on the metho cocktail that his voice trembled and cracked with emotion and tears turned his blue eyes into huge pools of fuming spirit. "*I wanted to live,*" he croaked. "I didn't want to die in some forgotten place that would be forever Lithgow. Just as we were about to collide I tore the Spit into a screaming starboard turn—and that's when the bugger hit me!"

Chisholm's shoulders had slumped, as though he were crushed by the memory of it. The tears streaked down his flushed face. He looked drained. Harry and Murphy sensed that his ravaged brain had finally topped the fiery peak of the methylated rocket ride and was toppling into the first stages of re-entry.

Harry asked: "What hit you? The priest?"

"No—the incense burner," Chisholm moaned, calmer now. "He'd flung the bloody thing through the back window of the Imp. The whole car filled up with the foul, acrid smoke. I couldn't see a damn thing for it. I was so bombed by that time I thought I was on fire. All I could think about was getting the hell out of there and back to base. So I headed for the first break in the clouds, and shot out the same church doors that I'd come in. The descent down those bloody steps to the street shook me up so much that I nearly rolled the car. I sped back to the safety of Kalkara, dumped the Imp behind the police station and took refuge in the bar owned by Pal Joey's stepmother. Thanks to Joey's influence on my behalf and the fact that the church at Concepcione was confusingly situated in the middle of the main thoroughfare, thanks also to my well-known struggle against the devil drink—the Catholics, you know, have a splendid understanding of evil as something that man carries with him, like cancer or athlete's foot, and is rid of only by death and salvation . . . Anyway, thanks to all that, I got off on a dangerous driving whilst under the influence conviction and agreed to leave the island. I also agreed to leave Habeeba, who was with child and unable to cope with further emotional strain—watching me fly out each day and never certain whether I would return. There are many churches in Malta."

If Harry Pearce was suspicious of most things around him, there was a reason for it: He was a naturally suspicious type of bloke. He was also not the sort of man who sought and made casual friendships. Real friendship was almost a love affair for him. It had to be all or nothing at all—no buggering about, no holding back, no backing down, no tricks, no piking, no bullshit; and complete and irrevocable commitment on both sides. So Harry rarely had any friends.

During his life on the outside, his only real mate had been Roy "Blooch" Boots, of whom it could be said no better cobber a man ever had. Blooch, whom the old-timers in the pubs of Surrey Hills still acclaimed for his performance on Anzac Day, 1958, the year before Harry got married, when he brought the house down at a pre-dawn rum-and-Bovril binge in the Randwick Returned Servicemen's League Club by suddenly bending over in the packed, medal-festooned main bar, shouting "Fire! Fire!" and letting rip with an almighty fart that Harry ignited into a sheet of blue flame with a cigarette lighter. Unfortunately, the blast of fire had a blow-torch effect on the president of the club who was standing nearby, scorching a bloody great hole in his best bag-o'-fruit—the result of which was outrage, followed by a brawl which caused several of the veterans to limp painfully when it came time to join the Anzac parade, thereby heightening the emotion of an already heart-tugging annual event.

Blooch, who never once gave Harry reason to regard him as anything but a true friend; whom Harry felt he had literally betrayed when he married Shirley and inherited her bitch of a mother at Coogee, the Eastern Suburbs beach community, on June 14, 1959, and got sucked into a deadly *bombora* of domesticity and hate. Blooch, whom Harry hadn't set eyes on since a day in March, 1965, when his mother-in-law—might she one day rot in bloody hell!—triumphantly informed him that a court order had been obtained restraining Blooch from entering her house again, causing further mental strain and anguish to her and her suffering daughter and otherwise committing indiscretions at the dinner table.

It was the loss of Blooch and the subsequent cold, horrible reality of a life chained to two spiteful, vengeful, mentally barren women that set in motion a train of torment that eventually carried Harry to the culminating mayhem of the axe—a blind, maniacal lapse of sanity, a sudden and terrible rampage with the heavy blade that ended in murder most foul and shocking, along with a life sentence to Parramatta Jail.

When Harry arrived at the jail he went into solitary confinement in the Blockhouse for his own protection, which was something of a laugh when you consider how many men would care to tangle with an axe-murderer. But prison procedure said he needed protection, because within the spare but strictly enforced code of infringements in the criminal world there are two particular types of offenders whose crimes are abhorrent even to criminals: rapers and murderers of children. And Harry Pearce had murdered not only his wife, Shirley, but his child too.

It mattered not that the boy had been slain in the insane collapse of a mind tortured to complete breakdown by almost eight years of combined torment from his wife and her bloody mother. It mattered not that Harry had loved the cuddly, flaxen-haired little chatterbox more than anything else in the whole world. It mattered not that the two women had instituted a divorce suit and were claiming custody of the child just before Harry blew his stack. It mattered not that, during the terrible bloodbath with the axe, a pinpoint of peculiar reasoning at the back of his crazed mind had told him that his wife already bludgeoned to death and he himself now facing the wrath of God and society, there was no-one to look after the little boy except his mother-in-law, who had fled in terror from the house. And that was one thing his ravaged sanity could not accept.

All that mattered when Harry finally reached Parramatta Jail was that he had murdered a child. So he went into the Blockhouse, a forbidding, featureless concrete building with no windows that was segregated from the rest of the prison by a barrier of tall stone walls crowned with glass and barbed wire.

Solitary confinement was a miserable routine even for Harry, who wanted nothing more than to be left alone with his misery. He existed in a tiny cell with a bunk, an open toilet box, his soul-consuming grief and a stunted wooden table that offered, rather pathetically, a cheap plastic-bound copy of the Holy Bible. Harry eventually got so desperate that he read it cover to cover, three times.

For twenty-three hours of the day, Harry saw no daylight, nor the features of a fellow human being. He lived in the subterranean gloom of wire-netted, low-watt lightbulbs, or the darkness of night, and learned to measure his empty fathomless time by the rude clang and clatter of a narrow letterbox hatch set into the bottom of his cell door, as, three times a day, an unseen hand thrust his food through to him. His thoughts dwelt almost entirely on his mother-in-law.

For one hour each afternoon, chain-linked manacles were locked to Harry's ankles and wrists and he was led out into the piercing, almost blinding sunlight of a small and private exercise yard. There, as he clanked and jingled around a path worn in loose cinders by other feet before him, moving as mindlessly as an automaton, he found he was not alone in his solitary hell. Behind him, always about ten paces behind, walked what was obviously the only other inmate of the Blockhouse, a tall, gaunt creature with a hooked nose, long sandy-coloured greying hair that was spreading in ratty lanks over his ears and down to his shoulders, and eyes that were steel grey and cold as Christ on a mid-winter's morning.

The mysterious figure was shackled, as Harry was, in his green prison fatigues. Other than that, Harry knew absolutely nothing about him, nor could he find out anything—for on the one occasion that he turned to speak to the man, a carbine-toting warder who watched over them told him to shut his guts, keep his eyes to the front and keep moving. The man himself never once, in the whole three months, made any attempt to communicate with Harry; but he became the subject of much discourse when Harry finally emerged from the Blockhouse and joined the other convicts, and Henry Trembler—quick off the mark as usual—became one of the first to start drawing Harry out of his numbness.

"Heavens above!" Henry exclaimed. "Three months in that morgue would just about drive me around the bloody twist. I'd go blind from self-abuse."

"Yeah," said Harry.

"That," said Henry, pointing at the tall, wire-fringed walls, "is where they put the real dinkum evil criminals. They call them *intractibles*."

Harry took a look at the multiple murderers, sex-killers, baby-slayers, rapists, armed holdup artists, strong-arm merchants, cheats, liars, thieves, sodomists and various other transgressors at large in the open section of the jail, and whistled.

"Christ," he breathed. "There's a bloke still in there."

And in doing so he set off a wave of speculation on what horrible, bestial, unimaginable crime anyone could possibly commit that would be considered worse than murder, rape, grand theft, sodomy, demanding money with menaces or beating the living shit out of some poor bloke for reneging on his SP betting debts.

Anyway, Henry Trembler's sleazy advances toward Harry stopped rather abruptly the day Harry took that punishment of sorts from Willie Crewe, then knocked him out cold in the ring. Thereafter, Harry kept completely to himself, despising everybody; and it wasn't until Kevin Murphy bounced into the jail four years later that he began to respond to friendly overtures. It was hard not to respond to Murphy—a tall, lean, thirty-year-old bank robber with a schoolboyish face, a lemon-rinsed shock of honey-blond surfie hair, a joking personality and a comic, hopeless capacity for fucking up everything within arm's reach that suggested arrested development, an overgrown teenage delinquent in need of care and protection, largely from himself. When Murph stuck a beautifully hand-painted sign on Harry's cell door saying WARNING: THESE PREMISES ARE PATROLLED BY GUARD DOGS, it occurred to Harry that anyone with his sort of bloody cheek definitely needed protection. When Murphy sauntered into his cell one day, took a look around the bare walls and said: "You know what? I reckon you could use a bloody great picture up there," the first tenuous bonds of something approaching a friendship began to form. But even then, it was not until the (Rev) Clement C. Hunt Arts and Crafts Society was established, a year later, and Murphy dropped the first hints of his plan to escape, with Harry, that their friendship began to blossom into something comparable to the affair of the soul that had been Harry's relationship with Blooch.

And now Harry was being asked to place his trust in a bloke who drove cars through bloody churches!

Noel Chisholm was draining the last dregs of his metho cocktail. Harry and Murph were still regarding with flabbergasted stares this strange, nihilistic man. Harry finally broke the stunned silence by asking:

"What brought you home, Nole?"

"I had the choice," Chisholm explained, "of either Australia or Tierra del Fuego—the only other island left. I chose Australia because I felt the need to go back to my roots as an Australian, in much the same way that Nolan came home and madly painted pictures of Ned Kelly. Besides that"—Chisholm gazed solemnly into his empty tin mug—"I came home to die."

"You're dying?"

"We're all dying," Chisholm explained. "As for me, death said *Coming, ready or not* the day I saw something in the Pacific. On that day my heavens cracked and shattered. I faced the choice of suicide or immediate retreat to the funny farm. Being opposed to all premeditated forms of violence, and already convinced I was existing in a loony bin anyway, I had no alternative but to remain condemned to life. But that life, thank Christ, is nearly over."

Harry glanced hard at Kevin Murphy, and Murphy raised his eyebrows.

"Can you still fly?" he asked Chisholm.

"I flew Spits in the Pacific and Ansons on the discipline run."

"Can you fly a Cessna?"

"Same thing," said Chisholm. "The old Vickers Wellesby and the Concords share one common characteristic: They both need speed, open space and the correct angle of flaps to get off the bloody ground."

There was a long thoughtful silence, Chisholm still orbiting on the soft wings of his cocktail, Harry and Murphy preoccupied with a mental analysis of Chisholm's attributes. He was a man obviously afraid of nothing, defiant of everything around him. He was a flier and, if the escapade in Malta was not just alcoholic fantasy, he was a bloody good driver too. He was dying, so he had nothing to lose. He was a playwright, so he had something vital to offer. It was Harry Pearce who finally popped the magic question.

"You want to break out of this jail?"

Chisholm laughed. "My dear fellow, I am a prisoner of my own mind. I carry my jail within me, and I've been trying to break out of it for as long as I can remember. I've rattled its bars and blown holes in its walls with bangalores of booze. However, I would like to break out of this joint. I take it you have a plan."

"Yeah," said Harry. "And the way Murph's got it all worked out I'd say it'd be something right up your alley."

Murphy leaned forward, and the others joined him in a tight huddle. Murphy explained the plan.

"Old Clemency's organising a big open day and exhibition to show off the work of the arts and crafts society," he said. "There's going to be some big-wigs coming in from outside to see the paintings and shit that we've done, including, from what I hear, the Minister for Corrective Services, who's a right little bastard, and the Mayor of Parramatta. We're all going to be asked to recite poetry and sing songs and generally perform like a bunch of rehabilitated little angels. It'd be a fucking crime, wouldn't it, if a couple of little darlings grabbed the visitors and held them as hostages and busted out of here— blowing the entire fucking jail to the ground as they went?" Murphy sat back proudly and asked Chisholm: "What do you think?"

Chisholm was by now shakily topping up a second mugful of methylated spirits and orange juice.

"That," he declared, "is about the craziest, most ridiculous, suicidal, half-arsed example of man's indomitable folly that I've ever heard in my life. I hesitate to compare it with the fool who jumped off Sydney Harbour Bridge with a lighted candle jammed up his backside singing 'A Star Fell From Heaven.' I can only equate it, in fact, with the blockhead who leapt after him, trying to blow the candle out. However," he grinned, "it is, as you say, right up my alley. What do you want me to do?"

"Write us a play," said Murphy. "That'll do for starters, anyway."

"That'll certainly be for starters," Chisholm confessed. "I've never written one before."

Harry Pearce let out a huge sigh of exasperation. "Do you mean to say this whole fucking charade has been a complete waste of time? You're supposed to be a great playwright, aren't you?"

"I am," Chisholm assured him. "What do you think my whole bloody life's been about? There's a book, poem, sculpture, painting or play in every man's experience. Mine happens to be a play." He grinned again as Harry and Murphy thought that one over. "However, it's going to be very interesting to actually write one. How long do I have?"

"Three weeks," Murphy told him. "Can you write a play in three weeks?"

"I don't know. I've never written one. Durrell, you know, wrote each segment of his *Alexandria Quartet* in an average of just six weeks, and look what a masterpiece that turned out to be. However, that was a quartet of novels, and I take it you won't want something as ambitious as the *Quartet*."

78

"We couldn't give a fuck what it is," Harry pointed out, "as long as it's ready three weeks from today. We'll leave the subject to you."

Chisholm arose from his bed, took a deep slug of his meths and orange, jerked as though a lightning bolt had hit him, stamped his feet in a while Apache war-dance, then floated euphorically over to a book-strewn desk placed in an alcove similar to the one in Harry's cell. "How about a prison theme—*The Unknown Convict*, or something like that? I'm currently engaged in study of Australia's convict era for reasons that are somewhat dear to me, and it appears that this prison, right where we are now, could well be regarded as the only legitimate monument to this nation's real past. Hardly had this little inland settlement progressed from log cabin to stone hut, it seems, when . . . Let me see . . ." Chisholm produced his spectacles and put them on, then thumbed through one of his books. "Ah yes. Here it is. In 1796, Governor Hunter decreed that each settler and housekeeper had to supply each week ten straight logs, nine feet long and seven inches in diameter, for the construction of the colony's first jail. The convicts naturally had to work a little harder—they had to supply twenty logs a week. But life was all beer and prawns for them, so to speak," said Chisholm, reaching for another volume, "compared with the women in the penal stockade at Toongabbie, less than three miles from here. There, they were worked to death dragging brick-carts for the construction of the settlers' homes. And if I may quote from this record: *The women who misbehaved were put in iron-spiked collars. Six hundred out of eight hundred died in six months at Toongabbie.*" Chisholm snapped the book shut. "Is it any wonder that Australians are renowned for their inherent contempt for the forces of law?"

"Fucking cops," Murphy gnashed.

"Ah, but don't place all the blame on the boys in blue. Men in uniform are disciplined to obey orders without question, and the orders ultimately come not from the barrack floor but the quiet, civilized drawing rooms of our society. Take dear old Nathaniel Payten, for example . . ." Chisholm opened another heavy volume, casting his owlish eyes through the pages. "Now here's a real pillar of decent, civilised society as it reigned then. *Nathaniel Payten, born 1800 of English settler parents; wealthy landowner; builder and stalwart of the established church; a man of little ostentation, a man of action, not of words; his architectural masterpiece was the beautiful All Saints Church of England; he also built the Convict Barracks, the Female Factory and the stone wall, that still survives today, around the infant town's gaol*. That's this jail," Chisholm added, putting the book down and removing his glasses. "Now there's a great Australian monument that you won't see commemorated each bloody centenary. We have the dubious privilege of being incarcerated right slap-bang in the middle of the Cradle of the Nation."

"And," said Murphy, "that bloody wall must be about a hundred and fifty years old by now. No wonder we can never get near it."

"OK," said Harry. "Looks like we've got a break going. Anything else?"

"Yes," said Chisholm, draining the last drops of his second cocktail and collapsing back on the bed. "I need something in return for my work."

"What's that?" Harry demanded suspiciously.

Chisholm held up the empty tin mug. "A constant supply of this exquisite brain-mash, and enough money to set me up in Tierra del Fuego when we get out of here. Like Australia, it's situated at the absolute arsehole of the world, and it's populated, I'm told, only by sheep and goats. So it's the one place in the world where I won't be able to get into any more strife. It's also the only place left."

Harry asked: "How much dough would you want?"

"Two thousand bucks."

"Forget it. You're mad."

"That's how much it will cost to get Habeeba from Malta. Also, Tierra del Fuego is the place I have chosen to die. Is that asking too much?"

Harry sighed and said: "OK, if you put it that way. I think I know where I can raise it."

"It's all settled then," Chisholm beamed, mixing another batch of brain damage.

"Except for one thing," said Kevin Murphy. "We keep this scheme strictly to ourselves. The others'll go with us, when the time comes. They'll create havoc out there and give us a better chance of pulling the whole caper off. But one man doesn't go with us. Henry Trembler stays inside."

"Why's that?"

"Christ, it's obvious, isn't it? That creep's a bloody menace to society. He'll fuck anything that moves. I've got two beautiful young daughters, just out of primary school. I'd never get a wink of bloody sleep knowing Trembler's on the loose."

"OK," said Harry.

"And another thing. Nole, you've raised a lot of hell in your life, but from what you've told us you've always been a bit too bloody friendly with cops."

Chisholm smiled. "No doubt something that has its roots in our convict-jailor heritage. I remind you that the cops have always seemed to come off second best."

"Yeah, well . . . There's another thing that worries me, quite frankly. We still don't know exactly what put you on the wrong side of the law when you came home."

"My luck ran out," Chisholm explained, gazing into the foul yellow depths of his third drink. "When I came back I went to live in a little hamlet near my birthplace, Lithgow, bloody Lithgow, that coal-mining hole in the ground on the other side of the mountains. The police sergeant in my little retreat was an old schoolmate of mine, and naturally we swiftly established a close drinking friendship. His little police post, in which he and his wife had living quarters at the back, had a corrugated iron roof. Every couple of nights or so, when the devil possessed me, we enjoyed a harmless ritual in which I would stand outside, hurl a number of rocks onto the roof and, as they clattered and clanged down the iron, I'd shout: 'I'm the greatest fucking playwright in the world—and all you cops are cunts!' And the sergeant would race out, buckling on his revolver and yelling blue murder for the benefit of his missus, and accompany me to the local pub.

"One particular night, I vividly recall, I threw my rocks, and as they clattered and clanged down the roof I bellowed: 'I'm the greatest fucking playwright in the world—and all you cops are cunts!' And out of the station poured no less than ten uniformed and plainclothesmen who, unbeknownst to me, had been sent there to organise a search for a party of lost bushwalkers. The entire detachment beat the living hell out of me and charged me with drunk and disorderly behaviour."

eleven

(Rev) Clement C. Hunt was a fifty-five-year-old self-defrocked Presbyterian minister who'd spent most of his life married to the church. It was a spiritual union that he'd once tried to explain to a young, beautiful and high-spirited grazier's daughter—the one and only girl whom he had considered joining in holy and temporal matrimony. He warned her that he was married to his faith. She said: "Go fuck your faith, then." And that was the end of that.

Actually, to continue on a crude note, his faith had since been well and truly fucked for him. It showed in his occasional encounters with the Sydney press and various politicians and sociologists who had visited Parramatta Jail since the formation of the revolutionary (Rev) Clement C. Hunt Arts and Crafts Society. To all of them he rather incongruously described himself as a "reformed rehabilitationist," and then defined his role as prison superintendent in this fashion:

"Rehabilitation, in the strictest sense of the word, means to restore to a former capacity, rank or right. Now, I ask you—how can one rehabilitate a creature like Henry Trembler without again putting at stake the safety and sexual dignity of half the adults, children and livestock of Sydney? Take Kevin Murphy—he may well develop into one of Australia's greatest landscape artists. But do you think that when he walks out of here in four years' time he'll have turned his back on banks, shotguns and fast cars? It's far more reasonable to assume that he will adapt his newly discovered talent and appreciation for art to ransacking the Art Gallery of New South Wales. *Rehabilitation*," (Rev) Hunt would submit, his clapsed hands resting gently on his office desk in an attitude not unlike prayer, "is a much confused and misinterpreted theory. I should know, by God. I've tried it."

And, by God, he had. After graduating from theological college he had spent some twenty-five years close to the dead heart of Australia, an ardent troubleshooter of the church's Inland Mission, fighting to bring education and the word of Christ to young aboriginals and isolated whites on and around the cattle stations, mission outposts and hot, barren Far West desert townships of New South Wales—far farther west than Bourke, beyond the mythical Black Stump, where, as Hunt often joked, the crows flew backwards to keep the sun and the flies out of their eyes.

The trouble is, Christ's word went over like a lead balloon amid the fierce heat, the flies, the vast hopeless loneliness of desert vistas that shone like lakes with mirages that stretched interminably from horizon to horizon. The only salvation that interested most of the cheeky-faced, spindly-legged black kids, and the young whites, was that which beckoned them from the City of Sydney, that great coastal oasis, that Garden of Eden, of shade, excitement, of material riches. So, much of (Rev) Hunt's desert mission was spent interceding with the authorities on behalf of kids who'd been caught robbing a post office or general store to grubstake their escape from the wilderness, who were destined for the infamous jails at Bathurst or Grafton, who, with (Rev) Hunt's help, were sent instead to prison farms and training schools.

Almost invariably, they returned home twelve months or two years later and robbed the same post office or general store, this time in a highly professional manner. And when they were caught again, and (Rev) Hunt sought Christian counsel with them again in the lock-ups, he was horrified to hear of the things they'd learned at the farms and reform schools: Certainly not the error of their ways.

In desperation he would put Christ aside and threaten them instead with the dreadful damnation of Grafton and Bathurst, and be shocked to learn that they didn't give a damn. It was all very perverse: But for the thin red line between Good and Evil, they were simply struggling up the ladder of life like anyone else. They were students of the anti-Christ, swotting like hell to gain a place in a tertiary institution, from which they inevitably graduated and returned home, flushed with maturity, to show off their new skills by robbing both the post office *and* the general store, then headed east to much greater opportunities awaiting them in the banks and betting offices of Sydney. And, just as perversely, (Rev) Hunt's country flocks would follow their escapades in the newspapers with the same parochial pride that they'd have for any local boy who made good.

It was this ever-turning circle of lawlessness that finally induced (Rev) Hunt to go east himself and find out where the system was going wrong. He enlisted in the New South Wales Department of Corrective Services, so convinced was he that rehabilitation was needed where it was needed most, in the jails. So anxious was the department to take up his services that he was offered a chaplaincy at the minimum-security Emu Plains prison farm. Hunt responded by telling the department to go to that place from whence he was supposed to save men's souls: He hadn't come east to teach hymns and wipe noses; he had come to strike at the core of habitual crime.

(Rev) Hunt would have been shunted back west on the next Tippuburra Express had not fate intervened at the right time in the form of Dickie King, a half-caste aboriginal and former pupil of one of Hunt's Far West mission schools, who broke out of Bathurst jail, stole a shotgun, fifty cartridges and a Ford utility from an outlying sheep grazier's homestead, then headed west along the Bathurst-Orange highway to the sanctuary of a long-abandoned gold mine in the ghost town of Lucknow—taking the grazier along as a hostage. Just before he reached the mine he ambushed two detective-constables from Orange who, in the interests of promotion, had caught up with him well ahead of the rest of a wide noose of Central West police. Dickie didn't shoot the two cops; he handcuffed them both to the grazier and took all three with him down the mine.

For two days, well over a hundred and fifty police from all over the lush sheep- and wheat-farming area staked out the mineshaft, threatening with loud-hailers to blast Dickie back to the Stone Age if he didn't let his hostages go and come out firing. Dickie didn't even have the decency to reply.

"That's just like a bloody boong," complained the Chief Inspector who was orchestrating the entire police seige. "They haven't got the bloody guts to fight man-to-man without a skin full of cheap plonk. Jeezus, they're decadent."

"I know Dickie personally," said (Rev) Hunt, who'd just arrived on the scene, believing that if Dickie hadn't gone insane with paranoia by now he might be able to talk him into laying down his arms and surrendering peacefully. "I'm convinced," he said, "that if I can get into the mine—*alone*—I might be able to persuade him to surrender peacefully."

"Look, padre," the Chief Inspector said, "a hundred and fifty heavily armed cops haven't been able to persuade that black bas—er, boy to surrender peacefully. For all we know he's already shot the poor souls in there with him. Might have eaten them, for all we know. He's had no food for three days."

"Let me at least try," Hunt pleaded.

"Yeah? And what if he shoots you?"

"Then," said Hunt, bland as can be, "at least he'll die on a full stomach."

After more haggling and entreaties, and after signing an agreement absolving the Chief Inspector of all blame for his death, (Rev) Clement C. Hunt finally strode forth into the no-man's-land between the cordon of police guns and the narrow timber-propped mouth of the mineshaft, a loud-hailer in one hand and a white handkerchief in the other. He was within twenty yards of the pithead and the rusted, twisted rails and long-abandoned machinery strewn around it, when the mouth of the shaft exploded and buckshot whistled high over his head.

"Fuck off, Reverend!" the voice of Dickie King screamed. "You ain't gonna fool me with that white flag!"

"Dickie, I've come to help you," Hunt called through the loud-hailer. "Haven't I always tried to help you before?"

"You ain't never done nothin' for me except bullshit about Jesus Christ! An' look what the bastards did to him!"

"OK, Dickie, let's forget Christ," Hunt yelled, and to show he was on the level he slowly removed his white dog-collar and tossed it to the ground. Although he didn't realise it at that time, it was the most profound act of his life: He would never take up the collar again. "There!" he called. "Now can we talk as one ordinary human being to another?"

"Are you crazy? How can I be a ordinary fucking human being when a couple-a hundred fuckin' cops out there are ready to shoot me?"

"All right, Dickie. All right. Let's forget about human beings. What if I offer myself as another hostage? With a farmer, two detectives and a Presbyterian minister in there with you, you should be able to hold off the entire New South Wales police force."

There was a long, tense silence that was broken only by the wind that whistled mournfully through the rusting, decrepit struts of an ancient gantry that had long ago toppled from the pithead. Then Dickie bawled:

"OK, Reverend—I tell you what I'll do! You can come in here and replace one of these fuckin' cops. He's shit his pants so much the stink is makin' me sick. But don't you try anythin' smart, or I'll fill your guts with lead!"

The exchange went smoothly, (Rev) Hunt almost gagging on a

shockwave of stench that hit him as the lucky detective—ashen-faced and shaking—waddled past him and headed across the wasteland to freedom. Once inside the mine, Hunt groped his way ahead of Dickie, both barrels of the shotgun prodding him in the small of the back, down a dark winding shaft that finally broke out into a wider man-made chamber where the fortunes of the gold-fevered prospectors of old had obviously petered out. The cavern was lit dimly by a single candle, a box containing the best part of a whole gross of them lying nearby. The halo of light weakly illuminated the shadowy, sweating figures of the grazier and the other detective, who were handcuffed together, stripped to the waist and hacking feverishly at the pit-face with a pick and a rusty shovel.

"What in Christ's name are they doing?" Hunt gasped.

"I thought we were gonna leave Christ out of this," Dickie King reminded him. "They're digging for gold."

"Why?"

Dickie's dark face broke into a broad, sardonic grin. "Because I told 'em I'd kill 'em and eat 'em if they didn't. An' they're so shit-scared they'd believe anything. That's when that other fuckin' cop starting crappin' his pants. He just sat there an' shat himself. A grown man, doin' a disgustin' thing like that . . ." Dickie shook his head sadly, then he prodded the grazier with the muzzle of the shotgun, and the grazier tore frantically at the black soil and rocks with his pick. "C'mon feller, you aint gonna make me very rich at that rate."

"Dickie, I know why you're doing this," (Rev) Hunt appealed. "And believe me, this isn't the right way to go about it."

"So what am I supposed to do?" Dickie snarled. "Get a fuckin' bulldozer down here?"

(Rev) Hunt wiped beads of nervous sweat from his forehead and tried again.

"Dickie, I know how life must seem to you. You're black, and it's almost as if the whole rest of the world is white. You're the victim of two hundred years of white oppression and prejudice, and whatever you do to try to raise your voice above theirs, they are still the bosses and the prosecutors, judges, juries and jailors. I know, Dickie. I *know*."

Dickie again prodded his two slaves with the shotgun, and the grazier whimpered with terror. "Keep talkin', Reverend," Dickie muttered.

"I know how it is when your proud forebears have been slaughtered by men with horses and dogs and guns, men who called you savages, yet committed pogroms of untold savagery themselves. I know how the diseases and the alcohol brought by the white man have reduced the pathetic remnants of your people to a status little better than that of camp dogs. I've seen the shanty hovels on the fringes of the country towns where your people are condemned to squalid ghetto life. I've heard the screams of babies weak from malnutrition—with white supermarkets just down the road. I've pleaded with doctors to devote one day a week of their wealthy practices to the care of your people. I've seen education denied you, your dignity stripped away, your racial pride trampled underfoot by the greed of this country's exploiters, young men like you prodded into drunkenness and crime and a life without hope, a life with nothing to offer but the bars of the white man's prisons. I've seen it, Dickie. I know what it's all about!"

Dickie looked stunned. For what seemed like an eternity he gazed sightlessly into Hunt's appealing face; then his eyes went red with sudden, seething rage, and he swung the shotgun back on his terrified hostages.

"You filthy white bastards!" he screeched. "I'm gonna shoot you lousy cunts dead, right now!"

"No!" Hunt shouted, lunging forward to snatch at the shotgun. "No, Dickie! This is not the way!"

"I'll beat their fuckin' brains out then!"

"No, Dickie!"

Hunt fought a furious tug-of-war with Dickie for control of the gun. Finally he managed to turn the muzzle away from the terror-stricken targets. "Don't you see, Dickie, that it is the white man who is the real victim? When the Day of Judgement comes, and all of us, every man and woman and every little creature of the earth, stand before Him, then the colour of a man's skin is going to mean nothing, for we shall all stand naked as the day we were born, our sins stripped from us and held high for Him to see. And when He sees the foul stains of the white man's linen, then the heavens will tremble with His wrath, and the eternal agony of the Fires of Damnation will be His judgement for all those who did thy people wrong!"

Dickie eyed the two gold-diggers venomously and asked: "This Judgement Day—when's it gonna happen, Reverend?"

"One day, Dickie. One day when the earth stinks with the rot of man's corruption, and nothing is left untouched by his putrid smell."

"Yeah, but when, Reverend? *When?*"

"Who knows, Dickie. It may come tomorrow. It may come a year from now. Ten years. Ten million years. Only He knows."

"I can't afford to wait that long," Dickie snarled, raising the gun again. "I'm gonna blast these two white bastards right now!"

And Hunt resolutely folded his arms across his chest and said: "All right, Dickie—shoot them. Shoot them in cold blood. And then you'll be no better in His eyes than they are."

The two prisoners finally cracked completely, spinning around from the pit-face and falling on their knees, sobbing with terror and pleading for their lives. "Reverend!" the grazier screeched. "What the fuck did you come down here for anyway? What have you got against me? I've got a wife and three kids and a two-hundred-acre sheep property out there! That may not mean nothin' to you, but to me it's my whole fuckin' life! *I don't wanna die!* I'll do *anything* to stay alive! I'll dig clear through to the Queensland border for gold for this black bas—er, boy if I have to! Why don't you just fuck off an' leave us alone!"

"There," Hunt murmured, turning to Dickie. "You see that? Why, killing a poor broken wretch of a man like him would be a waste of good buckshot."

"Yeah," Dickie agreed, watching with contempt as the grazier fell forward on his face in the dirt at his feet, dragging the terror-stricken cop with him. "Yeah," said Dickie. "He ain't worth the bloody trouble. Besides, he's gone an' shat hisself like the other one. Christ, these people have go no fuckin' idea of hygiene. Let's get out of here, Reverend, before I throw up."

"Good boy," Hunt smiled, throwing a protective arm around Dickie's shoulders as they made their way back through the darkness of the tunnel toward the mouth of the mine. "You've shown mercy, Dickie, when your body and mind were possessed by the instinct to kill. You came here a frightened boy. You leave here a man who has triumphed over the darkness of his own soul and goeth forth now into the light of everlasting peace and salvation."

They stepped out into the blinding glare of daylight at the mouth of the tunnel, and Dickie, squinting through the sun's blaze, saw a hundred and fifty cops with shotguns, carbines and submachineguns waiting for him.

"They won't hurt you," Hunt assured him. "Nobody's going to hurt you, Dickie. Walk with me."

"You go first, Reverend," said Dickie.

"As you wish."

"Walk right in front of me, Reverend," said Dickie. "They won't shoot a preacher."

"Of course, Dickie."

They walked slowly out into the teeth of the police cordon, stepping carefully over the warped rails of the old diggings, (Rev) Hunt's head held high with majestic bearing and Dickie not more than a pace behind him, shielded by him. And when they were within twenty yards of the police, Dickie lifted his shotgun and shouted:

"Throw your guns down, the whole fuckin' lot of you! Or the preacher gets both barrels in the back!"

"He means it!" Hunt yelled. "He's got nothing to lose! I beg you not to do anything rash!"

There was a massed clatter of metal on rock and shale as the entire police force threw down their weapons; and Dickie shouted:

"Now clear out, right away from here! The whole fuckin' lot of you!"

"Do as he says!" Hunt pleaded. "He's a desperate man!"

Around them the cops stepped back in a mass from their discarded guns, and like the Red Sea the cordon parted at the middle and the blue uniforms melted away to right and left. When he was certain that their way was clear, Dickie handed the shotgun to Hunt, and the minister unsnapped it, took out the two twelve-gauge shells and threw them away.

Dickie said: "What d'you think's gonna happen to me, Reverend?"

And (Rev) Hunt said: "You'll go straight back to jail, Dickie."

"Well," said Dickie, "at least I made a few people shit."

"You certainly did," said (Rev) Hunt. "You certainly did."

Dickie King not only went back to Bathurst jail, but the file of offences covering his dramatic three days of freedom was so long and varied that he ended up with another ten years added to his original sentence. As for (Rev) Hunt, his cup ranneth over with acclaim for his single-handed capture of Dickie and reward for his Christian empathy—the greatest reward of all being the very one that he had been seeking: a temporal post with the Department of Corrective Services. Amid much publicity he was appointed deputy superintendent of Parramatta Jail, where, within the space of a year and the time it took for the incumbent superintendent to drop dead at his desk of a heart attack, Hunt now reigned supreme. Within a week of his triumph he had already set into motion his long-cherished theories on rehabilitation. The first thing he did was to rehabilitate Dickie King from Bathurst and have him transferred to his own prison. Dickie had changed.

"You know, Reverend," he said when Hunt had a little personal chat with him before committing him to Bull Sanderson's care, "I been thinkin' day and night about all those things you told me down in the mine."

"Good," said Hunt. "And don't you agree now that it was better to turn the other cheek and live to fight another day?"

"You bet," said Dickie. "Only next time there's gonna be a fuckin' bloodbath, man. We blacks are gonna kill every white bastard we can lay our fuckin' hands on."

Turning first to the prison's industries, (Rev) Hunt halted the dull, monotonous, unrewarding manufacture of General Post Office mailbags and replaced it with something of far better use and dignity to the prisoners: a full-scale engineering workshop capable of repairing or manufacturing anything from a tin can to a ten-ton truck. After a great deal of lobbying by Hunt around the city's growing secondary industries, orders began to pour in for work on parts and components that the factories couldn't afford the capital investment to make themselves. And out of the workshop poured an incredible variety of weapons—knives, revolvers, rifles, even replicas of the simple .45 U.S. Army "grease gun," a piston-action submachinegun and an assortment of hand grenades, all in perfect working order, all so professionally manufactured that they were rounded up in a one-day emergency swoop by Sanderson and his warders and locked away in a steel cabinet in Clement C. Hunt's office as a vivid reminder of how badly his prison industries scheme had failed.

Unvanquished, Hunt removed the workshop's main production capability—mainly the lathes—and turned it over to panel-beating and minor automotive repair work. This worked well for all of a year, until the city's Chief Inspector of Police threatened to expose the plant as the source of a sudden large wave of car-stealing in which the swiped cars were unrecognisable and untraceable after rolling out of the jail.

(Rev) Hunt's market-gardening scheme, established on a patch of wasteland behind the main cell blocks and under the watchful gaze of the armed guards on the main prison wall, was hastily terminated when a visiting study group of trainees from the New South Wales Department of Agriculture identified most of the flourishing crops as cannabis. Animal husbandry went the same way after a rash of heavily wagered cockfights and a particularly nauseating scandal involving Henry Trembler and most of the animals.

In desperation, (Rev) Hunt turned to sport, and the now-defunct gardening area was transformed into a rugby league football pitch. A prison team was formed and it proved, after several weeks of heavy training, to be a promising one—so promising, in fact, that the city's mayor took up a challenge from (Rev) Hunt and persuaded the city's A-grade league team to try them on for size. On the day of the historic encounter, with Hunt positioned proudly in the middle of an improvised grandstand with the city's press and leading dignitaries packed around him, the visiting team trotted out onto the pitch, jumped and skipped and shrugged around a bit, warming up, then formed a line to handclap the prison team as it emerged from the toilet block. The prison team looked splendid in their black shorts, bottle-green socks and bulky green guernseys—chests out and heads high, a credit to prison reform. The line of men reached the waiting city team and trotted past, warmly shaking each outstretched, friendly hand—then ran like the wind to the prison wall, every one of them, where they pulled coiled ropes out from under their guernseys and hurled them, tipped with grappling hooks, over the wall. Only three team-members were left, still struggling up the last few feet of their ropes, their hands almost clutching the rim of the wall, by the time the spectators, the visiting team and the prison warders recovered enough from their shock to raise the alarm.

Three days later a burly police sergeant, every inch a cop from his peaked cap to his shiny black regulation boots, walked out of the tailoring class that had taken over the now-defunct workshop, casually strolled right through two wire-meshed iron gates leading to the prison's administrative block, negotiated the corridors of the block itself and even poked his head through the open door of (Rev) Hunt's office.

"You run a good prison here, Mr Hunt," he said. "The Chief Inspector asked me to say hullo before I go."

"Oh. Oh, thank you, sergeant," said Hunt, glancing up from a pile of paperwork. "Give the good man my kindest regards and tell him my door is always open if he's around this way."

"Right you are, sir."

Boldly, the sergeant tipped his hat at another wire-meshed, manned checkpoint between the office block and the main gates. Casually, he signed the visitors' log in the guard-room before making a little joke. "You got so many locks and bolts in here you'd think it was a bloody prison," he quipped at a warder who swung open a small hatch in the main gates and bid him a cheery "Gidday, sarge."

Outside the jail, in the sudden shock of traffic noise and birdsong, the sergeant paced slowly and purposefully through back streets leading to the city's main north-west thoroughfare. Not a bell had clanged; not a siren had shrieked. Reaching the main street, breathing deeply the exhaust fumes of a crawling cacophony of peak-hour traffic, he was about to run for a bus when there was a sudden screech of tyres and brakes and a crash of metal close to him, and a sudden gathering of people around the scene of a collision.

The sergeant was about to turn tail and run for his life when a little interfering old lady grabbed at his sleeve and said: "Sergeant, are you going to stand there and do nothing? There may be people bleeding to death in those cars."

With a moan, the sergeant approached the scene of the wreck and found two Holden cars locked together and only slightly damaged, and an angry, red-faced man arguing in English with an hysterical Italian migrant.

"You see what this fuckin' dago did?" the Australian gentleman complained. "Jeezus, they don't speak fuckin' English, they don't bother to learn to read the fuckin' road signs, and they drive around in fuckin' brand-new cars while their families live ten to a room on bread an' fuckin' tomatoes. This wop bastard ran right into the fuckin' front of me!"

"Well, punch him in the fuckin' head then," said the sergeant— and that, of course, was where he blew the whole beautiful escape. The ensuing brawl attracted the real police, who took a very dim view of the aggrieved Australian driver's claim that "the sergeant told me to belt the dago bastard!" and grabbed the escapee as he was about to board another bus a few hundred yards down the street.

The incident also blew completely all (Rev) Clement C. Hunt's remaining hopes of prison rehabilitation. For weeks he procrastinated between reverting the conditions in his jail to the old punishment system or leaving the prison service altogether. He began to withdraw from everyday duties, brooding bitterly for hours on end in his office on the absolute bloody fool that the prisoners had made of him.

God only knows what might have happened if, in absolute desperation, he had not hit upon the idea of arts and crafts and artistic endeavour as a means of keeping the prisoners' minds off escape. Nothing could go wrong with paintbrushes and potter's wheels, he told himself. Even a determined man with a sculptor's chisel would take months to chip his way out of the jail. The only possibility of escape that he could see was for Murphy and the others to leap into the landscape Murphy had painted for Harry Pearce's cell and run off with the sheep. Out of the arts scheme grew the revolutionary (Rev) Clement C. Hunt Arts and Crafts Society, and still another venture which this time was beneficial to the community at large yet required tools no more lethal or dangerous than fine wooden needles—Project Kiddie Kare, in which soft toys were turned out for the State's orphanages.

For one whole year now, the (Rev) Clement C. Hunt Arts and Crafts Society had flourished in an atmosphere of creative, peaceful endeavour. The men worked like little beavers on their paintings, novels, sculptures, pottery, jewellery and batiks. Not one had tried to break out. Not one had so much as looked like trying to shoot through. (Rev) Hunt had triumphed. He should have been pleased. He was. But his faith had been well and truly fucked upon. His vocation had been destroyed. A light had gone out in his soul.

As he often told visitors to his jail, his hands clasped in silent communion on the desk-top in front of him:

"Rehabilitation is a dead issue in the Corrective Services Department and in this jail. I tried it, and look what it did for me . . ." And, rising from his desk, he would unlock the steel cabinet at the rear of his office and show his visitors the arsenal of knives, revolvers, rifles and grenades that he kept there to remind him of his unfortunate folly.

twelve

(REV) HUNT WAS AGAIN DISPLAYING THE ARSENAL OF weapons in his office, this time to a new recruit to the prison staff, a twenty-two-year-old rookie warder named Bruce Greenwood. Fresh out of training school and a neat, shining credit to the Corrective Services Department in his crisp new deep-blue uniform, Bruce instinctively stepped back a half-pace, almost stomping on one of Bull Sanderson's highly polished, steel-reinforced toecaps, as Hunt waved the snub snout and flash suppressor of the "grease gun" at him.

"Do you mean the prisoners have actually made a submachine-gun, sir?" Bruce gasped.

"Oh yes. That, and an assortment of other weapons that would equip a whole army platoon," (Rev) Hunt said. "We've not only got some of the most dangerous, intractible criminals of the Commonwealth in here, we've also got some of the country's finest gunsmiths."

Sanderson coughed politely and stuck in his two-cents' worth. "Don't you take your little blue eyes off those buggers for a second, Greenwood, or we'll be whippin'' round the hat for your bloody funeral."

(Rev) Hunt smiled patiently and said: "Mr. Sanderson may have a rather earthy way of expressing his concern for your safety, but you can take it from me, Greenwood, that there isn't a finer and more experienced prison officer in this whole State. As you get to know the routine here you'll find that Mr. Sanderson virtually lives for his work, and he expects the men under him to follow his example. Why, on years in the service alone, he's been here longer than most of the prisoners."

"Twenty-eight years, sir," Sanderson reminded him proudly. And he told Greenwood: "I was two years younger than you, boy, when I joined the service in 1946. Things were different in those days, feller—criminals were put in bloody jail to be punished."

"Er, yes," said (Rev) Hunt. "But you'll find we have a unique policy in this jail, Greenwood. We allow the prisoners to explore their creative abilities, on the premise that if they're kept busy at work that interests and actually stimulates them they'll be too preoccupied to think about escaping."

"I was about to remark, sir," said young Greenwood, "on that portrait of Her Majesty behind your desk. Is that the work of one of the inmates?"

"Er, yes," said Hunt, turning to admire a portrait in oils of the Queen that Kevin Murphy had painted especially for him to mark the inception of the (Rev) Clement C. Hunt Arts and Crafts Society. "Yes, that was painted by Kevin Murphy, who once ran rings around the New South Wales and Queensland police forces as one of this country's most talented bank robbers. It's a rather, er, unusual study, wouldn't you agree? There's something intrinsic in her smile that I sometimes compare with the elusiveness of the Mona Lisa."

"He's certainly captured Her Majesty's radiance, sir," Greenwood agreed. "Yet one can almost feel the inner loneliness of her authority. Marvellous brush-work, and such subtlety of colours."

"You sound as though you have an expert's appreciation of art, Greenwood."

"Oh, I've dabbled, sir," Greenwood confessed with a blush. "Though I must say, I could never hope to achieve the brilliance of that portrait. You must be very proud of it."

"Actually," said (Rev) Hunt, "It's an absolute embarrassment. Brilliant, yes—but an embarrassment, all the same. I keep it on the wall to remind me that a prison officer must have eyes in the back of his head to spot the mockery and malice that go on when his back is turned. Mr. Sanderson, with his wealth of experience and keen insight into the criminal mind, has never been fooled by this portrait. What was the opinion you expressed when it was unveiled, Sanderson?"

Sanderson shifted his big boots and coughed politely again. "I was of the opinion, sir, which I later conveyed in no uncertain terms to that dingo Murphy, that Her Majesty looks as if she's just alighted from her Royal Coach and stuck her foot in a dog's dropping."

(Rev) Hunt smiled at Bruce Greenwood's fiery embarrassment. "The King who wore no clothes, eh? Now what do you really see, Greenwood?"

Greenwood's mouth flapped silently for a few seconds, then he finally confessed: "Yes, I must admit, sir, that the subtle downward curl of one side of Her Majesty's lips does sort of suggest repugnance. However," he added with blushing defiance, "I still say, with all due respect, that it is the work of a genius."

"Of course. I wouldn't dispute that for one minute. But it's an *evil* genius, Greenwood, and it's there on display to remind you and every other officer in this prison of two cardinal rules of conduct, rules that Mr Sanderson will make sure you religiously adhere to from the moment you begin your duties. Mr Sanderson?"

Bull Sanderson drew himself up to his full six and a half feet of authoritarian brawn and regarded Greenwood with the look of a man who'd break his young body in two if he ever stepped out of line. "Rule number one," he growled. "Behind the smiles and constant friendly banter of those little bloody beavers out there, there's just one simple thing on their rotten little minds—*escape*. Know it, Greenwood. Be constantly aware of it. Recite it to yourself in your sleep. Keep your eyes open and your trap shut. And don't turn your bloody back on 'em for one second, or I'll kick your silly arse from here to Surfer's Paradise! And that brings me to rule number two: as deputy superintendent, I'm the only officer in this, apart from Reverend Hunt, who's allowed to have any personal contact whatsoever with the inmates. As far as you're concerned, you give the orders that I tell you to give, and other than that you keep your bloody self to yourself. If any of 'em give you any backchat, you say nothing—you come straight to me!"

"There's a good reason for this, Greenwood," (Rev) Hunt explained in gentler tones. "These men will only be friendly with a prison officer if they think they can get something out of him. And ultimately, the things they want are things that will help them escape."

"They pick on the junior, inexperienced officers straight away," Sanderson warned. "It starts with tobacco—and ends with a gun."

"It's been known," (Rev) Hunt explained, "to take less than twenty-five miɪutes for a young warder, new to the game, to be compromised as such. And I don't think I have to describe what happens to prison warders who allow themselves to be compromised."

"They get *destroyed*," Sanderson rumbled. "And I'll tell you right now, boy, that if any officer under my command dishonours the service in any bloody way whatsoever, there won't be enough left of him for his bloody mother to recognise by the time I've finished with him and chucked him in with the rest of the miserable scum on the other side of the wire!"

In the short, shocked silence that followed, even (Rev) Hunt's hands trembled slightly as he unlocked another steel cabinet behind his desk. "Well," he said cheerfully, "we'll have a cup of tea, Greenwood, and then you can accompany Mr Sanderson and me on a tour of the prison. It will give you the opportunity to get your bearings. But first"—(Rev) Hunt emerged from the cabinet with a bunch of large keys on an iron ring—"here are the most precious tools of your new trade. There is a key on this ring for every office, compound, cell block, facility and gate. Keep them always on your person. Always ensure that they are handed to Mr Sanderson to be locked away at the end of each shift. Treat them as if they are part of your very body and soul."

"Guard them with your *life*," Sanderson snarled. "And if you should ever lose them, well . . ." For once, words momentarily escaped him. "Well, just start running, and pray to bloody Christ that I don't catch you before you can get on a bloody plane for Brazil!"

Emerging fifteen minutes later from Hunt's office, the three men strolled down a gloomy green corridor leading through the administration block, then Greenwood was introduced to a warder manning a steel-barred checkpoint opening out into the jail itself.

Sanderson told the warder: "Spread the word around that I want Murphy and Pearce watched like hawks. Those two have been getting a bit too bloody pally with Chisholm lately, and I've got a feeling they're up to something."

Passing through the gateway, Greenwood was momentarily dazzled by the harsh sunlight bouncing off the prison's ancient sandstone buildings. (Rev) Hunt pointed out the cookhouse and mess hall, located to their right and adjacent to the administration block. Before them lay the vast open quadrangle skirting up to the tall, domed cell blocks which were arranged on the other side in the shape of a fan, their steel doors looking straight back at the office complex.

"There are six cell blocks, Greenwood, each containing two double-tiers of fifteen single cells. That's sixty men to a block and a total capacity of three hundred and sixty inmates. We're keeping ten cells empty at the moment for emergencies."

"Emergencies?"

"Conditions in this jail are becoming so well known that I fear there'll be trouble soon at Grafton or Bathurst or even Long Bay from men who want to get transferred here."

To their right, between the last cell block and the prison's main wall, they could see the slate roof and encircling wall of the Blockhouse.

"There are four armed guard-points on the main wall, one at each corner," said (Rev) Hunt. "Each point is manned by two men around the clock on three sight-hour shifts. They are all crack shots with revolvers, carbines and machineguns."

"What's that building underneath, if you don't mind me asking, sir?"

"We call that the Blockhouse," Hunt explained. "It's a halfway house, a sort of quarantine, for child-killers and rapists, and a place where we confine the intractibles."

"Intractibles?"

"Intractibles," Hunt echoed. "Men who can only be described as having sunk to the level of savage animals. Men to whom the very principle of human dignity has about as much value as raw sewage. Men who violently resist any form of cooperation with the warders."

"Is there anyone in there?"

"One man," Hunt said solemnly.

"What has he done?"

Sanderson said curtly, "He's not a man, he's a bloody beast. Let's leave it at that for now."

To the left of the quadrangle, they showed Greenwood the The Pen and explained its purpose, gave him a brief look at the auditorium, then led him through a double wire-meshed and locked checkpoint that opened onto a stone stairway at the foot of one side of the auditorium. This staircase dropped down to an underground complex housing the (Rev) Clement C. Hunt Arts and Crafts Society.

In a room whose walls were packed with paintings, batiks, pottery and sculptures, some eighty prisoners, watched over by six warders, were hard at work on Project Kiddie Kare, making soft toys for orphans. As Hunt explained the details of the charity work, Sanderson led them over to a table where Willie Crewe was slaving away in the middle of a crowd of cons, sewing multi-coloured felt patterns together.

"Willie Crewe," Sanderson announced for Greenwood's benefit, as Crewe stitched away with his wooden needle. "Willie's the prison's chief cook, when he's not hard at work making bunnies and duckies."

Crewe stiffened, and his thin, murderous mouth curled with venom.

"Watch it, mate," Sanderson warned him, "or I'll tear your bloody arm off and belt you to death with it." Then he turned to inform Greenwood: "Willie used to do a lot of work for the boys up in The Cross. He's knocked off at least three blokes for them, that's apart from the number he went soft on and just permanently maimed, and he would have been convicted for a fourth but they reckon they'd have to tear the Sydney Opera House right down to the bloody waterline to find the evidence. Never turn your back on Willie Crewe. Oh, yeah—Willie also runs the SP book in here, and they say he's made a bloody fortune with it."

And that made Willie really boil inside, his hands shaking violently as he punched the felt with his needle—for Willie had just been neatly conned out of most of his SP profits by Harry Pearce. Willie had made two thousand five hundred dollars out of his betting franchise, and only the day before, Harry had tripped while shuffling with the other prisoners in his lunchtime shift past the service counter in the mess hall and dropped his entire tray of shepherd's pie and potatoes and peas and apple pie with custard all over the floor at Willie's feet.

"You bloody drongo," Harry spat angrily. "Now help me clear up this shit."

And while he and Willie were crouching close together, slowly mopping the horrible mess together, Harry hissed: "I want two thousand bucks, and you're going to bloody get it for me."

"Like hell I am," Willie whispered. "Where would I get dough like that?"

"Don't bugger about with me—you know where."

"What if I don't want to give it to you?"

"Then Murphy and me will make sure your life's not worth living in here. Simple as that."

Willie sneered obscenely. " 'Murphy and me,' eh? I didn't know you two were goin' steady."

"Don't get smart, Willie. Just get me the dough. I beat the shit out of you with one punch, remember? I can do it again, every day, and so bad that you'll need that money to buy a new bloody head by the time I've finished."

"I want twenty-five percent interest, payable within twelve weeks."

"You got it."

"And I want Botham."

Harry snarled: "You keep your dirty hands off that kid."

"Why? Is he yours, Harry?"

"No, he's not mine. But I'm lookin' out for him against bastards like you. And no-one's laying a bloody hand on him."

"I'll look after him."

"No you won't. I've seen what you can do when you get fed up with 'em."

"He likes me," Willie sneered. "He's a man like the rest of us, an' he can make his own decisions. Why don't you let him decide?"

Harry thought that over for a while, wiping up the last of the scattered peas, then he said: "All right, we'll let him decide—when he's a man like the rest of us. When he's twenty one."

"When's that?"

"A month from now."

Willie licked his thin lips. "OK. Done."

And now, working away on his duckies and bunnies, Willie sensed that he certainly had been done. What would Pearce need money for, except to pay off contacts for an escape? Why would he so willingly let Timothy Botham go, unless the break was timed to take place sometime during the next month? Willie had lost two thousand bucks and the heady, violent, sadistic delights that he brooded about when he thought of young Bothams. He was going to make Pearce pay for that, he seethed, as Sanderson and (Rev) Hunt and Bruce Greenwood moved on from his table, and Sanderson announced:

"Backs to the wall, gentlemen. It's none other than Henry Trembler—stuffing another duck, I see."

Henry giggled as he stuffed cotton wadding into the hem-stitched, empty toys that came from Willie Crewe's worktable. "I've got more pride than that, Mr Sanderson," he whined. "Besides, they make a hell of a racket. Some people keep them as watchdogs, you know."

"Go on, Trembler," Sanderson growled. "You'd screw a good-looking rat if you could run fast enough to catch one."

Henry's spectacle lenses shone like twin mirrors as he glanced up, grinning wickedly, at Sanderson. "Only if it was female," he giggled. "There's nothing queer about me."

100

"Henry Trembler," Sanderson casually informed both Bruce Greenwood and (Rev) Hunt, both of whom were blushing furiously, "has interfered in a sexual manner with just about every animated bloody object you can name. He's probably the world's greatest living sex offender, old Henry. He's also the only man in history who raped a whole bloody convent of nuns in one go."

"Mr Sanderson," (Rev) Hunt appealed. "Do we have to?"

"With all due respect, sir," Sanderson replied, "I'd like young Greenwood here to know just what sort of animals he'll have to deal with in this prison."

"It wasn't a whole convent," Henry Trembler whined. "It was just one dormitory. Ten nuns."

"And the Mother Superior, Henry."

"I didn't lay a finger on her."

"You didn't have to, you dirty old swine. She dropped dead of shock."

"Well how was I to know the poor old bird had a weak heart?" Henry's spectacles flashed again in the room's neon lighting as he shook his head sadly. "It was all going beautifully up to the time she came in on the scene. It was like a bloody dream. Christ, I was like a fox in a bloody chook-run. You should've heard them squawk— flapping about in those lovely long habits and masses of white under-garments. They couldn't get out because I'd locked the door. And the windows—God bless the rigours of their Order—were naturally bar-red. Oh, it was gorgeous! I remember standing at one end of the room, exposing myself and muttering the usual obscenities, and they clung together at the other end like a flock of frightened penguins, praying and crossing themselves, their beads clicking like hailstones on a tin roof. One of them thrust herself forward and threw herself on the flood in a position of supplication, begging for mercy—and I'm afraid that's when I lost my head completely. In the carnal pan-demonium that followed, all I can remember is the plumpness of the flesh beneath all those long flying garments and prayers and screams and entreaties. A couple of them even laid about me with their rosaries, which made it all the more exquisite. I was a man trans-ported, possessed—a mindless machine, systematically ravishing them all, one by one, until finally the tumult died to a few sighs and sobs, and I stood alone and naked in the middle of the room, my victims strewn around me in various stages of exhaustion and undress, and I took my spectacles and hung them over my still-erect doodle and I said: "Take a good look around you, Big Boy, and see if there's anything you missed!" And that's when the Mother Superior unlocked the door and swung it open, saw me standing there in the middle of all that carnage, saw a cock with glasses on staring at her and dropped dead on the spot."

All work in the room had long since ceased. In the shocked hush, (Rev) Hunt's features had drained to the shade of alabaster. Bruce Greenwood gulped and said: "I think I need some fresh air."

"I didn't know she had a bad heart," Henry mumbled, "or I wouldn't have done that stupid thing with the glasses."

Sanderson said: "Henry, you'd better pray that you go to hell, because God's gonna bloody well get you for that."

"Oh no he won't," said Henry. "I'll kill myself first."

Outside the arts and crafts centre, back on solid ground above the subterranean complex, Greenwood breathed deeply the fresh air and felt that he himself had just had a glimpse of hell.

"God, what a monster," he gasped.

"Never turn your back on Henry Trembler, lad," Sanderson said with an obscene chuckle. "About the only thing he hasn't had a go at yet is a bloody prison warder."

Greenwood said: "But that man in the Blockhouse! What in God's name did *he* do?"

"All in good time, Greenwood," said (Rev) Hunt, finally recovering from his own shock. "First I want you to meet a very special and distinguished inmate of this jail."

They found Noel Chisholm in his cell in cell-block C, asleep on his bunk, face-down in a pile of books, some of which were opened at tracts of print underlined with red pencil. Bull Sanderson lifted a heavy history book from Chisholm's study desk and dropped it on the floor, and the loud thud immediately sparked Chisholm into life. He leapt up from the bunk, made as though to greet (Rev) Hunt with an outstretched hand, then fell flat on his face.

"Good Lord, man," Hunt gasped as he and Greenwood rushed to help the stricken playwright to his feet.

"Forgive me," Chisholm begged. "I seem to have temporarily lost the use of both bloody legs."

As they helped him back on to the bed, Hunt said: "You look as though you're a very sick man, Mr Chisholm. I think we'd better get you straight to the sick-bay."

"No, it's no use," Chisholm replied bravely, his face sweating profusely and his limbs twitching violently with ague. "It's nothing but a touch of malaria. Comes,upon me every few months. Caught it in Calcutta, where I once enjoyed the distinction of pissing from a great height on a Maharajah's head."

"Then I think the sick-bay is certainly the best place for you," (Rev) Hunt insisted; but Chisholm dismissed his concern with a courageous limp wave of a hand.

"No, my dear Reverend. Not when I'm about to complete my life's work. I have so little time left, you know. Mr Sanderson, if you'd be so kind as to look in the corner under my desk you'll find a bottle with some yellow medicine in it."

Without so much as a comment, Sanderson reached under the desk in the alcove, brought forth the bottle and handed it to Chisholm.

"I was working with a United Nations relief team at the time," Chisholm recounted, his voice and hands trembling as he uncorked the foul draught. "I'd been out in the bush for six weeks watching doctors and nutritionists from all over the globe trying to fight the double calamity of famine and an epidemic of cholera in the State of Bihar. The stench of death and the unearthly scenes of suffering are something that I will forever be struggling to erase from my mind." Chisholm took a huge gulp from the bottle and, as his head snapped backwards, almost dashing his brains out on the wall, the tiny cell quickly filled with the acrid fumes of methylated spirits. "*Jeeeezussssss!* That's fucking good!" he gasped, his eyes filling with tears. "I recall that the horrors of, Bihar State followed me even to Calcutta, a city not unknown for its own terrible misery and a place where, if you happen to fly in around dawn and take a bus or taxi from the airport to the city terminal, the landscape on the way literally blossoms with thousands upon thousands of black arseholes, all defecating in the sand for as far as the eye can see." Chisholm took another swig of his medicine and went a deep and distressing purple in the face, clutching wildly at his heaving stomach, his heels drumming on the concrete floor. When the spasm had passed he held out both his hands, palms down, and said with a twinkle in his bloodshot blue eyes: "You see? It's gotten rid of the shakes already. I'll soon be in a condition favourable to work."

"Good man," said (Rev) Hunt. "Is there anything we can offer that will hasten your recovery?"

"Plenty of rubbing alcohol—for my legs," said Chisholm. "A

103

couple of dozen bottles of a brand of tonic water known as Schweppes—it's loaded with quinine, you know. And perhaps some angostora bitters, if there's any handy."

"What about a bloody coffin to go with it, Nole?" Bull Sanderson growled.

"I once made an agreement with a Macquarie Street specialist, Mr Sanderson, that when I die my body will be preserved for medical science. I am simply upholding my end of the bargain."

Sanderson laughed heartily at that one; and Bruce Greenwood, unable to contain his surprise and confusion any longer, turned to (Rev) Hunt and blurted: "Do you mean, sir, that this man is dying?"

Noel Chisholm eyed Greenwood directly for the first time. "Young man, we are all dying. How else can we make room for other people? You're dying as you stand there gaping at me right now. You'll go to the grave as surely as I—the only difference between us being that I'll drop off the twig in some style, never having stooped so low as to become a prison officer."

"Now, Nole," Sanderson cautioned him, "there's no need for that."

"Of course," Chisholm agreed. "We need prison officers. They are part of the proud tradition upon which this great nation was built. Young man, whatever your name is," Chisholm continued, addressing the confused Greenwood as he swept himself off the bed, tested his legs and took a history book from his desk, "you are part of a tradition that began the moment Captain Phillip and his First Fleet sounded shallow water in Sydney Cove in 1788. I think it says something for the character of his historic endeavour, and the strange character of this country now, that within no time at all the pioneers of your profession were shipping hundreds of poor, doomed petty thieves and Irish rebels fourteen thousand miles to penal servitude on a vast, sun-struck, semi-tropical wasteland surrounded by two mammoth oceans—and then building prisons to put the poor bastards in!" Chisholm, riding an alcoholic roller-coaster by now, wrenched open the history book and poked a bony finger accusingly at Greenwood's pale face. "Let's take dear old Nathaniel Payten, whom we all know now as a pillar of the established church of this infant colony, devoting his efforts not only to the wall around this very jail—"

"I didn't know that," (Rev) Hunt interrupted.

"You know now, Reverend," Chisholm snarled, getting progressively angrier as methylated spirits and emotion came together within him. "In 1818, it says here, Nathaniel Payten built a three-storeyed building commissioned by the Reverend Doctor Samuel Marsden—another great benefactor of our squalid history—and sponsored by that great humanist Governor Lachlan Macquarie himself, which they called the Female Factory. This institution was built to hold a hundred and seventy-two women, sleeping two to a bed, who had either committed a punishable offence after arrival in the Colony, or had arrived and *were not yet assigned to some service.* Governor Macquarie graced the opening ceremony of the completed building with his great presence, and according to this little snippet of public record here *gave the workers four gallons of spirits to drink to the success of the building.*" Chisholm paused and took another swig of his own spiritual aid. "Eeeeeyuh!" he gasped, then rounded again on his transfixed audience. "The Female Factory wasn't a success, it was a fucking scandal! For a start, old Nat Payten had neglected to provide baths or laundries. Within a few years the number of inmates had grown from a hundred and seventy-two to two thousand, and in the 1830s, long after the black hole had been condemned by the Colonial Architect, it was still operating and doing a roaring trade as a matrimonial agency-cum-brothel where a man could go along and apply to the superintendent to have all the willing ones paraded like bloody cattle before him. One can perhaps understand the complaint of a visitor who commented at that time: *It would be difficult to imagine a more difficult community, and those who visited the establishment could scarcely realise the possibility that Great Britain could have produced such an assemblage of ugly creatures.* Poor bastard! Obviously all the pretty ones had been snapped up by then!" Chisholm slammed the book shut with a violence that made Bruce Greenwood start. Once again, he'd ridden out a fiery ride, only this time he felt an exhaustion, the drained, empty weariness of a man who has seen not colours, but nightmares of the mind. He fixed Greenwood with a steely stare and said: "There's your heritage, young man, in one brief glimpse of Nathaniel Payten's distinguished biography: booze, brutality, bondage and the beginnings of a brothel syndrome from which the women of this country have never since been emancipated—they still have the general status of sex machines—and from whence came, I would personally speculate, that much-cherished Australian male phrase: *Put a bag over her head and you won't know the bloody difference.*"

"You should've seen my wife, Nole," Bull Sanderson said, as

casual as could be. "She looked bad even with the bloody bag on."

Chisholm stared furiously at Sanderson for a moment, then shook his head and burst into laughter. He laughed without rancor. He laughed because there was little more he could do but laugh. Then Bull Sanderson started laughing, and so did (Rev) Hunt. Only Greenwood was left, tense and poker-faced, confused and bewildered and wondering what in God's name the joke was all about.

"Mr Sanderson," Chisholm choked, tears streaming down his face, "under circumstances far bloody removed from these, we might have enjoyed throwing rocks on a few tin roofs together."

And Sanderson said: "What? And end up in bloody jail like you?" And that set off another gale of laughter that finally subsided when (Rev) Hunt noticed a sheaf of papers among the books on Chisholm's desk, upon which were scrawled words that he suspected were of a creative nature.

"I see you've started work on your play, Mr Chisholm."

Chisholm said: "Yes, as a matter of fact I've actually been commissioned to write it for the arts and crafts open day."

"I hope your work is progressing well."

"Modestly," said Chisholm. "I'm having trouble with the title at the moment."

Hunt took another look at the sheaf of papers, blinked and said: "I trust the substance of the play won't prove so difficult."

"I'm torn at the moment between a one-man narrative epic of the magnitude of Ezra Pound's *Cantos*—delivered by me alone from within the solitary radius of a single spotlight on an empty stage—or perhaps a parable in music and mime for several players in the tradition of *The Soldier's Tale*. Or maybe I'll just confine myself to the orthodox drama in three acts with six scene-changes and apologies to the audience for the author's profound disregard for curtain calls. Whatever, it will be a bloody beauty. And, of course, it will be set in a prison."

"I wish you every success," said (Rev) Hunt. "And I'm sure that with your great wealth of experience you'll not thirst for inspiration or material."

"My dear Reverend, I can feel the inspiration coursing through my veins right now," Chisholm grinned, up-ending the medicine bottle and grinding his teeth violently as the mixture burned through his system. "As for the material," he croaked, "I fear that a great deal of it is going to need more than the restricted dimensions of the ordinary stage. Unless I indulge in symbolism, for example, I'm going to need a bloody circus tent in which to express the intense profundity of my actions at that moment when I stood on the balcony of the sixth floor of my hotel in Calcutta, a can of cold Foster's lager in my hand and a macabre pageant of dead, skeletal, fly-blown babies still parading through my mind, and watched the Maharajah's pompous arrival. My balcony was actually inside the hotel, overlooking a sort of vast enclosed courtyard that comprised the lobby and reception area, an opulent lush-carpeted affair in which fountains played amid exotic indoor foliage, a string quartet squeaked away discreetly in one corner and turbaned Sikh pageboys glided about ringing the bicycle bells of long-poled placards upon which were chalked the names of the guests they were seeking. It was a gracious, civilised scene, broken suddenly by the sound of drums and the hideous wail of goatskin pipes as the advance guard of the Maharajah's entourage marched in through the main entrance. Dark-skinned, turbaned giants, clad in crimson uniforms of a private military design, heavily braided with gold, formed a guard of honour, the blades of their swords flashing in one single blaze of disciplined precision as they raised them in salute. And as the drums and pipes reached a climactic thunder and shriek of homage, in came the Maharajah himself."

Chisholm was pacing back and forth between his bed and the workdesk, his medicine bottle now empty but clutched tightly in one hand, his bloodshot gaze glued blankly to the floor as his mind relived one of the greatest moments of his life. "I recall that he was a tiny, pudgy, pompous little shit amid all those hulking guards and retainers. Wealth and power glittered in the vulgar gold thread of his robes, the exquisite gems that shone in his turban, the sapphires and diamonds of rings that literally dripped from his fat fingers. The fanfare of his arrival died suddenly to a dramatic silence as he waddled through the two ranks of the honour guard, heading my way, his soft pink lips pursed with impatience as the hotel staff bowed and scraped before him. In the silence, in the deathly hush of the entire lobby, I waited until the corpulent little creep was almost underneath me, heading for his private lift, then called:

" 'Hey, you! Here's a present from Australia!' And, from my great height, I dropped the half-empty can of Foster's beer. Having delivered my little gift, and watched him recoil with shock as the foaming missile flew at him, I then called upon the only weapon that I had at my disposal, the only means by which I could express my rage and contempt, the one terrible, ultimate insult to the pride and honour of a high-caste Hindu: I shouted, 'And here's something else from the babies of Bihar!'—and drenched him with pee.''

Outside, once again, in the harsh glare of sun on sandstone, Hunt, Sanderson and Greenwood made their way across the quadrangle toward block C, and (Rev) Hunt said: "Remarkable man, eh? What do you think, Greenwood?"

"With all due respect, sir," said Greenwood, "I'd say he's nothing more than an incorrigible larrikin and a drunk."

"A distinguished drunk, Greenwood. Most drunks drink to celebrate their own miseries. Chisholm's misery is that the rest of the world won't urinate on Maharajahs. By the way, Mr Sanderson, do you think that we can find him something a little less debilitating than methylated spirits and rubbing alcohol?"

Bruce Greenwood looked aghast. "Do you mean, sir, that you are actually pandering to his lust for alcohol? In prison?"

"Noel Chisholm is dying," Hunt said. "He's lived his life on his own terms, and I don't see why he should die on anything else."

"But sir—you heard what he said in there. He's obviously used the threat of death for years as an excuse for his excesses."

"Not an excuse—a justification," said Hunt. "Besides, he may not know it but he *is* dying. When he came into this prison he was given the customary physical examination, and the doctor's confidential report shows, in so many words, that Chisholm's small intestine is so full of holes that it looks like a sock that a dog's been chewing. And his liver is the size of a rugby football. The momentum of the alcohol racing through his system is the only thing keeping him on his feet at the moment. It's estimated that he has only three to six months left to live. As soon as the arts and crafts exhibition is over, I propose to rehabilitate him in the strictest sense of the word and have him paroled so that he can spend his last days free to do whatever wild deeds he wishes." Hunt paused to push open the steel door of cell-block C. "But first," he told Greenwood, "I want to see his play."

thirteen

IN THE SANCTITY OF HIS CELL ON THE second tier, right-hand side, of block C, Harry Pearce was standing with chisel and mallet in hand perusing a smooth, unviolated two cubic feet of dressed sandstone when (Rev) Hunt, Bull Sanderson and Bruce Greenwood popped in. It was Harry's second block of stone; in four nights of frenzied creativity he had transformed his original block into what he considered to be an absolute bloody triumph. It rested now on the floor by the side of his bunk, its artistry veiled completely with a towel. Harry was poised, now, to make his first nervous cut in the new butter-coloured stone when the three prison officers walked in and Sanderson barked:

"Times have changed, eh, Pearce? That sort of bloody thing used to be called hard labour."

Harry's hands jumped, and he slowly put down his tools. "You're not making it any bloody easier, mate," he said. "I wish people would have the decency to knock before they come in here." Then he turned away from his desk and saw (Rev) Hunt and Greenwood, and he said "Nice to see you, Mr Hunt" to Hunt and gave Greenwood a perfunctory nod.

"I hope we're not delaying your work, Mr Pearce," said (Rev) Hunt.

"No, sir," Harry sighed, sitting down on his bed to roll a cigarette. "I've got all the time in the world."

And Sanderson crowed: "That's right, Pearce. What's ten minutes when you've got another fourteen years up your sleeve?"

"Up yours, too," Harry muttered, and Sanderson laughed maliciously.

"Now then, Pearce, let's not have any outbursts of artistic temperament, or you might end up wearing that bloody chisel for a collar."

"Mr Pearce," (Rev) Hunt informed Bruce Greenwood, "was a stonemason before he, er, transgressed and came to this jail."

"A monumental mason," Harry reminded him; and Bull Sanderson stuck his two-cents' worth in again.

"You're not exactly monumental on modesty, are you, Pearce?"

Harry coldly ignored Sanderson and explained to the others: "A monumental mason carves monuments. My line of work was religious monuments—statues and headstones for Rookwood Cemetery. Angels and cupids and inscriptions for the dear departed. Maybe an occasional Madonna or crucifixion for the local churches."

"That's before he carved up his missus," Sanderson informed Greenwood; and as Harry's body tensed, his fingers crushing his lighted cigarette to a pulp in the palm of one hand, Sanderson added: "Watch yourself, mate—or I'll ask your bloody mother-in-law to come and visit you."

"You do that," Harry growled. "There's no-one I'd rather see at the moment."

"Of course, stonemasonry was once the predominant science of civilised man," (Rev) Hunt pontificated to no-one in particular, glancing at Harry's bookshelf, next to the workbench, which was packed with illustrated biographies and critiques of Michelangelo, Marini, Lipchitz, Henry Moore and Barbara Hepworth. "Before even the Renaissance the freemasons, as they called themselves, enjoyed a status throughout Europe that we award to the biophysicist today. It's hard to imagine that men who worked with nothing more than ordinary compasses, calipers, T-squares, right-angles, plumblines and spiritual inspiration were able to build astounding monuments like the cathedral of Rhiems, for instance, a one hundred and twenty-five foot masterpiece of the principle of the flying buttress. Yours is a craft that goes back over eight hundred years, Mr Pearce.'

Harry sighed and said: "I wouldn't know a flying buttress if I saw one, Mr Hunt."

"You'll see one in a minute, mate," Bull Sanderson snarled, "if you curl your lip like that at the superintendent."

"I'm just an amateur sculptor, Mr Hunt," Harry explained, ignoring Sanderson's withering stare. "Doing my best for next month's arts and crafts exhibition."

"It's often intrigued me," (Rev) Hunt declared, "how a sculptor actually expresses his inspiration. The mechanics of the thing, I mean. Does he seek his idea in the shape or grain of the stone, or does he make the grain conform to his idea? Or, as Michelangelo, I believe it was, once wrote:

When that which is divine in us doth try
To shape a face, both brain and hand unite
To give, from a mere model frail and slight
Life to the stone by Art's free energy."

"I wouldn't know, Mr Hunt," Harry confessed. "All I know is that marble's different to sandstone because you've got to hit it harder. But you've got to be a lot more bloody careful, too, because it'll shatter if you don't treat it right—like cutting a diamond. Sandstone's just like cheese by comparison. You can do anything with it. Cut it with a knife if it's young enough."

"Young rock," Hunt mused. "It's compelling to imagine that something as inanimate as rock actually has life. And to think that your skilled hands"—Hunt gestured at Harry's untouched cube of sandstone—"will bring life and beauty from within that lump."

"Actually, it'll be more of a *memorial*," Harry explained. "All six of them. A sequence of different ideas that I'm thinking of calling *In Loving Memory*."

"How apt," (Rev) Hunt said, thinking of Harry's former profession. *How apt*, he thought, blushing slightly with horror as he remembered Harry's terrible murders. To skirt away from the subject he turned to Bruce Greenwood and asked: "Do you dabble also in sculpture, Mr Greenwood?"

"No sir, only paints," Greenwood replied, his ears colouring self-consciously. "In fact, I was about to remark upon the very unusual perspective of that landscape on the wall there. Is that another of Kevin Murphy's works?"

"Indeed it is," said Hunt. "Unorthodox, to say the least."

"Abstract, I would have said, sir."

"*Bizarre*, Greenwood. Another example of genius mocking the eye of the beholder. God only knows what Murphy is trying to say with only half a combined harvester, but he's certainly challenging us with something."

"Oh, I wouldn't say that, sir," Greenwood insisted, tilting his head at a painful angle in search of the right perspective. "I'd venture to suggest that he's commanding the eye of the beholder to seek its own reward, rather than rely on the artist. It's almost as if he's telling us to complete the full picture ourselves."

"He's starting on the other half next week," Harry Pearce blandly told them, and both Greenwood and (Rev) Hunt retreated quickly from the painting.

"Well," said Hunt to Harry, "I trust you'll have all your work finished in time for the exhibition."

"I'll make sure of that, sir," said Bull Sanderson, eyeing Harry threateningly. "I'll personally keep this dingo and bloody Murphy under constant surveillance."

"I see you've completed one sculpture already," Hunt said, pointing at the towel-covered shape beside the bed. "May we take a quick look at it?" And he was reaching down, his fingers all but touching the hem of the towel, when Harry panicked.

"No!" he snapped. "I mean—that bust is part of a sequence, Mr Hunt. It doesn't mean a bloody thing on its own. I don't want anybody to see anything of it until it's all finished."

"Of course. I do apologise," (Rev) Hunt said, flustered as he straightened up. "That's the prerogative of any artist. Good luck, Mr Pearce, and in moments of doubt take comfort from Michelangelo's advice that *'to break the marble spell is all the hand that serves the brain can do.'* "

"And don't get up to anything funny, Pearce," Bull Sanderson snarled, "or I'll break both your bloody hands."

Down on the ground floor of cell-block C, Kevin Murphy had organised a dozen men, including the aboriginal militant Dickie King, Arthur Hancock, a sixty-year-old incorrigible pickpocket who was the prison trusty, and even Lyle Walker, to help him work on the second-greatest artistic endeavour of his life. After completing the mural of the hunting dogs on the wall outside Timothy Botham's cell, Murphy had taken a good look at the rest of the block's four walls, the untouched spaces covered only with depressing State Government regulation green paint, and decided to keep going.

His vision was immense—to cover the entire ground-level wall, right around the inside of the block, with one inter-connected mural depicting Australia's colourful history: the landing of Captain Cook, the arrival of Phillip's First Fleet, the merciless flogging of the convicts in the penal settlement that once fouled the earth upon which this very prison stood, the infamous massacre of the aboriginal population of Tasmania, the bloody goldminers' rebellion of the Eureka Stockade, the tragic death of Ned Kelly, the abortive baptism of fire at Gallipoli, which gave birth to the myth of the Anzac nation. Murphy's technique was similarly ambitious: He was going to paint the various scenes in relief, using putty and plaster to build up the facades that he wished to emphasise and, he explained it, "lift it right off the wall." His time was severely limited: He had to complete the project for the arts and crafts exhibition. And that's why he had enlisted the help of as many fellow convicts as he could muster.

He had them hard at work, now, each man stenciling onto the wall his sketched and numbered rough outlines of each historical sequence, the next step being to pack certain areas with putty—when Murphy could get his hands on the putty that he wanted. As the men struggled and swore with huge sheets of tracing paper, trying to pin them flat against the wall to transpose Murphy's simple line-drawings, the sound of Timothy Botham's harmonica wafted mournfully over the coarse chatter and curses as he practised "Danny Boy" in his cell. Murphy was bawling out Dickie King for insisting that Captain Cook's historic landing at Botany Bay didn't happen quite the way he'd drawn it.

"The abos didn't stand there and fuckin' welcome him," Dickie insisted. "They speared the bastard to death!"

"That was in Hawaii, you dumb shit," Murphy raged. "And for Christ's sake, stick to the bloody plans the way I've drawn them—those boongs are not supposed to tower right over him like that!"

"Why not? Maybe he was smaller than them! Why does the bastard always have to look like he was the second coming of Christ?"

"Look, Dickie," Murphy sighed, wiping sweat from his brow, "if you don't like this scene, go and do something else—go and do the Tasmanian massacre if you want to prove a bloody point."

"Are you kiddin'! The only massacre I'm gonna fuckin' do is when I get out of this stinkin' white man's jail and start organisin' these stupid bastards into some action! Then I tell you what, man—the fuckin' streets are gonna run with blood!"

"So what's new? They run with blood every Saturday night when the pubs close."

"An' look what caused that!" Dickie screeched. "The white man got us pissed on his liquor, then banned us for years from his fuckin' pubs! Jesus, man, they're the first places we're gonna hit when the fightin' starts."

"Dickie," Murphy pleaded, "why don't you go and change places with Lyle Walker and work on the convict flogging scene, huh? All those poor white bastards bein' lashed to death? That should make you feel bloody good."

And that's when Murphy glanced down the cavernous bowel of the cell block and saw (Rev) Hunt, Bull Sanderson and Bruce Greenwood stepping down the steel stairway leading from the upper catwalk and Harry Pearce's cell. Murphy turned to Arthur Hancock, the trusty pickpocket, and said: "You ready?" Then he turned to the rest of the gang. "All right, they're briefing the pigeon."

(Rev) Hunt was, of course, absolutely amazed at the breadth and magnitude of this, Kevin Murphy's second-greatest artistic endeavour.

"It's for the arts and crafts exhibition," Murphy explained, ignoring Bull Sanderson's suspicious leer and nodding casually at Bruce Greenwood. "The idea is to brighten up the cell block a bit and give the visitors something interesting to see. Show them that prison life is not all bars and bloody blank walls. After we've finished with this block I'd like to have a go at the other five—with your permission, of course."

"Of course," (Rev) Hunt beamed. "I think it's a marvellous idea. Not only is it personally rewarding to you, Mr Murphy, but it's obviously helping to get some of the other men involved in creative work."

"Some of them couldn't create a decent bloody stink," Bull Sanderson sniffed. "You're taking a risk, Murphy, letting them loose on something like this."

"They're only helping with the outlines, then I'll get them to build up some of the figures with putty."

"Putty?"

"I'm doing some of the work in relief, to sort of make it stand out from the background. Like that bloke over there being flogged to death on the rack. Do you know some of those poor buggers were given a thousand lashes? I got that from Nole Chisholm's books. They reckon that when the penal stockade was really going strong, you could see some convicts wandering about permanently crippled, almost bent bloody double, from the injuries of the whips."

(Rev) Hunt coughed delicately and said: "Yes, I'm afraid those were the Dark Ages of our nation's past. Thank God our prisons are a little more enlightened today. Yes, this is all very illuminating," he said, turning to study again the various scenes, "but don't you think perhaps we should include a few of the more positive aspects of our history?"

"Like what?" said Murphy. "The Depression?"

"Watch it, Murphy," Sanderson snarled. "You'd look funny trying to paint with both your bloody arms in splints."

"Well," Hunt declared, glancing around the walls again, "I must say that this will certainly prove to be one of the major highlights of the exhibition. You'll need a great deal of putty, of course. Write down exactly what you want and I'll arrange it with the department. This will stand as a testimonial to your talents, Mr Murphy. In years to come, men from all walks of life will say it was your vision and skill that made the hardships of their confinement perhaps a little easier to bear."

"It'll be the second greatest endeavour of my life, Mr Hunt."

"Oh? And what will be your greatest endeavour?"

Murphy said: "I've got another vision in mind which'd go even further than this cell block—with your permission, of course."

"Of course. What is it?"

"I want," said Murphy, taking a deep breath, "to paint the inside face of the main prison wall."

(Rev) Hunt said: "Good Lord." And Bull Sanderson broke into a vulgar howl of laughter.

"You must be going mad from sniffing paint, Murphy," he hooted. "Do you think we're stupid enough to let you go within ten feet of that bloody wall?"

"Just hear me out a second, Mr Hunt," Murphy pleaded, ignoring Sanderson's rude cackle. "I'm not trying to con you. I want to paint a mural covering the entire inside face of the wall—a mural showing the city outside as it was in the 1820s. Here, I got this from Chisholm's books." Murphy handed (Rev) Hunt a sheet of paper upon which was written the impressions of a visitor to the settlement in 1819: *Hailed as the City of Vines, the best feature of the town is its wonderfully peaceful airs as its spires and towers and house-roofs peep out from amidst an exquisite framing of vines and greenery and flowers. From the top of the toll-hill, the whole town is seen spread out before you: the church with its double-topped steeple peering out of the middle; the elegant Government House with its extensive and tasteful domain bounding the town beyond, and the handsome brick house of the Rev. Dr. Marsden crowning a fine rising ground to the left, surrounded by thriving clumps of trees.*

(Rev) Hunt looked momentarily as if he were emotionally overcome by the graphic description. He folded the paper carefully, handed it back to Murphy and murmured: "Beautiful. Beautiful, Mr Murphy."

"That's exactly the way I want to paint it," Murphy explained. "I'd paint that scene, just as it's written there, and you'd be able to stand in the jail and look around the wall, and instead you'd see the trees and vines and the church and old Marsden's house."

"My God," Hunt gasped, "I see it all now. The illusion would be incredible—almost a prison without walls!"

"Almost," Murphy reminded him; and even Bruce Greenwood, having stood there in silence for ten minutes in Kevin Murphy's presence, full of seething excitement and mute tribute to the great painter's genius, finally cracked and broke the first of Sanderson's cardinal rules.

"Amazing, Mr Murphy," he bubbled. "You certainly are a man of immense artistic vision."

"Hey, watch it," Sanderson reminded him, and then glowered at Murphy. "Are you, by any stretch of the bloody imagination, trying to con us into getting rid of the main wall?"

"Of course not! The bloody wall will still be there, but instead of just rock you'll see the town as it was a hundred and fifty years ago."

"I don't like it, Mr Hunt," Sanderson growled. "I mean, your new policy is all very well and good, but the first principle of a prison is still a bloody great wall to remind the buggers that society doesn't want them."

"Walls do not necessarily a prison make, Mr Sanderson. Besides"—and (Rev) Hunt laughed at his own humour—"any man who was rash enough to try to run away would still be in for a nasty shock, wouldn't he? Mr Murphy, I think this idea of yours is astounding, visually and aesthetically, and as far as the morale of the prisoners is concerned it is revolutionary. You'll need a lot of paint, of course. What else?"

"The help of every man who can use a paintbrush and count up to twenty. I'll be using numbered patterns, chalked on the wall."

"Ah ha!" Sanderson bawled rudely. "Now I see what you're up

to, you bloody dingo! You'll have every bugger in the place up and over the wall the minute you get close to it."

Murphy ignored Sanderson and said to (Rev) Hunt: "I give you my word, Mr Hunt, that no-one will try to escape while they're working on the wall. You can shackle us all together and have armed guards watching over us the whole time. But I give you my solemn and honest pledge that there'll be no funny business."

(Rev) Hunt said: "Of course, there will have to be strict security measures. But I don't see why an atmosphere of distrust should interfere with such a grand scheme. Do you, Mr Sanderson?"

"I'll have armed men spaced every six feet along the top of that wall," Sanderson said. "And I personally will be manning a bloody machinegun in the grounds right behind Murphy and his crowd. And if one of them so much as raises his bloody head from his work for a second, they'll be shipping his remains out of here in a bloody bucket."

"Well, there you are," Hunt said, a trifle shakily. "Good luck, Mr Murphy, though I'd say that you'll have to work night and day to complete all your visions in time for the arts and—"

And that's when the voice of Harry Pearce suddenly bellowed through the cell block: "Sanderson—up your big hairy fat arse!"

And as Bull Sanderson swung away from the group with a coarse answering roar, Harry appeared on the catwalk outside his cell at the other end of the block, waving his mallet furiously above his head. "I can't stand it anymore!" he screeched. "I can't take it any more! Another fucking fourteen years! I'll kill myself! I can't go on any longer!"

And as Harry hurled his mallet across the cell block and slipped, weeping, to his knees on the catwalk, (Rev) Hunt quickly took charge of the situation. "Come, Mr Sanderson. I'll call the Medical Officer while you pacify him. Mr Greenwood—you remain here and watch these men."

No sooner had they gone than Kevin Murphy and old Arthur Hancock the incorrigible pickpocket swung on Bruce Greenwood, and Murphy said: "You strike me as being a bloke who appreciates art, Bruce."

"Oh, I do," said Greenwood, breaking another rigid rule.

"Well, how would you like to help me with this stuff?" Murphy asked, gesturing at his mural.

"I really don't see how I could," Greenwood said apologetically. "Being a prison officer, you know."

"Ah, but you *can*," said Murphy, glancing aside at Arthur Hancock and winking. "That putty I was talking about. It's special stuff, see? It's gotta be the type that won't crack or go silly when it's been painted over with acrylics. There's only one place in Sydney where you can get it. Here's the address." Murphy thrust a note at the flustered Greenwood, and Greenwood's fingers recoiled from the slip of paper as if it were poison.

"I can't do a thing like that," he protested.

"Yes you can. The address is written clear enough. All you've gotta do is pick up the stuff twice a week and figure out a way of getting it in to me. And also keep your bloody trap shut."

Greenwood's mouth trembled with outrage. "I'm afraid I'll have to go straight to Mr Sanderson about this."

"You do that," said Murphy, grinning wickedly.

And Arthur Hancock said: "While you're at it you can tell him you've lost your keys."

"*What*?" Greenwood frantically searched every pocket of his new uniform for the precious keys, his features now quaking as though he were about to cry. "Give them back," he ordered Hancock, tears springing into his eyes.

"Sorry, mate," said Arthur, "I haven't laid eyes on them."

"You've got them!" Greenwood cried. "Give them back, or I'll go straight to Mr Sanderson!"

"And do you know what Bull Sanderson will do to you? He'll *murder* you. Jesus, a young bloke like you. First day on the job, isn't it? Lost your keys. He'll go right off his bloody head."

"You wouldn't wanna see him when he loses his nut," said Murphy. "Jesus, it's *horrible*. I only saw it once. Young warder, just like you. Same age, I'd reckon. Lost his keys. Shit, you could hear the screams from one end of the prison to the other."

"I remember that," said Arthur. "They had to call in the cops to drag Sanderson off the poor little bugger."

"They say that poor kid's never been right in the head since," said Murphy, studying young Greenwood's pale, terror-stricken features. "I wouldn't want a thing like that to happen to you, Bruce. So here's the address, and I'll expect the first shipment the day after tomorrow. And you can rest assured, mate, that none of us will so much as breathe a bloody word about it."

Bruce's mouth opened and closed spasmodically for a few seconds, his eyes popping with horror. Then he managed to croak: "My keys. He'll want to see my keys."

"You'll get them back the moment the first shipment comes in," Murphy promised. "In the meantime, Arthur's got another set here for you. They're exact replicas of the ones he lifted, only they don't fit any locks in here. Make sure Sanderson or one of the other blokes doesn't try to use them. OK?"

As Murphy and Hancock turned back to their work, leaving Bruce Greenwood to cope with his fear and agony, Arthur said: "Sweet as a nut, eh? What's it all about?"

"Don't ask silly questions, Arthur."

"All right, but when it happens I don't want anything to do with it. I don't want to know about it. I'm happy where I am."

"That's sweet with me," said Murphy, then he grinned evilly again. "Hey, how do I go about this for the record book? Do I claim the twenty-five minutes it took from the moment young Bruce walked in here, or the five minutes it took to break him?"

"Claim the twenty-five," Arthur advised him. "Why make it hard on the next bloke?"

fourteen

•

TIMOTHY BOTHAM WAS IN A BAD, BAD way. All of a sudden it was as if age had crept up on him prematurely and robbed him of all his blushing youth. He had become pale, listless. He had an unhealthy inward-looking glaze in his blue eyes, and bleakness of spirit within which he had withdrawn completely to the confines of his cell and the metallic agony of the one tune that he'd managed to master on his harmonica.

Harry Pearce watched the young man's steady deterioration and became so worried that even "Danny Boy" didn't drive him insane with irritation anymore. It was not only Botham's collapse that worried him, but the damage that the boy could do to the escape plan if he cracked up entirely. And it was obvious to Harry that the strain of one more visiting day would be too much for Botham's weakened morale to cope with.

On visiting days the wives and children of the inmates, or those lucky enough not to have been deserted or divorced, flocked through the prison's main gates and congregated in a compound situated between the guardroom inside the wall and the administration block. There, they were able to talk to their men through a high wire fence, up which their children clambered and swung when the novelty of the situation wore off and left them bored.

Husbands and wives were allowed to converse freely, but were strictly denied any physical contact through the fence; they had to observe unmarked but rigid limits two feet back from both sides. Other than that, the arrangement played an important part in the men's morale—as Kevin Murphy reminded his stunning red-headed young wife, Marcie, a Queensland country girl, who turned up with their beautiful, bouncing ten- and twelve-year-old daughters on the one visiting day that drove Timothy Botham close to the point of cracking.

"What the bloody hell are you wearing that long dress for?" Murphy complained, pointing furiously at Marcie's long, ankle-length woollen dress.

"It's the latest fashion, darl," Marcie explained, doing a slow pirouette that made her long hair flash like beaten copper in the sun. "It's the maxi."

"So what happened to the bloody mini you usually wear?"

"Oh, that sort of thing's out of fashion now, love."

"Well, it ain't out of fashion with me," Murphy raged. "I want to see every bloody inch of you when you come here, especially your legs. That's what we've got this bloody wire fence for. An' you have to turn up wearing a bloody dress right down to your ankles!"

Marcie pouted beautifully and tossed her hair again. "Don't be rude," she said. "I would've thought you'd have a lot more important things to think about in here."

"Listen—what else could I have on my bloody mind, night and day, except you and your legs?"

"Well," Marcie sniffed, "if it's as bad as all that—here they are." And with a sudden cheeky grin she swept open the front panels of her maxi to reveal the exquisite long, slim, unblemished legs and thighs that made Murphy moan in his sleep at night, along with a tiny but shattering glimpse of frilly white panties. But for the ever-vigilant guns of the armed guards on the main wall above them, Murphy would have torn a hole in the wire fence, then and there. As it was, he groaned and said in a hoarse low whisper: "Jesus! If I don't get out of this fucking place soon I'll end up as nutty as old Henry Trembler."

"Don't do anything rash, darl," said Marcie. "It'd be a pity to crack now and spoil the whole thing.'

"Don't worry about me," Murphy assured her. "I'm working on the main wall right now, you know. Everything's right on schedule. By the way, I've got a mate—a good one. He'll be coming with us, after he's settled a bit of business here in Sydney."

"What's he in for?" Marcie asked.

"Life," said Murphy. "He carved up his old lady and, uh, some-one else with an axe."

Marcie said: "You really pick your mates, don't you, Kev?"

"I told you, he's all right. He's no sex maniac, if that's what's—" Then Murphy sensed a hulking presence right behind him, and saw a warning flicker through Marcie's hazel eyes, and he said: "Well, how are the kids doing at school?"

"Cheryl's just had two teeth filled, haven't you, Cheryl? Show Daddy how nice they look now."

And Bull Sanderson, who had just loomed up behind Murphy, literally sniffing with undisguised suspicion, said: "That's a very nice dress you're wearing, Mrs Murphy."

"It's called a maxi, Mr Sanderson," said Marcie, modestly pulling the drapes of the skirt together.

"My, my," Sanderson breathed. "Fashions seem to be changing day by day, don't they? Makes you wonder what's coming off next, doesn't it, Mrs Murphy?"

"You should see some of the things the girls are wearing these days," said Marcie. "You'd swear they were walking around in the nutty."

"Which reminds me," said Sanderson, talking now to Murphy, "what's wrong with young Botham? He's gone sour all of a sudden. I just had to threaten him with bloody solitary to get him out of his cell and into the fresh air."

"You know what's wrong with him," said Murphy. "It's just

121

dawned on him that he's gonna spend the next four bloody years of his life in jail."

But that was only half young Botham's problem, and, as he was telling Harry Pearce right then, strolling with him around the sun-blistered tarmac of the quadrangle, the other half was driving even deeper into his tortured soul.

"I thought she'd come and see me this time, Harry—I really did," he said mournfully. "I reckon like it's her bloody husband. I reckon he's found out about our affair, and he's keeping her prisoner in her own home."

"Yeah, maybe you're right," said Harry. "Maybe she's waiting till things cool off a bit, then she'll come and see you."

"*D'you reckon?*" For one beautiful split second, Botham's strength returned; then he sank back again into a hopeless lethargy. "No, I know I'll never see her again, Harry. I'm goin' crazy thinking about her. I can't get her out of my mind. An' then I like keep thinking that I've got four years to go in here without her. That's *forever*, Harry."

"Hang on, mate," Harry said consolingly, glancing quickly around them as Botham began sniffling. "You know, you've gotta face up to the face that she didn't do a bloody thing to help you at your trial."

"How could she?" Botham sniffed. "Her whole name and reputation were at stake. How could the wife of a city councillor stand up in court in front of all those people and say straight out that she'd been having a love affair with a twenty-year-old motor mechanic? An *apprentice* motor mechanic . . ." Botham's spirits sank so low now that he was practically slinking along with misery. "I think she did it to protect me, you know that? My Mum would've had a blue fit if she'd known I was messin' about with women."

Harry sighed impatiently and said: "Look, mate, if she was really in love with you she would've spoke up alright."

"She was . . . She *is*," Botham insisted, tearful again. "She told me there was no-one else like me."

"Well, at least she was telling the bloody truth then. Look, Timothy, four years isn't forever. It'll go like lightning, believe me, if you don't spend all your time mooning about . . ."

"What d'you mean, four years?" Timothy gasped. "I thought we were like gonna break out of here!"

"Keep your voice down, and keep walking," Harry hissed. "Look, d'you know what the bloody chances are of successfully breaking out of here? Ninety-nine percent of the breaks fail before you've even got near the bloody wall. And even if you manage to get over without being shot full of bloody holes by those guards, the average time spent on the run from every bastard in uniform outside is about two weeks. Then you're back in here with another bloody stretch added on to your sentence. Sanderson's got this place sewed up as tight as a fish's arsehole."

Botham said: "But you're still gonna try, aren't you, Harry? Like I heard Murphy raving about it the other night."

"No, we canned the whole idea, Timothy. Too bloody risky."

"I don't believe you," Botham sniffed. "Willie Crewe says you an' Murphy are up to something, and I know you are too."

"It's too bloody dangerous for you, mate," said Harry. "You're a nice enough kid and you got lumbered by a rotten magistrate, and I don't want to be responsible for getting you bloody killed in the bargain."

Botham said: "I'm desperate, Harry. I've got to get out. I want to get out so bad that if I don't go along too, nobody'll be going—you like know what I mean?"

Harry halted and looked Botham straight in the eyes with a gaze that was absolutely murderous. "I'll pretend I didn't hear you say that, Timothy. Kid or not, you should know what happens to anyone in here who dobs somebody in."

Botham suddenly started crying, clenching his teeth on the harsh, upward thrust of his grief. "I've gotta get out, Harry," he wailed. "I've gotta like see her soon, to settle my own mind, or I'll go nuts. I don't care if they catch me—I just wanna see her and be sure. You've got to take me too!"

"Pull yourself together," Harry rasped, his eyes searching about them for onlookers. "OK, you want to escape? This is how we escape. We knock a hole in the wall of my cell, jump out, run across the quadrangle to the corner of the wall near the Blockhouse, throw ropes up the wall, climb up, overpower the guards and grab their weapons, then shoot through before the alarm's raised. It's bloody risky, mate. You still want to try?"

"Sounds beaut, Harry," said Botham. "What night do we go?"

"Who said any bloody thing about night? We're gonna do it in broad daylight. Catch the guards when they're least expecting it."

"You can count on me, Harry," Timothy pledged, sniffing up the last of his tears. And Harry sighed deeply and shook his head.

"Jesus," he breathed. "Anyhow, do you feel better now?"

"Yeah, now that I know I'm getting out. When do we like go, Harry?"

"I'll tell you when we're going when we're ready to go. Meantime, just pull yourself together and stop getting bloody uptight and be ready to move the moment I give the bloody word."

An hour later, the visiting session over, Harry Pearce and Kevin Murphy were shackled together by the ankles along with some sixty other men, working on the mural on the inside of the main prison wall. The workers were shackled in pairs with a heavy chain running between their legs. This allowed them freedom of movement, in tandem, up and down the wall, but restrained those who had any ideas of making a suicidal bid for freedom over the twenty-five-foot monument to old Nathaniel Payten. Sanderson's fail-safe machinegun and armed pickets had been discarded that morning when he and the other warders took a look at the brassy skies and decided the day was going to be a bloody scorcher. However, the hexagonal tar-paper-roofed, glass-sided guardposts at each end of the wall were literally bristling with guns.

Murphy said to Harry: "You fix Botham up?"

"Yeah. I told him we're going to break out in broad daylight and wipe out one of the guardposts as we go over the bloody wall."

"Good. If he goes to Sanderson with that he'll get his arse kicked in for trying to be funny."

Harry asked: "How's Nole Chisholm doing with the play?"

"He's finally done the title."

"What's he calling it?"

"*Bars.*"

"*Bars?*"

"Prison bars," Murphy explained.

"You sure the piss isn't hitting him too bloody hard?"

"If it is," said Murphy, "he's giving it one hell of a bloody thumping back. I've never known a bloke who could take so much of it and stay on his bloody feet."

Harry shoved a paintbrush into a can at his feet, straightened up with a jerk that rattled the chains connecting them and slapped pea-green paint into a chalked outline of the foliage of a tree. In the
124

fierce, seething heat, both he and Murphy were wearing wide-brimmed, war-surplus Digger hats with wet towels draped over the backs of their necks. "Jesus," Harry moaned, "what I wouldn't bloody do now for a can of cold beer."

"Don't even think about it, mate," Murphy murmured. "I some-times wonder what'd be the first thing I'd make a grab for when I get out of here—Marcie or a bloody great ice-cold jug of that Queensland Four-X. Jeez, that's powerful bloody piss. I used to drink it in Roma—that's a little half-arsed cattle town about two hundred and fifty miles west of Brisbane, just off the Darling Downs. That's where I met Marcie. Roma's a weird place, all right. Like a real Wild West town you see in the movies—batwing doors on the bloody pubs and all these cockies walking about with ten-gallon cowboy hats on and fancy riding boots. Population about two and a half thousand, if you don't count the cockies and their bloody cattle. It's got a meatworks and an oil-drilling depot and a bloody great fat bottle-tree just off the main street. And rough! Shit-a-brick, you only have to look twice at some of the blokes in that town to get thumped in the bloody head. There's one particular pub there, the bloody Commercial, where I used to do most of my drinking. On a Saturday night, around about eleven, the town's police sergeant used to march into the public bar and make a big fuss about how the proprietor was contravening the licensing laws if he didn't kick every bastard out and close up right away. So the owner used to kick us all out and lock the doors and pull down all the blinds, and I tell yer, within a few minutes the whole of that town's main street would look like everybody had dropped dead and been buried. We'd all wait around for about fifteen minutes, pissing up someone's passion-fruit vine or something, then we'd creep around the back of the pub and knock on the door. The old sergeant himself would open it and invite us all in, and next thing we'd all be in the back saloon bar hollering and kicking on till dawn."

Murphy paused abruptly, glaring up along the chain-gang, and bawled: "Hey! What's that bastard doing flat on his bloody back?"

"He's fainted," someone called. "Jesus, Murph, it's a hundred and twenty degrees in the shade here."

"Then you're lucky you're not in the bloody shade, aren't you?" Murphy yelled. "Pour some water over that lazy bugger and keep him working. I promised Old Clemency we'd have all this finished a fortnight from now."

Amid the groans and curses of the chain-gang, Murphy filled his

125

brush with yellow paint and began working subtle highlights into Harry's pea-green leaves. "I tell you, Harry, you could drive down the main street of Roma any time after midnight on a Saturday night thinking everybody was tucked up and fast asleep in their beds, and if you weren't a local there was no way in the bloody world you'd guess the whole bloody male population of the town was getting pissed and yahooing and gambling and fist-fighting in the back rooms of the pubs. And the local abos too—the jackeroos from the cattle stations. They weren't allowed in any of the pubs, except in the back room of the Commercial on a Saturday night to gamble. And every Saturday night, after they'd all get pissed and lost all their dough, there'd be an almighty fucking brawl. Every time it'd be the same bloody routine—they'd stand in a line on one side of the bar, drinking like it was about to go out of fashion, and we'd all stand on the other side. They'd be bad-eyeing us, and we'd be slinging shit at them. Then one of 'em would drop his glass and go crazy, and both sides'd get stuck into each other. Jesus, there was one black bastard we called Bad Bennie who used to get so savage that it'd take me, the sergeant and a dozen other blokes to hold him down and stop him from killing someone. That's after we'd done the rest of them, of course."

"Sounds a bit like this best mate of mine," said Harry.

And Murphy said casually: "Oh yeah?"

"Anyhow, he used to be my best mate. Blooch, his name was. He and me were mates from bloody way back. Blooch used to be able to drink any bastard under the table, then beat any bastard you'd like to name in a fight. There was only one bastard he couldn't beat, an' that was a big red boomer kangeroo called The Aussie Battler . . ."

"Wait a minute," said Murphy. "You're not having me on by any chance, are you?"

"This is the God's honest truth," Harry swore. "Every year old Blooch and me would get pissed in the pubs around Randwick and Blooch would end up in the ring with The Battler at the Royal Easter Show. That bloody roo was six feet tall, weighed about fifteen stone and they used to put boxing gloves on his paws and stick him in the bloody ring and challenge any bloke to go five minutes with him. And I tell you, that Battler fought like a bloody threshing machine. Every year for six years, old Blooch had a go at the bastard, and every year he ended up flat on his arse on the canvas. You couldn't keep up with the bugger. He'd jump around so fast you couldn't lay a decent bloody punch on him. Blooch used to fall for the same bloody routine every year. Soon as he was out of breath and ballsed-up from chasing the bastard all around the ring, The Battler would butt him up against the ropes and whip in under his guard and pummel the Christ out of his chest with his gloved paws. Then he'd sit back on his tail, bring his hind legs up and boot old Blooch right in the guts."

"That's pretty dirty," Murphy observed. "Even for a bloody kangaroo."

"Yeah, well old Blooch got a bit cheesed off after a few years. Then one Easter we were raising bloody hell in a pub in The Cross, and Blooch was getting himself worked up for another bloody go at The Battler, and we fell in with this bloke from out West who'd done a lot of roo-shooting for the dog-food factories. And this bloke told Blooch how he could always stop a kangaroo on the run just by whistling at it. They're very inquisitive bastards, you know, and this bloke said he used to whistle and they'd stop dead in their tracks and look around to see what was going on, and they he'd give 'em a good clean shot right in the bloody head. Anyway, we all rolled on out to the Show, and there's The Aussie Battler waiting in the ring to give Blooch another bloody thrashing. I got myself into the crowd on one side of the ring, and Blooch put the gloves on and climbed in the other side. The bell rang and The Battler went straight into his usual routine, leaping about all over the bloody place. I waited till Blooch had worked him into a corner, then I put two fingers in my teeth and let out one hell of a whistle. The Battler stopped dead, stuck his nose up in the air and turned to see who the bloody hell was calling him, and Blooch let rip with a bloody killer of a punch that caught the bastard full in the side of the bloody head. The Battler snapped back like a bloody express train had hit him. He rocked right back onto his tail with his hind legs flapping about in the air. Every bastard in the place was going wild and throwing money about, and Blooch was just about to whip in with another haymaker and finish him off when that bastard Battler sprung off his tail like greased lightning, caught Blooch in the guts with both his hind legs and mule-kicked him across the ring, through the ropes and right into the bloody spectators!"

A howl of disbelieving laughter rolled down the line of chained, sweating men, and as Harry began protesting that most of the story was true, a distinctive savage snarl erupted behind them.

"That's the biggest load of bullshit I've ever come across in my life, Pearce."

"You should know what bullshit looks like, mate," Harry muttered, not even bothering to turn away from his work.

"*Mr* Mate to you," Bull Sanderson growled. "An' I'll tell you something, Pearce. You wouldn't know if a train had run up your backside until the bloody people started getting out. So don't think I don't know what's goin' on between you and that other bloody ratbag next to you."

Murphy, bending close to the wall to pick grit out of his paintwork, said: "We're just good friends, Mr Sanderson."

"You'd better be, because you'll both be spending a few bloody years together in Grafton if you so much as look like trying to break out of here. And you know what it's like in Grafton, don't you? The warders up there bash you around with rubber truncheons every day for three months from the bloody moment you arrive there."

"If I was gonna break out of here," said Murphy, "I sure as hell wouldn't be standing here in chains trying to paint my way through the bloody wall, would I?"

"Yeah, well just to make sure, I'm leaving Mr Greenwood here to keep an eye on you. He's armed with a three-o-three rifle, and he hasn't had much experience with guns so don't do anything to shock him or it might go off." Sanderson drew breath for a second, then left them with a final threatening blast: "And if I see any more of you bastards lying down resting I'll make the lot of you double-time round the bloody quadrangle for an hour in your chains. You're here to work, not to enjoy yourselves!"

Kevin Murphy waited until the sharp crack of Bull Sanderson's steel-capped boots had died away before turning to Harry. "This wall's in a shocking bloody condition, Harry," he said. "Look at this . . ." He reached up to scratch at the mortar between the stones, and the ancient bonding crumbled to a plastery dust. "Look at that stuff, Harry. It's so old you can dig it out with your bare hands."

"I know. It's terrible," Harry agreed. "If young Bruce wasn't here guarding us we'd be able to take the whole bloody wall to bits and walk out. You'd think they'd build prisons to last, wouldn't you?"

"It's bloody scandalous," said Murphy. "We'll have to fill in these seams before we can paint over them." He turned and eyed the rookie warder. Young Bruce looked tense, sweaty and sweltering in his new uniform, his knuckles white from the ferocity with which he was gripping his heavy rifle. "What d'you say, Bruce? We can't have a prison with a weak wall, can we?"

Greenwood's mouth started twitching, and his eyes fluttered away from Murphy's leering gaze.

"You don't look well, Bruce. You look pale and wan, like you haven't been sleeping enough and eating the right food. Something troubling you?"

"Y-you know what's troubling me, Murphy," Greenwood stammered, the rifle now shaking slightly as he held it rigidly across his chest. He breathed deeply to steady himself and then blurted: "I'm not going to bring in any more stuff for you, Murphy. I don't care what happens to me, I'm not going to do it."

"That's a pity, Bruce. D'you remember the little receipt you had to sign when you picked up the first lot? That came in here with the second lot, and I've got it safely tucked away and ready to show to Sanderson if you start losing your nerve."

"You swine," Greenwood gasped, his eyes watering with tears of distress amid his pale, sweaty features. He looked like a man in the grip of a high fever. Which was understandable, considering the slather of fear and desperation that he'd been through over the previous week trying to smuggle Murphy's stuff into the prison. He'd finally stumbled upon a solution which would have done justice to the criminal cunning of the very man who'd forced him into this awful situation.

Right across the street running past the main gates of the jail was an unassuming two-storey brick and weatherboard cottage—the home of prison governors in times long past—which had no bars on the windows, no lock on the front door and a garden gate that was invariably open. Yet it was literally a jail in itself. It was a Periodic Detention Centre for thirty or so men of varying ages and backgrounds who had been convicted of crimes ranging from carnal knowledge to culpable driving and given sentences that would remove them from society and their families at weekends but otherwise not interfere with their occupations.

It just so happened that Greenwood found himself rostered to go back and forth between the jail and detention centre twice each Friday night, escorting Arthur Hancock, the light-fingered prison trusty, whose job it was to wheel over a huge hotbox containing evening meals from Willie Crewe's cookhouse, then bring it back full of empty plates. Greenwood found that he could load the box with Murphy's stuff, stashing the plastic-wrapped packages between the empty plates, and simply give the guards on the main gates a cheery smile as Arthur rolled it in right under their noses. Once back in the kitchens it was Arthur's job to smuggle the stuff past Willie Crewe and get it to Murphy's cell.

Twice so far the scheme had worked like a dream. It was fool-proof: The warders at the gate and guardroom didn't give the hotbox so much as a glance as it trundled back and forth. Why should they, if a fellow warder was escorting it? But had they looked a little more carefully at Bruce Greenwood they might have seen the fear shining in his eyes, sensed the utter panic about to spring from his twitching limbs, caught a glimpse, perhaps, of nerves so badly frayed by the whole nightmarish affair as to be on the point of snapping altogether—as they were in great danger of snapping right now on this blazing hot afternoon when Bruce stood trembling and close to collapse before Kevin Murphy's cobra-like grin, the bulky war-surplus rifle dancing in the sweaty grip of his hands.

"If I'm a swine, Bruce, what does that make you?" Murphy grinned. "You're in shit up to your neck too, you know."

"No I'm not," Bruce protested. "I can still go to Mr Sanderson and tell him how you trapped me."

"Then he'll want to know why you didn't go to him ten days ago when it first happened. That's if he hasn't already beaten you to a bloody pulp by then."

Harry Pearce turned away from his paintwork and added casually: "Prison warders don't like scandals involving their own kind, Bruce. It lets down the whole bloody side. When they get them on this side of the bars they treat them worse than the bloody intractibles."

Bruce nervously licked sweat from his upper lip. "I can tell Sanderson I went along with the whole business to learn more about your plan."

"Sanderson doesn't like rookie warders who show that sort of initiative," said Murphy. "Besides, you don't even know if there is a plan, let alone what it is."

"What about the stuff I've been bringing in for you?"

"What stuff? If you can find it, mate, you can have it. Then you can take it along to Sanderson and tell him how it bloody well got in here. While he's strangling you."

Bruce passed a twitching hand over his eyes, wiping away another flush of sweat; then, raising the rifle suddenly and pointing it at Murphy, he played his pathetic last card. "I'm going to shoot you, Murphy," he hissed, "unless you come with me right now and tell Mr Sanderson exactly what's been going on."

Murphy put his brush in the paint tin, straightened up very slowly, glanced at the muzzle of the rifle and glared coldly at the rookie warder. "Never point a gun at anyone, mate, unless you mean to use it," he said. "And you shoot an unarmed prisoner in chains, Bruce, and the whole fucking Corrective Services Department'll drop on you like a ton of bricks. Even Sanderson'll say that's nothing but cold-blooded murder. An' he'll really take you apart then. And you won't be able to prove why you did it, because I won't be alive to bloody corroborate it."

"And I'll make sure you get a knife in your guts the moment they put you away," Harry Pearce vowed.

For a few moments, Bruce stood ashen-faced and swaying in the shimmering heat as though about to pass out. Then he lowered the rifle, wiped sweat again from his brow and gazed blankly, uncomprehendingly, at the ground.

"Don't worry, Bruce," Murphy said cheerfully. "It'll all be over soon, and then I promise no-one will ever know that you were anything but a bloody credit to the prison service. Unless they check the last couple of deposits in your bank account, of course. Now before you bring in the last shipment of stuff, I've got just one more little job for you. I want a copy of the key to the big cabinet in Old Clemency's office. You know the one I mean, don't you? Get it to me with the other stuff next Friday and that'll be the last thing I'll ever ask you to do. Except keep your young mouth shut tight."

And with that, Murphy and Pearce turned back to their work on the wall, leaving Greenwood in his lonely, ludicrous position of armed grief. And Murphy said: "Roma would be a pretty good place to head for, Harry, when all this is over. That's, uh, unless your old mate Blooch is waiting for you."

"He won't," said Harry. "We broke up about ten years ago, and I haven't seen him since. My bloody mother-in-law took out a court order stopping him from coming near the house. That's what did it."

"Your mother-in-law?"

"It was her house. Like, mistake number one. She's the reason why I did what I did and ended up in here." And Harry savagely slapped his paintbrush at the wall.

Murphy said: "She wouldn't be the unfinished business you've got lined up when we get out of here, would she?"

And Harry simply said: "The old bitch had it in for me in one way or another from the bloody moment I met Shirley. Jesus, I still don't know why I got caught up like that. Blooch and me were having the time of our lives. I didn't need to get married. Maybe I thought I needed something a bit solid underneath me, like a wife and kids. I was close on thirty at the time. I know I wanted a son. Maybe I wasn't having such a great bloody time after all. Anyhow, I met Shirley at a dance at the Randwick RSL Club. Actually, Blooch cottoned onto her first, but he got so pissed he couldn't scratch himself, and she and I sort of came together while we were trying to pull him out of the bloody toilet. She was a good-looking girl, a bit skinny but very quiet and lady-like and sort of timid, like she needed someone close by all the time to protect her. We didn't say more'n a few words together the whole evening, but she stuck close to me and wouldn't dance with anyone else, and when one bloke she'd turned down started getting a bit nasty with her, I was up out of me bloody chair and had him by the throat on the bloody floor before I'd even realised what I was doing. And naturally old Blooch was right up next to me, quick as a bloody flash, kicking the shit out of the bloke's offsider, before we could figure out why it had all started. Anyhow, to cut a long story short, Shirley and me started going steady after that."

"That's what I like to hear," said Murphy. "A love story."

"It was, for a while," said Harry. "Shirley and me and Blooch went everywhere together—the races, pubs, dances, pictures, you name it. She really fitted in well with us, though she got a bit cheesed off when Blooch had a chuck or a fight at a party. Especially when I went to help him. Everything was going real sweet. Then she took me home to meet her mother, Ruby."

"Ruby," Murphy echoed. "Mine's called Florrie. Funny how they all seem to have names like that, isn't it?"

"Ruby wasn't funny, mate, I can tell you."

"Florrie ain't exactly a barrel of bloody laughs either."

"She couldn't be half as bad as Ruby, mate. Jesus, that old bag came on like a bloody steam train from the first night I met her. You know, like how Shirley was a good girl who'd been brought up to be a lady even though she'd had to slave hand and foot ever since she was born to feed her and raise her since her old man got blown to bits making a bloody hero of himself at Tobruk . . ."

"War widow, eh? They're the worst."

"Ruby was worse than that, Murph. Her old man didn't die in Tobruk at all. Shirley told me he got pissed and shot through the moment he got home and took off his bloody uniform. Can't say as I blame the poor bastard, either."

"That's the trouble, see," Murphy said philosophically, dabbing away with his paintbrush. "That's where all the Rubies and Florries came from. Not from another bloody planet, like you'd think. It's all those blokes who came home from the bloody war and started hitting the piss like they thought they'd never have a good time in their lives again. That's what caused it. Same thing happened to Marcie's old man. Most of them got stuck into their RSL Clubs and only came out when it was time for a feed."

"I don't know about that," said Harry. "But I know I should've had the brains to see what the score was then. Shirley took me back for another visit, then another, then we were staying home with the old bag three nights a bloody week—then practically every bloody night! When I complained to Shirl about it she said the old dragon never had any company and got scared when she was left alone in the house . . ."

"Probably haunting herself every night."

"Blooch started coming over with me every couple of nights to stop me from going crazy, but then he said 'fuck' or farted or something at the dinner table, and the old bitch started criticising him from then on. Then we started into all the bloody *diseases* . . ."

"That's when it starts to get rough," Murphy observed. "How many did she have?"

"More than you could poke a bloody stick at. You know, that old bag looked healthier than you or me, and she was built like a brick shithouse. She had a bloody good figure, actually, for her age, which wasn't that close to fifty. But the way she complained about her health you would've thought the bloody funeral procession was already on its way down the street. In one week alone, she came down with insomnia, migraines, gallstones, palpitations of the heart,

anaemia, thrombosis, pleurisy, cancer of the breast, a collapsed lung
and fallen arches—and that was all on top of her usual aches and
pains and giddy spells!"

Murphy said: "Marcie's old lady used to come down with things
she called *girl's troubles*. I finally fixed that by refusing to dry myself
on any of the bloody towels in her bathroom."

"Yeah, well, in the end I realised that the only thing Ruby was
suffering from was a chronic lack of what her husband had taken with
him. But it was too bloody late by then. I'd lost me marbles completely and proposed to Shirley, and Shirley had somehow talked me
into moving in with the old lady for a while until we could afford our
own home—and on June the fourteenth, nineteen bloody fifty-nine,
we got married at a church in Coogee with the old lady practically
throwing herself all over the floor with grief and old Blooch so pissed
out of his head that he dropped the rings as he was handing them to
the minister, then fell arse-over-bloody-head at our feet trying to pick
'em up."

Murphy said: "Yeah, well, I did it a bit more cunning than that.
I ran off with Marcie after I'd knocked over the Commonwealth Bank
in Toowoomba, and married her in Surfer's Paradise. Then I took her
back home and told Florrie if she didn't like it she could stuff it."

"I wish I'd had the bloody sense to do that," Harry said sadly.
"It's funny—I really did feel keen about Shirley. I must have done, or
I wouldn't have put up with all the bloody trouble I had with Ruby
when we moved in with her. It wasn't such a bad place, a two-
bedroom cottage down at Rosehill. I liked it because it was opposite
the racecourse, and I used to go out at dawn just about every day and
roam around the stables in the back streets, yarning with the appren-
tices and trainers as they saddled up for exercise. It was about the
only moment's peace I could get, except for the cemetery."

Murphy said: "Don't tell me what happened then. I'll tell you.
You wanted to get out of the old lady's clutches but Shirley was too
scared to move because of the money situation, so you got pissed off
with Shirley and started fighting with her, and the more you fought
the more she needed the security of her old lady."

"Jesus, it was worse than that," said Harry. "From the moment I
moved in, Ruby started to get really flirty with me, touching me all
the time and telling me how bloody handsome I was. Every time I
bent down to do anything she'd practically break a bloody leg trying

to pat me on the backside. Then she started walking about with her housecoat half open, and trying to barge in on me by mistake when I was in the bathroom. And winking! Jesus, I thought her bloody eyelashes were gonna fly off. Then she started doing a fast canter every morning from her bedroom to the bathroom—detouring through the kitchen!—with nothing on but her drawers and bra. I tell you, that was the last bloody straw. There's nothing that'll turn you off your bacon and eggs quicker than half a bloody ton of tits and bum flying in all directions around you. Finally I thought, this has gotta stop. And there was only one thing I could think of that'd put a bloody stop to it."

Murphy said: "You bastard. You didn't."

"One morning," said Harry, "I waited outside her bedroom door, and when she flew out I grabbed her and pushed her up against the wall. It was like trying to berth a bloody zeppelin. Anyhow, she went all strange and shivery and acted like she wanted to get away. And I said: 'Listen, Ruby, you keep running through the house like that, and you know what's going to happen to you, don't you?'

"And she pretended to be angry and said: 'And you know what Shirley would do if she saw you doing this.'

"So I sort of leaned up against her a bit and said: 'What Shirley doesn't see, Shirley doesn't know, eh, Ruby?'

"Well, she started to pant a bit then, and she fluttered her eyelashes at me and said: 'Go on, I'm old enough to be your mother.'

"And I said: 'Well, I'm not so young that I don't know how to slip you a little bit of what you've been missing.'

"And she went really coy then, wiggling about like a lump of bloody blancmange, and she said: 'You wouldn't dare.'

"And I patted her on the bum and said: 'Listen, Rube, don't dare me because you might end up experiencing a big shock.'

"And she started to get red around the neck then, her big tits pumping up and down like barrage balloons, and she said: 'Yeah, if pigs had wings.'

"And that was the bloody moment I'd been waiting for, Murph," Harry said excitedly. "That was when I got right into her! I leaned closer to her and put my mouth right up to her ear and I said: 'Listen, love, if pigs had wings you wouldn't need a bloody broomstick to fly around on all the time.' *JESUS, DID SHE HIT THE FUCKIN' ROOF!!*"

Murphy stood motionless, his brush suspended chin-high and a foot away from the wall, dripping yellow paint into the baking dust at his feet. Gazing in absolute wonder at Harry, he said: "Jesus, I can't say as I'm bloody surprised. That was a *horrible* bloody thing to say, Harry." Then he shook his head and added: "Why couldn't I ever think of something like that?"

"Yeah, well, I paid for it, mate," said Harry. "Eight years of it. And every single bloody day of it was pure hell. Until I finally went nutty and—well, you know."

Murphy said: "We'll have to start filling in these bloody seams before we can paint any further. We'll do that just before we knock off. Then we can get the paint over it the first thing in the morning." He stepped back a few paces from the wall, dragging the main chain with him—and Harry—to study their work. "That tree looks real nice, Harry. We'll move on a bit and do the church next. I want it nice and big and bold so that it stands out well from the trees." Murphy turned to a mute, morose figure standing beside them. "Looks nice, doesn't it, Bruce? How about doing me a little favour and trotting over to block C and getting me a couple of cans of grey and blue paint?"

Greenwood said: "I'm not allowed to move from my post, Murphy."

"Go on, Bruce. Jump to it. I'll hold your gun so's you can run faster."

Greenwood was so deep in his misery that he started to hand the rifle to Murphy. Then he froze, blinked furiously for a moment and, with a suffering moan, turned and shuffled off toward the cell blocks. Murphy turned back to Harry and said: "Right. While he's away let's get that bloody mortar out of there. Dig back into the wall as far as you can, Harry. But only on the sides of the slabs, not underneath. I don't want you losing both your bloody hands if one of the bastards slips down."

As they worked, digging the rotten mortar out with small plastering trowels, Harry asked Murphy: "How many banks did you know of altogether, Murph?"

"Dozens, mate," said Murphy. "I lost count after a while. It took them two years to catch me, too. And then they only got me because some bastard dobbed me in."

"The same bastard you're gonna fix when we get out of here?"

"Ask no questions, Harry. Hear no lies. You've got enough bloody problems of your own."

"What are mates for, Murph? If you've got a good one you stick with him all the way. Share and share alike."

Murphy grinned broadly and said: "OK, mate. But I'll do the fixing, and you can just hang around, like, in case he tries to fix me. Jesus, I tell you what, that bastard's got a lot coming to him. He not only dobbed me in, you know. He did something else almost as bad as that."

"Like what's as bad as dobbing someone in?"

"Like he *robbed me*—the ratbag! I still can't get over how he did it, too. See, I was running a beautiful little racket in those days. Sweet as a nut. I lived a respectable life in Roma with Marcie and the kids—they were just babies then—and told her old lady and everyone else I was a travelling salesman. Men's clothing, suits and stuff that I'd flog around the cattle and sheep properties. If anyone looked like getting suspicious, I had about six big trunks of samples to show them, too. Every couple of weeks I'd drive east to Brisbane, check my car into a parking station, put on one of the suits—a different colour and style each time—stick on a big bushy false beard, then go and buy a cheap old second-hand bomb of a Holden or Falcon. I'd change its number plates to New South Wales or Victorian ones, then drive down into New South Wales and knock off a bank in one of the northern towns, you know, Moree, Gunnedah, Glen Innes, those sort of places. Nothing so big that they'd have a big man-hunt out for me afterwards. Just a nice little cosy country branch making a nice little fortune living off the banana or pineapple growers or dairy farmers. After I'd done the job I'd take off the beard, change into a clergyman's outfit, then stroll to the railway station and get a train back to Brisbane. Beautiful, eh?"

Harry said: "Don't tell me you could stroll anywhere after knocking off a bloody bank."

"Ah, but the way I knocked 'em off was sheer bloody style, mate. None of this tearing in with a stocking over me face, waving a shotgun and clubbing people about and threatening everyone with bloody death. Attracts too much attention, that. The excitement gets everybody's adrenalin working, and next thing you've got some silly cunt of a teller having a bloody go at you. Blokes who pull jobs like that only want to show how bloody tough and horrible they are, anyway. They usually forget what they're there for, cause a lot of distress to people and then find half the State's police force hot on their bloody tails. No, I liked to work in an atmosphere of peace and tranquillity. I'd walk into the bank looking very respectable in my suit, carrying a neat business-like attaché case, smiling at everyone and nodding politely to all the ladies. I'd even have a light raincoat over one arm to cover up the sawn-off double-barrelled shotgun. I'd fill out a withdrawal slip, casing the joint for alarms and guards as I did it, then pick my teller and walk up to his or her window with a big friendly smile on my mug. Now there was no need for noise, threats or nothing. I'd just hand the teller the slip of paper, on which I'd written my customary withdrawal request, which always went like this:

> *HAND OVER YOUR FUCKING MONEY*
> *AND DON'T MAKE A FUCKING SOUND*
> *OR FUCKING MOVE OR I'LL BLOW*
> *YOUR FUCKING HEAD OFF WITH*
> *THIS FUCKING SHOTGUN*

"That's friendly enough," said Harry.

"Well, I used to put in the 'fucking' bit just to make sure they knew I was bloody tough and horrible. Jeez, it did the trick, though. They'd freeze like a bee had stung them on the bum. Completely buggered. Most of them didn't recover from the shock until I was halfway down the bloody street with my case packed with loot, heading for the nearest public toilet. By the time they'd raised the alarm and brought the cops in I'd be a minister of Christ heading for the station to go to a convention or something in Surfer's."

"Sweet all right," said Harry, hacking away with his trowel at the mortar between the blocks of stone. "So how did you get caught, with a nice little routine like that?"

"I still have bloody nightmares about it," said Murphy, shaking his head. "I'd knocked over dozens of banks and not one thing had gone wrong. Then I lined up a prosperous-looking little branch of the Rural just outside Kempsie. Lovely little place. Only two tellers, with one of those great big old-fashioned strongroom doors stuck right behind them. I went in respectable, like, opening the door for a little old lady and her dog, humming a little tune. As I filled out my withdrawal slip I picked my teller. Christ, he was a weedy little bloke—only a couple of strands of hair left, sort of slicked across his dome, a pair of funny old wire-rimmed spectacles and wearing a bloody awful cardigan that his missus obviously made him wear every day. He looked like she forced him to cook the bloody dinner every night, too. I felt so sorry for him that I was thinking of crossing out a couple of the fuckings. Anyhow, I gave him a big friendly smile and handed him the note, which said, naturally:

> *HAND OVER YOUR FUCKING MONEY*
> *AND DON'T MAKE A FUCKING SOUND*
> *OR FUCKING MOVE OR I'LL BLOW*
> *YOUR FUCKING HEAD OFF WITH*
> *THIS FUCKING SHOTGUN*

"He studied it for a moment, adjusting his glasses, then, for Christ's sake, he got a pen and wrote something on it and handed it back to me! He'd written under my stuff: *HOW MUCH DO YOU FUCKING WANT?*

"I should've turned tail and run right then, but I wrote on the paper: *STOP FUCKING ABOUT—I WANT ALL THE FUCKING DOUGH YOU'VE GOT.*

"He looked at the note again, and Jesus if he didn't write on it again and hand it back. This time it said: *HOW DO YOU FUCKING WANT IT—LITTLE BILLS OR BIG FUCKING BILLS?*

"I wrote back: *CAN'T YOU FUCKING READ—I WANT FUCKING EVERYTHING.*

"And he wrote back: *GIVE ME YOUR FUCKING BRIEFCASE THEN.*

"I wrote: *DON'T TRY ANYTHING FUCKING SMART—LIKE TIPPING OFF THE FUCKING MANAGER.*

"And he wrote: *I AM THE FUCKING MANAGER.*

"I should've got right out of there right then, Harry. Jesus, by this time I was sweating blood. Anyhow, he took the attaché case and opened up the strongroom, and I'm standing there with a couple of people queueing up behind me feeling like I'm gonna bloody faint or something if he doesn't hurry up. Then he came back and handed the case to me, and the bloody thing was packed so tight with dough I could hardly carry it. Then he handed me another note which said: *GO OVER TO THAT FUCKING BENCH AND FUCKING WAIT FOR ME.*

"I wrote back: *ARE YOU FUCKING CRAZY? I'M FUCKING OFF MATE.*

"And he wrote; *NO YOU'RE FUCKING NOT—I'VE GOT MY FOOT ON THE FUCKING ALARM BUTTON.*

"I don't know how the people behind me didn't twig to what was going on. They must have thought I was a deaf-mute or something. Anyhow, I started to panic, and I wrote: *DO YOU WANT ME TO BLOW YOUR FUCKING HEAD OFF WITH THIS FUCKING SHOTGUN?*

"And he wrote back: *DO YOU WANT ME TO BLOW A FUCK-ING HOLE IN YOUR GUTS WITH THIS?*

"I looked down, and there in his right hand, poking at me from under the rim of the window, was the biggest bloody Smith and Wesson revolver I'd ever seen. Jeez, I nearly shat myself on the spot. I could see the little bastard was tough and horrible enough to use it—he had nothing to lose with me standing there with a bag packed with his dough. Besides, the last thing I wanted was a bloody commotion. So I went and sat down on the bench and he served his other customers, then he told the other teller to take over the shop, put a jacket on and came around to me.

" 'Start walking,' he whispers. 'An' don't try anything funny or I'll scream blue murder, an' then every bastard'll be onto you.'

"As I followed him out of the bank and down the main street, the little rat walked right in front of me, stiff-like, as though he'd crapped in his pants or something. People said hullo to him, and he just nodded quickly and kept walking. If I'd been the killing type I would've let him have both bloody barrels in the back right then. Anyhow, we got down the street a bit and he said: 'OK, where's your getaway car?'

"I said: 'Why the bloody hell are you doing this to me?'

"And he said: 'I've been waiting twenty fucking years for some-one like you to come along. Now, where's your car?'

"I took him to the old bomb I'd bought to bring me down from Brisbane, and he took one look at it and said: 'Jesus Christ—that old heap wouldn't outrun a cop on a bloody pushbike.'

"I told him it wasn't supposed to, and he said: 'Anyhow, get in and drive me into Kempsie.'

"Christ, the town we were in was practically on the Kempsie city limits as it was. As we tooled along I couldn't find one deserted spot where I could maybe knock him on the bloody head and throw him out of the car. We were just getting into the Kempsie suburbs when he said: 'Right, pull over here.' And Jeez, we were right outside a bloody police station! When we'd parked, he tapped the attaché case and said: 'There's close to a hundred grand in there, feller. Ten percent of it's yours. The rest is mine.'

"I said: 'Like buggery.'

"And he said: 'You want me to start screaming?'

"So I had to just sit there, Harry, with both hands glued to the bloody wheel, while the little bastard helped himself to close on ninety thousand dollars of my dough! When he'd got it all into his bag he looked at me through those funny little glasses of his and grinned. 'Nice to do business with you,' he said. 'Now gimme your driver's licence—your real one. And take that beard off so's I can get a good look at you.' And after I'd done all that, he said something to me that I'll never ever bloody forgive him for, Harry. He said, *Piss off*—like I was a two-bit bloody hood! And then he said: 'Don't come near my bank again or I'll have the cops onto you so fast you'll think the fucking sky fell in on you.' Then he got out of the car and I got out of Kempsie like my backside was on fire."

Harry said: "I'm sorry to say this, Murph, but that's about the neatest con I've ever heard of. What happened to him?"

"I read about it all the next day in the North Coast newspapers. *One Hundred Thousand Dollar Bank Heist—Manager Tells of Nightmare Ride With Killer Bandit*. Lousy little bastard! Then the next day the papers said he was going on extended leave to recover from his terrible ordeal."

"When did he dob you in?"

"Not then—six months later. He had to make it look as though I had time to stash all that ninety thousand bloody bucks away, see? Marcie and me were sitting in the Beer Garden at Surfer's Paradise, watching a Maori floorshow and minding our own business, when every bloody cop on the Gold Coast suddenly jumped on me. As they dragged me out of there, who should be sauntering in but that same little bastard—with a blonde on his arm who looked like she'd just stepped off a King's Cross strip stage. As the bulls tore me past him, I looked at him, and he looked at me, and he laughed like a bloody drain. That was the worst part, Harry. That was worse than everything else he'd done. That was what turned him from a bloody rotten con man into a filthy lousy no-good criminal bastard in my mind. He'd dobbed me in just for bloody laughs!"

fifteen

WHEN WILLIE CREWE A-WOOING WENT, Henry Trembler would sure as God be hanging on his tail, a voyeuristic fly on the wall, avidly watching Willie's gradual, systematic advances from encounter to courtship to dalliance to final conquest. To say that a perverse bond existed between Henry and Willie would be putting it mildly. Henry played Mephisto to Willie's Faust, encouraging with satanic relish the young ex-thug's pursuit of young Bothams like Timothy.

Henry had no qualms about his role in this two-man pack-rape relationship. "If you distilled everything that was evil from every man, woman and child in this country," he would candidly confess to various State Health Commission psychiatrists who tried regularly to find something worth rehabilitating within him, "you'd be left with the essence of me. Which is not surprising, because I had a very strict Catholic upbringing—*Blessed is the Fruit of Thy Womb*, and all that—and in my formative years was destined, in fact, for the priesthood. I was a pious little bastard in those days. I had it so bad I used to dream up imaginary sins to please the local priest at confession. Every week at St. Joseph's I'd step into the box with my little curly head spinning with mortal temptations that I'd fallen victim to—horrible nasty sweaty thoughts like looking up little girls' dresses, pinching ladies' undergarments from clotheslines or writing *bum* on the toilet wall. After I'd babbled them all off, old Father O'Leary would let out a weary sigh on the other side of the confessional and say in a tone that I could tell was close to bloody boredom: 'Recite three Hail Marys, pray for forgiveness and make sure you wash your hands before you come to confession." And I'd think: 'Christ, what does the bastard want from me?'

"Then, one day, I was sitting there in the gloomy box, and old Father O'leary was practically nodding off on the other side as I told him how I'd pressed myself up against a woman in a bus, pinched some dough from my old lady's purse and dropped a cat's turd through the bloke next door's letterbox, and the good Father was starting into his 'Recite three Hail Marys, pray for forgiveness and wash your hands—' when, on sudden impulse, right on the spur of the moment, I said: 'That's not all. Father, I fucked a duck.' And old Father O'Leary said: 'I hope you prayed for that little duck's soul and gave it a Christian burial. God is the Father of all living creat—" 'No,' I said. 'Not that way—the other way.' And old Father O'Leary started again into his Hail Marys. Then he said: '*What!*' And I said: 'That's right, Father. I fucked a duck.' And he sort of spluttered about a bit, then he said: 'Do you mean to say you've had *carnal knowledge of a duck?*' 'Yes, Father,' I confessed. And the whole box started to rock about as he went off his nut in the next cubicle. 'That, my child,' he said, with his voice shaking, 'is a terrible, *mortal* sin!' And I thought, *Ah, now we're getting somewhere.*

"So the next week I'm back in the box again, and this time I can tell old Father O'Leary's all ears on the other side of the grille—I could almost hear them flapping with curiosity—and I said: 'Father, I've sinned.' And he was right on the ball this time. Quick as a flash he said: 'Tell me everything, my child.' And I said: 'Well, I opened my fly in front of a lady on the train, I said a rude word to a little girl in our street and I cut a hole in one of the toilet doors at school.' Old Father O'Leary was silent for a couple of seconds, then he said: 'Is that all?' And I said: 'No, Father—I poked a possum.' He said: 'You what?' And I said: 'I poked a possum. That's after I got up a goat.' And he said: '*You got up a goat?*' And I said: 'Yes, Father—I got up a goat.' And he exploded and yelled: 'Holy Mother of Christ! That's the most wicked sin I've ever heard of in my life!' And I thought to myself: *Hell, what more does he want?* So after that I dropped all the usual preamble about belting through stores pinching ladies' tits and peeping through bedroom windows at night, and stuck to the good stuff like mounting marsupials, banging bullocks, shafting sheep, rooting rabbits, copulating with cats, fornicating with ferrets, humping horses, screwing chooks, raping rats, compromising cows, pronging pigs and other gross offences of a bestial nature.

"After six months I was running out of local livestock and fauna, and old Father O'Leary had just about exhausted all the acts of absolution that he could think of. Then I slipped up very badly. One day I'm sitting there in the box and old Father O'Leary is leaning so close to the grille that I can practically hear his heart thumping, and I say: 'Father, I've sinned.' And he says: 'Yes, child, what is it this time?' And I crossed my fingers and took a deep breath and said: 'Father, I penetrated a penguin.' And Christ—that did it! That made him go right off his bloody rocker. He was in such a rage he started kicking at the side of the box, and his voice thundered in my ear: *'That, my child, is the absolute evil!!'* And I thought to myself: *Ah, success at last.* And as I was sitting there giggling and congratulating myself, old Father O'Leary suddenly leapt out of his side of the box, tore the curtain across on my side, dragged me right out of the confessional and started slapping me about the bloody ears. 'You told a *lie!*' he hollered. 'There are no penguins within a thousand miles of Sydney!'

"And the old bastard dragged me right out of the church, belting the hell out of me as we went, and when he got me to the front steps he said: 'It is a mortal sin to tell a lie!' And I shook my head to stop the bells ringing and said to him: 'So much for the sanctity of the bloody confessional, Father.' And he said: 'There is no sanctity in my church for little boys who tell lies!' And I said: 'Well fuck the church'—which, of course, I finally did, ten years later when I collared those nuns in the dormitory of the convent.

"I remember the court case vividly. A great deal of it had to be held in camera, of course, particularly the evidence of old Father O'Leary, who came forth to testify about my horrendous, bestial malpractices as a child. I remember spitting across at him from the witness box and screaming: 'So much for the fucking sanctity of the confessional, Father!' before my police custodians dragged me down to the cells and lay about me with their rubber truncheons. My crowning glory, though, was the judge's remark, after sentencing me to penal servitude for the duration of Her Majesty's pleasure, that in all his long years as an arbitrator of justice he had never been compelled to tip the scales on so evil and revolting a monster masquerading in the form of a human being. It was at that moment that I finally felt close to God, or at least on his level."

In prison, Henry Trembler carried the keys to his self-appointed kingdom with a sort of progressive benevolence, a walking encyclopedia of sin, a sociologist of evil. Where the godly could counsel that there was only one way to be *good*, Henry could offer advice on a thousand ways to be *bad*. And he had the added advantage of being able to relate badness to a million and one encompassing influences of man's environment. Thus was he able to justify Willie Crewe's brutally evil character in these broad terms: "Australia has too much of two things—drunken fathers and bitter, matriarchal mothers. The result is too many homosexuals. At the same time, there are too many repressive laws and bloody prejudices against homosexuality—and the result is you, Willie Crewe."

With Timothy Botham it was something a little the same, yet a little different. But for the complete loss of his father at a tender age, Botham might well have been prowling the prison alongside Henry and Willie, or submissively awaiting them on the other side of the jail's line of sexual demarcation. As it was, he was an innocent bird of prey in between.

Botham was so innocent that, in prison terms, he was completely "straight." And as such, his entire future depended upon the tacit protection given him by Harry Pearce. If he lost that protection he would have to choose between the two sides of the line—to be a Willie Crewe or one of the others. If he chose neither, Willie or someone else on his side would catch him savagely in the middle, and, thereafter, that's where he would stay, in a defenceless, pathetic limbo.

From Willie Crewe's point of view there were only two stumbling blocks between him and his beloved Botham: Harry Pearce and Mrs Muriel Everingham. Harry Pearce was not so much a problem anymore, so long as Willie could woo Botham away from him before Harry made his break. Mrs Everingham was something else—like a siren, she sang songs of torment from the distant rocks of her tawdry marriage, plucking at Timothy's taut heartstrings with fingers that bore within them, still, the promise of his body's young warmth. So Mrs Everingham definitely had to go.

The exorcism began as the cool breezes of evening began sweeping away the dead, heavy heat of the afternoon on which Murphy and Pearce had worked on the inner face of the main wall. After the evening meal, Murphy had been marshalling his troops for further work on the mural in cell-block C and Pearce had gone to his cell to begin chipping away at the sixth and last sculpture of his mysterious *In Loving Memory*. Willie and Henry had followed Timothy back to his cell, where Timothy cheerfully entertained them with an awful, nerve-wrenching rendition of "Danny Boy" on his harmonica.

"How d'you like it?" Botham asked them, slapping the infernal instrument against the tight, softly rounded curve of his thigh, after having treated them to no less than ten renditions.

"You play beautifully, Timothy," Willie Crewe cooed. "But don't overdo it."

"It like helps keep my mind off things," Timothy explained, blushing a slight pink that made Willie's guts crawl.

Henry Trembler's glasses flashed like twin sephamore beams in the glare of the ceiling light as he promptly stepped in with: "What sort of things, Timothy?"

Timothy blushed again and flicked spittle from the harmonica to the floor beside his cot. "Like things," he muttered, flushing a deeper pink, now, from the roots of his blond hair to the dimple of his soft, girlish chin. "Like the woman I love."

Willie Crewe's amorous smile tightened as he said: "Tell us about her, Timothy."

"Oh, there's nothing much to tell . . ."

"Go on," Henry insisted wickedly. "There's no woman on earth who hasn't got a word or two going for her. Tell us what she looks like."

"Yeah," said Willie. "Like, is she ugly?"

"No, she's not," Botham replied hotly. "She's the most beautiful woman in the world. She's beautiful in a *mature* way, you know, like—"

"So she's an old woman?" Willie interjected hopefully.

"No, she's not," Timothy protested. "She's like quite young for her age . . . I mean, she's not that much older than me."

Soothingly, Henry Trembler suggested: "Age doesn't count, Timothy, when a woman is in love."

"Yeah," Willie agreed. "A bit of the right thing'll turn any old bag into a raving bloody princess overnight."

"She's not an old bag!" Timothy cried, and the mirror-like lenses of Trembler's glasses swung warningly on Willie Crewe.

"He didn't mean your woman, Timothy," Henry said. "I'm sure a young man as prett—er, handsome and clean-cut as you wouldn't be seen dead with any old bag. Tell us what she looks like."

"Well," said Timothy, his inner torment flaring brightly into his nutbrown eyes, "she's got long black hair that sort of comes right down to her shoulders. And she's like got a nice face, and her lips are sort of big and red . . ."

"Sounds like a woman, all right," said Willie.

Trembler licked his lips and said: "That's nice, Timothy. But what does she look like?"

"I just told you what she looks like!"

"Has she got big tits?"

Timothy looked terribly shocked. "They're not tits," he protested.

"What are they, then?"

"They're not like just *tits*."

"What are they like, then?"

Botham's arms flailed the air around him with frustration. "That's not a nice way to like speak about a lady," he said indignantly.

"That's true," Trembler said soothingly. "She can't help if it she hasn't got any tits."

"She has got tits!" Botham cried. "She's got the biggest tits you blokes have ever seen!"

"Jesus," Henry breathed, licking his lips again. "Tell us about them, then, Timothy."

"Well, they're sort of like . . ." Timothy had his hands cupped to his chest. Willie Crewe caught his breath with an audible gasp. Timothy paused and blinked and said: "Wait a minute! Why should I tell you blokes anything? You're just a couple of pervs."

Henry said: "Go on, Timothy. I'll bet you've never even seen her tits."

"Yeah, you've been pulling the pud too much, Timothy," said Willie. "I bet you've been dreaming it all up."

"I have not," Timothy gasped, his brown eyes moistening with injury and anger. "I saw 'em like every other day for six months. *Naked!*"

"Naked!" Henry Trembler echoed, whipping his spectacles off

and polishing them feverishly with a handkerchief. "What were you doing, Timothy, peeking through her bathroom window?"

"I'm not that type!" Botham insisted. "I was like in the bathroom with her!"

Trembler cackled obscenely and asked: "What were you doing in a lady's bathroom, Timothy?"

"You're a real sticky-beak, aren't you?"

"Well, you must have been doing something, Timothy, if you were both in the same bloody bathroom and her tits were naked."

"It's none of your business," Timothy declared sullenly, his lips pouting effeminately.

Willie Crewe felt a mixture of lust and hatred boil through him. "Ah, shit," he rasped, "he's been having bloody wet dreams, that's all."

"I have not!" Botham cried. "Anyhow, how do you blokes know, anyway? You weren't there, were you?" For a moment the agony flared again in his eyes, and he said in a half-whisper, more to himself than his inquisitors: "She was like teaching me things."

Henry Trembler rose up from his cross-legged position on the floor alongside Willie Crewe and sat down next to Timothy on the bed. With bated breath he asked: "What sort of things was she teaching you, Timothy?"

Botham glanced away from him with blushing self-consciousness and mumbled: "She was like teaching me how to scrub a lady's back."

Trembler and Willie Crewe looked at each other incredulously and then burst simultaneously into filthy laughter; and Botham, his features crimson with embarrassment and anger, cried: "What's there to like laugh about? She was a beaut lady. She was always teaching me things. She *loved* me."

Trembler was polishing his spectacles again, still choking with evil mirth. He pulled himself together and said with mock earnestness: "I'm sure she was a beaut lady, Timothy. But why was she teaching you things? I would've thought a lov—er, attractive young man like you would know enough to give her a few lessons to get on with. Know what I mean?"

Botham glanced agitatedly about the cell as though seeking a path of escape. Then, in hushed tones, he confessed: "I never like knew any girls before I met her. I went to a boy's school, and we weren't allowed to, you know, have anything to do with the birds in the other block."

"Ah," Henry sighed, smacking his lips with relish and glancing meaningfully at Willie Crewe. "So you were a virgin when you met this woman."

"I'm not anymore!" Botham declared manfully. "I know like everything there is to know now. She taught me *everything*. She loved me."

"Yeah," said Willie Crewe, his lips curling with malice. "When she saw a young virgin like you coming along she must've thought all her bloody Christmases had come at once."

"That's not true! She loved me, I tell yer. She told me so."

"Like when you was scrubbing her back for her in the bath?" Willie's malicious snarl turned to a sardonic sneer. "You know what I reckon? I reckon she saw you as the answer to all her bloody prayers."

"You dirty rat!" Botham sprang off the cot and stood over Willie, his fists clenched furiously at his chest; and Henry Trembler jumped up and threw a skinny, pacifying arm over the young man's shoulders. "Calm down now, mate. Willie's only trying to help. We're both trying to help—we're your cobbers, aren't we?"

"Help what?" Timothy sniffed, close now to tears as Henry eased him gently back onto the cot.

"Well, Willie and me are both men of the world. We know about these things. You say she loved you. We only want to protect you, sort of like make sure you didn't get a bum steer."

"She was no bum steer. She loved me."

"Well, you tell us everything that happened, and Willie and me being much more experienced in these things than you are—we'll be able to tell you whether she did or not."

"I can't do that!" Botham gasped. "It's like *intimate*."

"Aw, c'mon Timothy. Wouldn't you like to know for sure, one way or the other?"

"Yes," Timothy moaned, cradling his suffering head in his hands. "I'll like go nuts if I don't know for sure."

Henry's mirrors flashed again on Willie Crewe, and a wicked grin flickered as fast as a snake's tongue across his lips. "OK, Timothy. Let's start at the beginning—when you first met her."

Botham heaved a big sobbing sigh and then muttered into his cupped hands: "It all started when my boss sent me to her place to fix her big end—"

Willie Crewe's pent-up breath exploded through his teeth with a

149

whistle, and Timothy's head flew up from his hands: "See? You're just like having a go at me!"

"Sorry, Timothy," Willie choked. "I was thinking of something else. Go on, mate."

"It was like her car I had to fix, *see?*"

"Go on, Timothy," said Trembler, fighting to keep a straight face.

"Well, I like fixed her car in the garage at the back of the house, then I went to the back door and called through the fly-screen that everything was like fixed. She didn't answer, and I had this receipt that she had to sign saying I'd like done the job. I called again and she still didn't answer, so I opened the fly-screen door and like called her again. She still didn't answer, and I knew she couldn't have gone anywhere because I was fixing her car. So I thought she might be in the living room and like couldn't hear me, so I opened the door and went through the kitchen and down this hallway to look for her, and I saw this open door halfway down. I just looked in, like, to see if she was there. I didn't know it was her bedroom—and there she was, standing in front of a mirror with just a brassiere and a pair of panties on!"

"Holy shit," Henry Trembler breathed. "What happened then?"

"Well, I tried to like back-pedal up the hall as fast as I could, but she must've seen me because she called out something like: 'Come back here, young man.' I didn't know what to do, but before I could shoot through she was out in the hall, and she'd put a housecoat on, and Jesus, *was she angry!*"

"I'll bet she fucking was," Willie Crewe sneered nastily.

"She said to me: 'How dare you spy on a lady in her bedroom like that.' And I like started to apologise, and she said: 'That's a terrible thing to do. I've a mind to telephone your employer and tell him what you did.' And I said: 'No, Jesus, no, lady! I didn't do it on purpose.' She sort of looked at me for a while, like she was trying to make up her mind what to do, and then she like said: 'Well, I'll let you off this time. But you'll still have to be punished.' And I said: 'I'll do anything, Mrs Everingham, only please don't tell my boss. He'll tell my Mum.' So she said: 'Come into the front room and I'll decide what to do with you.' "

Botham paused, lowering his head to his hands again. And Trembler, furiously polishing his spectacles, said: "Yes. Yes."

"The next bit's like *personal*," Botham moaned.

"Go on! Go on!"

"Well, we went into the living room, like, and she sat down on the settee and leaned back, and the housecoat like fell apart as she crossed her legs. I just stood there like a shag on a bloody rock staring at all that naked flesh. Then she said: 'Take off your trousers and underpants.' I said: 'Jesus, I can't do that in front of a lady.' And she said: 'Do you want me to phone your boss right now?' So I like took off my strides and Y-fronts and then stood there wishing the bloody floor would open up and like swallow me. I couldn't like keep my eyes off her bare legs, and then Jesus if I didn't start to get a big hard-on. It just came up and stuck through the flaps of my shirt like a bloody flagpole. And she looked me up and down, very slow like, and she said: 'How old are you, Timothy?' And I said: 'I'm nineteen, Mrs Everingham." And she said: 'Well, you're certainly a big boy for your age.' And I said: 'My Mum always says she wonders when I'll ever stop growing.' And she like laughed about that."

"Exquisite," Henry Trembler moaned, rocking gently back and forth on the cot beside Botham; and he shot another purposeful look at the agitated Willie Crewe. "Don't stop now, Timothy," he said.

Botham now looked as though he'd like to hide his entire body in his cupped hands. "Well, after that," he mumbled, "she stretched out her long legs, like, with one crossed over the other, and like put her feet up on a coffee table. My doodle grew so big then that it was almost tapping me on the stomach. And she said: 'Do you like my legs, Timothy?' And I said: 'Yes, Mrs Everingham, they're like very nice.' And she sort of uncrossed them and like crossed them again, and said: 'I'll bet you'd like to touch them, wouldn't you Timothy?' And I said: 'Oh no, Mrs Everingham. I wouldn't do a thing like that to a lady.' And she looked at me a bit funny, like, and said: 'What's wrong with them? Aren't they bloody good enough for you?' And I said: 'No, I mean, like yes, Mrs Everingham. They're like very beautiful. It's just that I've never like felt a lady's legs before.' And she said: 'Don't give me that sort of shit, Timothy. I'll bet a young man with a big cock like yours have never had any trouble finding enough girls' legs to feel.' And I said: 'No, honestly, Mrs Everingham, scout's honour and all that—I've never known any real girls, except for my sisters, like.' And she said: 'Are you trying to kid me?' And I said: 'No, God's honour, Mrs Everingham.' And she sort of took a big breath and like shifted about a bit on the settee, then she said: 'You poor sweet little bugger. We'll have to do something about that, won't we?' And I said: 'Do you know any girls, Mrs Everingham?' And she said: 'Do you want me to call your boss right now?' And I said: 'Jeez, no, please, Mrs Everingham, don't do that!' And she said: 'OK, now here's your punishment. I want you to stand there and look at me and think of all the naughty things you'd like to do to me.' Well! I stood there and looked at those legs of hers and like the parts of her ti—er, bosom that was like showing through the housecoat, and my dong started throbbing like it was going to burst. Then she lay right back on the settee with one leg sort of bent up over the other and her head propped up on a cushion so's she could watch me, and she said: 'Now Timothy—masturbate!' "

"Oh, good Lord in heaven," Henry Trembler gasped, his spectacles fogging up with a vile, sweaty mist again. "Go on, dear boy. Don't stop now."

"Well, like that's all there is," said Timothy. "I was so worked up by then—her sort of spread out in front of me like that—that all I had to do was like put my hand down there and it was all over. Then Mrs Everingham sighed like she was tired or something and got up and said: 'That was beautiful, love. Now let's go and have a cup of coffee and you can tell me all about yourself.' Timothy raised his head from his hands and asked Willie Crewe, who was fidgeting about and running his tongue feverishly around his dry mouth: "How's that? Now do you like believe me?"

"Let's hear some more," Willie said hoarsely.

"Just because she used the word *love*, Timothy," Trembler patiently explained, "it doesn't necessarily mean she loved you. You'll have to come up with more than that if you want an expert opinion."

"Yeah, let's have some more," said Willie.

"Well," said Botham, lowering his curly blond head to his hands once again, "we had some coffee in the kitchen and she like got to talking about me and she said it was terrible, like, that a decent young man like me had never had any experience with women. Then she said she'd like to help me, and that if I promised not to like breathe a word to anyone I could come back on the following Monday and she'd start giving me lessons on how to behave with girls. I said: 'That's real beaut of you, Mrs Everingham,' and she said: 'Don't thank me—thank my big end.' "

"So you went back on the Monday?"

"Yeah, I like went back on the Monday and she gave me a cup of coffee in the kitchen and she said: 'You haven't told anyone, have you Timothy?' And I said: 'Honest to God, Mrs Everingham, my lips are sealed.' And she said: 'Well, we'd better do something about that too.' And she gave me a big kiss, real passionate like, and then she said: 'Now let's begin the first lesson . . .' "

"Details, Timothy. *Details*," Henry Trembler snapped. "Like did she have any clothes on?"

"Oh yeah," said Timothy. "She like had this beaut dress on. It was sort of like blue, and a bit low in the front, and made of that sort of pimply nylon that—"

"Stick to the details," Henry snapped. "What happened next?"

"Well, she took me into the front room, like, and closed all the venetian blinds so that no-one could like stickybeak from outside, then she sat down on the settee and told me to sit next to her. Then she said: 'To start with Timothy, I'm going to teach you how to make advances to a lady without being rough and frightening her. So many Australian men think they just have to jump on and crack the whip and we'll get up and gallop the full eight furlongs.' "

"Priceless," Henry commented gleefully. "Priceless. Carry on, dear boy."

"Well, first she taught me how to put my arm around a lady, gently but firmly, like I meant business. Then she showed me how to like tenderly pull a lady towards me and kiss her without almost breaking her neck. Then she said: 'No, Timothy—that's how you'd kiss your sister. Now try again, and this time put your tongue in the lady's mouth.' Well, I thought: *Strewth, that sounds a bit bloody unhygienic*. But I like did what she said, and we like played around with each other's tongues for a bit, and after a while I sort of started to enjoy it. Then she pushed me away a bit and like panted for a while, catching her breath, then she showed me how to put my hand up a lady's dress, tenderly like, without alarming her."

"She was moving pretty fast for a first lesson, wasn't she?" Trembler observed.

"She was very patient with me," Timothy retorted.

"Yeah, patient like a bloody tiger shark on a lump of fresh meat," Willie Crewe gnashed.

"Now, Willie," Trembler cautioned him, "let's hear Timothy out before we jump to conclusions. What happened next, Timothy?"

"Well, I had three goes at putting my hand up a lady's legs,

153

under her dress, before she said I was doing it right, like *tenderly*. Then she showed me how to like slip it gently in between a lady's thighs where it was all warm and moist. After I'd got that part worked out properly she showed me how to like put my hand on a lady's er, like her, um . . ."

"A lady's what, Timothy?"

Timothy blushed furiously. "You know. Like her, um, *thingummyjib*."

"Oh," said Trembler. "Her thingummyjib. Do you mean her genitals?"

"I don't know about that," said Timothy. "I was too busy feeling her thingummyjib. Anyhow, she showed me how to like caress it and fondle it, first outside a lady's panties and then like inside. Mrs Everingham started to breathe very fast then, and her eyes were like closed, and I said: 'I'm not hurting you am I, Mrs Everingham?' And she said: 'Oh, sweet Jesus—you've got fingers of silk, my love. I think I'd better show you how to take a lady into the bedroom for the next lesson.' "

"Fingers of silk, eh?" Trembler glanced quickly at Willie Crewe, and Willie began fidgeting about again on the floor.

"Yeah, well anyhow, we went into the bedroom, like, and she said: 'Now I'm going to show you how to undress a lady without ripping half her clothes in the process.' Well, then she showed me how to like unzip a lady's dress without getting it caught in the material, and then how to slip it over a lady's shoulders, like, and let it drop slowly to the floor so that all a lady had to do then was like step out of it and kick it across the carpet. Then she like sat down on the bed in her brassiere and panties and she said: 'Now, Timothy, I want you to show me how you'd cuddle a lady and fondle her breasts without climbing all over her.' So she showed me how to like put my arm around a lady's shoulders and feel her ti—er, boo—er, bosom at the same time. Jesus!—they were so big I like thought her brassiere was going to explode, especially when she started breathing heavily. The damn thing was so tight I thought: *Shit, is this all I've been missing out on?* It was like trying to get a good grip on a big watermelon in a canvas bag. Then she said: 'Now for something very tricky, Timothy. The next step is to see if you can fondle a lady's breasts with one hand and unsnap her bra with the other.' Well, it took me like the best part of ten minutes to do that—Jesus, it's hard to get your fingers around those little hooks an' eyes when the whole bloody thing's like stretched as tight as a drumskin. Anyhow, I finally got the last hook undone, and the whole thing like flew off so fast that one end nearly caught me in the eye. And her tits sort of tumbled and rolled free like they was . . . Like they was so big . . . Like I remember that all I could think of was a big fifteen-foot surf, a big dumper, breaking and crashing over at Bondi . . ."

"Lord, how poetic," Henry Trembler gasped, cherishing the vision in his mind's eye. "What happened next, dear boy?"

"Then she like put her arms around me and held me close," Timothy recounted, the pitch of his voice rising passionately, "while I like squeezed and caressed those beautiful big tits. Oh Christ, it was like I was a baker up to his armpits in fresh dough, like I was the king of the whole world and every tit in the kingdom was mine to play with. And then . . . And then . . ." Timothy paused, breathing feverishly now, gulping deeply. "Then she like rolled back so she was lying back on the bed, and her breasts sort of like flattened and spread on her chest, and she cried out: 'Now show me how you'd suck a lady's nipples!' And she grabbed me by both ears and pulled me to her big brown nipples and it was like I didn't need any bloody lessons anymore! I just pulled one into my mouth, like, and sucked on it and rolled it around with my tongue, and she like started making funny sounds and she threw her legs into the air, like, and I put my hand on her tummy and began stroking it while I was sucking her tits, and I pulled my head away for a second and said: 'Oh, Jesus, Mrs Everingham—let's get on to the next lesson.' And she said: 'Lower, Timothy—*lower*.' So I like dropped my voice a bit and said: 'Oh, Jesus, Mrs Everingham—let's get—' And she shouted: 'No, for Christ's sake! Your hand! *Lower!*' And next thing I'm showing her how I'd like tear off a lady's panties, and she's like rolling about on the bed with me as I sucked her tits and messaged her thingummyjib, and I remember it like opened up and it was hot and sticky inside, and all I could like think of was things opening up, like flowers and seeds and fruits, and like big beanshoots rising up out of the ground, and she was like tearing at the belt of my strides with one hand and ripping at the zip with the other, and she like got a hand inside and squeezed me hard and then she like threw herself on her back and opened her legs wide as could be, with her knees up in the air, like, and she said: 'Now kiss me, Timothy.' And I like said: 'I

155

thought we'd like finished with that part.' And she shouted: 'Kiss me there, Timothy. Oh, please kiss me *there!*' So I like started kissing her there . . ."

"Where?" Trembler demanded, almost beside himself with obscene excitement. "Where? *Where?*"

"In her bedroom, like. On her bed."

"No, you bloody dope! Where did you bloody kiss her?"

"On the thingummyjib," Timothy cried excitedly, his big brown eyes glazed and milky with renewed desire as his tongue babbled off the vivid flashes in his tortured mind. "I kissed it, then I like kissed it again, and Mrs Everingham said: 'Oh God, put your tongue in, Timothy.' And I like thought: *Stone the crows—that's a bit bloody close to the bone, like.* But I gave it a little lick, and it like tasted alright, sort of like a bit salty, like when you lick your arm after a day at the beach. And then I put my tongue right in and Mrs Everingham let out a little scream, and it was like I was eating a hot mango—all sticky and gooey and salty and sweet—and I like started to enjoy it, and then I like felt something warm and wet like close over my cock, and then Mrs Everingham rolled again, and next thing everything went black and sort of funny and muffled, like I was skindiving and hearing noises from above the surface of the water, and Mrs Everingham had closed her thighs right over my head and I couldn't hear anything and I couldn't like see anything and I couldn't breathe properly, and I was just like starting to panic when I was suddenly up above the surface again, gasping for breath, and everything was like flashing and popping around me, and I'm on my knees and Mrs Everingham's legs are like spread out around me, and she leaned forward with her breasts all squashy and hot against my chest and she grabbed me by the shoulders and pulled me right down on top of her, and I like thought I was going to fall off for a moment and then her hands were like down between my legs and she was guiding me into her! And oh, Jesus!—*I'd never known a feeling like it in my life!* I felt like my toes were gonna fall off! I felt like everything inside me was swelling up and going to blow apart! It was like catching the best wave of the day off Whale Beach! It was like the time I cried when the Anzacs marched down Pitt Street with the pipes like howling and the drums beating and the medals jingling on the old blokes' chests, and I like thought I saw my Dad in amongst them . . ." Botham had leapt off the bed and to his feet now, so emotionally overcome was he by his visions. Trembler and Willie Crewe sat transfixed, open-mouthed, as the young man's fists beat at the air in front of him and his voice rose with each escalating step toward his final joy. "It was like the day they took us all in the school bus to see the Queen, and all those thousands of kids like went crazy, screaming and waving their flags, and I like bawled my eyes out because the noise made me so happy! It was like belting out onto the Sydney Cricket Ground with a million other kids, all fighting for the stumps, when Redpath whacked that six over the scoreboard to thrash the hell out of the Poms! It was like I wasn't just *me* anymore! It was like I was part of the *whole thing*, like . . . And I looked down at Mrs Everingham, heaving about underneath me, her long black hair like tumbling all over her face, and I felt like crying again because it was all so beautiful! And Mrs Everingham like cried out: 'Oh Timothy, I can feel you inside me!' And I said: 'I can feel you too, Mrs Everingham.' And she yelled: 'Timothy, you're beautiful!' And I said: 'You're beautiful too, Mrs Everingham.' And that's when she cried: 'Oh Timothy, I love you! *I love you!*' And I like said: 'I love you too, Mrs Everingham.' And then she like shouted: 'Fuck me, Timothy!' And I like shouted: 'Fuck you, Mrs—' "

"That's enough!" Willie Crewe screeched, jumping to his feet.

"—Everingham!"

"That's enough!" Willie yelled again, his unabashed jealousy flaring hotly to his cheeks and brow.

"Don't stop him now," Henry Trembler protested. "We're just getting to the best part!"

But Willie, trembling with rage and hatred, spun on his mentor with a nasty snarl. "Can't you see what that bitch was doing to him? She was just bloody using him!"

"No she wasn't!" Timothy cried. "She loved me. She told me so! Didn't I just tell you. . . ?"

"She was just using you, you dumb bastard! An' then when her husband lumbered you both she dropped you like a bloody hot brick!"

Trembler grabbed Timothy's arm and pulled him back down onto the bed. "He's right, you know, Timothy. Now, if you want my opinion—"

"You just shut yer guts," Timothy bawled, his face screwing up and grievous tears welling into his brown eyes. "And that like goes for you, too!" he yelled at Willie Crewe. "You're just a couple of dirty pervs! She loves me, an' nothing you say can like tell me any different."

"Well you'd better just start thinking differently, boy," Willie growled menacingly, standing over him. "Because you're about to start learning a few new tricks."

"I don't need any more lessons," Timothy sniffed. "She like taught me everything. Everything there is to know." And his anger and frustration boiled up again as he turned on Henry Trembler and said: "I don't care what you think! She loves me, an' I love her. And we'll like be together again soon, so you can both go jump in a bloody lake!"

Willie said: "So you'll be together again soon, eh? How soon, Timothy?"

Timothy blushed deeply and muttered: "Soon."

"Soon?"

"Soon."

"How soon, Timothy?"

Timothy turned away from Willie's menacing stare and murmured: "Just . . . like soon."

Willie Crewe looked hard at Henry Trembler and his cruel lips became all but a thin gash of venom amid a face that was now white with fury. Then he suddenly leapt at Timothy, tearing at him with both hands, and he savagely caught hold of the front of the young convict's green denim shirt, yanked him viciously off the cot and heaved him up close to him, up on the tips of his toes. "Now you listen to me, you little jerk-off," he snarled, his mouth so close to Timothy's face that Timothy flinched as the hot, bitter breath buffeted him. "You put that bitch right out of your bloody mind, right now. Because you're not going anywhere, boy. You're staying here, with me, and I'm going to teach you a few things you never even dreamed of before."

"You leave me alone," Timothy wailed, squirming in Willie's vise-like grasp, trying to pull away. And Willie slapped him hard across the face with a violence that sent him crashing back on to the bed.

"You fucking bastard!" Timothy shrieked. "You wait till Harry Pearce hears about this! He'll like fucking murder you!"

Willie stepped forward and struck him again, backhanded this time and so savagely that Timothy's blond head plunged sideways into the pillow and rumpled blankets at one end of the cot. Then Willie leaned down and spoke close to Timothy's ear. "You're mine now, not Pearce's. You do what I say, mate, and we'll get on fine together. You give me trouble and the next couple-a years are going to be sheer bloody murder for you."

Timothy, sobbing with terror, looked up from the bedclothes, looked at Willie, looked at the sinister, dispassionate beacons of Henry Trembler's bi-focal glasses—and finally read the message in them. "I'm not that type!" he cried.

"That's fine by me," Willie crooned. "I prefer a bit of innocence, don't you, Henry?"

"Harry'll kill you dirty bastards for this!" Timothy insisted; and Willie leaned down again and put a hand firmly around his shrinking Adam's apple and said in a hissing, viperish tone that made Timothy's eyes bulge with horror: "Pearce doesn't own you anymore. I do. I paid him two thousand bucks for you, sonny, and that's a lot of bloody dough to go throwing around on anything. Now you'd better start giving me my money's worth, Timothy, or I'll get really rough with you."

There was a long silence, during which Timothy's frightened sobs slowly dried to a chilled exhaustion. In this numbness he stared sightlessly at the floor at Willie's feet. Then he slowly raised his head, frowned strangely and murmured: "Harry did that?"

Willie patted his breast pocket. "I got his IOU here if you want to take a dekko at it."

Timothy said quietly: "He said he was going to like get me out of here."

Willie said: "You mean a break?"

"Like over the wall," said Timothy, staring again at the floor. "In the middle of the day, when the guards like aren't expecting it."

Willie looked at Trembler and both snickered with amusement. "You're not doing very well for yourself, Timothy. That's two people who've taken you for a bloody ride." Willie glanced again at Henry, then sat down next to the stricken Botham and cautiously slid his arm around his slumped, defeated shoulders, gently squeezing the nape of his neck on the way. "You need someone who'll really look out for you, for a change, Timothy."

Timothy turned his head and looked blankly at him. "He like

told me we'd break out of his cell and belt across the yard to the—"

"Wait a minute," Willie snapped, his eyes darting again to Henry Trembler's glasses. "Break out of his cell? How?"

"Like through the wall," said Timothy.

"That's bloody craz—" Then Willie jumped to his feet and let out a loud whoop. "Jesus," he hollered. "Now I bloody see it! Christ, I've been waiting seven bloody years to get even with that bastard, and now I've got him bloody cold. Don't you go away, Timothy," he said, turning toward the cell door. "There's gonna be shit flying in all bloody directions in a little while—then you an' me an' Henry'll have another little chat!"

sixteen

WILLIE FOUND BULL SANDERSON IN THE TV ROOM, next to the underground arts workshop. Sanderson was in one of his rare good moods. He and a big crowd of cons were watching the latest assault on Sydney's criminal elements by Inspector Bill Mainline, star of the weekly homegrown police thriller, "Calling All Cops." Sanderson liked watching "Calling All Cops" for the precious moments when a crook or cop angrily slammed a door and the walls of the cheap studio sets trembled.

The cons enjoyed it for the inevitable moments in the buildup of each dreary plot when the crims shot a cop or bashed a nightwatchman or manhandled a sheila or belted the living daylights out of Mainline himself, who, in real life, was a refugee of the collapsing British film industry, a former immortal player of such one-line triumphs as "The Yard have come up with the information you wanted, sir" in dozens of B-grade Pommie regional police dramas. Right now a long-haired, angry young immigrant Croation terrorist with a bestial grimace on his face and an insane obsession about blowing up the Sydney Opera House at the climax of the jewel-spangled opening night of an Australian prima donna's first homecoming in ten years was wrestling with Mainline on a rocking pontoon at the harbour's edge, with quick intercut flashes showing the seconds ticking off on the timebomb stashed away in the Opera House while the celebrated soprano and a cove in leotards and a funny wig screeched at each other in Eyetalian on the main stage.

Mainline was in the process of being simultaneously strangled and beaten about the head with an iron bar by the evil Croat when Willie Crewe slipped into the flickering blue haze of the room. He found Sanderson looking quite pleased—the prison chief didn't like cops any more than the men who were whistling and stamping their feet with joy around him.

Willie slithered into an empty seat beside Sanderson, leaned close to him and said: "I've got some pretty interesting news for you, Mr Sanderson."

Sanderson reluctantly tore his eyes away from the TV screen and said: "Don't tell me you're going to have a baby."

"Listen," Willie hissed angrily, "you know that, uh, business with Murphy and Pearce that you've had on your mind lately? I think I can clear it up for you."

Sanderson looked Willie straight in the eyes and dropped his voice to a harsh, secretive whisper. "Before you go dobbing anybody in," he said, "you get it clear in your little mind that I can't be in a dozen places at once when they decide to get you."

Willie put on a bland, matter-of-fact smile. "I don't know what you're talking about, Mr Sanderson. All I was going to tell you was that Harry Pearce's just finishing off his sixth sculpture. Ain't that good news?"

And with that, Willie slid away, leaving Bull Sanderson somewhat bewildered. The burly deputy superintendent scratched his head, then shook it, then turned back with a sigh to the TV set just in time to see justice done on the Croation hood in a horrible, flailing, screaming plunge into the boiling foam at the foot of The Gap, the nationally famous suicide spot at the narrow bottleneck entrance to Sydney Harbour.

Then Sanderson suddenly booted his chair over backwards in his frantic haste to get out of the room. Once outside he tore up the footworn sandstone steps leading up to ground-level, taking them two at a time, his big boots cracking on the stone like rifle shots. Emerging onto the skirt of the quadrangle he charged around the entrance to the auditorium, reached the locked cyclone-wire checkpoint leading to the administration block and, as Bruce Greenwood, the warder on duty there, fumbled with his key in the lock, he shouted: "Raise the bloody alarm!"

The prison siren was already wailing hideously as Sanderson stomped down the main corridor of the office block and charged unceremoniously into (Rev) Clement C. Hunt's office just as Hunt, working late that night, was jumping out from behind his desk to find out why in God's name the siren was howling.

"Murphy and Pearce!" Sanderson bawled, tearing at the receiver of an intercom on his desk to order carbines from the armoury.

"I knew those buggers were up to something," he snarled as he slammed the receiver back in its cradle.

"I don't understand," (Rev) Hunt said helplessly.

"You will," Sanderson growled. He snatched two rifles from a warder who'd just hot-footed into the office from the armoury, then rudely hustled (Rev) Hunt out into the corridor.

"I don't understand," (Rev) Hunt insisted as they hurried out to Greenwood's checkpoint, their senses suddenly bombarded by the awful scream of the siren and a blaze of searchlights aiming like air-raid beams from the four guardpoints on the main wall, searching the tall structures of the six cell blocks.

Sanderson tossed a rifle to Greenwood and bawled: "Right, you—fall in with me! If you see any bastard moving where a bastard shouldn't be, shoot the bastard on sight!"

"I still don't understand," (Rev) Hunt cried plaintively, his voice almost drowned out by siren's metallic screams as a squad of six armed prison officers joined them on the way to cell-block C.

"Don't anybody go in there till I give the bloody word!" Sanderson shouted as they approached the block's steel doors. "You three get on one side, and you lot get on the other with me. Mr Hunt, would you mind keeping right out of the way until we're in there. Greenwood, you get right behind me—and cover me when I go in. And try not to shoot me in the bloody back!"

The siren shrieked and the spotlights gathered together to nose like a pack of hounds at the half-opened doors of cell-block C. Both groups crouched tight against the walls on either side. Sanderson pulled on the bolt of his rifle, ramming a shell into the chamber, looked hard at the warders opposite him, licked his lips and then shouted: "Right! I'm going in!"

With a brute speed that would have done justice to Inspector Mainline's men, he crashed through the steel doors like a crazed steer through an abattoir fence, his rifle gripped firmly at waist-level, ready to counter the hail of bottles, bricks, bullets or fists that he felt certain would rain upon him—only to find a couple of dozen curious heads turned towards him along both sides of the block's walls, bewildered faces wondering what the hell he was up to, paintbrushes and putty knives poised passively in mid-air as all work stopped dead on Kevin Murphy's great mural.

And Murphy himself bawled from the distant end of the block: "What the bloody hell's going on? Jeez, you might let a bloke know when you're going to stage a bloody drill!"

"Shut yer guts, Murphy!" Sanderson raged. "Get both bloody hands up against that bloody wall and stay there! And that goes for the rest of you bloody ratbags!" As the entire complement of convicts froze at the wall, Sanderson snapped at Greenwood behind him: "Take four men and cover these turds. And keep a close watch on Murphy. The rest of you follow me."

As they mounted the steel stairway leading up toward Harry Pearce's cell, (Rev) Hunt said: "You certainly are a man who sticks rigidly to the book, Mr Sanderson. I had no idea you were holding a drill."

"This is no drill, sir," Sanderson barked. "You'll soon see what it's all about."

They burst unheralded into Harry Pearce's cell just as Harry was about to take the first delicate tap at an intricate bit of carving around the eye of his sixth and last bust. Harry froze as Sanderson barked: "You make one bloody move, Pearce, and it'll be your bloody last!"

"I really don't understand," said (Rev) Hunt, glancing around the peaceful, creative scene.

"That makes two of us, sir," Harry muttered.

"Keep your trap shut," Sanderson snarled. "Get over there against that wall and keep your hands up where I can bloody see them."

"I still can't see what it's all about," (Rev) Hunt complained, his voice peevish now as Sanderson ploughed on into his apparent fool's mission.

"You will, sir," Sanderson promised him. And he waved a hand around the cell in a triumphant flourish. "But first take a good look around and tell me if you can see anything that is in any way suspicious."

(Rev) Hunt gazed about the room and shrugged his shoulders. "All I can see is a bed, books, pictures, five pieces of sculpture on the floor over there covered with sheets and towels and Mr Pearce's half-finished work there on the bench. Oh, and I see Mr Murphy has completed the other half of his landscape."

"Right," Sanderson barked. "Now, sir, can you tell me where Pearce got the stone from for his bloody sculptures?"

(Rev) Hunt shrugged again. "I can't say as I can. Where did you get it from, Mr Pearce?"

"Pearce knows, don't you, Pearce?" Sanderson crowed mockingly. "So does that ratbag Murphy."

"I don't know what you're talking about," Harry muttered, turning slightly away from the wall.

"Keep your face to that bloody wall, you lying dingo! Or you'll end up giving it a new coat of bloody paint. *Red paint!*"

(Rev) Hunt frowned impatiently and said: "Mr Sanderson, would you mind telling me exactly what all this is about?"

Bull Sanderson puffed out his brawny chest and strutted like a pigeon-cock over to the wall that was now almost entirely covered by Murphy's twin landscapes. Murphy had certainly completed the other half of the painting: It was an exact replica of the first, right down to the same peculiar chaff-chute and tantalising glimpse of seed separator of the half a combined harvester. Only it was painted in reverse, flowing left to right across the canvas, so that the chutes and seedboxes joined to form not a whole harvester, as one might have expected, but a disjointed affair with none of its vital machinery or tractor showing. The result was not only bizarre, it was infuriating.

But that mattered not one iota now as Sanderson, poised at the brink of glory, turned from the painting to ask (Rev) Hunt: "Now, why would Pearce want a painting this bloody big on his wall?"

(Rev) Hunt frowned again—then his face began to go pale.

"And why would he want *two* big paintings—especially when the two combined, like, practically cover the entire bloody wall?"

As Sanderson reached up, spreading his beefy hands to pull the first painting from the wall, (Rev) Hunt's features drained even whiter, and he gasped: "You don't mean. . . !"

"See for yourself, sir," Sanderson crowed, and with another great flourish he tore the painting away from the wall—and there, in the space that it had covered, there for all to see, there, shrieking at them in indelible witness to Harry Pearce's clandestine sins, was a normal, untouched, bland-faced stone wall, every whitewashed stone set neatly in its place.

Sanderson looked hard at the wall as though expecting it to fall apart at any second. Then a fiery red flush broke out at the base of his thick neck and seeped slowly up through his stunned features. (Rev) Hunt coughed delicately. Sanderson suddenly tore at the second painting, wrenching it furiously from the wall and tossing it to the floor—and again, the wall behind it looked just like any other wall.

"I don't understand, Mr Sanderson," said (Rev) Hunt.

"Neither do I, Mr Hunt," said Harry Pearce, his eyes and hands glued to the opposite wall.

"Shut up, Pearce," Sanderson hissed furiously. "There's something going on here—I can bloody *smell* it! Crewe wouldn't have told me if—"

"So it was Willie Crewe, eh?" said Harry.

And this enraged Bull Sanderson so much that he grabbed Harry's chisel off the workbench, rushed at him and thrust it threateningly close to the back of his head. "Listen, you ratbag," he rumbled, "you tell me where you got that bloody stone from, or so help me you'll end up wearing this bloody chisel in your bloody skull!"

"Mr Sanderson!" (Rev) Hunt snapped. "I fail to see how violence of that nature will help uncover something that apparently isn't there."

"I *know* it's there!" Sanderson roared. "I know this bastard's up to something. And so help me I'll crack his bloody lying skull open if he doesn't tell me!" Sanderson raised the chisel. Then, with a shudder that shook his entire frame, he took a tight grip on his composure, turned and with a moan of rage of frustration hurled it at the opposite wall, the one which had been hung with Murphy's landscapes—where, with a soft thud, it stuck like a knife in the whitewashed stonework.

For a few silent, stunned seconds Sanderson and (Rev) Hunt stood studying the embedded chisel as if it were the most incredible thing they'd ever seen. Which it was. Sanderson then looked at (Rev)

Hunt, and the prison superintendent looked aghast. Sanderson then strode over to the wall, pulled the chisel out, then began hacking away at the stonework—flaky dust pouring out of each deep gouge.

"It's painted plasterboard!" he cried triumphantly. "I knew those buggers were up to something!" And to prove the point he rammed the chisel right through the panel—another of Murphy's many masterpieces—and wrenched the entire facade from the wall. There, in its place, was a neat rectangular hole, six feet wide in the inner part of the block's double wall, the exact size, in fact, of six blocks of workable sandstone. Sanderson peered into the alcove. "Jesus," he said. "The bastards even chipped all the mortar out of the outer stonework. All he and that ratbag Murphy would've had to do is kick the blocks out with their bloody feet and climb through!"

(Rev) Hunt gave Pearce a look that was both amazed and exasperated. "What in God's name made you attempt such a stupid thing?"

"I can't work without stone, can I?" Pearce replied.

"You're a bloody fool, Pearce," Sanderson barked. "And don't make things worse for yourself by telling lies. Now put your hands behind your bloody back while I put these handcuffs on you. You're going to the Blockhouse, and so is that ratbag mate of yours, while Mr Hunt and I make reservations for you at Grafton."

"Murphy had nothing to do with this," Harry said as the steel bracelets clicked around his wrists.

Bull Sanderson let out a mocking laugh. "Do you mean to say you let him paint those bloody pictures for you and make up that false wall, and not once did you tell him you wanted them for a break? Pull the other leg, Pearce—it's got bells on it."

(Rev) Hunt coughed delicately and said: "I think we'll have to investigate this business a lot more thoroughly, Mr Sanderson, before we jump to any conclusions."

"I don't see why, sir," Sanderson replied stiffly.

"You will, Mr Sanderson, when we've had a chance to sit down and weigh up several important matters . . ." (Rev) Hunt sighed heavily, so deep was his disappointment in Harry Pearce. "In the meantime, you'd better escort Mr Pearce to solitary."

Sanderson said: "There's just one other thing, sir. I think we should take a look at the work Pearce did on those blocks while we're at it."

"As you wish," the superintendent sighed.

The next few minutes were filled with what can only be described as cold, unadulterated horror, as Sanderson tugged, one by one, the sheets and towels off Harry's five finished sculptures. As each work of art was revealed (Rev) Hunt's features flinched with increasing shock, starting with the first bust, a head-and-shoulders nightmare of a woman whose face was screwed up in agony, whose eyes bulged hideously and whose tongue rolled forth, revoltingly swollen, from a mouth that was wide and gasping on the choking, crushing strictures imposed by a rope that was knotted tightly around her neck. The second bust showed the same women with an axe embedded deep in her skull; in the third little masterpiece, someone had cut her throat from ear to ear; the fourth bust was something that its viewers could only guess, from the terrible facial convulsions, was a vivid example of death by arsenic or some other deadly poison; and the fifth showed eyes that were swooning upward in a bizarre fashion as though actually searching for the bullet hole set neatly in the centre of the forehead. At the base of each bust, carved neatly into the stone and filled with gold paint, were the words *In Loving Memory*.

(Rev) Hunt, gulping repeatedly as though on the brink of being sick, finally broke the ghastly silence. "That's the most horrible, disgusting thing I've ever seen in my life," he croaked.

"It's a pity you missed the last one," said Harry. "I was going to have her run over by a bloody bus."

Even Bull Sanderson had gone ashen-faced. "Jesus, Pearce," he murmured, "even your mother-in-law couldn't deserve a terrible thing like that."

Harry said: "You haven't met my mother-in-law, mate."

(Rev) Hunt, wringing his hands with grief, said: "Mr Sanderson, you'd better take Pearce to the Blockhouse right this instant. And please make arrangements to have these—these *demented spectacles* destroyed as soon as possible."

"Right, sir," said Sanderson, guiding the handcuffed Pearce toward the cell door. "We'll pick up that other bloody ratbag on the way."

"I would suggest," (Rev) Hunt suggested quietly as they moved out onto the catwalk, "that we let Mr Murphy stew for a while. I have matters that must be discussed with you in private first."

Down below, amid a curious, strained silence, Murphy and his workmates glanced up from their spread-eagled positions along the wall and watched the handcuffed Harry Pearce being led along the catwalk and down the steel stairs. Murphy turned his head and shot a look that was black as thunder along the wall to where Timothy Botham was leaning against it alongside Henry Trembler. Botham's face was white as a sheet, and his lips were twitching as though in prayer. Then Murphy heard Pearce yell: "See you later, Willie Crewe!" And he heard a shifting, rustling murmur of anger ripple through the men around the walls. Then he heard Bruce Greenwood addressing him quietly from behind.

"It looks as though I don't have to worry anymore, Murphy," Greenwood hissed happily, actually prodding Murphy in the back with the muzzle of his carbine. "I'm afraid that looks like the end of your little plan."

"Don't bet on it, Bruce," Murphy said, grinning at the wall. "That wasn't the bloody plan, old mate—that was the bloody diversion."

seventeen

BULL SANDERSON USUALLY SIGNED HIS NAME *A. Sanderson*. Apart from that he was a large, forbidding question mark to the three hundred and fifty jailbirds in his charge. Even to his fellow prison officers he was a walking, talking mystery: What other label could they possibly paste to a man who, in twenty-eight years of devoted service to the Department of Corrective Services, had rarely stepped outside the prison walls?

It was a standing joke, in fact, that Sanderson, who had been in jail longer than most lifers, still had ten more years to serve before his parole—his retirement. That much was known and joked about; the rest of his half-century on earth was little more than a series of brief, disjointed flashes of information, or speculation, that inevitably flared and died quickly from want of further fuel in pub-talk. He'd once had a wife. They reckoned she deserted him soon after the wedding. He had no children. He was a tough old bastard. A stickler for the book. Trying to get anything more out of him was like trying to squeeze money out of the Federal Government at budget time.

A few characteristics that all could agree on, no matter which side of the bars they stood, were the obvious ones. Sanderson was as straight as a ramrod, totally incorruptible, and was possessed of a voice that, given full range, could blister the Dulux white gloss off a weatherboard cottage. And he had an incredible vocabulary to go with it—one that the entire prison heard on the evening that he busted Harry Pearce and, after escorting Harry out of cell-block C, subjected him to a record forty-five seconds of unbroken abuse, during which he never once appeared to draw breath.

"Pearce," he bawled, "you are a bloody lop-eared, snaggle-toothed, drippy-faced, feeble-minded, piss-weak, bird-brained, bloody-minded, arse-aching, ugly-faced, bile-bellied, shit-filled, sloppy-headed, weak-kneed, dick-dipping, pud-pulling, breast-fed, flop-featured, foul-faced, fuck-witted, mutton-minded, pin-headed, dooble-daft, dill-brained, tit-twisted, slack-arsed, rough-headed, goggle-eyed, bandy-legged, pigeon-toed, knock-kneed, fuck-faced, knuckle-headed, muff-diving, mickey-munching, saddle-sniffing, double-dealing, doodle-dumb, pea-brained, lame-brained, pig-headed, fart-faced flip of a fucking galah! And a bloody pelican, if you really want the truth!"

As the shocking stream of obscenities echoed around the moonlit walls of the jail, Harry said: "What do you expect me to do—say I'm sorry or something?"

Sanderson dropped his voice a few decibels and pointed his prisoner out onto the inky-black tarmac of the quadrangle. "You've really disappointed me, Harry," he said. "I thought you had more brains than the rest of the blockheads in here."

"I've got bloody brains all right, mate," Harry said. "Enough bloody brains not to sit on my backside doing nothing for the next fourteen years."

"Yeah, well that's a matter of opinion, isn't it? The way you fancied getting out of that cell, I'd say it's your brains you've been sitting on, not your bloody backside."

"OK," Harry breathed. "You lumbered me fair and square. Now I suppose you're pretty pleased with yourself."

"No, I'm not," Sanderson snapped. "I've got to make out a report now, and that report might just send you and bloody Murphy to Grafton!"

"Murphy didn't have anything to do with it. It was my idea and my break."

"Don't insult my intelligence, Harry," Sanderson growled. "You just pray that I can persuade Old Clemency and a few other people in the department to keep you and that other dingo here."

"Grafton doesn't scare me," Harry sniffed, and Sanderson grabbed him roughly by one shoulder, pulling him to a halt in the eerie, moon-bathed wilderness mid-way across the vast yard.

"Listen, you bloody fool," he hissed angrily. "Get this into your thick head, right now. No-one's got any bloody idea what Grafton's like until they get there—and then it's too bloody late! This jail's a kindergarten compared with that one. They've got warders up there who make me look like an old plonko playing Father Christmas. You don't get sent to Grafton to be rehabilitated or even punished, mate. You go there to be *broken!*"

Harry stared silently at the shadowed pools of Sanderson's eyes, then dropped his gaze to the ground. Sanderson said: "You can get done over with truncheons up there, Harry, just for lifting your eyes from the ground for a second at the morning muster."

Harry swallowed hard, then said: "So what d'you want me to do? Go down on my knees and beg for mercy?"

"I'd kick you right in the teeth, Harry, if you did that. And I'm not what you'd call a violent man."

"That's true," Harry admitted.

"I might have a bloody rough tongue," said Sanderson, "but you know, as well as the rest of the blokes in here, that I've never once laid so much as a finger on anyone."

"I know that," said Harry.

"I play the game, strictly by the rules, right?"

"Right," said Harry.

Bull Sanderson sighed wearily, glancing back toward the silvery, moonstruck wall of cell block C. "And what do I get in return? You have to pull a stupid stunt like that—right at the time when the bloody department's got its eye on blokes my age to see if we're still up to the job. You shitheads don't realise how lucky you are! Instead of Old Clemency and me, you could have a couple of real monsters in charge of you!"

"I know that," Harry sighed. "But it still doesn't make those fourteen bloody years seem any shorter."

Fourteen years! You should be laughing, old mate! I've been in here twice that long already, and I've another ten years to go to retirement."

"Yeah," said Harry. "But you can get out any time you feel like it."

"Yeah," said Sanderson. "And lose my long-service pay, superannuation and Christ knows what else. One more bloody stunt like yours and I'll probably lose my pension too!"

Harry said: "You can still walk out of that main gate any time you feel like it."

And Sanderson said: "Can I? Do you know what happened to me the last time I went outside? May 1970 it was. I remember it distinctly because it was the twenty-second anniversary of the day my bloody missus shot through. I got done up in my best bag-of-fruit and got a bus to the railway station, then took a train into the city. I got off at Wynyard and walked down to Circular Quay and knocked off a couple of middies or six in my favourite pub, The Ship Inn. I was sitting there on my stool, contemplating the foam on my seventh, when this red-faced bloke wearing a rugby union club blazer sat down next to me. And me, being friendly like and not the sort to turn a blind eye to any bloke, well I turned to him and said: 'How yer goin', Ocker?' And he got real stroppy and said: 'You trying to take the bloody piss out of me or something?' And I thought: *Jeez, that's strange.* So I left The Ship and I'm strolling up George Street, stickybeaking in the shop windows, and suddenly I hear this weird music and singing—and along comes this bloody line of blokes all done up in orange bedsheets with their hair all shaved off except for a funny little knot at the top, like. And they're all dancing about in a file, banging drums and clanging these funny little cymbals together and singing about this cove named Harry Crystals. I thought: *Strewth, it's a bit bloody late in the year for the Waratah Spring Festival.* Then one of them stuck a little stick in my hand that smelled something like a lady's bath-salts, and he said: 'Peace, love, brother—a fragrant gift from Harry Crystals.' And I said: 'What am I supposed to do with it, stick it in my bloody garden and water it every day?' And he said: 'You can jam it up your bloody bum if you like. That's twenty cents, please.' So I said: 'Like buggery—I didn't ask for it.' So he said: 'All right, give the bloody thing back, then.' And I thought: *Shit a brick! What's happening to this bloody country?* So I walked on a bit, turning it all over in my mind, and next thing I saw this place called the Adult Boutique which had a little sign saying it was restricted by law to people eighteen years and over. I thought, well, at least I'd be able to have a look in there without being pestered by blokes in bed sheets. So I sauntered in, and there were all these blokes, and a couple of birds, crowded around these peep-show machines, like you see at Luna Park. I thought, Christ, it was years since I'd seen *What the Butler Saw*—so I put twenty cents in one of them and watched a little screen and this film came up showing this sheila in a negligee doing the washing-up in her kitchen. Then her husband came in and started feeling up her backside. I thought: *Christ, that's a bit bloody rich*. And then, Harry—I tell yer, if I'd been the bloody butler in that house I would've called the bloody police. The things those two got up to was bloody disgusting—right over the bloody breakfast table, too! So I got away from there as fast as I could and had a good look around the shop. Jeez, it was a real kinky place—all these books and stuff called *Mama's Boy*, and *She Took it All* and *Parisian Dildo Girls*. And next thing, Harry, I was standing by a glass cabinet trying to figure out what this long, plastic-looking thing was in there. I looked and I looked, and then it bloody dawned on me—it was a bloody great rubber doodle, big as a bloody horse's doover! Well, that was just about the bloody limit! I turned around and there was this sheila standing next to me, and I got really angry and shouted: 'You should be bloody ashamed of yourself—looking at things like that!' And next thing, everybody in the place is laughing like hell, and I give the sheila a prod on the shoulder, real angry like, and *Jeezuss!*—she wasn't a bird at all, Harry, she was made of rubber! Well, everybody was pissing themselves by now, and I got out of that bloody place like a rocket."

Sanderson pulled Pearce to a halt again as they reached a lofty, heavy-studded steel doorway set into the outer wall of the Blockhouse. Sanderson was in no hurry to leave Harry. He tugged a packet of cigarettes from his tunic, offered Harry one, then lit it for him.

The intense frown on the prison overlord's broad face faded with the dying flare of the match.

"I just sort of wandered blindly about the streets after that, Harry," he said. "It was like I was in a real nightmare. Only I didn't know what was the dream and what was real. The whole thing had put me right off my beer, too, so I just walked an' bloody walked, trying to figure it all out in my bloody mind. Anyhow, I wound up in the bloody Cross in the end, and I'm standing around on this street corner feeling like the spare prick at a bloody wedding, and I see this big sign saying *Les Girls—Non-Stop Revue*. So I said to myself: 'Right, Arnold, things have changed, mate, and you'd better get up with the rest of the bloody field, or you'll find yourself left out completely.' "

"Arnold?" Harry's face was tinged with a faint pink in the glow of his fag-end.

"My Christian name," Sanderson grunted. "*Arnold*. Sounds like a bloody cabinet-maker, doesn't it? Anyhow, I thought a good girlie show, you know, a smile and a bit of tit, would help me pull myself back together, so I went in and up these swish-looking stairs, found the bar and ordered a whiskey and took a good bloody dekko about the place. It didn't seem too bad. The floorshow was pretty good, you know—it was just starting when I walked in. A couple of really beaut birds did a song and dance act, then a blonde girl and a bloke with a big moustache did a French bedroom skit that started me laughing a bit. But I tell yer, there were some sheilahs along the bar who looked as rough as bloody guts when the lights hit them. I should've bloody known, just looking at them, that something was on the nose, like. But I was starting to relax and enjoy myself, you know. I had another whiskey and watched this bird and bloke jumping in and out of bed together, then this soft little voice next to me said: 'I like a man who's not afraid to laugh.'

"I said: 'Beg yours?'—nearly dropping me bloody drink all over the bloody floor—and there was this cute little sheila standing there. Jet-black hair cropped close to her ears, sort of like a pageboy cut. Big brown eyes. Nicely dressed, a sort of mini-dress with fluffy bits around the wrists andb—er, up here. Tits were a bit on the small side, but you can't have every bloody thing, can you? Small all over, as a matter of fact. Hardly tall enough to reach my shoulders. She said her name was Monica, or Monique, or something . . ."

Sanderson suddenly thrust his chin aggressively at Harry Pearce's shadowed features. "You ever breathe a bloody word about this to anyone, Harry, and so help me I'll make sure you rot in that Blockhouse for the rest of your bloody life."

Harry's teeth caught a sharp dart of moonlight as he grinned. "What happened, Bull? She put the hard word on you?"

"Not right away," said Sanderson. "First she asked me whether I came here very often, you know. And I tried to act like I did this sort of thing every bloody night of the week, and I said: 'Only during the mating season, love.'

"She said: 'What do you do for the rest of the year? Eat grass?' And that had me completely buggered right away. I felt like a real fuckwit. And I said: 'Yeah, well, I asked for that one, didn't I?' Then I got sort of scared that she might shoot through on me, so I said: 'Sorry, love—it's just that I'm a bit out of practice. To tell you the truth, I don't come to these sort of places very often.' She smiled. And then I said: 'To be completely honest, I've never been to a place like this—*ever.*'

"She smiled again, sort of warm like, and then she said: 'You don't know what you've been missing. How do you feel on your first night out?'

"I said: 'A bit queer, you know.' And she sort of giggled a bit about that. I said: 'In fact, the whole day's been a bit bloody strange all-round. The way I feel at the moment I don't know whether I'm Arthur or Martha.' Well, that really made her laugh. It made me feel a bit more sure of myself. Then she slipped her hand very lightly into mine and said: 'Well, you just relax a bit and buy us a couple of drinks and we'll see about sorting you out.'

"She sat up on the stool next to me, very close, and we watched the floorshow for a while. I didn't take too much of it in, to tell you the truth. I was trembling like hell and trying to figure out something to say. I remember that most of the skit was the old doctor's surgery routine—a lot of gags about full physicals and open wide and all that sort of caper. Then everybody fell about all over the place when he got to the bit about where to stick the bloody thermometer. Then there was a break for dancing, and this Monique turns to me and says: 'You haven't told me your name.' And I got a bit smart like, and said: 'That's for you to find out, isn't it?' And she put a finger in her mouth, real child-like, and said: 'I bet a big strong mature feller like you would have a big strong name.'

"Well, that had me completely buggered. I mean, I couldn't very well tell her it was Arnold, could I? So I said: 'I'll give you three guesses.'

"She said: 'Arnold?'

"I said: 'You must be bloody joking. I wouldn't be seen dead with a bloody silly name like that.'

"She said: 'Of course not. You're not the Arnold type at all. You're more the strong, silent, animal type.'

"I said: 'You're getting warmer.'

" 'Bongo?' "

"I gave her a bit of a playful nudge and said: 'No, come off it, you're playing silly-buggers now. You've got one more guess left.'

"She said: 'Now let's see . . . What's strong, silent and animal?'

"I said: 'Shall I give you the first letter?'

"She said: 'No, I give up.'

"I said: 'It's Shane.'

"She took a quick sip of her drink and said: 'Now we must find you a nickname. Or have you got one already?'

"I said: 'Most people call me Shane.'

"And she said: 'What else do they call you?'

"And I said: 'That's for you to guess, isn't it?'

"And she leaned close to me and put her arms around my neck. Then she kissed me on the cheek and whispered in my ear: 'Do you know what I think? I think there's only one word to describe you—*Bull*.'

"Jesus, she was quick, that Monique. I said: 'Bingo! Right first-off. Give the lady a prize.'

" 'I've got one,' she said, putting her arm through mine and snuggling closer to me.

"I said: 'You know what? I think you're a pretty smart sheila, Monique. D'you follow the football much?'

"And she said: 'Wouldn't you like to dance?'

"And next thing, we were out in the middle of this crowd on the dance-floor, leaping up and down like a bunch of boongs around a bloody plonk-bottle. I didn't go much for that sort of dancing. Neither did she after I'd threatened to thump the sheila behind me for kicking me in the back of the legs. 'Don't take any notice of that bitch,' she said; then she was in my arms, pressed close to me, her head resting gently on my chest and her elfin face gazing up at mine, and I thought to myself: *Hullo, you're in like Flynn here, mate*.

"And she said: 'I like a man with big powerful shoulders.' And I said: 'Yeah, well, I used to exercise a lot. That was then I played front-row for Balmain.' She said: 'That must have been exciting.' And I said: 'Yeah, well we were all set to win the League, you know— then this mongrel bastard stiff-armed me in a tackle, and as I went to punch his bloody head in he booted me right in the bloody kneecap. I was out of the game for two seasons after that with a buggered-up cartilage.' She sighed and said: 'That must have been terrible.' 'Yeah,' I said, pulling her real close like. 'For six months the quacks were drawing a pint of bloody fluid a week off that knee. They said I was lucky I didn't lose the whole leg.'

"She went quiet for a while, her head tight against my chest, and I said: 'You know, you're the first sheila I've talked to—intimately, you know—for years.' And she said: 'You're not married?' I said: 'I was once. Till my old lady shot—till I lost my missus.' She said: 'Oh, I am sorry. How long is it since she passed away?' I said: 'She didn't exactly pass away, love. She bolted. Slipped her harness at the Auburn lights on Parramatta Road, and next thing you couldn't see her arse for dust. Good riddance to her.' She looked up at me then with a little pout, and she said: 'That's not a nice way to speak about a lady.' And I said: 'She was no lady, love. And the nicest thing she ever did for me was to bugger off.'

"Then she frowned a bit and batted her eyelids at me and said: 'Isn't there anything nice that's ever happened to you, Bull?' And I guess the whiskey must have got to me then, because I got a bit choked up and said: 'Yes. *You!*' Then I lost my bloody marbles completely and swung her around and around on the dance-floor until some bastard elbowed her in the back and she gasped out loud, and I was just about to fill the bastard in right there on the spot when this bloody spotlight hit us both full in the face and someone announced that we'd just won first prize in the bloody dancing competition.

"Everyone around us was making a big bloody deal about the whole thing—the birds shrieking and cackling like a bunch of bloody chooks, and this stupid bastard up at the microphone going off his nut and telling everyone that we'd not only won ourselves a bottle of bloody champagne, but in the great tradition, or something, of *Les*

Girls I was King for the Night, and like everybody give a big hand for his charming Queen. Everyone went completely ape then, and the band started playing the bloody Wedding March, so help me, and then Monique threw her bloody arms right around me and gave me a big smouldering kiss, full on the lips, right there in front of every bastard. I felt like a real dope.

"Then I thought to myself: *Don't spoil it for her, mate.* And I lifted her right off the floor and we clung together kissing like it was about to go out of fashion while the band played its bloody head off and everyone whistled and screamed, and Monique poked her tongue right into my mouth, and I thought: *Jeez, this sheila's really hot in the pants for me.* And I put my hands over her tight little bum and pulled her up so that she was practically sitting across my bloody chest, still kissing me and running her hands through my hair, and then some bastard threw a pile of confetti over us, and while I was trying to get the bloody stuff out of my eyes the band started playing a waltz, and next thing we were all on our own in the middle of the bloody floor standing like a couple of bloody shags on a rock with every bastard watching us.

"Monique said: 'Don't be scared. Let's dance.' And I managed to follow her around the floor without breaking any of her bloody toes, and after a while the other couples started to join in and I could breathe easy again. Monique said: 'How do you feel now, Bull?' And I said: 'A bit of a bloody drongo.' And she laughed and said: 'You should learn to let your hair down a bit. There's a first time for everyone.' Then she nestled her head against my chest and said: 'Tell me all about yourself.' And I said: 'There's nothing much to tell.' She said: 'You really are the strong silent type. Go on, I bet you're the sort of bloke who's done a lot of interesting things.'

"And you know, Harry, I looked back over my life, and for Christ's sake, I couldn't think of one interesting bloody thing that would interest anyone. Except when I made that touch-down right on the final whistle, the week before that bastard buggered up my knee, and put Balmain in the semi-finals. Then she reached up and whispered in my ear: 'Don't worry, I'll get it all out of you later.'

"I said: 'Later?'

"She said: 'When we're alone.'

"And I said: 'Like tonight?'

"And she giggled and said: 'We just got married, didn't we?'

"And I said: 'But Jeez, I've gotta get back to the bloody clink tonight.'

"And she stopped dead on the spot and said: 'The clink? You mean jail?'

" 'Er, yeah.'

" 'What are you doing in jail?' "

Sanderson offered Harry another cigarette and touched a lighted match to it. Pearce was shivering slightly in the night's chill. "Harry," Sanderson said, "I was on one hell of a bloody spot. There's this beautiful little sheila practically breaking her neck to get me into bed, a half a dozen whiskeys already under my belt, a bloody great bottle of champers waiting for us at the bar and everybody's falling arse-over-tit to make sure we were having a bloody good time. What would you have said?"

Harry flicked his ash at the ground. "I wouldn't have stuck my neck out and told her I was a bloody prison screw."

"Right. I lied. I told her I was doing ten years. Her eyes got real wide, and she said: 'What for?' And I lied again. I said: 'Armed robbery.' Her eyes were so big they were like bloody dinner-plates. 'Armed robbery?' 'Yeah,' I said. 'With grievous bodily harm.' She gazed at me for a couple of seconds like a kid in front of a Christmas tree, then she threw herself at me and said with a big sigh: 'Wow, Bull—I thought for a moment you were going to say you were a prison screw or something.' And I said: 'Don't be bloody dumb. I hate fucking screws.' And she said: 'Don't get mad at me, Bull. I was only joking.' And I said: 'Yeah, well I don't go for those sort-a jokes.'

"And she said: 'Armed robbery! Wow! Tell me about it, Bull. Who'd you stick up?' Jeez, I really had to think fast. I said: 'Aw, banks, payroll trucks, you know.' 'Wow!' she said, sort of grinding herself against me. 'How'd you get caught? Somebody dob you in?'

" 'Naw, some stupid mug of a bank teller got smart and raised the bloody alarm. Fuckin' cops were waiting for me as I came out. That teller got his, though, I can tell yer.'

" 'You shot him?'

" 'Naw, just pistol-whipped him into a coma.'

" 'Wow. You sound like a real tough crim, Bull.'

" 'Yeah,' I said. 'That's my speciality, see?' And I gave her a big bloody wink. 'Like, assault with a deadly weapon.'

"That really turned her on, I can tell yer. I thought she was gonna faint right at my bloody feet. Then she stepped back a bit from me, looked deep into my eyes and said: 'How come you've got to go back to jail tonight?' But I had her cold on that one. I said: 'It's simple, love. I took a day out. Cost me a few fiddlies in the right places, but there you are—you don't get anything for bloody nothing these days, do you?' She looked like she was going to swoon again. 'Wow, Bull. You mean you just walk out for the day when you feel like it?' And I said: 'Sweet as a bloody nut. I've got that bloody place sewn up as tight as a prostitute's purse. When I say jump, every bastard from the superintendent down starts jumping.' She snuggled into my chest again and said: 'Bull, do you have to go back?' And I said: 'You stupid or something? Where else am I going to get such a bloody good alibi?' Well, she really gasped over that one. '*You don't mean. . . ?*' And I said: 'Let's put it this way, darl. If the bloody superintendent knew the full extent of the vast empire of crime being directed from one of his cells, right under his bloody nose, he'd be back west hammering on his church door before you could say Ned Kelly.' And that sort of shut her up for a while.

"But only a while, mind you. Next thing, she comes up with something that makes me go completely weak in the bloody knees. She points over at the tables near the bar and says: 'Wow, what a coincidence! See those two fellers over there? One's got a scar down one cheek and the other's got a broken nose . . .' And I say: 'Yeah, what about them?' And she says: 'They're good friends of mine. And they're both just out of the clink too! One got done for manslaughter—the one with the busted nose—and I don't know about his mate. Let's go over and talk to them. They'll be knocked out to meet a big-time crim like you.'

"Well, I'm not kidding you, Harry. I nearly shat myself right on the spot. Monique was tugging me across the floor towards these two evil-looking bastards, and the crowd around us was breaking up at the end of the dance bracket, and the bloke with the scar right down the middle of his ugly mug was already looking our way and taking a good bloody close dekko at me. It was all I could do to stop from running for my bloody life. Anyway, I managed to whisper loudly at her: 'You trying to get me fucking killed or something?'

"Monique stopped pulling at me, and her face got a bit scared, and I softened my voice a bit and said: 'Look, you know what'd happen to me if anyone recognised me in here? They'd be straight on the blower to the bloody cops. There's blokes in this town who'd give their right arms to get even with a crim like me. Even dob me in to the bloody law. And how would I be able to explain how I'm out for a night buggerising about with a sheila when I'm supposed to be doing ten years' hard bloody labour for armed robbery?'

" 'Sorry Bull,' she said, her lips trembling a bit. And that buggered me too. If there's one thing I can't cope with it's a bloody sheila getting emotional about something. So I said: 'Hey! Have a bloody go at this, will you.' And I popped the cork on the bottle of champagne that the management had set up in the middle of a special table for us, close to the stage and right in the box-seat for the gala finale of the bloody floorshow. And of course, the bloody mug of a waiter must have shaken the hell out of it on the way, because the bloody stuff shot straight up to the ceiling and sprayed all over the place. There were birds screaming all around us, and blokes flapping about all over the place with handkerchiefs, and Monique and me sitting there not knowing whether to laugh or bloody cry, saturated from arsehole to bloody breakfast time with bubbly.

"Then Monique said: 'Oh, Bull . . .' And she leaned forward and kissed me right on the lips, but I'd already finished telling the bloody ding waiter what a fart-faced bloody dago dope he was, and I held her close to me as he and a couple of his bloody Eyetie mates stripped the table off and set the bloody thing straight again, and Monique said: 'Bull, why don't you like *not* go back tonight? Why don't we just run away together? Head north or something. Get a car and just hit the road. We could shoot through to Surfer's and like spend a couple of weeks there getting a suntan, and . . . you know . . . get to sort of know each other a bit, and then get a caravan and head up the coast to Townsville and Cairns and I can take turns driving, you know— I've got a licence and I can do the cooking while you—'

" 'Hey, hold your horses a bit,' I hollered, pouring us both a glass of champers. 'I can't run off just like that. I'm a jailbird, you know. I'll have every bloody cop from here to Woop Woop after me.'

"She said: 'You could dye your hair, Bull. Dress a bit differently. Grow a beard or something. Change your name. Can't you see it, Bull? It'd be just you and me.' She started struggling with her handbag, and bugger me if she didn't come up with a bloody Commonwealth Bank savings book. 'I've got some money put away, Bull. It's not much, but I reckon it'd be enough to get us a station-wagon or something, or maybe an old Volkswagen camper. We wouldn't need anything else, Bull. Just *us.*'

"And I swear, I was nearly choking on my bloody drink. 'Listen, are you crazy or something?' I said. 'You know what life would be like, on the run with a dangerous bloody criminal like me—a *wanted man?* Jesus, darl, you'd never have a moment's bloody peace. It'd wear you down. You'd have no time for cooking or cleaning or sunbathing or enjoying yourself, or all the other bloody things that sheilas like to do. You wouldn't like it, I tell you. Running for your life all the time. Here today, and gone tomorrow. Every town the bloody same. Looking over your shoulder every five minutes, never knowing if the knock on the door's going to be some bloody Jehovah's Witness doing a bit of God-bothering or half a dozen bloody great CIB men loaded down with bloody submachineguns and tear gas . . .'

" 'I don't care, Bull,' she said, her eyes all misty with tears and her nose going pink. 'I'd go through *anything*, if it was with a man like you.'

"Well, I tell you, Harry, I didn't know if it was the bloody champagne getting to me, or what, but I couldn't tell if I was coming or going. I mean, for a while there—just a while, mind you—I couldn't think of anything else that I'd rather do than shoot through in an old Falcon or something with that chick. Just me and her, and the open road. Head up to Surfers and spend every day on the bloody beach, every day in the beer-garden knocking back schooners and every night . . . Jesus, Harry, I had it all right there before me. All I had to do was say the right bloody thing and goodbye misery, goodbye all those rotten lousy gut-twisting days looking at brick walls and bars and ugly bloody faces, trying to keep my guard up against a pack of murdering, thieving, lying, cheating, snivelling, fucking rat-bags who thought it was all a bloody great game . . . All I had to do was say the right word, Harry. And stone me, if I didn't balls the whole bloody thing up. I said: 'What'll we do for dough, darl?'

"And she said: 'You could stick up a bank or two, Bull.'

"And I said: 'What d'you mean, *stick up a bank?* D'you want me to end up in bloody jail or something?'

"And she said: 'You're shouting at me, Bull.'

"And I said: 'You know what happened to bloody Bonnie and Clyde, don't you? They ended up so full of bloody holes you could've strained your bloody soup through them.' And she pouted and

flounced a bit in her chair and said: 'I thought you were supposed to
be a big dangerous crim.' And I said: 'You bet I am. But there's no
way I'm going to spend the rest of my bloody life shooting it out with
the bloody cops.' And she said: 'I think you're a load of bullshit, that's
what I think.' And she started sniffing and snivelling and grabbing
about for her handbag, like she was about to jump up and go, and
next thing she knocked her drink all over the table and then swayed
sideways so far that she nearly ended up on her arse on the floor.
'And now look what you've done,' she wailed. 'I'm pissed.'

"And I could see that every bastard was looking at us, so I
straightened her up and put my arm around her shoulders and gave
her a clean handkerchief for her mascara and said: 'Look, darl, it's not
the end of the world. I've only got a couple of years to go, and I can
get out just about any weekend I want. We can have a lot of fun together, just the two of us here in Sydney. We'd have two whole days
a week together, with nothing to worry about but where we'd go
next. There's a million bloody things we could do. We could even
rent a flat somewhere, and you could like stay there and keep it
warm for me. What d'you say?'

"She stopped sniffing and wiped away the last of her tears, and
then she sat twisting the soggy handkerchief around her fingers.
'You'd come and see me every weekend?'

" 'Like a rat at a lump of bloody cheese.'

" 'You wouldn't shoot through and leave me with the rent?'

" 'Jesus, what sort of a bloody bloke d'you think I am?'

"She screwed the handkerchief around a bit, then she bit her lip
and said: 'It'd have to be somewhere close to town, Bull. I couldn't
stand living in the suburbs. And I'll definitely need a car to go shop-
ping with. You wouldn't believe the dirty old pervs who get about on
the trains these days.

" 'Atta girl!' I hollered, and we toasted each other with champagne, and I felt I was riding on cloud nine or something. It was like
life was suddenly all wine and roses for me. A bird of my own. A
little nest to go to at weekends. A bit of love and *dignity* for a
change—something to wash away all the slime and grime of those
bastards in the bloody jail. I hugged her, and then we drank to each
other again, like lovers, holding hands as we sipped the bubbly and
gazed into each other's eyes—and then the lights suddenly dimmed
and there was a loud crash of drums and the stage lit up for the grand

finale. The curtain rose and the band struck up a Gay Nineties number and a whole bloody chorus line of birds appeared, kicking their legs up in the air and throwing their skirts all over the place in one of those French can-can things.

"Christ, every one of them looked like she'd just carried off the first prize in the Miss Australia contest. All squealing and kicking and blowing kisses all around the place, and then sweeping about and bending over to wiggle their bums at the audience. I was so full of plonk and happiness by this stage that the whole show became a mindless bloody whirl of tits and bums and garters and frilly drawers. I felt Monique squeeze my arm, and I kissed her on the ear and felt myself to go soft and dribbly inside that I wouldn't have raised so much as a bloody murmur if I'd melted all over the bloody floor . . ."

Sanderson stopped abruptly and turned and peered into the empty gloom of the quadrangle, as though searching for something. His breath heaved once, deep as an old dog's weary sigh, and watched something in the night that Harry Pearce could only wait patiently for him to share. It was a long lonely time before Sanderson, sniffing harshly, turned back from the darkness and murmured: "I was *alive*, Harry. I was enjoying myself for the first time in my bloody life."

Harry said: "So what happened, Bull?"

There was another long, agonising pause before Sanderson answered. "It was a good show," he said quietly, almost wistfully. "Songs and dances, lots of gaiety and dirty jokes. They went from the French can-can to a steamboat and minstrel routine, then into a big tableau of artists and models, with a half a dozen birds posing with nothing on but a bit of silk to hide the maker's name. Then it all came to a head in a grand spectacle of flowing gowns and powdered wigs—you know, minuets and polkas and all that sort of jazz—and right at the last bloody blast of music and drums, right at the point when the whole bloody place was jumping and everyone was going crazy and stamping and whistling and screaming for encores, every bird, every single bloody bird from one end of the bloody stage to the other, curtsied to the floor, blew kisses at every bastard, then whipped her bloody wig off and threw it up in the air! And Harry, I kid you not, every one of them had hair like yours and mine! They were all bloody blokes!

"And then it dawned on me that the whole bloody show, and the whole bloody crowd around me, was a pack of *screaming bloody poof-tas!*"

This time the silence was horrible. This time it was Harry who turned away, staring at nothing in particular in the general vicinity of the Blockhouse gate. Without looking back, he asked: "Monique too?"

"Don't ask me," Sanderson muttered gloomily. "There was a lot of turmoil."

"Well, *was* she?"

"Naw," Sanderson sighed. "She wasn't."

"Don't bet. I did me block completely. Went right off the twist. All I can remember is that I was yelling like hell at her, and a couple of huge bouncers were climbing over everybody to get at me, and I was so mad I like went to tear her wig off like the others and throw it up on the stage . . ."

Sanderson sighed heavily again. "It wasn't a wig at all. I nearly tore her hair out by the bloody roots."

Harry said: "Got another weed to spare?" And Sanderson handed him one, then lit it for him, and Harry's bland moustachioed features glowed macabrely over the cupped furnace of his hands. He pulled deeply on the cigarette, then said: "You could still have all that, Bull—a bird and a bit of enjoyment. One mistake's not going to mean a whole bloody life of bad luck. Why don't you stop being a bloody mug and go get it while you still can?"

"It's too late now, Harry. A couple of years ago, maybe. To tell you the truth, I've never had much courage when it comes to kicking over the old traces. I'm old enough to remember the Depression, you know. It did strange things to a lot of blokes. It buggered my old man completely. Then he turned around and buggered me. I can still remember the old bastard on his death-bed, tears in his eyes and my old lady's Bible in his hands, making me swear on God's oath that whatever happened to me, however many tries I scored, I'd give up trying to be a professional footballer and join the bloody Public Service. 'Security first, Arnold,' he told me. 'Get that quid in your pocket—and stuff everyone else.' "

Harry laughed. "Go on, you miserable old coot. I'd still change places with you."

"I bet you would," Sanderson growled, pulling himself together and tugging at a panel set into the wall to one side of the Blockhouse gate. Behind the cover of the panel there was a red button. Sanderson pressed it and they heard a bell buzz softly on the other side of the steel doors. "Instead of that," said Sanderson, "you're going in there, mate, where dangerous bloody intractibles like you belong. And Harry, I mean what I said—you'd better pray that I can sweet-talk Old Clemency into giving you another break. Because if I can't, you and me won't have any time for any more little man-to-man talks in the middle of the night. You'll be fighting for your bloody life in Grafton."

With a clang that rudely punctuated Sanderson's final warning, a small grille popped open in one of the doors and they heard a deep yawn as two bleary eyes appeared at the slit.

"Got another customer for you," said Sanderson. "Artistic type. Likes to carve things in stone. So don't give him anything sharper than a bloody plastic mess-knife or he'll be through the wall before you can say Mickey Flynn."

One of the Blockhouse gates was opening, creaking slightly as it moved with monolithic reluctance on its hinges. Sanderson looked at Harry, and Harry looked at Sanderson. Then Sanderson dropped his gaze and said: "In you go. And take these with you." And he handed Harry what was left of his pack of cigarettes.

"You're not a bad sort of a bloke, Bull—for a bloody screw," said Harry, turning and taking his first steps towards solitary confinement and another scintillating communion with the Holy Bible. Then he halted and turned back to the prison boss.

"Bull," he said, shaking his head, "you must be about the most hopeless bugger I've ever met. I can't get over it. D'you mean to tell me you spent half the night in a club full of bloody queers and didn't wake up to it?"

"Oh, I woke up all right," said Sanderson. "There was a lot of bloody things I woke up to that night. Like for one thing, life outside these bloody bars is *dangerous*, mate. Most of the people out there haven't got a shred of bloody decency left in them. They'd shaft you as soon as look at you. Christ, Australia's not a land of honest ordinary cobbers anymore, and everyone pulling his bloody weight to make us proud to stand tall in the sun and all that shit. It's Sodom-all and fucking Gomorrah!"

"Hey, steady on. You're not going to tell me that one balls-up in a bloody nightclub made you turn your back on the entire outside world."

"It wasn't that, Harry," Sanderson sighed. "It was what came after."

"You mean there's *more?*"

"Yeah, there's more . . ." Sanderson stepped closer to Harry in the open gateway. "It's all right," he told the waiting guard. "Give us a couple more minutes, and he's all yours."

As the guard shrugged and melted into the darkness, Sanderson said to Harry: "Somehow I got out of that club in one bloody piece. I remember hitting the street, dazed like, and all I could think of was getting back to the clink as fast as my bloody legs would carry me. I didn't fancy another minute of life on the outside. Anyhow, I walked back down William Street, heading away from The Cross, trying to dodge the strip-joint touts and stumblebums, and finally made it to Hyde Park, where it was all dark and peaceful and completely deserted at that time of night. Christ, it was good to be alone, I can tell you.

"So I'm strolling across the park, like, breathing the fresh air and starting to feel like a decent human being again, and I suddenly realise that I'm busting for a pee. I could see a public dunny up ahead, next to St James's station, but there was no way in the bloody world I was going to take any chances like that. I'd had enough trouble for one night. So I did the obvious thing and slipped behind a couple of bushes, then gave the old ferret a good run. I was standing there, minding my own business, pissing like a brewer's carthorse and letting all the pain and anxiety flow away—and next thing a voice says: 'Hello, Tinker Bell. What's that you've got there? Your wand?' "

Harry Pearce let out a short, incredulous hiss of laughter. "You don't mean. . . ?"

"Yeah . . . I mean, no. No, it wasn't a bloke—if that's what you're thinking. It was Monique! She'd followed me all the way from Les Girls. Christ, Harry—have you ever tried to whip the old feller back into your tweeds in the middle of a pee? The pain was *excruciating*. 'Bloody hell!' I remember yelling at her. 'Don't ever creep up on me like that again!' And she sort of shrank back, all shadowy-like in the darkness, and she let out a little sad moan and shook her head and said: 'Jeez, Bull—I don't seem to be able to do anything right, do I?' Well . . ." Bull Sanderson's voice was low and sad now. Harry had never seen him sad before. Enraged, yes. But not sad. "Well, she looked so little and upset and sorry for herself in the dark, and I was bloody tired and still half-pissed and, quite frankly, I was pleased as bloody punch that she'd come after me like that. Anyhow, I put my arm around her and said: 'Ah, come on, brighten up. It's not the end of the bloody world, you know.' And she said: 'I'm sorry, Bull. I shouldn't have got you into that mess back there.' And I said: 'Not to worry. I should've had me wits about me anyway. I'm sorry I pulled your hair like that.' And she said: 'It's all right. It's been pulled before.' And I held her tight, like, and she was shivering a bit, and I said: 'It sounds like you need someone to look after you.' And she looked up at me and said: 'You got anyone in mind, Bull?' And I said: 'Well, I'm thinking about it.' And she said: 'Well, I've got this little pad up in Darlinghurst. It's not much. Just a room and a TV set. But you're welcome to come and have some coffee with me while you're thinking it all over.' I said: 'That sounds nice. I might just take you up on it.' And she said: 'Do you mind if we walk there? There's something I've got to tell you before you like make up your mind.' I said: 'Oh? What's that?' And she said: 'Let's wait till we get a bit closer to home. If I tell you now, you'll run a mile and I'll have to chase you all over town again.' "

Harry waited while Sanderson stared into the darkness again. The prison chief's boot scraped loudly on the concrete as he squashed a wandering cockroach. Harry lit another cigarette. "What did she tell you, Bull?"

"Nothing I didn't already know. It didn't matter anyway by then. My mind was already made up."

"So what went wrong?"

"A couple of cops got in on the act, that's all. We were both halfway up William Street, arm in arm, heading back towards The Cross, and I was waiting for her to tell me, and I guess she was like trying to work up the courage, and a bullwagon pulled up next to us and a cop shone his torch on us and said: 'Hey, Monique! Business is booming tonight, is it?'

"I tell you, Harry—I bloody near tore the door right off that bullwagon dragging the bastard out of there. His off-sider came running around from the other side while I was belting the shit out of him and pulled a bloody gun on me. I whipped the gun out of his hand and threw it up the street and thumped him to a bloody pulp too. Next thing, there's police cars and bullwagons coming out of the bloody woodwork, and I'm yelling at Monique to get the hell out of there and there's about a dozen huge wallopers trying to get the bloody cuffs on me . . ."

Sanderson paused abruptly, his eyes searching the darkness again. Then he turned back to Harry with a shake of the head and a heavy, sardonic laugh.

"It was lucky I was a prison screw, Harry," he said. "I nearly went to bloody jail for that."

Harry said: "You seen her since then?"

Sanderson said: "She came visiting once. Asked to see a big crim named Bull. I sent word out that Bull was in solitary for a couple of years. She sent a letter in telling Bull she'd never met a man like him in her life. She said she'd wait for him. She said she'd always be waiting. Bloody ridiculous, isn't it?"

eighteen

KEVIN MURPHY WAS MOVING FAST NOW. HE had to. From the moment Pearce had disappeared into the Blockhouse his own position in the jail had become, quite frankly, without a shadow of doubt, in Noel Chisholm's educated tongue, *untenable*.

"What does that mean?" Murphy demanded suspiciously during a lightning visit to the great playwright's cell, where Chisholm was absorbed in his one hundred and fiftieth attempt at the title of his play.

"It means you're knackered," Chisholm replied. "And so too, I'd imagine, is the great escape."

"Like bloody hell it is," Murphy swore, peering over the shoulder of the literary genius. "I'm ready for 'em when they come for me. I've got a few tricks up my sleeve that'll delay every bloody attempt them make to get me in with Pearce or shoot us both off to Grafton. Old Sanderson's just gotta lay one finger on me and I throw an epileptic fit, right there at his feet, that'll put me in the sick-bay for two weeks, I reckon, while they do all the medical tests."

"They'll probably have a good look at your medical history and charge you with attempted fraud," said Chisholm. "People with epilepsy don't just suddenly flop to the floor and start kicking—they usually have a long history of attacks, right from childhood."

"OK," said Murphy. "So I'm a late developer. I had chronic asthma as a kid, anyway. I had to spend a lot of time off school laid up in bed. That's how I got around to painting and drawing."

"Then wouldn't it be easier to stage a massive asthma attack?"

"Not on your life," said Murphy. "They're no bloody joke, mate. The pain's incredible, and you feel like you're going to explode. I wouldn't like to go through that bloody caper again."

Chisholm blinked, then reached for his familiar unlabelled pint bottle of amber-coloured liver tonic. "Of course," he mused, uncorking it. "I didn't think of it that way."

"The main thing," said Murphy, "is that I've got to move fast now and get all that painting done before Sanderson and Old Clemency move in to grab me. And you've gotta get that bloody play finished fast, Nole, because time's running out, and the entire bloody break hangs on it." Murphy glanced at Chisholm's pile of papers and sniffed. "Is that all you've done so far?"

But Chisholm was engaged in a series of savage snapping motions with his teeth, simultaneously drumming his chest with a clenched fist. Then he leapt to his feet, hurling his chair away behind him, and did a little dance that appeared to be a combination soft-shoe and shimmy.

"Shiiiiii-ettttt!" he gasped, trembling violently. "You sure this is ordinary meths, or are you trying to palm high-octane jet fuel off on me?"

"Since when did you start becoming a connoisseur, Nole? If I gave you a dose of bloody battery acid you wouldn't know the difference. You sure you're going to be able to write this play?"

"*Am I sure?*" Chisholm snatched a pile of papers from his desk and waved them furiously at Murphy. "Does the sun rise in the morning? Does the moon. . . ?" He stopped yelling, grabbed a pencil from the desk. "Hey, that's not bad. *Is the Sun Rising?* That's got a strong feeling of imprisonment in it. *Reach for the Sun*—the agony of the locked soul. Or better still, the paradox of the human being behind bars—*The Sun Also Rises . . .*" He sighed and slumped back in his chair. "Balls. That was good for one run, but never again. It was good then because life was good then, and life was good then because we knew it was good then, and we knew it was good then because a man was a man and a woman was a woman, and we knew what being a man and a woman was all about because we talked a lot in short bursts and sipped the frozen *grappa* and felt the old Mauser wounds flare with pain again as the wild ducks skidded down toward the dawn-misted ice . . ."

Murphy said: "What happened to *Bars?*"

"Same thing. It didn't sound right anymore. It didn't say what I wanted to say."

"What is it that you want to say, Nole?"

"That I'm the best bloody playwright in the world—and the rest of you are a pack of cunts."

"Why don't you call it *A Pack of Cunts,* then?"

"That's not bad," Chisholm admitted. "It has a certain jolly, matey, desperate sort of Australian ring about it—like *The Desert Rats* and *A Hatful of Arseholes.*"

"Be serious, for Christ's sake," Murphy moaned. "You can't put on a play called *A Hatful of Arseholes.* There might be sheilas in the audience."

But Chisholm had just taken another quick slug of firewater, and his entire head had gone blood-red like an overripe tomato, and Murphy flinched as he watched the troubled sage bend and pound it repeatedly on the surface of the desk. There were a number of horrible strangling sounds during which Chisholm recovered his breath, then he spun on Murphy with winds playing through his hair, an insane, slightly crooked gleam in his eyes and a bony finger stabbing at Murphy's chest.

"Don't underestimate this bloody country, mate," he croaked harshly. "We've got a language so rich that practically every bloody indigenous phrase we utter would make a knock-out title for a book or play. And we used to have an innocence so boundless that it had to be honest—how else could one of our most noted composers write a symphony to celebrate the intrinsic beauty and poetry of the sun, wind and hot sands of his native Swanbourne Beach and call the first movement 'The Dance of the Beach Inspectors'? What courage! What audacity! Old Pembarthy looked at Swanbourne Beach and he didn't only see a rapsody of sand and sea for strings and woodwind with full orchestral climaxes to portray the beer cans and meat-pie wrappers swirling in a southerly buster . . . He saw a lot of beery, obscene, fat-gutted old RSL layabouts who all acted like vulgar personifications of Bob Menzies and intimidated healthy young women in skimpy bikinis with an idiotic righteousness that was reciprocal only of Bob's own unabandoned sycophancy when he practically hurled himself at the feet of the Queen and penned the immortal words that made Australians like me cringe in the company of others:

> *But once I saw her passing by,*
> *Yet I shall love her till I die.'* "

Murphy cautiously backed away from Chisholm as the playwright burst into verbal flames, erupting like a gasoline dump on fire. *"What did we ever need the bloody Queen for?* So that we didn't feel so naked and lost down at the other end of the bloody world? So that we could all make our mandatory little trips to London to get laughed at? It was one of her great-great grandfathers who dumped us down here in the first place! And instead of trying to kick Britain back in the arse for what it did to us, we looked there, we looked *everywhere* for a sense of identity, and ignored the very ground at our bloody feet. We had it here! We were standing on it all the time—sovereigns, newly-crowned, every bloody one of us, and a whole new reign of the common man about to begin. But we let ourselves get fucked by everyone who came bearing gifts. We lost our virginity somewhere between the woodchip heaters and colour TV. We abdicated, and then we didn't even have the damned courage to screw up our own pioneer dreams in our own inimitable way—we had to import all the shoddy, tinselly, hand-me-down bad taste of five-and-dime Americana!"

"That's Australia," said Murphy. "Love it or leave it—that's what I say. Besides, you didn't exactly play your bloody part in its downfall. You pissed off and spent thirty years overseas."

"You're right, I did," Chisholm muttered, winding down now, settling back again into his writing chair. "And a lot of the other yahoos went with me. Except Gorton, and look what happened to him. They're all dead now, the ones who got away. Finch was the last to go. The rest were killed off by suburbia, and Federal grants to the arts. And I, too, am dying . . . So let's get on with this fucking play."

"That's the spirit," said Murphy, reaching inside his prison shirt. "And before you get going, here's something that might give you some extra inspiration, like." And he dropped a fat wad of banknotes, secured with a rubber band, on the desk. "It's the two grand you said you needed to get Habeeba to that bloody island of yours. Now, does that convince you that the break's going ahead as planned?"

"That convinces me," Chisholm snarled, "only that you and the rest of the inmates of this mental asylum need your bloody heads read. Don't you know that giving money to a writer before he's even put pen to paper is tantamount to murder? It's like giving whiskey to the aborigines, electric blankets to the Eskimos. It saps our will to survive the stench of our messy little adolescent fox-holes. It robs us of that blind compulsion to spill our brains on the ground at our feet and say, 'Look Mummy, poo-poo!' " Chisholm feverishly up-ended the bottle of jungle juice, and a violent, involuntary muscular spasm made him slam it back onto the desk so hard that the vile contents sprayed all over his papers. Murphy backed away toward the bed as the stricken playwright began slapping and punching furiously at something horrible that was crawling up his left leg.

"The world is littered," Chisholm bawled, "with the sorry wreckage of our breed—glowing, clean-cut, well-bred PR hacks and social darlings who, had it not been for society's thoughtless attempts to expose them to money, would have remained good honest mental cripples—happily leaping from shadow to shadow nursing their warts and deformities, contentedly shuffling around in the twilight zone looking for kids to play with, busily building schizophrenic fantasies with the constancy of self-reproducing amoebas . . . Bloody legions of them who ask nothing more from life than a new definition of insanity! A Royal Commission into Vapours of the Mind! So that we can all file in, dragging our smelly rags and pathetic handcarts full of old indiscretions and shards of coloured glass and, one by one, at the Chairman's invitation, crawl up into the witness stand and give evidence to the effect that *You're all full of shit!*"

Chisholm spun on Murphy with huge steaming tears pouring from his eyes, his fists clenched tightly in front of him.

"For Christ's sake, Murph, the spirit must *fly!* Without wings we are condemned to a life on this bloody planet that's as meaningless as moss on a garden wall. Sentenced to be born, to exist and then to die wondering what the bloody hell we were here for in the first place. Is it nobler in the fucking mind to treat this idiotic bio-chemical manifestation we call living like a prolonged holiday in the head, voyaging wherever our thoughts, or the colours, take us? Or to sit the whole bloody show out in some vast brick-and-fibro parking lot watching *Number Ninety-Six* because we've fooled ourselves into thinking that cretinous garbage represents *something we've lost!*"

Chisholm suddenly snatched a handful of paper from his desk, rolled it up and then rammed it into the neck of his near-empty suicide bottle. Then, as Murphy watched, horror-stricken, he grabbed a cigarette lighter from his drawer and lit the fuse. "Out there, Murph, all around us," he gnashed as the Molotov cocktail blazed in his hand, "is a vast army of people who've lost sight of their heritage so badly that their most reckless idea of being Australian is to assemble in Martin Place once a bloody year to indulge in two minutes of public breathing!"

"Put that bloody thing out!" Murphy yelled, leaping to grab the alcoholic firebomb; but Chisholm danced away from him, the fuse of the bottle burning dangerously close to the neck.

"We need something that'll shake this fucking place up, Murph! A *revolution! Insurrection!* Murder in the bloody streets! Drag some of those blue-rinsed old ducks out of their frangipani gardens and make them watch atrocities being committed on their bloody poodles. . . !"

But Murphy had made another desperate lunge at the bottle, and this time he knocked it out of Chisholm's hand so that it hit the floor and smashed and then there was a dull WHUMP! as the meths ignited; and Murphy rushed to the bed, tore off the blanket and began beating at the flames, and when the blanket itself caught fire he used his feet, stomping and kicking and dancing until the flames had been crushed and all that remained was a pool of soggy cinders, a lot of smoke and an unimaginable stench. With a deep, shivery sigh, Murphy settled back on Chisholm's cot, shaking his head.

"You could've blown us both . . . Aw, what the hell. The thing that amazes me about you, Nole, is that if you wrote down everything that comes out of your bloody mouth we'd be rehearsing that play right now, instead of buggering about with the title."

"The title is the most important part of the whole project,"

Chisholm said indignantly. "Once I've got that right the rest of the play will fall into place without any worries."

"Well, you'd better get your finger out, Nole, because we've only got about a week now before the exhibition. And we need at least a couple of rehearsals, because we can't allow for any bloody mistakes. And another thing, that play's gotta have a good death scene in it—lots of blood and drama. And it's gotta have one good line towards the end that'll be the signal for the entire bloody break-out."

"That gives me a lot to work with," Chisholm sighed, settling back in his writing chair. "In the meantime, I guess you and Pearce will be making last-minute corrections to the script from your cells in Grafton."

Murphy slapped his forehead with exasperation. "Listen, Nole, didn't I just tell you there's no way that's going to happen? Didn't I tell you I got it all worked out? I tell you, Nole, I'm a slippery bug-ger when it comes to trying to get me to do something that I don't wanna do. I'll fight them every inch of the bloody way, and if every-thing else fails I'll kick off a bloody riot in here that'll make Attica look like a bunch of bloody uni students on a pantie-raid."

"I used to do a bit of pantie-raiding myself," said an oily voice from the cell door, and Henry Trembler snaked in, his spectacles switching to high beam as they reflected the neon lighting in the ceil-ing, his nostrils wrinkling with disgust. "Phew! What's been going on in here? Barbequeing a garbage bag?"

"Bugger off, Henry," Murphy snapped.

Trembler threw up his skinny arms to feign shock and horror. "Is that the way to treat an angel on an errand of mercy?"

"Maybe," Chisholm mused, mostly to himself, "I could farm the bloody play out and get everyone to write a scene and then call it *Naked Came the Sex Offender*."

"Precious," Henry sniggered, clapping his talons together. "And I could appear at the climax doing a glorious full-frontal. Which is something I never found time to try when I took up pantie-raiding. I used to race through the backyards at night with a bloody great pair of tailor's scissors, cutting the crotches out of women's drawers on the clotheslines. I had a real knicker fetish in those days. I used to have to take a pair to bed with me every night or I couldn't get a wink of sleep. All I could think about was soft sweet bums in silk panties. Or gym knickers—you know, those old-fashioned navy blue types that the girls were at school. All that lovely innocent healthy puppy-fat leaping about with gay, youthful abandon and those bloomers ballooning and straining every time they dived, squealing with excitement, for the ball. I became a permanent fixture at netball carnivals, you know. Until I got caught interfering with a heap of sweaty underthings while a bunch of them were showering in the changing shed after one particular match."

Murphy, thinking of his two young daughters, said: "Jesus, you're depraved, Henry."

"Not depraved, dear boy. *Deprived*. I couldn't get enough of them. In the end I solved the whole problem by sewing all the crotches together and making a quilt out of them. I slept like a log after that. It became my security blanket . . ." Then Trembler's evil gaze caught the wad of banknotes on Chisholm's desk. "Good Lord! Is that Mickey Mouse money or the real thing?"

Murphy answered that by grabbing Trembler roughly by his shirt-front and gazine menacingly into the satanic creature's thick lenses. "You didn't see any money, Henry. You've never seen any money. And if you open your silly mug to anyone about this, you'll be sewing your own crotch into the next quilt. Do I make myself bloody clear?"

"Of course," said Henry, squirming like a trapped goanna. "Though I must say, this is a fine way to treat a good samaritan who's come here to help you stay out of Grafton."

"What do you mean?"

"Sanderson's on the prowl. He's looking for you. It looks like this is the moment of truth."

"Oh shit," Murphy groaned, releasing the struggling pervert. He turned to Chisholm. "What'll I do?"

Chisholm looked cross-eyed at him. "I was under the distinct impression that you had it all worked out."

"Yeah, but this is all happening so fast. It takes time to start a bloody riot." Murphy began pacing up and down the cell. "I've gotta bloody think . . ."

Luckily, Chisholm took matters firmly into hand. He reached below his desk and emerged with yet another bottle of amber-coloured firewater. Then he began rolling some sheets of paper into a fuse.

"No. No more of that, Nole," Murphy pleaded. "We'll *all* end up in Grafton." He turned to Henry Trembler. "Piss off, Henry," he snapped. "Go find Sanderson and stall him as long as you can. Tell him I'm crook and I've gone to the sick-bay."

As Trembler scuttled out, Chisholm said: "It looks to me as if you've got little alternative but that massive asthma attack."

"I can't," Murphy wailed. "It takes days to build up to one of those things. Besides, I'll never be able to fool Sanderson. The symptoms are so bloody horrible there's no way I'll be able to fake them properly."

"What about epilepsy? You don't have to fake any symptoms for that. You just suddenly collapse in a heap on the floor and throw a pink fit. And bite anybody who tries to intervene."

"I can't," Murphy moaned. "I can't do it. I know I'll blow the whole thing."

"Maybe you need a little bit of help," Chisholm suggested, reaching again for his bottle of combination death-juice and embalming fluid.

"No, we'll save the firebombing for the last resort," said Murphy. Then he realised what Chisholm was really getting at, and he backed away toward the wall, his eyes wild with horror. "*No!*" he protested hoarsely. "*Never!* Never again in a million fucking years! Are you crazy? That stuff's nothing but a one-way bloody trip to the funeral parlour. D'you think I wanna *die?*"

"Better to die amongst friends, and swiftly," Chisholm said brightly, "than to go through a lingering form of suicide in Grafton. Maybe you haven't been listening to the radio lately. If you had, you might have enjoyed a delightful little programme which appealed to me because it brought old Nat Payten immediately to mind. Do you remember Simmonds and Newcombe, the two Sydney boys who killed a warder about fifteen years back, and the police responded with one of the biggest manhunts in Australian history?"

"Who'd ever forget Simmonds and Newcombe? That's like asking me if I remember Ned Kelly."

"Kelly had it easy," said Chisholm. "He only got shot in the legs and hanged. Simmonds and Newcombe ended up in Grafton. Simmonds killed himself in there, and Newcombe served his time and managed to emerge in one piece, paroled, and he's now a businessman living under another name. He was on ABC radio just recently, chatting about his life in Grafton, and if I were not a man already committed to strong drink I think I would have smashed my way out of here with my bare hands and headed for the nearest pub, there to drink myself into complete paralysis, or worse. You see, Newcombe described how he and Simmonds arrived at Grafton, flown there in handcuffs and chains, and at the reception centre they were both ordered to strip down to their birthday suits . . ."

Chisholm glanced at Murphy, and it was like looking at a man waiting for a house to fall on him. Murphy's mouth hung open, his eyes had a funny, glazed, cringing look about them.

"I'd better not tell you the rest. It might upset you."

"What happened?" Murphy croaked.

"Well, I won't frighten you with the details. I'll just skim quickly over the surface . . ."

"Nole, get to the bloody point!"

"Well, it seems that Simmonds was then taken into an adjoining room, and the door was left wide open so that Newcombe could watch his mate being beaten unconscious by half a dozen uniformed Neanderthals with rubber batons. The way Newcombe described it, I recall, the violence he was compelled to witness was shocking enough, but the worst terror of all was the realisation that he was inevitably going to have to walk into that room and submit to the same relentless thrashing himself." Chisholm shrugged and threw his hands into the air. "Of course, the whole thing might have been embellished a bit. I mean, who can trust a con to tell the whole truth? But by the same token . . ."

Chisholm halted. Murphy looked very sick. His features were the shade of antique, undecorated bone china. His eyes darted helplessly about the cell, searching for a way out. Finally, he sank into a defeated huddle on Chisholm's cot.

"Nole, promise me you'll give me a safe dose of that stuff," he pleaded. Then he put his head in his hands. "On second thoughts, maybe you'd better give me the whole bloody bottle."

nineteen

BULL SANDERSON WAS PROWLING THE PRISON LIKE an old dog pacing its territory—sniffing into every nook and cranny in search of that ratbag Murphy. Sanderson had just emerged from a critical meeting with (Rev) Hunt at which the immediate future of Murphy and Pearce had been irrevocably decided. And he wasn't happy. At a time when he was expecting sullen restlessness or even open hostility over Murphy's predicament, the prison was too quiet, too subdued—everything running too smoothly. It made the hairs on the back of his neck stand on end.

There wasn't so much as a hint of malice around him. No angry mutters about Pearce's stretch in the Blockhouse. No network of seething, ill-concealed whispers that might signal the way to Murphy's hiding place. Even Willie Crewe, who now accompanied Sanderson wherever he went, sticking to him like a fly on a toilet wall, failed to arouse any unpleasantness.

"They're gonna get me, I know they are," Willie whined at Sanderson's elbow as they emerged from the exercise yard and headed out across the quadrangle towards the cell blocks.

"Yeah, I reckon they probably will, Willie," Sanderson said grimly, taking advantage of the only enjoyment he was having that day. "I wonder what it'll be. A knife in the back when you're taking a pee? A couple of feet of piano wire around your throat when you're totting up all your bookie's winnings? Maybe they'll go easy on you and just blow a hole in your head with a zip-gun when you're asleep."

"You've gotta protect me, Mr Sanderson. I'm a witness for the Crown, remember? If I hadn't been keeping my bloody eyes and ears open you'd never have lumbered Murphy and Pearce. The way I see it, you *owe* me, Mr Sanderson."

"I don't owe you the bloody time of day, Willie," Sanderson growled. "I told you, I can't be in a dozen bloody places at once. If they're out to get you, they'll get you—nothing's more certain than that. All I can do is make sure you get a decent bloody burial if they're civilised enough to put you out of your bloody misery when they've finished with you." Sanderson let that little bit of hilarity drive home, then he halted and gazed straight into Willie Crewe's horrible little shit-scared eyes.

"You know the form well enough, Willie. How many times did you do the same thing when you were on the loose in what we laughingly bloody refer to as decent, law-abiding society? I can promise you one thing, Willie—your killers will not go free. Now, doesn't that make you feel better?"

Turning away, Sanderson raised a hand to shield the sun from his eyes and surveyed the work in progress around the jail's inner wall. No sign of Murphy, but Murphy's prison-without-walls mural was progressing very nicely: The prison was already beginning to look as though it had no walls. In fact, the effect was uncanny. It was as though the tall, brooding cell blocks had been set down like wheat silos in a rustic nineteenth-century Australian country town. The "City of Vines" was being re-created in splendid living detail by the chain-gangs sweating with their brushes and cans of paint along each wall. The inside face of the wall to Sanderson's right, beyond the Blockhouse, showed the toll road to Windsor, another of the nation's first settlements, curving up over the toll-hill in a pastoral setting of gums and eucalypts sprinkled with rude, squat, bark-thatched heaps of stones that were the convict cottages of that era. At the peak of the hill a ragged figure was laying into a team of bullocks with a whip that snaked and curled so viciously that Sanderson could almost hear its pistol-shot crack.

As the prison boss's suspicious gaze moved left around the walls, trying to pick Murphy out amongst the toiling convicts, the whole panorama of spires and towers and roofs, vine-framed in the "wonderfully peaceful airs," unfolded. There, on the farthest wall, the one beyond the cell blocks and football pitch—the scene of the abortive rugby-league breakout—stood the church of St John with its double-topped steeple, sleeping with Christian tranquillity in a sunlit blaze of greenery and flowers that lent such an authentic air to the scene that Sanderson imagined he could wander up the wide pebbled carriageway that reached up to the entrance, mount the broad stone steps that led to the doors and step right into the nave. Except that he'd never be seen dead in a church.

To the left again, Sanderson could see the columned, Georgian facade of Government House, set amid a copse of tall trees on the slope of the landscaped domain—now, in this present time, a rather tatty city parkland, infected by used condoms and paspalum and presiding over one of the most filthily polluted rivers in New South Wales—that climbed up to the Observatory. From there, the eye followed the downward sweep of the governor's estate to the house of the notorious Reverend Samuel Marsden, whence the scene took in the infant town itself, a huddle of cottages, liquor establishments and more solid two-storey brick and slate-roofed banking and mercantile houses, these themselves looking out over a scattered pageant of horse-carriages and over-dressed ladies with parasols delicately negotiating the potholes of the broad, unsurfaced main street and a mangy dog that had chosen this particular moment to cock its leg against a hitching post.

And there was one other incongruity which, for one moment, Sanderson suspected Murphy had added deliberately in another of his bizarre, smart-arsed pokes at ordinary people's feelings: Armed guards seemed to be suspended in the clouds over the roofs and vines and treetops as though victims of a mass hanging—standing with their carbines cradled at their chests along the top of the wall. If Sanderson's appreciation of art had gone anywhere beyond well-thumbed *Playboy* centrefolds, he would have compared the effect immediately with the best works of Magritte. As it was, he was forced to admit to himself that Murphy, for all his ratbag ways, was one hell of a fair hand with the old brush. Even with some sections of the vast mural uncompleted—rough mono-coloured outlines awaiting Murphy's final life-giving touch—the whole picture was beautiful, magical. And even Willie Crewe's psychopathic instincts were moved beyond his fears of retribution and thoughts of punching the shit out of people.

"Shit, it looks like real history. Like the stuff we had to read in school."

"Yeah," Sanderson agreed. "And I tell you someone else who's going to be history once I get my bloody hands on him."

"Maybe he's in one of the cell blocks. Jeez, I'll be glad to see that bastard Murphy behind bars, I can tell you."

But there was no sign of Murphy in cell block B, no trace of him at all amid a gang of whistling, cursing interior decorators, led by the aboriginal militant, Dickie King, who were hard at work undercoating and stencilling the well for the final sequences of the second-greatest artistic triumph of Murphy's career, the patriotic pageant he had decided to call *Advance Australia Fair*. And Sanderson again heard sirens whine in his head as the cons greeted him cheerfully, without so much as a curled lip of defiance or a grimace of malevolence, and even appeared to welcome Willie Crewe, who still slunk along at his side.

"Gidday, Willie," Dickie King grinned happily. "Owyergoin', or-rite?"

Willie responded by practically fastening himself like a limpit mine to Sanderson's brawny elbow.

"Hi, Willie," the rest of the cons echoed. "Wanna join us?"

"I'm looking for Murphy," Sanderson growled. "Where the bloody hell is he?"

"I think he went to the sick-bay," Henry Trembler informed him, emerging from the line of paint-spattered workers who'd been colouring in a series of numbered shapes to form the basis of a mural celebrating Australia's historic gold rush. It was a compelling scene, graphically depicting the rough-and-tumble hardships, fierce human bonds and inherent violence of that wild era. It showed a band of Caucasians engaged in coarse banter with an immigrant Chinese prospector and his family.

Sanderson peered closely at it, then stood back to get a wider perspective. "What are they doing to that Chink?" he asked.

"They're stringing the bugger up to that tree—by his pigtail," Dickie King informed him. "In the next scene they rape his wife and daughters, beat up his son, kick his grandfather down an old digging, set fire to his belongings, pinch all his equipment and then torture him with whips to find out where he stashed his nuggets and dust."

Sanderson blinked and shook his huge head. "Christ, he's lucky he's not Greek. What did he do to deserve that?"

"Nothing much!" Dickie gnashed. "He just forgot to mention to God that he was on his way to Australia when he was born. With a bit of luck, Old Hughie might have felt sorry for him and painted him white!"

"So where were you when your name came up? Stuck in a bloody pub somewhere?"

Dickie casually laughed it off and booted a half-empty paint can all over the floor. "Good joke. I like that," he laughed. "Ha-ha-ha-ha-bloody-ha! Another white Anglo-Saxon Protestant racist slur like that and your name goes right on top of the fucking death-list!"

Willie Crewe stiffened and moved into the shadow of Sanderson's back. "What death-list?"

"*Assassination list*," Dickie hissed. "Every bloody politician,

Bible-basher and bloody cop who gave us shit and denied us our rights as Australian citizens and human beings is gonna get his fucking head blown off the moment the revolution starts! Christ, man, there's gonna be white blood spilled from arsehole to breakfast time!"

"Yeah," Sanderson sighed. "Well, you'd better learn to bloody read and write first, or you'll never remember all the names."

"We'll remember," Dickie snarled. And he tapped his curly, Afro-cut head. "It's *written*, man—up here! That poor bloody Chink had a birthday party compared with what we're gonna do to the fucking whites when the fucking balloon goes up!"

Sanderson took another squizz at the gold-rush mural and grimaced with disgust. Then he ran his gaze down the wall and picked out a war-time battle scene in which troops with Digger hats, fixed bayonets, submachineguns, grenades and beer bottles were locked in ferocious house-to-house street fighting with a savage pack of sub-human beasts who all appeared to be wearing United States Army helmets and fatigues. One brute had a maniacal smile on his horrible stubbled chops and was pawing the bare breasts of a half-naked blonde as his burp-gun spat fury from his other hand.

"What bloody battle is that?" Sanderson demanded.

"That," Dickie announced, "is only the most glorious fucking episode in Australian military history. That's the one bloody battle that was fought on Australian soil against a ratbag bunch of Yanks who whipped in behind our backs and started knocking off our women and booze while we were all away fighting Rommel at Tobruk!"

Sanderson sighed heavily again. "The Battle of Brisbane Street," he muttered. "I might've known it. What happened to that other great military episode—Gallipoli?"

"We didn't win that one. Murphy said we should only present the positive bits of Australian history."

"What, like Chinks being strung up by their bloody pigtails?"

"They're doing the positive bits in the next cell block," Henry Trembler explained helpfully. "It's a whole artistic feast of ordinary down-to-earth Australiana. Murphy calls it *The Lucky Country*. There's blokes fighting for their lives in raging bushfires, shooting all their cattle and sheep in bad droughts, dragging their families onto the roofs of their homesteads in the floods, picking up the pieces of their towns after the cyclones and tidal waves, fighting sharks . . . You name it. It's all there. Why don't you go and see for yourself?"

"I've seen enough," Sanderson snapped. "You go and get Murphy right now and drag his arse back here. And don't come back without him or you'll spend the next couple of months in solitary. And you know what that means . . ."

"I'll go blind," Trembler admitted, slithering away. And as he went, Sanderson took another close look at the Battle of Brisbane Street, particularly at the way in which the bestial features of the central figure—the GI manhandling an armful of fair, unblemished Australian womanhood—stood out starkly from the rest of the mural. In fact, the face and most of the rest of the slavering beast's body, along with the more prominent points of his victim's ravishing anatomy, had been modelled in relief and protruded several inches from the wall. Sanderson fingered it, then tapped it lightly. It seemed solid enough.

"What's this? Papier mâché?"

"Putty," said Dickie King. "You remember Murphy saying how he wanted to use the stuff to make the pictures stand out?"

"Yeah," said Sanderson. "But he didn't say anything about bloody wires." He gingerly picked flecks of paint off a slim copper wire running from within the American infantryman's snarling face and into a thick coating of paint that formed the foundation of the next, yet-unfinished scene. "What's this bloody wire for? Murphy didn't mention anything about wiring."

"He uses it to hold the putty to the wall," Dickie explained. "Anyhow, that's the way he told it to me. I dunno a thing, anyway. I'm no bloody artist. Ask him yourself."

At that moment, Murphy was on his way from Chisholm's cell block, accompanied by Henry Trembler and convinced that this was going to be his last walk in the hot Australian sun. All at once it was as though the whole menacing reality of prison life had finally cracked his innermost defence—that shield of humour and conceit that is the mind's last-ditch stand against defeat and wholesale submission. Murphy felt as though he was a condemned man shuffling along Death Row for the last time. He was adamant that, whatever happened, the only way they'd transfer him out of the prison was feet-first in a wooden box. The trouble was, he had little doubt at all that the coffin was already open and waiting for him.

As they reached the doors to cell-block B, Murphy asked Henry for about the tenth time: "You sure Sanderson's going to ship me out of here?"

"He didn't exactly act like a harbinger of joyous news," Trembler replied. "But then, he never does, does he?"

"Well, looks like this is it," Murphy murmured. He heroically forced a tight, strained smile to his pale lips. "If I'm still alive fifteen minutes from now, you know what to do, right?"

"Don't worry," Henry assured him. "We're ready to stage a riot at the drop of a bloody hat. We'll tear this bloody slum down to its foundations, whether you survive or not. If you don't, it'll be a grand memorial."

"Thanks." Murphy shuddered. "That takes a lot of bloody worry off my mind."

Then he took a deep breath, glanced for perhaps the last time into his native sun and lifted a bottle of Chisholm's fearful home brew to his lips. He took a deep draught, almost a third of the shocking mixture, and a huge tremour that ran through his system with the violence of a lightning-bolt made him smash the bottle savagely against the cell-block wall. Then, with his teeth clenched tightly, his entire muscular apparatus fighting to stop his stomach erupting through his nose and ears, he stepped swiftly through the door and approached Bull Sanderson, prepared at last for his moment of truth.

If anyone, at that moment, had asked Murphy how he was feeling, he would have been inquiring about a state of body and soul that was far beyond the threshhold of interpretation in any known language. Even Murphy himself wasn't sure. All that his senses could tell him, signalling frantically from a dozen disaster points in his body, was that he was dangerously close to a terminal biological condition. All that he could see were the huge florid features of Bull Sanderson floating close to him like a great denizen of the deep against an aquarium window, and all that he could hear was a distorted far-away voice that was saying something like: "Ah, nice of you to drop in. Now listen to this—and I want the rest of you miserable bastards to hear this too! I've just come from an important meeting with Mr Hunt at which we thrashed out this entire bloody escape business, and we've decided we're not going to be the Mr Nice Guys anymore—you deceitful buggers can't be trusted for five minutes to act like bloody human beings. As for you, Murphy, and that ratbag Pearce, I can tell you right now that . . ."

But Sanderson had suddenly noticed that all was not well with Murphy. A horrible sickly flush, the colour of fresh blood, had engulfed Murphy's stricken face, starting at the neck and gradually

"Exactly," (Rev) Hunt agreed. "I myself have searched my heart for an answer to this dilemma, and I regret to say that the only possible conclusion I can reach is that there is a point in all affairs of men when compassion, understanding and the Christian instinct to give a fellow another chance are as prayers dashed to pieces on Satan's black shoreline. And then, sadly, the only possible mercy that remains is to *not* spare the rod."

"A flogging wouldn't do any good, Mr Hunt. Pearce wouldn't bat an eyelid, and Murphy'd probably scream the bloody place down."

"We must remind ourselves that flogging is no longer an alternative in this day and age, Mr Sanderson." (Rev) Hunt's hands were now locked together so tightly that his knuckles shone like new ivory. His gaze soared piously to the ceiling. "In fact, I can see no alternative but to make an example of these two men, remove them from this penal society and have them committed to Grafton."

Sanderson coughed again and squiremed uncomfortably in his seat. "I have to agree. We can't just ignore this business, Mr Hunt. And I understand how knocked-over you must be after all the privileges you've allowed these bloody dingoes out there. But, ah, do you think Grafton's really going to do any good? Pearce is as tough as bloody iron-bark, and so is Murphy under all that paint. Grafton would probably just make them worse."

(Rev) Hunt sighed and smiled ruefully at his prison czar. "I've thought very seriously about that too. But I really cannot see how an axe murderer responsible for two terrible murders and a bank robber whose record makes Dillinger look like an amateur shoplifter can possibly be seduced into a life of crime by the hardened criminals in Grafton. In fact I feel sorry for the men up there."

"They'll get broken into little pieces up there, Mr Hunt. I don't like to see any man get completely broken."

"Grafton didn't break Newcombe, Mr Sanderson. Newcombe is now back in society and living a totally decent and respectable life as a businessman."

Both men sat silently for a while, (Rev) Hunt contemplating the ceiling and Bull Sanderson brooding over his own little dilemma. As a human being his instincts told him to fight to the last to keep Murphy and Pearce out of Grafton's brutal clutches. As a loyal, highly regarded prison officer of the New South Wales Department of Corrective Services, his sense of duty demanded that he maintain law and order in his own jail—and discipline wasn't going to be maintained for long if he let two would-be jailbreakers hang around to become prison heroes. But then, there hadn't been many heroes in Bull Sanderson's boring, bureaucratic life.

"There'll have to be a court hearing, you know," he warned (Rev) Hunt. "The whole story will have to come out. And someone's going to look pretty bloody silly giving evidence that Pearce managed to carve five sculptures in his jail and he didn't once twig that he was getting the stone out of his cell wall. I'd hate to see a good, well-meaning bloke like you become the laughing stock of the department."

But (Rev) Hunt's resolve was as solid as granite. "We all have to bite the bullet once in a while, Mr Sanderson. And remember, two bad apples don't necessarily mean the whole experiment we've been conducting here is rotten. No, I'm afraid I can't see any alternative but to have both of them charged with attempted escape and submit them to the full process of the law."

"We've got the Blockhouse here, you know. Why don't we just shove Murphy in there with Pearce and throw away the key? Nobody's smart enough to break out of there."

"And who," (Rev) Hunt inquired, "is going to complete all the painting that has to be done for the arts and crafts exhibition? Murphy started it all, and he's the only man who can do it. And, by God, I'll make sure he finishes it."

Sanderson, puzzled, asked: "But how's he going to finish the work if you're . . ." Then he felt hope surge through him like a flash flood down an outback desert gully. "You mean they're not going to Grafton?"

"Oh, they're both going to Grafton, I can assure you of that. But *after* the exhibition. After the experiment has been unveiled and is shown to be a positive step forward in penal reform, and the departmental excitement has all died down. *Then* they'll go to Grafton." Sanderson watched (Rev) Hunt rise from the desk and walk over to his barred office window, there to gaze blankly at the grimy glass. "I've been a fool, Mr Sanderson," he said, his voice now low and sorrowful. "Goodness and mercy have blinded me to the realities of human nature. The beast that stalks within man cannot be handled with kid gloves. Being bestial, it has absolutely no appreciation of kindness and charity. Only when it is broken and knows there is no possible way in which it can win the struggle—only then can it accept virtue as its master."

(Rev) Hunt turned back from the window and, with sadness, returned to his seat. His hands assumed a position of prayer before him. "This nation still revels in its beastliness, Mr Sanderson. It was born a convict settlement and it is still the prisoner of dark, ridiculous emotional forces that are celebrated with vast quantities of liquor and sacrificial T-bone steaks. Almost a quarter of our adult population have serious alcoholic problems. Only a tiny few of them are gifted with Noel Chisholm's articulacy. Generation upon generation of our children grow up believing that the prime hallmark of Australian adulthood is to drink oneself into complete insensibility, throw up and then spend the next day sporting a crippling hangover. Thousands of our housewives are addicted in varying degrees to analgesic powders and tranquilisers. Apart from our drinking record, we are also the best cricketers in the world and among the global leaders in per capita road deaths and pack-rapes. My mind is firmly made up, Mr Sanderson. Pearce stays in the Blockhouse. Murphy completes his painting—forcibly induced, if need be. And when the exhibition is over, both of them are to be introduced to the same realities that I have had to face—in Grafton!"

Bull Sanderson continued to gaze furiously down at Kevin Murphy's sickly features, and he felt like booting Murphy's stupid arse all over the jail.

"You're a bloody fool, Murph," he raged. "You blokes had everything going for you in here. Now you can forget Old Clemency. He's a different sort of bloke now. One bloody peep out of you and you'll get belted so bloody hard you'll think a ton of bloody cement Bibles fell on you. He's going to be watching you like a bloody hawk over the next week while you finish that painting."

Murphy, with a voice still thin and weak with sickness, asked: "You mean to tell me I'm not going to bloody Grafton after all?"

"You've got work to do," Sanderson growled. "And by Christ, I'm going to make sure you finish it on time. Starting right now . . ." He turned to Dickie King and the rest of the cons around him. "One of you go to the sick-bay and tell the orderly that Mr Murphy requires a stomach-pump. The biggest stomach-pump he's got!"

twenty

IT WAS LATE THAT SAME NIGHT, AS MURPHY lay limp and sick and almost lifeless in his cot, as the rest of the prison slept, that Bull Sanderson quietly unlocked Noel Chisholm's cell door and aroused the great man from a shallow, dream-filled slumber.

"Not another flight!" Chisholm croaked, jumping bolt upright on his bed and staring sightlessly at Sanderson's broad face. "I can't take another flight with that lunatic!"

"Shut up," Sanderson hissed, shaking Chisholm's shoulder. "You'll wake up the entire bloody jail."

Chisholm's wild eyes gradually focussed on the prison overlord as his shocked senses recovered themselves. "Thank God it's you," he gasped. "I thought I was on ops again."

"There are no Japs around here," Sanderson assured him.

"I wasn't referring to Bloody Japs. I was having nightmares that I was back on the run to Broome."

"Keep your voice down," Sanderson hissed. "Get your duds on and come with me."

It was not until Chisholm had dressed, procured provisions for the mysterious mission ahead and been escorted quietly out of cell block C and into the vast, dark emptiness of the quadrangle that he asked Sanderson what in hell's name was going on.

"It's Reverend Hunt," Sanderson explained, keeping up a fast pace across the asphalt. "He's going through some sort of emotional crisis or something. He asked to see you."

"I'm not surprised," said Chisholm, hobbling along in the shadow of Sanderson's huge back. "Like me, he's lost his faith. It happens to us all the moment we realise that life is fundamentally a bowl of duckshit. And there's not even enough of that to go around."

"Yeah, that may well be," said Sanderson, and he halted and turned and blocked Chisholm's stumbling pursuit. "But this happens to be a little more serious than duckshit, Nole. I just happened to check Old Clemency's office—to see why the light was still on—and found him sitting in there with a bloody revolver in his mouth about to blow his bloody brains out. He needs help!"

"He certainly does," said Chisholm. "Go find another revolver and I'll join him."

"Stop pissing about, Nole," Sanderson growled. "Nobody blows his brains out while I'm in charge of this prison. Especially a nice bloke like the Reverend. Now, I've managed to talk a bit of sense into him, and calm him down a bit. The rest is up to you."

Chisholm said: "You're asking a great deal of me, aren't you? I'm not exactly a walking bloody advertisement for faith-healing."

"That's what I told him when he insisted I come and get you. But he says you're the only bloke who can save him."

They found (Rev) Hunt in his office, sitting at his desk, his hands clasped in front of him on the glass-covered surface, his pale grey eyes staring blankly at the opposite wall. The revolver lay to one side of him, filed neatly on top of a pile of departmental forms, letters and memorandums in his OUT tray. It appeared that in his own fastidious fashion, (Rev) Hunt had pigeon-holed suicide as a means of deliverance from his terrible dilemma. And terrible it was: Nothing short of a complete collapse of his vocation, his reason for living, his entire inspiration for *being*. His belief in Christian virtue had been crushed; his attempts at rehabilitation had been mocked and stoned. His very misery had been compounded by the awful revelations that had stunned him in Harry Pearce's cell. His soul was tormented with hate for Murphy and Pearce, and for all others who had done him wrong, and despair at that which he knew he must now do—send them to Grafton. His agony was such that his sanity now lay in the balance. As he himself defined this dilemma, his gaze flickering from the wall to reach out in tired appeal for Noel Chisholm's comfort and guidance:

"I am a jailor, when I was born to free men's souls."

Chisholm turned to Bull Sanderson with the funereal authority of an exorcist at the bedside of the possessed. "This will take a lot longer than I imagined," he said. "I suggest you leave us in privacy—and I beg you to turn a deaf ear to any screams, howls or piteous shrieks that may, in the course of this long night, ring from this room. Laughter, however, may be taken as a promising sign."

"I'll be down the hall in my own office," said Sanderson suspiciously, "if you need me." And with that he left the room, closing the door behind him.

Chisholm sat down in a chair to face (Rev) Hunt across the office desk. Long, and thoughtfully, did he gaze into the distraught man's tired, red-rimmed, watery eyes. Then he spake.

"Oh ye of little faith," he rumbled, an amused glint in his own blue eyes.

Pain knitted its coarse pattern across (Rev) Hunt's high brow. "Faith? Coming from you, that statement is an hypocrisy. I am appealing to you as one who has lived most of his life without faith, And you mock me."

"I've had faith enough to live this long," Chisholm retorted. "Certainly without resorting to the gun. Though I must admit, I have attempted to blow my brains out with other, more prolonged methods. And blown a few other minds along the way."

"That you, a man of strong religious background like me, should have lived for so long *without* faith—that is what fascinates me at this moment," (Rev) Hunt insisted. "It is vitally important that I learn how you have managed to do it, for the secret will decide whether I choose to carry on or deliver myself into oblivion. I am desperate, Mr Chisholm. *I must know.*"

Chisholm again regarded (Rev) Hunt thoughtfully, his lips pursed in an expression of calculation. "Have you considered spending the rest of your natural life pissed to the eyeballs?"

"I would rather die than suffer such degradation," (Rev) Hunt replied.

"A pity," Chisholm sighed. "Had your reply been in the affirmative we could have sorted this whole issue out right here and now. As it is, we must now tread deeper and more profound paths in search of your salvation, namely those that lead to the colours of the mind. Dallying here and there down insanity alley on the way." Chisholm reached into his green fatigues and brought out a full medicine bottle of methylated madness. (Rev) Hunt instinctively shrank back into his chair as the evil concoction was placed on the table.

"Mr Chisholm," he protested nervously, "I said a moment ago that I do not wish to become an inebriate."

"Then you are not desperate. You have not admitted that you are powerless, that your life has become unmanageable, that a power greater than yourself can restore you to sanity. Nor do you truly wish to know the secret of salvation." Chisholm began unscrewing the cap of the bottle. (Rev) Hunt's eyes were glued to the horrible urine-coloured contents; he licked his dry lips apprehensively. "I am not suggesting that you abandon your entire life to this vile fluid," Chisholm said, holding the bottle to his nose to test the bouquet. His eyes filled with tears. "No," he gasped. "That would be tantamount to putting a bullet through your brain anyway. What I am suggesting is that you abandon yourself for just this one night to my care and ministrations, during which we will indulge in a crash programme of faith-healing, a sort of emergency operation on the mind. *Shock treatment* may well be a term closer to the truth. I shall require your complete and absolute cooperation and trust. And as much personal courage as you can muster. You see, without this awful stimulant you will not behold the colours of the mind, and without the colours you will not begin to comprehend the essence of the philosophy to which I am about to introduce you—or re-introduce you, for the key to salvation lies, as a matter of fact, in your own misguided interpretation of faith."

(Rev) Hunt nervously licked his lips again. "I'm not sure I want anything to do with this," he said plaintively.

"The way I see it," Chisholm declared, "you have very little option. You're prepared to die anyway. And nothing, not even the terrors of this draught, can be as lunatic as putting the cold metal launching tube of an elementary combustion appliance between your teeth and discharging a high-speed nickle-plated projectile up through the roof of your mouth, thereby exploding your brains and various scalp and skull particles all over the—"

"Enough, Mr Chisholm," (Rev) Hunt pleaded, his sensitive features strained and slightly jaundiced. He sighed with heavy resignation. "I am willing to place myself in your hands."

"Good," said Chisholm. "You're already one step toward sanity. For our next step we shall join together in prayer. But first"— Chisholm thrust the medicine bottle across the table—"*Holy Communion.*"

"You mock me, Mr Chisholm!" (Rev) Hunt cried. "I ask for comfort and counsel in my hour of need, and you simply blaspheme!"

Chisholm grabbed the bottle back. "There! You see? You're jumping to false and totally fanciful conclusions already. And you haven't even touched a drop yet."

(Rev) Hunt was confused. "I don't quite understand what you mean."

"You have spoken of my lack of faith," Chisholm explained. "You have observed one side of the moon and ignored the other. In the natural order of all things, in the principle of cause and effect, in the Yin and Yang of our lives, for darkness there must be light, for good there must be bad, for up there must be down, for matter there must be anti-matter, and for faith there must be *anti-faith!* The dark side of the moon. The spiritual plane of no-hope. The twilight of the walking wounded, that place from whence we can observe the things that go on behind God's benign countenance. Where misery and injustice are manufactured, where bloody battles are fought and hunger and pestilence stalk the land, where the heavens moan in eternal agony with the cry of His only begotten son: 'My God. My God. Why hast thou forsaken me?' *Where God is the enemy of man!"*

(Rev) Hunt's eyes, wide now with fear, threw a cringing look at the ceiling, as though he expected thunder and lightning to crash upon them, for the whole place to be rent asunder in almighty wrath. Hardly had he realised how or why, than the bottle was in his hand, the small neck was at his lips—the first shocking flow of liquid lava burning its way down his tender throat. He gagged on the pain, his eyes brimming with tears. The bottle was whipped quickly out of his twitching fingers by Chisholm lest its vital contents spill all over the table. For moments, (Rev) Hunt's gaze remained heavenward, watching a gekko scuttle around a pale yellow pool that the grubby, fly-specked plastic shade of the light fixture was painting on the ceiling's white plasterwork. The gekko paused at the edge of the golden pool, as though about to drink, then glanced down at him, and its rubbery, translucent form turned blood-red and it grew from a tiny lizard into something horrible and prehistoric. Then the volcano erupted.

A thunderous blast tore (Rev) Hunt's entire body apart, his head bursting into smithereens and his legs and arms and feet and toes and other extremities flying off in all directions around the room, which, itself, pitched and rolled over like the stateroom of a sinking liner and, in a blaze of crimson and gold, boiled and whirled like fire out of a crater's mouth. Then things got bad. The fire curled, with another loud roar, into an enormous rushing whirlpool, and, into the gaping, racing vortex of this, (Rev) Hunt's senses—more a detached instinct, a tiny vessel of awareness; all that remained of his devastated body and soul—were irresistably drawn so that he was journeying at terrifying speed down a curling tunnel of flashing, kaleidoscopic lights and colours; and he watched the gekko rear its monolithic head and bare its gigantic blood-streaked fangs, and he heard, from the primal reaches around him, the Terrible Cry—and the earth was rocked, and the sky was torn asunder, and great oceans rolled together, and the seas were set afire, and graves were hurled about, and the sun ceased to shine, and the stars tumbled down, and mountains were blown away, and flames of fire were lashed upon him, and molten brass poured over him, and he was reduced to the lowest of the low and was engulfed by the scorching fire, and he was drinking from the seething fountain, and his only food was bitter thorns, and only boiling water and decaying filth could satisfy his craving hunger, and blackness and misery covered his face, and he was bound with chains and shackled, and his garments blackened with pitch and his head covered with flames and, groaning and wailing, he found himself on the edge of a vast, endless, glass-smooth landscape over which high blue heavens reigned and fluffy clouds gamboled like lambs. And a little man was running across the horizon. He was dancing as he went—little twinkling leaps and pirouettes. He was pissed. He was Chisholm, across the vast table-top, across the room, coughing and stamping and gyrating with the medicine bottle in his hand.

"HELP MEEEEEEEEEE!!" (Rev) Hunt screeched, and the tiny figure turned and rushed forth, speeding across the mirror-like landscape with terrifying haste; and (Rev) Hunt felt the gentle laying of hands upon his burning head, and he heard the voice of Chisholm, soft and reassuring above him:

"Long have ye carried the burden of righteousness. And deep hast thou ended up in shit."

(Rev) Hunt watched huge raindrops spatter on the glassy ground below him. He was weeping, watching his tears.

"Mr Chisholm," he choked, holding back a huge sob. "What did you see in the Pacific?"

"My dear Reverend," Chisholm replied. "I came here to save you, not destroy you."

"*I must know!*"

"You're not yet ready for it. You have to learn to walk before you can stagger and fall to your knees and open your heart to the plain, inescapable truth that there's no bloody hope for any of us. Just as that truth had been indelibly branded upon my soul by the time I was committed to the discipline squadron, flying transports to Broome, and turned up at the Darwin airstrip on my first morning, sniffing the cool desert-scented tropical air and bracing my legs against the reeling motions of a crippling hangover—only to find that there was a *common inebriate* staggering and weaving about beneath the underbelly of my plane. I was about to rush the bugger and kick his arse off the airfield when I realised, much to my surprise, that the distressed figure was not only the pilot of my plane, but my new Wing Commander too. We quickly recognised in each other a common suffering—we were both having extreme difficulty relating to the war. He, because he hated it. Me, because I couldn't forgive it. Both of us, because we were coincidentally pissed as ticks. From somewhere within his bulky flying suit he produced refreshment. We immediately discovered that we had common grounds for friendship . . ."

(Rev) Hunt accepted the proferred medicine bottle from Chisholm and took a second large swig. The desert airstrip and the stunted scrub around them began screaming with millions of cicadas. A great heat-wave passed over them, rolling like a cloud of steam, and it burned (Rev) Hunt's brow and cheeks and stifled him so that he tore at his clothes in his frenzy to escape it; and he staggered against Chisholm and grabbed at the lapels of his flying jacket, and his lips curled back savagely to bare his teeth as he snarled: "Is this your faith, Mr Chisholm?"

"It is my anti-faith, Mr Hunt," Chisholm explained, gently but firmly loosening the desperate hands from his person and guiding (Rev) Hunt back to his seat. "Like wine decanting, it has risen and strengthened in direct proportion to the rate of descent of the level in the other bottle. I have grown powerful in my despair. Girded have been my loins with antipathy. Over-runneth have I been in my cups with the revelation that heaven is a place for maharajahs, and the rest of us are being pissed on, constantly and with pin-point accuracy, from a great height. *Know that*, Mr Hunt! Admit it to yourself! And you are on the path toward salvation!"

"*I know it!*" (Rev) Hunt bawled, suddenly crashing his clenched fists down onto the table top. They had been joined, or rather delivered with, a navigator who was in even worse shape than they were—full as a boot and still singing songs left over from the night before as he fell out of the jeep that had ferried him down the runway. Staggering to his feet, he proceeded to kick violently at the vehicle before falling over again. "I know I've been pissed on!" he screeched insanely. "Good Lord in heaven—why do you think I want to die!"

"You don't have to die!" Chisholm bellowed, grabbing him by the shoulders to stop him from falling flat on his face. "You can stand and fight! You can carry the colours, enlist in the forces of the anti-
216

faith, get your name marked down in God's little black book, join the glorious crusade to turn the tables on Judgement Day, shove it right back up his almighty arse—that day upon which all the people of the earth shall gather upon the hills and rooftops and, at an agreed and appointed hour, supervised and coordinated by Swiss United Nations forces, with suitable and split-second allowances made for various time-zone dislocations, on the stroke of noon, GMT, every single voice on earth, every set of lungs, will join in one vast and terrible global shout. And the heavens shall resound with the almighty road: *FUCK YOU, GOD!!*"

"YOU'RE MAD!" the navigator shrieked, struggling violently in his seat. His eyes looked horrible. His charts were in such a disgraceful state that when the Wing Commander savagely careened them around onto the main runway for their third attempt at a take-off, none of them were sure they could even maintain a correct course along the tarmac. As they roared down the strip the Wingco uttered words to the effect that it was sure-as-shit lucky they had the West Australian coastline to follow down to Broome. If they could find the bloody coastline . . . Then Chisholm was grabbing at (Rev) Hunt grasping his trembling hands in a vise-like grip, his mad blue eyes burning holes in the poor man's head. "Can't you see it? Haven't you suffered enough? He doesn't want your faith! He wants to hear you *pray!* Almighty God, Beloved Father, constantly and with considerable finesse hast thou dumped shit upon us. All over our freshly laundered habits. We respectfully beseech thee to desist, and call upon thee to remove the letter H from thy little black book. And consider giving the Cs a break, too, while you're at it . . ."

"YOU'RE MAD!" (Rev) Hunt bellowed, fighting Chisholm's fierce grip. "Get us off the ground, for Christ's sake! We're going to crash!" He watched, horror-stricken, as the plane consumed the long runway at an incredible speed.

"He wants your pain, your anguish—your agony!" Chisholm hollered above the frantic roar of the engines. "His almighty ego *feeds* on your blind subservience, your pathetic pleas rising in a massed flutter and howl of hymns and chants and mantras and the spinning shriek of prayer-wheels, like a great cloud of ticker-tape confetti spiralling upward in a massive whirlwind of despair!"

The Wingco turned away from the shaking, rattling controls. He yelled at Chisholm:

"Go back and wind the bloody undercarriage up!"

"You're insane! You're an alcoholic psychopath!" Chisholm yelled back. "We're not even off the bloody deck yet!"

"Go do as you're told, you snivelling shit!" the Wingco raged, holding the joystick down with one hand and grabbing at Chisholm with the other.

"Go back and raise the wheels, for Christ's sake!" the navigator bawled in Chisholm's ear. "He won't lift us off until you do! Why torture him?"

With a strangled moan, Chisholm fought his way out of his flight seat, lurched back through the cabin and frantically began winding the undercarriage up. His mind's eye was already anticipating visions from the control tower of the plane sinking onto its fuselage as it sped along, showers of sparks and an awful scream of metal on asphalt as it skidded off the end of the runway, gouged its way through the surrounding grassland, tore through a barbed-wire fence, annihilated a herd of prime beef cattle, then turned its reckless attention to the one distinguishing landmark around that beckoned them to certain and instant catastrophe most foul—the neighbouring farmer's vine-covered, tin-roofed outside shithouse. Known locally as Theo's Thunderbox.

"However," Chisholm recalled, "I had sadly misjudged the awesome talents that still played from our Wingco's trembling fingertips. That man was no mere maniac, he was a bloody mad genius of man's mastery over machines and the principles of mechanical flight. He had it all timed perfectly. At the very moment that the wheels were due to disappear into the belly of the plane, lift speed was achieved and, with cries, he heaved on the stick and hurled us into the air."

(Rev) Hunt crawled back through the cabin to join Chisholm at the undercarriage winch. The bottle flew back and forth between them. "You'll never get into heaven," Chisholm informed him. "He only takes the creeps. The Fuckers of this world who go to church every Sunday and rob people blind the rest of the week. He sits up there watching a monolithic pyramid of struggling, screaming, fighting, gouging, kicking bodies trying to tear their way up the heap to Everlasting Life. And He laughs. And dumps another bucket of shit on the pile. Come over to our side, dear Reverend. Come join the army of the anti-faith. And while He's busy shit-canning everybody, we'll storm his battlements from the rear and claim the Kingdom of Heaven for our own."

"He always does it like that!" the navigator barked above the

218

howl of the plane's props. "And we've never crashed yet!" He stared balefully forward at the flight deck, where the shapeless, leather-helmeted heap that was the Wingco brooded over the controls. Then he began to weep. His shoulders heaved and tears splashed the shameful patches where decorations and insignias had once adorned his flying suit, soaking rapidly into the khaki material like rainspots into arid soil. "Maybe we did crash," he choked hoarsely. "Maybe we're dead, and this is some bastard's idea of eternal damnation. Every day, the nightmare of having to face another take-off with my life in the hands of that insane piss-pot! *No wonder I drink!*"

"What's *he* on about?" the Wingco inquired belligerently, set-tling down next to them on the fuselage floor and firmly prising the bottle from Chisholm's hands.

Chisholm informed him that the navigator was in the grip of a critical anxiety crisis. "He's lost his faith," he said.

That had an almost sobering effect upon the gallant Wingco. In fact, he looked quite hurt. "Don't you buggers trust me? Do you think I don't know how to fly this fucking crate? You think you can sling shit at me behind my bloody back and get away with it? I may be an officer and a bloody gentleman, but that don't mean I can't lower myself to indulge in a bit of arse-kicking in the ranks now and then!" He had the bottle in his hand, waving it dangerously close to Chisholm's face. Chisholm snatched it away from him, smashed it on the winding handle of the undercarriage winch and brandished the jagged end at his fat throat. "I warned him that if he made another threatening move like that against my person I'd cut his bloody guts out. It was an act of rank insubordination bordering on outright mutiny, but it calmed him. He sand back to the shuddering metal floor with a lazy grin on his fat chops, a certain grudging respect in his eyes. 'Jeez, you're a lucky man, Chisholm,' he said. 'That bottle could have had some booze left in it.'

"To give him credit, though, he never held a grudge for long— no matter how violently plastered he was. Within seconds he had produced yet another bottle of brain-damage, this one a homemade mango wine of dubious colour and vintage. I approached the evil fermentation with a trepidation that was borne out by my first sip. Had I been a connoisseur of fine wines I would have issued writs. The only merit I could possibly grant the brew was that it obviously travelled."

They were soon enjoying themselves—all thoughts of death, insanity and other unpleasantness forgotten as (Rev) Hunt entertained them with an almost word-perfect recitation of "Clancy of the Overflow," the Wingco himself responded with the entire unexpurgated ballad of "The Good Ship Venus" and Chisholm, struck as he was by sudden and alarmed curiosity, politely assured the Wingco that he was not trying to stickybeak or ask stupid questions or anything, but could he tell him who was flying the fucking plane?

"George," said the Wingco.

"Ah," said Chisholm. That explained why no-one was at the controls. "We continued partying, unbuckling our parachute packs for greater comfort and freedom of choreography. I recall that I brought the house down with a particularly well executed parody of the opening of that immortal radio show that almost got one of Australia's most beloved entertainers booted off the airwaves for the rest of his life. You will no doubt remember how he had become a coast-to-coast household name for his cheery, heart-plucking greeting: 'Hi ho, *ev*-verybodyyyyyyy!'—a clarion call that glued a nation's ears to its wireless sets like landlady's lugs to a honeymooning couple's wall. It brought sheep farmers in from their sheep, cattle graziers in from their cattle, wheat growers in from their wheat, leaving the blowflies to congregate in enraptured clusters on the fly-screen doors. All over the sunburnt country, throughout its sweeping plains, they listened as one vast continental ear surrounded entirely by oceans and waited with bated breath as the man who had captured their hearts and tickled their fancies strode up to the microphone and let rip with a highly imaginative opening that subsequently led to shocked apologies and hasty assurances that his personal and professional life had been under intense strain at the time:

'When roses are red
They're ready for plucking
When girls are sixteen
They're just ripe for . . .
Hi ho, *ev*-verybodyyyyyyyyyy!'

"There was a stunned national silence, then a huge gasp from the studio audience at the audacity with which he had pirouetted neatly around the magic word. Then he added, quite casually: 'And now you can all go fuck yourselves.' "

220

"YOU'RE A LIAR!" (Rev) Hunt bellowed, lunging at Chisholm's throat. "He wasn't even on the radio until well into the fifties!"

Chisholm fought him off, pinioning his hands behind his back. "The colours!" he bawled. "Watch the colours! Keep your mind off the supporting trivia. One more shocking lapse like that and I'll walk right out of here and leave you stuck half-way down insanity alley in a state of hopeless and irresponsible dementia!"

"Don't leave me!" (Rev) Hunt pleaded. "Please don't leave me!"

"Admit, then, that there is an anti-faith! It's your only way out!"

"I admit it!"

"Admit that God has done you wrong!"

"Oh God," (Rev) Hunt moaned. "We'll burn in hell for this."

"I'll pour the rest of this bottle over you and set fire to you myself if you try to pike-out now! You'll go up like a bloody weatherboard house on fire!"

"I admit that God has done me wrong!"

"Good. Now watch the colours. And repeat after me the words of Shakespeare: 'Some rise by sin/ And some by virtue fall.'"

"'Some rise by sin/ And some by virtue fall.'"

"Now take another slug of this."

The plane suddenly rolled to starboard, its screws tearing at the air with an outraged howl, and the Wingco, recalling that they were all aboard a flying machine, ordered Chisholm and the navigator forward to "take a quick dekko—see where we are." Chisholm staggered into the cockpit, suddenly concerned for the safety of all aboard, and was relieved to find that the plane was indeed in safe hands—the Wingco's controls jammed into level-flying position with a plank of wood, upon which was painted the word GEORGE.

"Where are we?" Chisholm asked the navigator.

"How should I know?" was the giggling reply.

"There's nothing out here but bloody clouds!" Chisholm shouted back at the Wingco.

"Maybe that's because we're twenty-thousand feet in the fucking air!" the Wingco yelled back. "Full marks for observation, Chisholm!" The gallant man was by now in a prone position alongside the undercarriage winch with the empty moonshine bottle cradled at his chest. "We must have missed the coast," he yelled at Chisholm. "We must be somewhere over the bloody Timor Sea!"

Chisholm, peering down through a sudden break in the snowy carpet below them, saw something that caused him to slightly revise

221

his faith in the Wingco's amazing capabilities. "Since when has Ayer's Rock been stuck in the middle of the Timor Sea?"

The Wingco accepted the facetious rebuke with good humour. "Watch yourself, smart-arse. You're addressing a superior officer. One more crack like that and you'll end up down there with Ayer's Rock plastered all over your bloody backside!"

Chisholm decided to take matters into hand before they reached the stage of outright catastrophe. "I realised that there was no point in prolonging the debate while he was confused of mind, hostile in manner and otherwise pissed as a newt. Besides, within a twinkling he had passed out cold on his back, still clutching the wine-bottle to him like a life preserver. Agreeing that our flight plan had been somewhat shot to buggery, the navigator and I marshalled our combined technical expertise and logic in a bid to put things right. If we were not over the sea, we agreed, then we must have gone inland from Darwin. And if that big red pebble that I'd spotted through the clouds was really Ayer's Rock, then we must be somewhere south of Alice Springs. *Alice Springs?* We checked the charts to see whether Broome was anywhere near Alice Springs and discovered, much to our chagrin, that GEORGE had fucked up badly—putting us nearly two thousand miles south-south-east of where we were supposed to be. 'We're in deep shit,' I informed the navigator. 'You're not kidding,' he said. 'We're running out of gas.' "

This was obviously a crisis that called for cool minds and keen leadership qualities—both of which neither Chisholm nor the navigator possessed. However, Chisholm quickly assumed command of the situation by ejecting GEORGE from the Wingco's seat and taking over the controls. He immediately thrust the plane into a steep, screaming dive.

"I'm just testing the ailerons," he explained to (Rev) Hunt, who had just deafened him with a terrified shriek close to his ear.

"They work perfectly!" (Rev) Hunt yelled. "Leave them alone!"

"OK," said Chisholm. "If you're such a great know-all, what do we do now?"

(Rev) Hunt checked the fuel gauges, rapping them professionally with a knuckle.

Chisholm said: "Why don't you step outside and kick the bloody tyres while you're at it?"

"Shut up!" (Rev) Hunt yelled. "Just shut up! I reckon we've got just about enough juice to make an emergency landing at Alice Springs."

"Have they got an airstrip in Alice Springs?"

"If they haven't, they're sure as well about to get one."

"What if we can't reach Alice Springs?"

(Rev) Hunt's reply was to rummage furiously in his desk drawer. So fierce was his haste that he tore the drawer right out of the desk and hurled it to the office floor. He emerged from the wreckage with a silver hip flask. "It's Scotch whiskey," he said. "I keep it for medicinal purposes. You never know when you might suddenly face the prospect of crashing and burning in the Simpson Desert."

Without further ado, both of them gulped courage from the flask. They then erupted into a series of retching convusions so explosive that the cockpit spun upside down and, for one horrible moment, Chisholm thought they'd been caught in the cannon fire of a marauding Japanese Zero. With big fuming tears in his eyes and a fierce blaze in his stomach, he instituted a rapid check of their situation. Which had changed considerably. They were now flying underneath the clouds, with a vast powder-blue lake stretching to the horizon below them.

"Stop that blubbering!" Chisholm yelled at (Rev) Hunt. "This is no time for emotional collapses. Leave that until we see if there's an airstrip there or not."

"I can't help it," (Rev) Hunt sobbed. "I DON'T KNOW WHERE I AM!"

"You're somewhere down insanity alley," Chisholm explained. "Flying over the Simpson Desert."

"Then what's that lake doing down there!" (Rev) Hunt screeched. "I can't remember ever hearing about lakes in the middle of the Simpson Desert! Only artesian bores." That made him let out with an even more grievous fit of sobbing.

"For Christ's sake!" Chisholm yelled, staring thunderstruck at the blue waters below them. "What's the matter now?"

(Rev) Hunt seemed to be looking down upon him from considerable height. That made Chisholm's disorientation even more nightmarish. "All my life the same terrible sense of failure has nagged me," (Rev) Hunt wailed. "I started out with such wonders in my head. And what did I become? Nothing more than an artesian bore!"

"Well that's a damn sight more preferable to being a subterranean outlet," Chisholm observed, still trying to make head or tail of that huge lake below them. "And there are a few of those running around. Besides, an artesian bore is someone who carries his brains around in his arse. Your brains are in your head, albeit in a horribly scrambled state. And you are already reaching beyond mundane intelligence. You are striking forth toward a totally new level of consciousness. You have admitted anti-faith. You have turned against God. You have decanted. You stand now on the other side of righteousness in His name's sake. Now, you no doubt wish to know what exactly *is* this new plane upon which you now stand."

"I wish to know," said (Rev) Hunt, "why I appear to be on the floor, and you on the ceiling. Or, vice-versa, why you are down there, and I am up here. *Am I cracking up?*"

"You know," Chisholm said, with a great sigh of relief, "I didn't want to say anything in case both of us were going around the bend. However, your intelligence is safe—that I can assure you. You have just resolved the phenomenon of the big blue lake below and the fact that you are stuck up on the ceiling. We are flying upside down!"

"Then turn us over, please, Mr Chisholm!"

"Your wish is my command," Chisholm assured him. "But first, let us push that intellect of yours another step, and define this spiritual world of no-hope into which you have now committed yourself. Reflect upon the words of Marlowe: 'I count religion but a childish toy/ And hold there is no sin but ignorance.' Or, as Oscar Wilde more bluntly put it: 'There is no sin except stupidity.' There is no sin where you now stand, Mr Hunt. That's for the poor struggling creeps on the other side. The only sin, Mr Hunt, is the stupidity of believing that wisdom and virtue will triumph, and that the meek shall inherit the earth."

Chisholm swung the plane over onto its right keel, and the navigator fell in a thrashing heap behind his flight seat. After a series of oaths and obscenities he rapped his charts, took bearings on the fuel gauges, then crossed his fingers and declared that they would probably make it. They celebrated this with a couple more belts of whiskey. Then (Rev) Hunt began kicking savagely at the instrument panel, smashing the glass-dialed gauges. Being in command of the flight and sole control of the plane, Chisholm naturally took umbrage at this.

"You should know that whiskey's not good for you!" he yelled.

"It goes straight to the brain! It turns mild-mannered little men into raving, self-annihilistic, fucking monsters!"

"Shut up! JUST SHUT THE FUCK UP!" (Rev) Hunt raged, confirming Chisholm's worst fears. Then he patiently explained: "I'm trying to give us a good excuse."

"What for?"

(Rev) Hunt's teeth grated with exasperation. "*A good excuse for suddenly landing at Alice Springs, two thousand fucking miles off-course with the Wing Commander flat on his fucking arse in an alcoholic coma in the back and you and I so fucking pissed we can't fucking scratch ourselves!*"

It made sense. They'd look silly just dropping in on the place, each of them falling arse-over-head out of the plane and doggedly insisting that this was not Alice Springs at all, but Broome, where they were supposed to be. Thereby confusing everyone. "However, it might just work," Chisholm observed, "if we remain united in absurdity." Driven to extremes they would show them the sign on the control tower. There, it says Alice Springs. No it doesn't—it distinctly says Broome. Wing Commander, what does it say up there? Up where? Up there—on the control tower. What control tower? Jeez, this heat's killing me . . . There you are, gentlemen—the Wing Commander is obviously suffering from a severe form of mental disorder caused by combat fatigue and the horrors he saw in the Pacific. That's why he has sought solace in strong drink. That's why he is now committed to a discipline squadron. That's why all three of us have been thus committed. If that repugnant sneer of the mouth, Colonel, is an expression of disbelief, then I urge you go consider the only realistic alternative—that you and your men have inadvertantly set up an air-base no less than two thousand miles from its proper and ordained position. You could be court-martialled for that. However, my colleagues and I are willing to overlook this whole scandalous affair and keep our lips buttoned in the future if you would kindly arrange for our tanks to be filled with high-octane gasoline, allow us to reprovision with in-flight refreshment, then point us in the general direction of the West Australian coastline . . .

"WAKE UP, CHISHOLM!" (Rev) Hunt screamed, tugging at Chisholm's flight jacket. "For God's sake, don't go to sleep on me now!"

Chisholm explained that he wasn't sleeping—merely resting his eyes, which were exhausted from the effort of fighting to uncross themselves. "You said something about an excuse," he murmured, searching the terrain below for signs of Alice Springs.

"All right," said (Rev) Hunt. "Instrument failure."

"Not bad," Chisholm admitted, glancing at the smashed dials. "There's certainly evidence to prove that they're not in perfect working order. Of course, the first thing they'll ask is how come they're all smashed. Then I'll be tempted to panic and tell them that shortly after take-off from Darwin the navigator suddenly and unaccountably went berserk, knocked the Wing Commander cold and then forced me to fly him to Alice Springs, plying me with liquor with threats of assault and battery and babbling crazily about some sheila he'd put up the stick whose father was waiting with a loaded shotgun in Broome."

As soon as he'd said it, Chisholm realised that (Rev) Hunt was in no condition to accept humour, however implied, let alone mockery and threats. Swiftly, the dear Reverend had snatched GEORGE up from the floor and was about to brain him with it. "You'll never live to tell the tale," he snarled, a glint of something close to psychopathic homicidal paranoia flashing in his crazed and horribly bloodshot eyes. So much for medicinal purposes. Chisholm realised he had another crisis on his hands. There's only one way to deal with the problem drinker, he told himself, and that's to keep his ravaged brain alive and thinking—prevent it from settling into one, single, all-consuming and possibly murderous thought-process.

"What about sandstorms?" he asked him.

(Rev) Hunt blinked. "What about them?"

"Or, better still, if you accept the theory that if you're going to try to pull a fast one, make it a bloody beauty . . . What about magnetic interference?"

That really set (Rev) Hunt thinking. The automatic pilot now hung limply at his thigh. But there's no accounting for the tortured logic of the drunk. "No, that won't do," he said. "Then we'll have to explain that we smashed all the instruments trying to make them work. And they'll never believe that."

"You have a point there," Chisholm agreed. "However, you'd better think of a good excuse fast. I can see something that looks like a human settlement off our starboard wing."

"I'm thinking," (Rev) Hunt moaned, wringing his hands with anxiety.

"You'd better wake up the Wingco, too," Chisholm suggested. "I can handle these crates once they're in the air, but I'm not too hot when it comes to taking off and landing."

(Rev) Hunt staggered off into the bowels of the plane. He returned very quickly, grabbing at Chisholm's shoulder.

"We've got our excuse," he announced in a slightly hysterical voice.

"What's that?"

"The Wing Commander's disappeared. He's no longer aboard the plane!"

Chisholm pondered upon the alarming news for a moment or two, as though examining its feasibility. Then he suddenly tore himself out of the pilot's seat.

"Grab this stick!" he yelled. "And hold it still. Don't mess about with it!" And, thrusting (Rev) Hunt behind the controls, he rushed back into the belly of the plane. He found that one of the loading hatches had been removed and ejected. In its place was a yawning hole full of shrill wind and a snowy glare that stabbed painfully at his eyeballs. Searching frantically, the only sign he found of the Wingco was the empty mango-wine bottle rolling and clanking about with the sickening pitch and yaw of the plane. "He must have wrenched the door open in his delirium!" he yelled. "Got sucked out by the pressure!" He shuddered at the thought of it. "What a terrifying way to go. We can only hope that he was still horribly pissed."

He clawed his way back to the cockpit, dragged (Rev) Hunt out of the flight seat. "What more can possibly happen, I ask myself . . ." He was scanning the outskirts of Alice up ahead, a wide municipal map of shiny sheet-metal rooftops, for a place to land. With a wracking cough, several loud popping sounds and a series of convulsions that shook the cockpit, the starboard engine died. Within seconds the port engine had run out of fuel too.

"Oh Lord God—save us!" (Rev) Hunt shrieked.

"It's no good appealing to Him," Chisholm reminded him. "You've denied Him, remember? Look at it this way: We no longer have to worry about excuses. We'll crash and tear the plane to bits anyway. They'll assume the Wingco perished along with us in the fire. You won't have to explain those wrecked instruments."

"*I don't want to die!*" (Rev) Hunt bawled.

"Well, you're recovering in leaps and bounds. You're now on the very threshhold of salvation. All I have to do is to bring this bloody kite down without killing us . . ." Chisholm watched the silver rooftops flash underneath them as he levelled the crippled plane to glide at breathtaking speed over the town. He banked into a wide starboard turn, searching for something remotely resembling a landing spot. He found one. "We can thank our distant forebears for the remarkably wide main streets that they laid out in these country towns. Never again will I take any notice of those who complain that you can fire a cannon down them at midday and not hit a living soul. That's exactly what we need at this moment." He levelled the plane out again, lowered the flaps and nosed it down. "Remember—name, rank and serial number only. If we survive. And unless the Chamber of Commerce or Rotary Club try to lynch us."

Wrestling with the controls with one hand, Chisholm offered (Rev) Hunt the silver hip-flask with the other. "Here, have a lost shot of this. And take courage from the anti-faith. Remember, there's no bloody hope for any of us. That way, we have everything in the world to look forward to."

(Rev) Hunt drew deeply on the flask and watched with horror as the town's wide main street rushed up towards them—cars careening to right and left of them and people scurrying, screaming, into shop doorways.

"The *key!*" he cried. "You haven't given me the key!"

"The key," Chisholm shouted, fighting to hold the plane's tail down for a belly-landing, "is *predestination!* Something you should have paid more attention to at theological college—the Calvinist heritage of your own Presbyterian faith. That God has unutterably destined some souls for salvation, if they're willing to spend their entire lives kissing his arse—while the rest of us are committed to the eternal damnation of fucked-up flight plans and crash-landings. Think about it! Close your eyes, confess that you have sinned by way of stupidity—*AND HANG ON!!*"

There was a piercing, grinding shriek of metal on clinkered bitumen, a terror-stricken scream from (Rev) Hunt. The cockpit heaved and bucked violently, hurling them both out of their seats. Then the entire world turned turtle on them, and a tremendous explosion lifted them up like a giant hand and carried them deep into unending darkness.

When (Rev) Hunt regained consciousness he moaned with pain,

then opened his eyes to behold the face of Chisholm hovering over him in a strange, holy aura cast like a halo around his head and shoulders by the light on the ceiling. Chisholm smiled and gently wiped a bubbly film of sweat from (Rev) Hunt's aching brow.

"Are we alive?" (Rev) Hunt whispered.

"Of course," Chisholm assured him. "That's what the anti-faith is all about. We always survive. How else can we remain available for further periodic crash-landings?"

Around them, the office looked as though a mob of crazed, Neanderthal ransackers had burst through it. The desk was upside down, its glass top smashed to a million fragments, its drawers torn out and strewn around it and their contents littered all over the floor. Chairs had been overturned. A desk-lamp lay twisted and smashed amongst them. A heavy metal filing cabinet had been tipped over and its manila-foldered files scattered around it in fanned piles like discards in a giant poker game.

(Rev) Hunt pulled himself up into a sitting position and groaned again as he surveyed the chaos. "What in Go—, er, hell's name happened?"

"We hit the colours. We crashed," Chisholm explained. "I'd forgotten to lower the bloody undercarriage. However, it's lucky I did, otherwise we would have shot right through the town and headed out into the desert. Never to be seen again."

"What happened to the Wing Commander?"

"We found him six weeks later. Or rather, we received a call from the police sergeant in a place called Alligator Creek, begging us to come and collect him. It turned out that he'd simply decided on the spur of some addled moment to go AWOL. So he'd strapped a parachute on and leapt out of the plane. Alligator Creek happened to be unlucky enough to lie in the path of his descent. During the course of his little sojourn there, he drank the pub completely dry and rendered the barmaid with child. Her husband, the publican, was hardly amused. Nor was her father, the police sergeant."

(Rev) Hunt passed a trembling hand across his fevered, throbbing brow. "And what happens now to me?"

"Ye shall go forth with a new faith and no hope—more fitted to cope with the cruel illusions of life. You are now on the side of the irredeemable and the damned. Don't try to save us—it's a hopeless cause. Try instead to equip those around you for the struggle ahead.

Turn pickpockets into highly accomplished thieves, bank robbers into respectable and intelligent white-collar crooks. Protect them from the vile retributions of our society, that they may develop and prosper in their creative endeavours and find satisfaction one day, like Kevin Murphy, as top-class art forgers. Most of the others get away with it very nicely. Keep Murphy out of Grafton. Keep Trembler away from little kids. Let your path be always lighted by the truth of predestination, remember to piss mightily on maharajahs and hark to the words of Luther, who saith: 'He who loves not wine, woman and song/ Remains a fool his whole life long.' " Chisholm rose to his feet, swayed a little, slipped (Rev) Hunt's heavy silver hip-flask into his back pocket, thereby swiping it. It was somehow symbolic of that moment that (Rev) Hunt saw him do it, yet said nothing. "Take a trip down insanity alley now and then. Keep the colours alive, virtue at a minimum and do unto others before they do unto you."

"I shall," (Rev) Hunt pledged softly. Then he passed out cold again.

Chisholm opened the office door and stumbled out of the room. He staggered right into the huge bulk of Bull Sanderson, who was lurking out in the corridor, listening for more screams.

"What the bloody hell's been going on in there, Nole?" he demanded.

"You said it—bloody hell," Chisholm told him. "Reverend Hunt is saved. The cancer of defeat has been routed, despair no longer possesses him. He is resting now—piecing together what's left of his mind. He'll live. He's got something to live for."

"What did you do to him?"

"I took him on a flight into the mind. It worked wonders with a similarly distressed navigator I once knew. It's performed nothing short of a miracle on Mr Hunt."

Sanderson escorted him back down the corridor and out through the checkpoints and onto the dewy, dawn-washed asphalt of the quadrangle.

Bull Sanderson said: "I know I don't have to say this, Nole. But you know what'd happen if even a bloody whisper of tonight's events go round."

"Fear not," said Chisholm. "The secret will remain with me." He paused, gazed up into a fanfare of pink and golden streaks fanning up into the early-morning sky.

"Up your gumboots, God," he murmured.

230

twenty-one

AFTER LITTLE MORE THAN A WEEK IN THE Blockhouse, Harry Pearce was facing a crisis of his own. Daily, he was locked in a struggle between mind and emotions. His mind knew the drill; after seven years in Parramatta Jail it had disciplined itself to hideous, unrelieved confinement.

The emotions were something else. Prodded and cajoled by the itchy, leaping physical hypertension of confinement in a tiny cell with only the ancients of the Holy Bible for company, they could erupt into screaming riots, insane rampages that could make the body hurl itself at the four walls, at the steel door, at the tiny wash-basin and adjacent open toilet bowl, or madly tear the stuffing out of the rough hessian mattress on the heavy, single-frame iron bed that was bolted firmly to the bare concrete floor.

Harry knew that the first two weeks of this purgatory were the worst. Here, the mind must triumph over the body's urge to let go and explode. Two weeks, and the panics would gradually subside, the fires would die and he could settle down and start doing some dirty drawings on the cell wall. He reckoned he had about another five days of emotional cold turkey to go.

He was a man to whom loneliness, on a more acceptable human level, was a blessing rather than a curse. He was also gifted with a tremendous, iron-hard will, an unconquerable stubbornness when he set his mind to it, but even he could not just dance over his inner geysers of panic and despair as he sat hour after hour, day after day, night after night, listening to the thunder of silence, counting every tick of the mental clock that measured off the eternities that lay between the clang of the tin plate on the narrow meal-hatch at the bottom of the door, the jangle of keys that heralded, with a sound as magnificent as a full fanfare of brass and drums, that the time had come for him to be ordered by mute signals out of his cell, then handcuffed and shackled at the ankles and led out into the blinding glare of the dusty exercise yard—there to spend an hour treading the cindered path like a dumb bullock hitched in perpetual slavery to some bloody Arab's irrigation wheel.

As always, the strange and celebrated monster of the lair, the mystery man they now called The Beast, followed him silently around the pit—a tall, thin, gaunt-featured apparition with long, shoulder-length hair and an unkempt salt-and-pepper beard who said nothing, made no attempt to utter a sound and shuffled in Pearce's footsteps like a dumb mule. And as always, when Pearce tried to turn and make verbal contact, a warder watching over them with a loaded carbine curtly ordered him to shut his guts, turn his eyes to the front and keep moving. Those were the only human sounds apart from his own mindless chatter that Harry had heard since Bull Sanderson committed him to solitary.

Christ! It was almost too fucking much to bear, this outer silence, with no word from Murphy. It was so bad that Harry sought solace in the Bible. Not in the spirit of the book, not even in the meaning, just the words, any words that he could repeat over and over again as he felt the tension rising out of the pit of his stomach, as he stalked back and forth in his tiny cell bawling like one of those funny misshapen men whose scrawny neck ligaments stuck out like whipcords as they hollered Hallelujah's at Billy Graham's old Down Under Crusades.

Harry's Bible was the New English version, and after eight days he'd covered the Old Testament right up to The Song of Sons 7–8, where the lucky bridegroom launches into an enraptured toast to his blushing bride before whipping her off on a two-week honeymoon in Surfer's.

" *'How you love to gaze on the Shulammite maiden,'* " Harry raved, pacing back and forth, the open Bible clutched fiercely to his chest, " *'As she moves between the line of dancers!*

> " *'How beautiful are your sandalled feet,*
> *O prince's daughter!*
> *The curves of your thighs are like jewels,*
> *the work of skilled craftsmen.*
> *Your navel is a rounded goblet*
> *that never shall want for spiced wine.*
> *Your belly is a heap of wheat*
> *fenced in by lilies.*
> *Your two breasts are like two fawns . . .'* "

Harry paused, wondering whether or not to go on. Mere words or not, this was pretty rich stuff for a seven-year con in solitary confinement. Then he heard a voice call unto him from somewhere outside his cell, a voice that spake in wrathful tones that filtered tinnily through the narrow hatch in his door.

"Shaddup, willyah!" it cried. "Read something else, for Christ's sake!"

Harry listened, his ears straining and the Bible poised at his beating breast. But there was no further sound. He shook his head. Maybe the silence and loneliness was really getting to him after all. Maybe he was starting to go crackers. Maybe that bloody so-called mate of his, Murphy, was swanning about out there without a care in the world—leaving him for dead! As the panic rose again he tore back into The Song of Songs:

> " 'How beautiful, how entrancing you are,
> my loved one, daughter of delights!
> You are stately as a palm tree,
> and your breasts are the clusters of dates.
> I said, 'I will climb up into the palm
> to grasp its fronds . . .' "

Harry paused again. And again the voice cried out:

"I'll bloody well grasp your fronds and tear the buggers off if you don't put a bloody sock in it! This place is bad enough, without you raving on about some sheila's tits!"

Harry dropped the Bible and rushed to the cell door. At that time of night, it could be the voice of only one man—The Beast. Trembling with excitement, he crouched at the door, put his mouth close to the narrow meal-hatch and shouted: "Why don't you stick yer nose up a dead bullock's bum!"

And as a mighty wind the voice replied: "How would you like a couple-a nuckle sandwiches to chew on?"

And Harry gave vent to great rage and shouted back: "You and who's bloody army—you long streak of gnat's piss!"

"You'll get yours, smart-arse! I'll see you in the bloody yard tomorrow!"

"Bring a couple of mates! You'll need 'em!"

"Like bloody-ha! No-one's ever beaten me, mate. And a bloody lot of blokes've tried. Including old Sanderson. An' I spit right in his bloody eye!"

Harry yelled: "If you're so bloody tough, how did you end up in here? Did you just decide to drop in for a bloody rest?"

"Like bloody hell I did! It took a dozen bloody screws to get me in here, an' I belted the shit out of most of 'em before one of the bloody mongrels laid me out with a rifle butt. An' even then I bit a lump out of his bloody leg as I went down. But I tell yer what—there's not one of 'em who'll try and mess about with me now! The first bloke who came in this cell to chain me up for exercise ended upside down with his silly bloody head in the toilet. Then I made a noose out of a strip of me blanket and caught a guy's wrist as he pushed a plate of that shit they call food through the grille. Bloody near tore his arm off! They started pushing the food in with a pole after that, so I made a slingshot out of the elastic of me underpants, fixed it to the hatch and when one of the bastards bent down to poke the dinner pan through I let him have it full in the bloody mug! No-one gives me shit, pal! They get it flung straight back at 'em! Still wanna have a go in the yard tomorrow? The warders won't mind. They'll figure it's good for me to work off some of me violent hostility an' aggressions! Saves *them* gettin' hurt, too!"

For once in his life, Harry Pearce was thinking twice about another man's challenge. No wonder Sanderson and the rest out there called him The Beast, he thought. Here was a man willing to fight dirty, below the belt, all the way down the bloody line—no holds barred, no quarter given in his weird one-man guerrilla warfare against authority. And at bay, no less! Fighting from the confines of his own cell! Compared with The Beast, Harry felt like a fraterniser, almost a conspirator, on the side of the law. He felt ashamed of his own weak, mealy-mouthed submission, which is all he could call his tacit acceptance of penal discipline when you placed it alongside the courage of a man who obviously never let a second go by without some shocking show of defiance and retaliation.

What manner of man could do this? What terrible rape of society's sacred flesh had motivated this war in the first place?

"Tell me one thing!" Harry bawled through the slot in his door. "*What are you in for?*"

"Mind your own bloody business!" The Beast's voice rang back.

"Well, how long have you been in solitary?"

"Two years, eight months and twenty-eight bloody days! Six hours to go to the twenty-ninth, if you want the full drum!"

Two years, eight months and twenty-eight bloody days! And Harry Pearce was scared of cracking up after only a day over one week. What did he need with the bloody Bible? The Beast's raw, uncompromising fortitude was suddenly an inspiration to him. It would pull him through, whether bloody Murphy left him to rot or not. The only trouble was, if he went brutalising the warders and catapulting shit through his meal hatch, he'd be on the plane to Grafton before you could say Dickie Doodle.

"What do you do in here to stay bloody sane?" he called. "Apart from trying to murder people!"

"Ah, there's plenty of tricks to keep yourself occupied with if you put your mind to it," The Beast replied. "Me, I like to swim a bit when the weather's real hot. I do a bit of surfing too—but the trouble is, you only get one bloody chance at a good wave an' then you've gotta wait around a whole day for the bloody tide to come back up. You'll see! I'll be shooting a bloody boomer tomorrow!"

But Harry was sadly pressing his forehead against the cold, enamel-surfaced steel plate of his cell door. He let out a gasping, exasperated chuckle as it all dawned on him. Of course! He should have bloody known. The Beast was as nutty as a fruitcake. And so would he be, if he spent two years, eight months and twenty-eight bloody days staring at four walls and a bed with only the Holy Bible for bloody company.

Harry retrieved the good book from where it lay sprawled open on the floor, smoothed out a couple of crumpled pages and resumed his mental battle against panic.

" '*May I find your breasts like clusters of grapes on the vine,*' " he chanted, pacing the concrete floor again.

> " '*The scent of your breath like apricots*
> *and your whispers like spiced wine*
> *flowing smoothly to welcome my caresses,*
> *gliding down through lips and teeth . . .*' "

"Read that bit about clusters of dates again!" The Beast's voice sounded from the other end of the block.

twenty-two

Young Bruce Greenwood, the rookie warder, was in a terrible mental state. By day he moved about the jail in a dream, doing each of his appointed tasks with the detached response of an automaton. At night he pitched and rolled on the storm-tossed seas of nightmares in which he was constantly trying to escape dreaded terrors that pursued him—running across the quadrangle, heading desperately for Murphy's toll-road that soared up the hill and away to the freedom of the bush beyond. And Murphy would be chasing him, shooting at him with a rifle, and as the bullets cracked and whined within inches of his head he would reach the foot of the hill and start climbing; but the hill was terribly steep and he would keep losing his footing on the dry powdery mud and gravel and slide back to the bottom. Where Bull Sanderson's brawny, hairy hand would clamp like a steel band around his ankle.

With Pearce in the Blockhouse and Murphy under constant guard as he worked on the last of the cell-block murals, Greenwood should have felt relief, free at last from the evils that he had been forced to perform. He had accomplished all that Murphy had demanded of him: He had smuggled the last of the *stuff* into the jail; he had dutifully, and in the face of great danger, made a duplicate set of the keys to the weapons showcase in (Rev) Hunt's office. And he had also brought in some mysterious electronic components which had been turned over to Timothy Botham, who went to work immediately on them in his cell, thankful that he was still in one piece after inadvertently committing his best cobber, Harry Pearce, to the Blockhouse and almost blowing the entire break. So anxious was Timothy to play his role in the escape—Mrs Everingham's opulent torso now seemingly within inches of his love-starved loins—that any visitor to his cell would never have guessed that he was doing anything more suspicious than fiddling with the insides of a couple of broken transistor radios.

"I'm just like fixing a couple of guys' trannies," he boldly explained to Bull Sanderson, his big heavy-lashed brown eyes dripping with innocence, when Sanderson wandered in and demanded to know what all the wires, circuits, fuses, condensers and other paraphernalia was doing littered about his desk.

"I like fiddling about with things," he told him.

"It was fiddling about with things that got you in here in the first place," Sanderson reminded him gruffly, thankful at least that the poor little bugger was now occupying his time with something a bit more useful than soul-wrenching fantasies about Mrs Everingham's big whatsits. "Keep your nose clean, son, and you'll get on OK," he said, unable to mention at this stage that as soon as the exhibition was over, (Rev) Hunt proposed to see about getting him paroled with Noel Chisholm.

With that last task accomplished, Bruce Greenwood should have found release from his misery. Instead he found that he wasn't yet free at all. Murphy had one final chore for him. Nothing difficult. Nothing serious. Something sweet at a nut, simple as standing on his head.

"I want you to run a few messages to Harry Pearce," Murphy explained. "That means you'd best get yourself posted with the guards in the Blockhouse. You're still on probation, so tell Sanderson you're just dying to experience every bloody facet of prison duty. Act keen. Make him see that you're a dedicated little screw who wants to be a big bloody screw. Now, off you go—and try and look a bit bloody happier. You're a prison officer, not a bloody prisoner."

Mercifully for him, Greenwood had little trouble getting a three-month special attachment to the maximum-security block. It seemed that finding men brave or stupid enough to hazard a twelve-hour roster guarding The Beast was one of Sanderson's 1. .-minable administrative headaches. Getting them to stay there for any length of time after their first encounter with the two-legged monster was like trying to persuade them to leap into Sydney Harbour on a calm, sultry midsummer night carrying a bag full of fresh, blood-soaked offal marked *SHARKBAIT*.

And so it was no wonder that when Greenwood reported for duty at two-thirty in the afternoon of his first day in the Blockhouse, the three other warders manning that particular shift suggested that because he was new to the game, like, perhaps he should start getting to know the ropes as quickly as possible by going and getting The Beast and Harry Pearce out of their cells and chaining them up for their one-hour break for fresh air and exercise.

237

"Here, you'd better take this with you," said the roster chief, handing Greenwood a rifle as his mates turned away, lips twitching with silent merriment. Greenwood instinctively shrank away from the weapon. In his tension-filled, inexperienced hands it was liable to accidentally go off and shoot someone.

"It's OK," said the chief screw. "It's not loaded. We never let The Beast get his hands near anything lethal. It's just for the sake of authority, like. Let him know you're the master around here."

"If he grabs it off you, start running," one of the other warders advised him while his partner went into a pantomime of convulsions behind Greenwood's back. "Then we'll throw in some tear-gas to quieten him down."

Greenwood licked his dry lips and asked: "Can't one of you come with me? Just in case something goes wrong?"

"Listen, Bruce, if you can't handle The Beast on your own on your first day, there's no way you'll be able to hold the bastard in the future. He'll walk all over you. Then you might just as well get transferred back to normal duty."

Where Kevin Murphy would be waiting for him, Greenwood thought. And Bull Sanderson.

When he reached the blank, forbidding steel door to The Beast's lair he somehow imagined he heard a muffled hoot of laughter from the watchroom back along the narrow, ill-lit, windowless passage. He stood there, unable to make a move for a while, his sweaty hands fidgeting with the barrel of the useless gun. Listening intently at the door, he could hear nothing from the other side. All that broke the terrible, menacing silence was the dull rhythmic thud of his own heart. The silence was too real to be true. He knew The Beast was waiting for him. He wanted to turn around and run.

He heard, or he thought he heard, the gentle, lazy slap and ripple of moving water. It was ridiculous, of course. Maybe The Beast was washing up at his basin. Maybe he was taking a bath. Ha-ha-ha! He felt like screaming with laughter, only he knew he'd never stop until they got him into a strait-jacket, hurled him into a padded room and rammed the hypodermic needle home.

He sank slowly to his heels, close to the door, and tried to peek through the narrow meal hatch, but the slit was blocked up with what appeared to be soggy toilet paper. The Beast was certainly up to something. Something he didn't want anybody to see. And that threw

Greenwood into yet another dilemma. What if The Beast was trying to do harm to his person behind that locked door? What if he'd committed suicide, or was lying there on the floor at this very moment, bleeding to death from the wrists—the deadly, razor-sharp, secretly honed-down blade of a plastic dinner knife tumbling from his limp, dying fingers—while Greenwood was buggering about outside his door too scared to make a move to see what was going on?

What a naive, unmitigated dingbat Greenwood was. With a sudden surge of no-nonsense courage, he snapped to his feet, thrust his rifle forward with one hand in a position of authoritative alert and used his other hand to unlock the huge door. And as the heavy lock clicked open, all hell broke loose at once, triggered by an earsplittingly shrill cry of triumph from The Beast.

"*SURF'S UP!!!*" he shrieked, like a man who wanted half Australia's eastern seaboard to know about it; and, at the same time, colossal unseen forces hurled the door open, slamming like a speeding express train into Greenwood, who was cannoned violently back against the opposite side of the corridor and who had little more than a dazed split second in which to marvel at the horrific, immense wall of water that hung in front of him and right over him, filling the entire cell doorway, before it let loose and turned into a mammoth tumbling torrent that crashed down on him, picked him up like a rag doll and bore him savagely back down the corridor, his head breaking the surface of the maelstrom just in time to be struck painfully by the edge of a flat aluminium dinner pan that The Beast was using as a board, riding it with his chest, his arms flung back like seal's flippers and one leg bent upwards behind him in excellent body-surfing style as he rode the crest of the big boomer that he'd patiently built up overnight by tearing his toilet bowl out of the floor, blocking the meal-hatch and letting his cell fill up almost to the ceiling with water.

"*GO, GO, GO—YOU BLOODY LITTLE RIPPER!!!*" the Beast bellowed as the huge wave careened towards the locked door of the watchroom at the end of the passage. There, it hit the door with a tremendous force that exploded it upwards, shooting The Beast and Greenwood at the solid concrete ceiling, then fell away and, like a mad thing on the rampage, seeking a way of escape, tore back down the corridor towards The Beast's cell. The Beast and Greenwood were carried helplessly with it, spinning over and over down the passage until the headwater of the torrent hit them like a Bondi dumper as it returned from whence it had gone after rebounding furiously off a blank wall at the other end of the Blockhouse.

This incredible to-and-fro tidal race continued, propelling the two men with it, until the bulk of the water had poured through the meal-hatches of enough cell doors to escape the corridor and form subsidiary whirlpools that tamed the main torrent, fed off it and lowered its level inch by inch until The Beast and Greenwood finally lay sprawled against the wall in about a foot of gently heaving water, groaning and gasping; then The Beast reached over, grabbed Greenwood by the hair and hauled his head up out of the shallows, shook him a couple of times and yelled:

"You bloody cretin! I was just about to try hanging five when you got in the bloody way! Now I'll have to wait all bloody day and night to try again!"

Bruce Greenwood, his sodden hair hanging in lanks like the fur of a drowned rat, opened his eyes and stared blankly at The Beast's indignant features. Then the blankness of his face began to metamorphosize into a curious questioning frown; then it changed again into a glint of recognition, and that in itself gradually hardened and transmuted into a progression of new optical effects and facial contortions that ranged from amazement through incredulity to umbrage, then anger and rancour and acrimony and virulence, then from rage and malevolence to outright fury—and suddenly, as though a lighted match had been tossed into the fierce, igneous gases of his mind, he fulminated completely into a boiling wrath that made his hands dart, quick as lightning, at The Beast's throat, lock around it like the jaws of a rabid cattle dog and, with The Beast too stunned to fight him off, pound the blond, bearded monster's head repeatedly and without caution against the corridor wall.

"YOU EVER DO THAT AGAIN TO ME AND I'LL KILL YOU!!!" Greenwood screeched, shaking the dangerous intractible with the brute, unrestrainable impulses of a dog on a dead rabbit, his maddened hands almost crushing The Beast's jugular as he bludgeoned the wall with the man's head. Then he hurled The Beast onto his face in the receding waters, scrabbled around him until he'd found his rifle, leapt to his feet and stood over The Beast's moaning, half-conscious, half-submerged body, the rifle poised above his head, its heavy mahogany butt ready to strike like a jack-hammer should The Beast so much as wiggle a pinkie.

"Make one move and I'll flatten you!" Greenwood spat. "Get up and get against that wall! Arms up, wide apart, and right up on your toes! And you so much as move a muscle and by God I'll *beat you to death!!*"

The Beast went up the wall so fast he looked like a gekko on its way to take care of a housefly. And as he hung there, balancing like a ballet dancer on points, Greenwood sloshed his way through the water to Harry Pearce's cell, unlocked it with a swiftness and resolution that had never been associated with this shy, gentle, sensitive, post-adolescent dummy before, and as the door swung open he thrust the barrel of the rifle into the room with a speed and efficiency that would have done justice to a TV cop raiding an urban guerrilla armoury.

"What the hell's been going on out there?" Harry yelled, backing nervously away from the gun.

"Shut up, Pearce!" Greenwood raged. "Get outside and up against the wall with The Beast! And don't you bat an eyelid until I've got the cuffs and chains on you both, or I'll beat the pair of you to a pulp with this rifle!"

Out in the corridor it took Greenwood only a couple of minutes to manacle both cons, with the very subdued version of The Beast hawking and blowing blood from his nose and Harry shaking his head at the wall with surprise and bewilderment. When the job was done, Greenwood ordered them both to turn about-face. Then he pulled a waterlogged piece of folded notepaper from his breast pocket and thrust it at Pearce.

"I'll carry your messages, Pearce," he rasped, his normally frightened, shrinking eyes still blazing with manic fury. "But I'm not going to be victimised any more, and I'm not going to stand for any physical violation by this *creature!* And I want to make one thing perfectly clear! When you and Murphy and whoever else is involved finally break out of this jail, *I'm going with you!* You're not leaving me behind to be mauled by Bull Sanderson and bunged behind bloody bars myself when they start investigating how all that plastic explosive got into the jail, how this whole place is wired up through Murphy's murals to blow sky-high, how Timothy Botham's almost finished work on the electronic detonators, how Willie Crewe is shitting himself to death out there because everybody's being friendly to him, how Murphy says you're to take it easy and don't panic because the escape's ready to go right on the dot and you're better off in solitary anyway because Old Clemency's gone nutty and is running the jail like a bloody Siberian labour camp. . . ! Oh, and also how Noel Chisholm's finally pulled his finger out and finished the title of the play, so everything's apples now and all we need is the exhibition to kick it all off!"

Greenwood gestured furiously at the soggy note that hung limply from Harry Pearce's fingers. "It's all in there! Read it! And don't forget what I said. I go with you. I'm gonna be your hostage, to cover myself from Sanderson and the law afterwards. I'm not spending the rest of my bloody life under suspicion for helping a jail-break. It's either that or, I swear it, you won't poke your nose outside solitary again!"

twenty-three

THE DAY OF THE (REV) CLEMENT C. HUNT Arts and Crafts Society Exhibition looked like being a bloody stinker. From the moment the sun blazed up over the horizon, the City of Parramatta began to boil in a heavy, flyblown, humid heat that melted the asphalt surface of Church Street and made the tyres of the dense morning traffic go *tack-a-tack-a-tack-a-tack* as it snarled and jostled its way through the inferno.

There is nothing that adequately describes the stifling summer heat of Parramatta and Sydney's western suburbs. Until the mid-afternoon sea breeze chooses whether or not to sweep in from Sydney Harbour, nosing its way along the crests and ridges of the North Shore, then funnelling down into the west through Dundas Valley, or until a thunderstorm breaks, Parramatta and its flat, spiritless, lower-middle-class suburbia suffers a deadening heat—rows of garish plastic flags and bunting hanging limp and lifeless over parades of baking chrome and duco in the rows of used-car lots along the major roads; the heavy air shrieking with cicadas; the whole brutal atmosphere an imprisonment in itself, locked into this vast suburban bowl by the high-rise undulations of the City of Sydney on the coastal front, and the Blue Mountains to the west.

The heat was even worse within the stone walls of Parramatta Jail. It blasted, with a dizzying ferocity, at the backs of the necks of the entire prison population, minus two, as they stood muster in neat rows in the quadrangle, sweating like hell in their clean, crisp, special-issue fatigues, suffering a last-minute pep talk by the man whose very name could be synonymous with prison reform from that day forth.

It belted the insides out of Noel Chisholm, the world's greatest living playwright, who, having finally completed his masterpiece, having been virtually hermitaged in his cell for the previous two weeks, only once stepping foot outside, decided the time had come to get out and take the airs on the birth of this most memorable day. After an alcoholic heart-starter that very nearly felled him like a poleaxed steer, Chisholm washed, shaved and toppled into his clean, starched fatigues, did a few discreet knee-bends to test his legs, and when they failed to buckle and cast him to the floor he made his way out of the cell block to join the muster, whistling, "Oh, What a Beautiful Morning."

As he sallied forth onto the quadrangle, a number of surprises shattered his delicate composure. First, he thought he'd done an Alice in Wonderland, stumbling mirror-wise into some evil fantasy that lurked at the back of his pickled mind.

"What happened to the fucking prison?" he wondered aloud, seeking support from the nearest wall as he gazed uncomprehendingly at the familiar prison installations, the cell blocks, exercise area, Blockhouse, administration building and main gate, and the paraded ranks of uniformed cons—all suddenly set down in the middle of the colonial era. What the fuck was that bullock track doing there, and all that bushland, and that mansion nestling into the landscaped hill, and that township with its buggies, parasoled ladies and a doggie taking a pee? And that church, with its wide pebbled driveway?

The the heat hit him. And it occurred to him, as his crippled lungs fought for air in the furnace-blast, that he may well have succumbed in his sleep overnight and gone to Hell. It didn't amaze him at all to find that Hell looked surprisingly like his native homeland. Then he heard voices, or rather a drifting excerpt from (Rev) Clement C. Hunt's pre-exhibition speech.

"I need not remind any one of you, I'm sure, that among the important visitors to this institution will be the Honourable Minister for Corrective Services and the Mayor of this historic city, whose impressions here today will have a strong and definite bearing on the future of every man gathered here now. In other words, any man who steps out of line today will regret it later when the Parole Board meets."

Chisholm, feeling a bitter nausea take possession of him, staggered back to his cell to fortify himself with another fuming belt of brain-mash. And as he reached his cell doorway, who should just happen to be slinking out—casting his reptilian gaze back and forth the way a snake instinctively searches its terrain for danger—but Henry Trembler. And Henry nearly jumped out of his skin with fright. He'd just made a swift, sneaky, unsuccessful search of Chisholm's cell for that two thousand dollars he'd seen on the playwright's work-desk.

"Good God!" he exclaimed, thrusting a hand to his skinny bosom with a theatrical flourish to calm his leaping heart. "You scared the living daylights out of me."

Chisholm, his own constitution still in a painful state of disorientation, brushed past the flushed pervert and rummaged under his bed for a bottle of instant escape. This he whipped to his mouth with the speed of a canvas water-bag to a thirsting man's lips in the middle of the Birdsville Track, then began coughing and kicking the hell out of the legs of his desk.

"*Hollllllly ber-luddddddddddy hellllllll!*" He gasped, making desperate gulping gestures as his eyes brimmed with tears and appeared almost to hiss with white steam like a laundryman's press. After doing a perfect mime of a barefooted beachgoer on a broken beer bottle, he managed to regain his lost voice. "What, may I ask, were you doing nosing about in my bloody room?"

Henry pouted, then pursed his thin lips and executed a little flounce. It was a bizarre gesture, not to say ugly and obscene. "Is that all the thanks I get for coming here to wish you the best of luck for your great event this afternoon?" he whined.

"I apologise," Chisholm said with great magnanimity, up-ending the bottle again and then biting savagely at the air around him. "I thank you," he gasped. "But I fear your kind wishes and felicitations may be a bit bloody premature. It won't be a piece of cake, getting out of here."

Henry drew breath, very quickly, as though the firm hand of the law had reached out and grabbed him unawares in the end cubicle of a public lavatory. "Out of where, Noel?" he asked, very matter-of-factly.

"Out of this bloody prison. Where else?"

"Here, let me get you a glass," said Henry, grabbing one quickly from a rack over Chisholm's wash-basin. "It must tire you out, drinking straight from the bottle."

"I've never actually sat down and thought about that," Chisholm confessed, allowing himself to be bent into a sitting position on the bed. Henry poured him a super-wallop of the liquid propellant and rammed it into his hand.

"Cheers! *Get it into your black guts*, as my father used to say when he partook of alcoholic beverages. Which was quite often. He was a man of merry wit and much joviality. Another of his classic exclamations was *If I catch you hanging around with girls I'll bloody well skin you alive!* I couldn't have been more than five at the time. So you reckon you'll be out of this place this afternoon, eh, Noel?"

Chisholm was still engulfed in the after-burn of yet another fireball. When his feet had stopped beating a tattoo on the floor he said: "Maybe drinking straight from the bottle does indeed sap you—over a very prolonged period of time. All that weight on the wrists and biceps. Not to say the neck, shoulders and spine. And from thence, the entire nervous system. Which in turn is rendered so exhausted that it cannot adequately cope with massive ingestions of alcohol—and thus the victim is liable to get as pissed as a parrot on his first couple of gulps." Chisholm raised a half-glass of his deadly mixture and idly watched the chemicals swirl and undergo various scientific experiments. "Maybe this phenomenon should be the subject of a nation-wide study," he mused. "I have always maintained, in the face of fierce resistance, that I'm not really an alcoholic."

"Of course you're not," Trembler agreed, topping up the play-wright's glass.

"Here's looking at you," said Chisholm, one eye fixed on the ceiling and the other gazing at the floor. "Join me," he invited, thrusting the glass at Henry.

"Just a sip," said Henry, and he raised the glass. "Well, here's to

245

the escape, Noel, old friend!" And while he managed to touch the glass to his lips and pretend to take a sip, the evil fumes made his stomach roll violently.

"Who told you about the escape?" Chisholm demanded. "You weren't supposed to know."

"Of course I know," said Henry. "Just think, in another eight hours we'll all be out of here. I suppose the whole business will go off on schedule, during your play."

"If you know all about it you don't need me to explain all the details," Chisholm replied bluntly, reminding himself to warn Murphy about keeping his bloody trap shut and not broadcasting the scheme all over the bloody jail.

But Henry Trembler now knew enough to convince him that the opportunity had come to finally begin realising the crowning ambition of his sordid life. Henry was bored. Life in jail, for all its depraved pleasures, was rapidly becoming a supreme pain in the rear end. With Willie Crewe swiftly degenerating from the exquisite sadist that he had been to the lily-livered paranoid that personified him now—clinging for his miserable life to Bull Sanderson—Henry knew it was time to go it alone. And this time, by Christ, the civilised world was going to tremble at his flat, smelly feet. And terrible would be the fear with which the people would ultimately hurl themselves to their knees, grovelling on their bellies, to proclaim him King of All Evil—Satan by any other name.

No more pantie-raids. None of this small-time, demeaning mass rape. The time had come, Henry had decided, to strike at the soft, throbbing heart of the entire Sydney metropolitan area and its encompassing environs. He could see it all now. During long lonely nights of fetid dreams he had mentally composed a complete Sydney tabloid front page that would shriek, in poster type normally reserved for a Gough Whitlam gaffe, *SATAN STRIKES AGAIN*—followed by a four-deck screaming subhead in 84-point bold upper-lower: *Sobbing Mum (19) Tells of Sex Terror Night Horror*. Next to the subhead, under the paper's floating masthead, there'd be a deep three-column picture of the sobbing young victim trying to shield her identity from the merciless photographers as she left the police station, and under that, running along the entire bottom gully of the page, there'd be a stark 48-point fifty-percent reverse arrow-shaped heading, directing the reader's revolted, avid interest to the details on page two and hollering: *Rapist Wore Mask, Cape, Desert Boots*.

246

He'd make The Prowler look like an outlawed chicken-thief. Compared with him, the Kingsgrove Slasher would be remembered as a slightly psychopathic nuisance. Even the Dirty Digger from Down Under would have to acknowledge that his leader writers had finally met their match. But to accomplish all this, Henry needed money. His costumes and various artificial devices alone would cost a small fortune. And his sophisticated animal senses told him that two thousand bucks was still stashed away somewhere in Chisholm's cell.

"Well, here's to life on the outside, Noel," he crowed, pretending to take another drink and feigning casual abandon. "I hope all that money of yours is safe. You'll need it out there. Prices have risen like a rat up a bloody drainpipe over the past couple of years, I've heard."

"It's safe enough," Chisholm assured him; and his next response, an automatic quick glance at the pillow of his bed, told Trembler everything he wanted to know. Right. You little beaut. He would be back.

Dickie King, the aboriginal guerrilla leader, also knew something was going to happen that afternoon. Not an escape—nothing as piddling as that. Dickie was planning a massacre. Along with outright revolution. Escape was the last thing on his mind because he was perfectly willing to die along with his intended victims, and quite confident that he would actually be killed. For one thing, he lacked artillery.

But Dickie had been making a knife out of a long flat bar of mild steel and a file that had long since disappeared from the inventory of (Rev) Clement C. Hunt's prison workshop scheme. And he was quite a knife-maker. The result of his secret toil was horrible to look at. When the light hit it, its wicked flash burned right into the brain. It could fall gently through yards of raw silk, or split a strand of fine hair. It could also, Dickie considered, carve up a few white trash, or bronze trash if you really wanted to get prejudiced about it, at some artfully contrived point during Chisholm's honky play. Dickie considered that the play represented the deepest, most crass white racism because he was the only black in it, and all the rest were whites. And that's also why he was certain he wouldn't survive this, the birth of the aboriginal revolution. But nevertheless, he would light the spark, and maybe those fighting in the future would remember it was Dickie King who was the first one to start making 'em shit—like, *really shit!*

Dickie would proclaim the revolution and its aims in a written testament which thanked (Rev) Hunt for "opening my eyes to the real plight of my people" and which would be discovered in his cell after Hunt, the Minister, the Mayor and an inestimable number of other people had been put to death in a bloodbath that would symbolise the rise of Australian Black Power. (Rev) Hunt would be the first to get it, Dickie had vowed, because he could now see as plain as the light of day that one of the fundamental plights of his people was that they were always getting fucked-on by phoney Christians.

Dickie considered that violence was the only real option left. The aboriginal leadership had tried to achieve at least a dialogue, and had failed because it wasn't articulate enough to win the arguments. Dickie King himself wasn't articulate enough to put it into those exact words—he could only draw rage from a strong emotional feeling that while Charlie Perkins, the chieftain of aboriginal militancy, had bravely illuminated the hopeless squalor of aboriginal life with his "Freedom Rides" into northern New South Wales and Queensland in the sixties, it was a different Charlie Perkins who tried to cope with the next step, the open dialogue with the whites.

Shit, Charlie had talked all right, and he knew what he wanted to say, but time after time Dickie had watched him on TV struggling with a vision and a *reason* that stood out like a spare prick at a bloody wedding, then collapsing into blind dogma and raw anger and frustration while some friendly, smiling fat-cat cunt of a politician or businessman or disguised racist whipped his arse with a silver tongue and a heap of condescending bullshit, making him look like a bloody moron—which everybody reckoned the boongs must be because how come they couldn't discuss anything rationally without getting rude and uncouth?

So Dickie's testament boiled down to one simple thing: No more dialogue. Make 'em shit instead, and then let *them* do all the talking. And if Dickie could get his razor-sharp knife into enough honky guts that afternoon, before they gunned him down and kicked him all over the jail, they'd be talking about this day as the day the boongs stopped swilling booze and started hitting back.

Dickie wrapped the knife's terrible blade in a handtowel, sheathed the weapon in his left sock and used a strip of bedsheet to tie the hilt snugly to his calf.

It just so happened that at that very moment Harry Pearce was arming himself too. But Harry wasn't buggering about with knives. Harry was packing a veritable cannon—a .45 Colt automatic service pistol that had enough punch, at close-to-medium range, in its fat snub-nosed bullets to blow a bloke's head off; or a leg, if it happened to be his lucky day. Harry prayed that he'd never have to use it. His knowledge and experience of guns was such that he had a novice's immediate and lingering fear that he was sure as bloody hell going to trip over his own feet, or sneeze at a critical moment, and accidentally blow a hole in himself.

Bruce Greenwood wasn't too happy about the gun either, despite the fact that it was he who had smuggled it into the Blockhouse, along with three loaded spare clips, and had just delivered it to Pearce in his cell. Bruce kept well away from the thing, out of its line of fire, as Harry gingerly checked the safety catch, re-checked it and then checked it again, and, though still not entirely satisfied that it would not just blow up of its own accord, stuffed it into the waistband of his prison strides.

"What's Murphy trying to do? Start a bloody war?"

"You'll need it," Greenwood told him. "The whole escape hinges on you breaking out of the Blockhouse at exercise time, getting through to Hunt's office and grabbing those guns and then busting in on Chisholm's play at the right moment."

"I didn't know it was that simple," said Harry with a cynical grin. "So while everybody's in the auditorium stuffing their mugs with popcorn and yelling *'Oh yes you will!'* I'll be fighting a running bloody gunbattle outside with most of the guards."

"You won't be fighting anybody," Greenwood assured him. "You'll have me with you—as your hostage, remember? All we have to do is to make it clear that my innocent, dedicated young life is on the line, and there'll be no trouble. But for God's sake, Pearce, promise me you'll handle that gun carefully. My part of the deal is that I get out of here alive."

Harry said: "The more I think about this lame-brained scheme, the more I wonder if any of us will get out of here in one bloody piece. OK—what's the right moment in the play when I'm supposed to burst in and blow a hole in my bloody foot or something?"

"It's all been carefully timed," Greenwood explained, none too confidently. "The play starts at two o'clock. Exercise is at two-thirty.

You'll have half an hour to take me hostage, break out of here, collect the guns and make it to the auditorium. At three o'clock precisely, Judge Payten will be saying to the prisoner: 'It is the sentence of this court that you be taken immediately from these premises to a place outside, and thence put to death by musket squad as an example to others of your foul, lawless breed. God Save the Queen.' At that moment, you're to break into the play, holding the gun at my head, and shout: 'Don't anybody fucking move!' "

"Couldn't we leave out the fucking?"

"It's Murphy's idea."

Harry sighed. "Yeah, I might've known it. I suppose anything could happen this time."

"Not if you keep your cool." Greenwood gestured at the bulky brown-paper parcel on Pearce's bed—another item that he'd smuggled past his colleagues in the watchroom. "Remember that you'll be wearing that outfit. You'll look so ridiculous that, for one thing, you'll have a strong element of surprise on your side."

Harry sighed again. "Maybe I should stay in here and serve those fourteen bloody years after all."

"You won't be here. You'll be in Grafton. Besides, there's no going back now."

"What about The Beast?"

"I'll take care of him. He's too dangerous to take along with us. He'd probably go murderously berserk and ruin the whole scheme."

Harry sat down on his cot and looked intently at the rookie warder. "Tell me one thing—and no bullshit, *please*. What did that bugger *do*?"

"He spat in Sanderson's eye."

"Yeah, but before that?"

"He beat up a warder in Grafton after catching him with that surfing routine. He nearly permanently maimed him, from what I hear—and that wasn't the first time. The superintendent had him transferred out of there to avoid the possibility of his men committing an official murder."

"How did he get sent to Grafton?"

"By setting fire to the solitary block at Bathurst. Before that he organised a riot in Long Bay, and before that he hung a guard by his heels from a tree at Emu Plains—then started a bushfire around him."

"For Christ's sake," said Harry, "just cut out the details and tell me—what did he *do?*"

"I don't know," Greenwood confessed. "Nobody ever talks about it. All I know is that it must have been something absolutely reprehensible."

"It must have been something bloody evil too," Harry observed.

But Harry's anxiety about The Beast was just a minor, niggling matter compared with the seething paranoia that by now had engulfed the psychotic mind of Parramatta Jail's most popular man of the year, Willie Crewe. Mind you, Willie had good reason to feel threatened. By anyone's standards it was difficult to reconcile his notoriety as a violent killer, thug, bully, sado-sexual beast of prey and, worst of all, a prison stoolie, with the overt, unashamed love and admiration that every con in the joint was now coddling him with. Not only that, but he had been persuaded, firmly and with jollity and good cheer, to take up an important role in Noel Chisholm's play. And that made him feel even worse.

"The bastards are up to something, I know they are," Willie whined as he accompanied Bull Sanderson that morning on a last-minute security tour of the jail.

"Now how can you honestly say that, Willie?" Sanderson replied, enjoying every minute of the snivelling ratbag's agony. "All I can see is a lot of nice friendly blokes falling arse-over-bloody-tit to be your best mate. Wouldn't you like to have friends like all the other little boys?"

"Who needs fucking friends?" said sweet little Willie. "They're only trying to suck me in so they can beat the shit out of me. They're always trying that. They're so fucking stupid they don't know I'm a bloody wake-up to it all. Nobody fools me, mate. I can handle any of 'em with one hand tied behind me bloody back. My old man was a champion boxer. He would-a won the Australian welterweight title if he hadn't got into that bloody brawl before the fight. I don't need him anyway. I can fight my own bloody battles."

"Of course you can, Willie," said Bull Sanderson. "Get 'em before they get you, right?"

"Bloody oath. Those bastards think they're so fucking smart, but I can see right through 'em, you betcha fucking life I can."

"That's the shot," said Sanderson, wishing he had the same miraculous powers. The hairs on his thick neck were still bristling with suspicion. Something was going to happen that afternoon. He could feel it in his bones. The whole bloody prison was too friendly, too relaxed, too cooperative for a bunch of cons about to be put up on show as a shining example of what society could achieve with its bloody outlaws and misfits. A bit of cynicism would have restored his confidence. A touch of naked vehemence against Willie Crewe would have reassured him that all was normal around him. As it was, even Timothy Botham—having already witnessed the darker side of Willie's confused personality—was an absolute bloody picture of sweetness and light when Sanderson and Crewe checked him in his cell.

"Hullo, Willie," Timothy said gaily, busily polishing up his silver-plated harmonica. "I took a squizz at you at rehearsals yesterday. Jeez, I didn't know you was like such a good actor."

Willie immediately went on the defensive. "What d'you mean by that? Got something to say, feller? Like to try yer luck outside?"

Timothy breathed on his harmonica and rubbed at a tiny speck of tarnish. "Naw, I wouldn't wanna tangle with a nice bloke like you, Willie. I'd rather be your pal. Like all the other blokes in here."

"Any time, pal," Willie gnashed. "Just say the bloody word. I'm ready for yer. An' that goes for any other bastard who fancies his chances."

Timothy fluttered his soft brown eyes guilelessly at Sanderson, and Sanderson felt an inbuilt siren begin to whine somewhere in the far reaches of his mind. For the first time in his career he sensed that he was helpless in the face of an obvious but unfathomable crisis. He sensed that something shattering was about to happen. It couldn't be something as simple as a break because he'd put paid to all that by separating Murphy and Pearce, and he'd made sure that the security arrangements for that day were such that a Sherman tank with supporting infantry couldn't have busted out of the place. With extra men around the walls and armed guards at all points inside—there would even be an armed detachment in the auditorium during Chisholm's play—Sanderson was convinced that a break was out of the question. So convinced was he of this that he'd not so much as batted an eyelid earlier that morning when he and (Rev) Hunt had gone over the security arrangements for the day in Hunt's office, and Hunt, himself satisfied that the jail was sealed up as tight as a drum, had glanced coolly at Sanderson for a moment, then said: "You are aware, of course, that if anything untoward happens today, I'm finished. And that means you're finished too."

"You don't have to tell me that, Mr Hunt," Sanderson had said confidently; and now he was wishing to God he could put his finger on the undefinable misgivings that were bugging him. Sensing danger even in Timothy Botham's bland, innocent demeanour, he found himself wishing for the first time in his career that he was right out of this bloody mess—out of the jail and out of the Corrective Services Department altogether. And with a shock that could have floored him, he even saw himself for a tiny split second of sheer insanity tooling a souped-up Falcon up the Pacific Highway towards Tweed Heads with Monique, or Monica, or whatever her bloody name was, chatting away sixteen to the dozen beside him. He mentally shook himself back to reality and gestured at Timothy's harmonica.

"Hasn't somebody trod on that bloody thing yet?"

"I don't let it out of my sight, Mr Sanderson," said Timothy. "It's precious to me. I helped me when I thought there was like no hope left, when my whole life was like plunged into darkness and I never thought I'd like see the light of free—, uh, a friendly face again."

Sanderson said in a very ironic tone: "What, are you planning a jailbreak?"

Timothy nearly shat himself on the spot, so stunned was he by Sanderson's casual, cordial, friendly, totally stupid crack. His harmonica nearly spun from his hands. He lost his breath, then felt a terrible red-hot dead-giveaway blush break out on his neck and climb rapidly up his face, making what seemed to him to be a hell of a lot of noise. He felt Sanderson's relaxed, amused aura begin to wane slightly. With tremendous effort he forced himself to meet the towering prison boss's gaze, then lifted the harmonica towards his cherubic lips.

"I learnt a couple of new tunes the other day. Would you like to hear them?"

"We'd love to," said Sanderson, suddenly in a hurry to leave. "But wait till we're down the other end of the block, will you?"

Left on his own, Timothy took a little while to fully recover. Then the excitement of this, the most beaut day of his young life, gradually flooded back into him. He was to smash his way to freedom that very afternoon. That much he was sure about. Just *how* he was going to accomplish it was still a complete mystery to him—Murphy's condition for letting him back into the scheme after Pearce's nabbing was that he relinquish all rights to the essential details of the plan "or the last time you saw Mrs Whatsit's boobs will be the last time you'll ever bloody well see them. Got it?"

Timothy had got it all right. He'd got it bad—worse than ever. He'd just written a note to his Mum, which, if it ever actually fell into her hands, would kill her stone dead on the spot.

Dear Mum, it read. *I know you must be disappointed in me, since I busted out of here and like there was that big gunbattle as we went over the wall and now I'm a wanted criminal with a price on my head. But if we killed anybody, you know, like a warder or a policeman or an innocent bystander, I want you to know that I didn't do it on purpose. It had to be done. It was like kill or be killed. I just wanted you to know I wouldn't have done it like in real life. By now you would have read about the kidnapping. Don't believe what they say, Mum. Mrs Everingham eloped with me of her own accord, and her stupid fat bastard of a husband wouldn't have been bashed up like that if he'd listened to us when we said we was deeply in love and wished to be married. You must have already read about that too. I had to like threaten to shoot the vicar and his wife so we could get it all done nice and legal. Muriel and I are now hiding out from the cops, waiting for the crash of rifle butts on the door, like, but I want you to know we are happy together and when the coast is like clear we'll come and visit you with the baby.*

Your loving son,
Timothy.

Timothy didn't know it at the time, but the letter would never reach his Mum. And neither would he see Mrs Everingham or her boobs again.

twenty-four

THE HONOURABLE WILLIAM LANCELOT PUFFIN, MEMBER of the Legislative Assembly and Minister of Corrective Services, Government of New South Wales, was a fat little roly-poly man who was so incompetent and inept at any given thing he turned his pudgy hands to that he compensated for it with a corresponding amount of bluff and bluster. That's why he was more popularly known throughout the state's political machine as Puffin Billy. His wife, however, was something else. At forty-five, against her husband's sixty-two, she was blonde, suntanned, exquisitely dressed on all occasions, particularly in bed, and was possessed of a tall, statuesque, well-stacked body that looked as though it had just glided down the false marble staircase of a Folies Bergère revue. In feathers, sequins and balloons.

A former Miss Australia whose candidacy and inevitable triumph had raised record sums for charity, she had climaxed her year of round-the-world publicity junkets and Australian Wool Board fashion appearances atop a pedestal of public admiration from which she could take her pick of Australia's entire population of eligible males. She chose Puffin Billy because she recognised that he was ambitious, potentially wealthy, headed for power once the Liberals got back in, stupid, unattractive to other women, hopelessly in love with her stunning body—and therefore wouldn't give her any trouble. Like most Miss Australias who'd risen from a discreet girlie snap in *The Sydney Morning Herald*—listing her interests and hobbies as swimming, tennis, music, modern literature and Tupperware parties—to society's top drawer, she abhorred trouble. And she abhorred trouble because, had her interests and hobbies been listed now, they would have read something like swimming, tennis, music, modern literature and being fucked rigid by young men, preferably around eighteen to twenty, with lithe, footie-strengthened bodies and associated attributes hitherto untouched by other female hands.

But trouble has a way of tipping itself on anyone, even former Miss Australias. And Puffin Billy and his good lady, Celia, were up to their necks in it as their black Daimler with a two-man police motorcycle escort cruised lazily through the boiling smog of heat and carbon monoxide and the road of semis and prime movers on Parramatta Road, edging towards a blaze of used-car yard banners that formed the outer fringes of the suburban city.

The trouble, on that particular day, was that Billy Puffin's political career was on the skids. And that in turn meant that Celia's secret life, a maelstrom of hot throbbing pricks and taut, teenage tummies, could soon no longer be afforded. And the thought of that threw her into little fits of pique that were never, of course, seen or heard in public, unless there were witnesses accomplished enough to lip-read Celia's poised, regal, obviously cultured small-talk through the Polaroid anti-glare windows of the Daimler as it swished past.

"You fat useless bloody little worm," she happened to be saying to the Honourable William, glancing idly at the tight uniformed buttocks of a PMG telegram boy on a pushbike as the Daimler wheeled at a set of lights and nosed its way into the city's main thoroughfare, Church Street. "You so much as make one fucking blue this afternoon and I'm going to shoot through with the first attractive piece of male arse that I see."

Billy squirmed and snorted through his nose—a sound that usually preceded a bit of bluster. "Really, my dear," he protested. "You must do something about your language. You are, after all, the wife of a Government Minister, even if you do behave like a randy Neopolitan street slut in private."

"Up yours for the rent," Celia riposted, hardly moving her soft, beautiful lips. She smiled warmly at a bunch of inquisitive housewives crossing in front of them as the Daimler waited at a second set of lights. "This time next week you won't be a Government Minister anymore, you fuckwit. You'll be stuck in the back benches shitting housebricks about the next bloody election. And Jesus Christ!—I hope it bloody hurts. *I hope it tears you to pieces!*"

Billy unhesitatingly switched his defence to pure bluff. "If I go, you go too, my love. Remember that. Then you won't be living in a mock-Georgian stately home in Pymble, gorging your disgusting desires on North Shore grammar-school boys, you'll be stuck in a Housing Commission slum in Blacktown trying to fellate some sweaty yobbo fitter-and-turner with skidmarks on his underpants."

"Screw you," said Celia, nonetheless frightened and revolted at the idea. If anything, she preferred her boys to have good clean top-pocket blue blood in their veins. "We wouldn't be in this damn mess if you didn't stick both your big feet in your stupid mug every time you open it."

It was painfully true that the Honourable William had the knack of executing a standing, static jump into his own mouth almost every time it emitted verbal sounds. And it was also true to say that Billy suffered from chronic verbal diarrhoea, along with another little eccentricity in which he constantly added new sounds to his spluttering vocabulary and either insisted on mispronouncing them or maintained absolutely no bloody idea in the world what they really meant. For example, just a week earlier he had sat down in the guest talent's chair, sweating through his greasy makeup, for a live interview on the ABC-TV current affairs programme, "This Day Tonight." "How can you honestly call for stiffer jail sentences," the interviewer asked, "when our jails are already overcrowded and most of them are little more than relics of the Victorian era?"

Billy blinked, shifted his fat backside about in his chair, then snorted through his whiskey-flushed nose.

"We'll build new jails," he blustered. "My Government and my Department stand firm on their proud record in the field of law and order, and the mandate that has been handed to us by the people of this Great State to strike at crime at its very source—cutting it off the way you would lop a sick branch from a healthy tree. Instead of pandering to crime with namby-pamby so-called progressive reforms that bear little relation to the realities we so vividly read about in our daily newspapers, I think I can say quite categorically and without fear of contradiction that the only real deterrent is *incasteration.*"

Now it was the interviewer's turn to blink. "You mean *incarceration*, of course."

Billy, nervous as hell, returned a fusillade of pure bluff. "Young man, I mean exactly what I just said. Nothing more, nothing less. And I will not have words put into my mouth in any attempt on your part to create cheap sensationalism."

"Let me get this clear, Mr Minister," said the interviewer, unable to believe his luck. "Are you in fact referring to a *surgical operation?*"

Billy plunged both feet right into it. "If that's the way you'd like to so bluntly put it—yes. A surgical operation would, I believe, be the correct analogy. Cutting away the diseased tissue of crime would be another way of saying the same thing. Now, I know that fighting fire with fire may seem to be socially repugnant to some in this enlightened age, but the shocking statistics speak for themselves, and, however reluctantly, we must face the fact that *incasteration* is the only answer. *Remove them*. Put them away. There's no punishment more abhorrent to the average Australian than to have his basic rights and liberties cut off."

By the time the Honourable William strutted off the set at the end of that historic interview, his political career was already on its way downhill with the speed of a runaway semi on the Hume Highway's dreaded Razorback. Even the Liberals could no longer shelter a moron like him in their front ranks.

So, as the Daimler pulled up at the massive steel gates of Parramatta Jail, where the Honourable Puffins could see (Rev) Hunt, Bull Sanderson and the Mayor of Parramatta, bedecked in his chain of office, waiting to greet them, Celia made sure that Billy fully understood the dangers that faced him that afternoon.

"Keep your stupid trap shut for once, and maybe we can ride this one out. But I warn you—you come a cropper once more and you won't see my delectable arse for dust. I've got a few friends in Canberra who're just itching to get into my pants. And I tell you—at least those Federal jokers appreciate a bit of fucking class."

The door next to her was wrenched open and out she sailed into the blistering heat, one slender white-gloved hand adjusting the wide, sweeping rim of her expensive powder-blue Pierre Cardin hat and the other thrust toward the Mayor with a condescending limp-wrist action as though she expected him to kiss her ring.

"My dear Mr Mayor," she purred. "We do hope we haven't kept you waiting too long."

"Not at all, my dear lady," the Mayor assured her, his insignia rattling violently like a chain on an abattoir's slaughterline as he executed a pompous, self-conscious little bow. "I trust the journey was not too tiring?"

"Not at all—we have air-conditioning in the Daimler, you know. We were quite delighted by the begonias in bloom along the way. It must almost be time for our native wattle to begin breaking out too. Not to say the kangaroo paws, waratah and gladioli. My husband and I are quite passionate about the preservation of our natural environment, as you may well know from his many speeches in

Parliament—within realistic bounds, of course. A great industrial nation like ours must also have its factories and oil refineries."

"Quite. Quite. My sentiments entirely," the Mayor oozed. "Ah, Mr Minister. How nice to see you again. You do us a great honour indeed by visiting us today."

"How do you do," the Honourable William replied, shaking hands. Then he feel silent, awaiting his wife's next cue, standing there like a fat overfed shag on a bloody rock. It was the Mayor who finally brought the paralysed tableau back to life.

"I'd like you both to meet the men who have made today's historic event possible—the Reverend Clement C. Hunt, superintendent of this fine institution, and Mr Arnold Sanderson, the chief prison officer."

"Charmed," said Celia, shaking (Rev) Hunt's hand and then slipping her long delicate fingers into Bull Sanderson's huge paw. "This must be a memorable day for you both."

"Indeed it is," said (Rev) Hunt. "A very proud moment indeed."

"It certainly is," Sanderson agreed, unable to restrain his gaze as it nipped right down into Celia's ravishing lace-trimmed cleavage with the speed of a rabbit down a burrow. He then shook Puffin Billy's fat little claw and found himself wondering what the hell the world was coming to these days. Maybe she had a father complex or something.

"My, you're certainly a very powerful-looking man, Mr Sanderson," said Celia, flirtatiously fluttering her eyelashes at him. "But then, I'd imagine that a man responsible for maintaining control in a jail full of dangerous criminals wouldn't last very long if he was short, fat and *spineless*."

"Too right," Sanderson agreed. "You've no idea what some of those buggers . . . er, ahem, well, I mean . . ."

With the Mayor and (Rev) Hunt looking daggers at him, Sanderson's mortified features broke into a horrible sweaty flush. But Celia responded to the *faux pas* awfully well: She cast her eyes shyly to the ground, blushed a little, then recovered her composure and let out a little peal of laughter.

"Come, Mr Sanderson," she chimed. "Being the wife of a politician isn't exactly what one would call a sheltered existence. You'd be surprised what I hear sometimes when the Minister is having one of his backroom sessions with his colleagues."

They all blew the tension away with a good laugh, and then Celia hooked her slim, suntanned arm around Sanderson's brawny bicep and said: "Well now—shall we venture inside and see how all your naughty boys are bearing up to their *incasteration?*"

twenty-five

THE BOYS WERE NOT BEARING UP TOO well, considering the itchy, sweaty, writhing frustrations that overcame them the moment Celia Puffin's incredible body swanned into view. Willie Crewe was already somewhat detached from his work with paranoia as he sewed his felt patterns together in the now-flourishing soft-toy department of (Rev) Hunt's creative labour camp. When he took a look at Celia's magnificent torso and long flanks garbed in a low-cut, lace-trimmed, knee-length pink chiffony diaphanous thing that masqueraded as a dress, he rammed his needle deep into one of his fingers. And while he was sucking furiously on it and cursing like a trooper under his breath, Henry Trembler, stuffing bunnies and duckies close by, caught sight of Celia himself and let out a long low whinny of agony and desire like a young colt encountering a brood of sexually inflamed mares.

Arthur Hancock, the old trusty, though not a day under sixty and long since released from man's baser desires, looked at Celia and calmly bent back to his work. Then he thumped his hand violently on the table, lifted it to his mouth and savagely bit it. Lyle Walker looked up, saw Celia bend over to take a close look at Timothy Botham's sewing circle, saw two breasts hanging like overripe mangoes, their tips only lightly kissed by the creamy satin of her flimsy bra, and he lay his head gently on his hands on the workbench and began to pray: "*Oh Lord, Sweet Jesus, Holy Christ in Heaven . . .*"

Dickie King, watching from the other side of the room, took a long lingering look at the soft spreading swell of Celia's beautiful buttocks against the pink chiffon and a terrible primeval lust rose up out of the deepest sludge of his mind like an ugly bunyip from the depths of a dark, misty, outback billabong. And, mentally, he added a new clause to his revolutionary testament: *White women are not to be harmed, but are to be treated with respect, if they agree to be fucked. If they don't, fuck 'em anyway.* Watching Celia's lovely bum, Dickie deeply regretted that he would not be around to enjoy it and other bums like it after he'd lit the first fires of insurrection. But then he took solace in the face that he'd definitely slip this honky chick a few inches before the cops and guards busted in on the scene of his bloodbath and made an aboriginal martyr of him.

And that left Timothy Botham to glance innocently up from his work to see what the sudden electrifying hush was all about and find Celia Puffin bending towards him, right over his desk, her pink lace-trimmed bodice sagging open and her breasts hanging like overripe Christ why go into all that again, her eyes meeting his with a smouldering, beckoning greed that scared the living daylights out of him and gave him a massive erection of such painful dimensions that when she offered her hand and said: "Hello. And who might you be?" he suffered the added agony of snagging it against the underside of the bench, so swiftly did he leap up to shake her hand.

Eyes watering slightly with pain, he replied: "I'm Timothy Botham, er, miss, madam, like ma'am."

"You look very young to be in prison, Timothy."

"My Mum always said I was like big for my age."

"Your Mum was quite right." Celia drew breath so deeply that Timothy experienced a wild moment of imagination in which he was being drawn bodily towards her luscious mouth. He glimpsed the strained, smiling features of Bull Sanderson, (Rev) Hunt and some little fat prick he didn't know hovering behind her, and blushed a red that was the colour of tomato ketchup.

Celia said: "What on earth is a nice clean good-looking young man like you doing in jail?"

"Burglary," Timothy informed her. "With other offences."

"Other offences?"

Timothy swallowed and glanced at Sanderson for help. But Sanderson looked like a man immobilised, waiting for disaster to strike and aware that there was no point in trying to do a bloody thing about it.

"Well," said Timothy, pursing his soft, madly kissable lips with an innocent eroticism that brought Celia Puffin almost within striking distance of an orgasm. "Well, some people might like call it rape or adultery, but it wasn't anything like that. We were like *lovers*—you know?"

But Puffin Billy was moving in with a gentle but firm "Shouldn't we think about moving on, my dear. We've lots to see and we do have a schedule to observe."

"Fuck your schedule," Celia said, smiling, in a voice only he could hear. But by then she had already been guided to the next table, where the twin mirrored lenses of Henry Trembler's spectacles probed her rather like searchlights seeking out the underbelly of a wartime Flying Fortress.

"Mrs Puffin, I presume," Henry said suavely, his horrible cesspit of a mind awhirl with images of long naked thighs and whips and chains and dark chambers and frilly underwear over his face and shuddering moans as he savagely tied her wrists to the bedframe with her gossamer pantyhose. "Of course, it was Celia Ramsbotton when I last saw you."

"Oh? And where, may I ask, was that?"

Through the slits in his leather mark, Henry watched her mouth curl into a beseeching *O* as she writhed on the bare wire of the bed, weeping and begging him to do whatever he would with her—anything that might satisfy her insane craving for bondage and humiliation.

"It was at a rather delightful garden party in Balgowlah, as I recall," he said. "You wouldn't remember me, of course. I was but a single face in a crowd of mass adoration as you moved amongst us, like a princess among her devoted subjects, collecting donations for the Meals on Wheels."

"Of course! I remember it well. That was just after I was crowned Miss Australia. What a marvelous memory you have."

"Dear lady, I am but a simple wayward oaf in the radiant beauty of your presence." And for a moment, Celia thought Henry Trembler was going to throw himself at her feet, as the dirty little snake bent down from his chair to pick a fallen duckie up off the floor and got a good close squizz at her exquisite legs, which tasted like heaven on earth as he hungrily licked and nibbled his way up from the ankles, around the calves, over the dimpled knees and up the cool, silky insides of the thighs and then into the bushy rendezvous of her womanhood from whence he could hear her ecstatic flight to climax as his tongue worked furiously on her swollen thingummyjig, you know, that thing that's supposed to send them raving.

Celia said: "Didn't something *awful* happen at that party? I vaguely remember there was a great deal of commotion and the police were called . . . Of course! Those two girls! Found naked and tied together in the shrubbery. My God, I remember it all now. What a shocking affair."

"I dare say," said Henry. "Though I'm glad to say I'd left to fulfill another social engagement by the time the police arrived."

Continuing their tour, the official party had climbed the stone steps leading up out of the underground workshop and were being ushered through a steel-framed, wire-mesh gate, manned by an armed guard, that opened out into the sun-flayed quadrangle when Celia turned to (Rev) Hunt and said: "What a sweet little man. And so refined. What did he do? No—let me guess. I'll bet he's an artistic type who was caught counterfeiting ten-dollar notes on the side."

Hunt said: "I'm afraid he did a little more than that, Mrs Puffin. And as for his talents, I shudder to think what an evil *impasse* civilisation would be coming to if his peculiar bent was classed as an art."

"Do you mean he's bent?"

"In many different directions, madam," Bull Sanderson gruffly assured her. "You might even say he's twisted, except that in plain down-to-earth language he's completely warped."

"So sad. But that often happens to artistic types. Such a waste. And obviously a man of good breeding."

"Well," said (Rev) Hunt. "You've seen our toy-manufacturing enterprise. Now, over here we have an exhibition that one would admit is truly of an artistic nature. Paintings, wood carvings, batiks, pottery, jewellery, straw and rattan handicrafts—all of them representative of the creative revolution that we have launched in this jail and which, if I might venture to suggest, Mr Minister, might bear some examination for possible inclusion in the general policy of the Corrective Services Department."

"We already have a general policy for Corrective Services, Mr Hunt," Puffin Billy said testily, sweating in the fierce heat of the quadrangle and already bored shitless by the whole affair. "And that is to lock people of a criminal nature away from the rest of society.

And I fail to see how this is to be achieved when, unless my eyes deceive me, I notice that this jail appears to have no walls."

There was a rude jangle of brass, as though a horse was shaking its bridle, as the Mayor spun away from the group to take a look for himself. And sure enough, at the distance from which they were looking, Murphy's mural of toll-road and virgin bushland rising up towards the Governor's domain blended in perfectly with the living sky and upper foliage of the trees beyond the wall. "Good Lord," the Mayor exclaimed. "Penal reform is all very well, but is it safe to allow hardened criminals this sort of liberty? What if they decided to just walk out of here and rape and pillage? I have my constituents to think about, you know. Decent, law-abiding citizens who expect to be protected from the lawless elements."

"The citizens of this city are quite safe, Mr Mayor," said (Rev) Hunt with an amused, condescending smile. "I can guarantee you that rape and pillage are totally inconceivable. If I might explain—"

"I think nothing less than a full explanation would satisfy *me* at this *junction*," Puffin Billy interjected rudely, the very concept of a prison without walls, combined with the dizzying heat, making him boil up into righteous indignation. "I don't recall giving my Ministerial Consent to the demolition of walls in any of the penal institutions within my authority, Mr Hunt. This is a blatant and serious violation of departmental policy, and one that I, as the Minister Responsible, view with the gravest alarm. How dare you allow murderers and bandits to roam at large, without the security of walls, with innocent women and children living within their evil reach?" Billy pointed furiously at the Church of St John. "And so close to a House of God! And you call yourself a man of the cloth? This is a *travesty*, Mr Hunt!"

"But there *is* a wall there, Mr Minister," (Rev) Hunt protested, unable to believe his own ears.

But Billy erupted into a fit of bluster. "Are you saying I can't see a wall that's not there when I'm standing here looking straight at it? Are you intimating that I'm blind? I assure you, Mr Hunt, that I have perfect twenty-twenty vision in both eyes. I am not in the habit of seeing things that aren't there, nor not seeing things that are there."

"What you are seeing, or not seeing," (Rev) Hunt explained dryly, "is simply a clever optical illusion."

"Are you suggesting I'm mad, Mr Hunt?"

"I believe the Reverend said *illusion*, dear, not *delusion*," said

Celia, smiling sweetly at the Honourable William. "A *deception*, not a symptom of insanity."

"That's all very well," Billy blustered. "But I do not take kindly to deceit, either. Throughout my entire Parliamentary Career I have adhered religiously to the principle of an open, honest and frank exchange of views and information at all levels, unlike my union-funded socialist opponents, who pay lip service to democracy in public yet allow their policy-making decisions to be formulated by a shady backroom committee of *faceless men*. As I have stated in the Legislative Assembly on many occasions, the welfare of a Free Nation like ours is too important to be decided upon arbitrarily by non-elected private citizens whose actions are not accountable to the voters. That's what we have politicians for!"

"A point well taken," said Celia, smiling with her teeth, her eyes casting fire at the silly puffed-up dickhead. "But perhaps we should allow Reverend Hunt to say what he was about to say."

"What I was about to say," (Rev) Hunt sighed, "is that what you are seeing is a clever *illusion* created to give the impression that there are no walls around this jail. In reality, it would take a platoon of well-equipped, highly-trained SAS commandos to break out of here. Mr Sanderson, would you be so kind as to demonstrate?"

"Right away, sir," said Sanderson, and he turned and walked back to the armed prison officer at the gate through which they had passed. After a short chat, the guard muttered a few words into a walkie-talkie strung over his shoulder.

"Now you'll see your wall," said (Rev) Hunt. And as they all watched the toll-road with its frozen tableau of bullock-driver and encompassing bushland, an absolutely amazing optical illusion took place before them. Like people's militia in a Chinese revolutionary ballet performed against a rural backdrop, two lines of rifle-toting guards trotted on-stage from right and left, dancing through treetops and along the ridge of Murphy's hill as though tippy-toeing on an invisible wire. As the two lines met, the figures halted, turned to face into the jail, then each sank to one knee, shouldered his rifle and took aim at a point that appeared to be right dead-centre of Puffin Billy's pompous pudding-shaped tum-tum.

The Minister passed a fat hand over his sweaty forehead and said: "Could we perhaps move out of this heat and into the shade, Mr Hunt?"

"Marvellous! Absolutely marvellous," Celia Puffin exclaimed as they all shifted into the shade of an awning strung over the exhibition of arts and crafts, which itself ran like a display of prizes in a fairground sideshow alongside the cyclone-wire fence of The Pen. "Just like a modern Peking ballet," Celia gushed. "Is this part of the play you promised us, Reverend?"

"No, simply a little demonstration of the tight security that exists here," Hunt replied, quite pleased with himself. "The play comes later."

"Quite stunning," said the Mayor. "I see it all now. My compliments, Mr Hunt. I had no idea that you possessed such a flair for the theatrical."

"Not I, Mr Mayor," (Rev) Hunt admitted, "but an inmate whose creative talents have done wonders to this prison, not to mention a number of banking establishments, and whom you shall all be meeting very shortly."

(Rev) Hunt glanced at Bull Sanderson and his eyebrows darted up and down in a gesture of satisfaction. Sanderson grinned and winked back at him. Everything seemed to be going along like a bloody house on fire.

"Well, Mr Minister," Hunt ventured as the group wandered slowly down the long sideshow of paintings, batiks, carvings, raffiawork and other artwork. "What do you think of our prison without walls?"

"Quite honestly," said the Honourable William, "I am at this very moment composing in my mind a Ministerial Memorandum of a confidential nature to be circulated with the greatest expediency to all penitentiaries and corrective institutions within My Department's jurisdiction . . ."

(Rev) Hunt again glanced at Sanderson, and it was he who winked this time and Sanderson's bushy eyebrows that shot up and down.

"This Memorandum," Billy continued, "will make it clear in the strongest and most irrevocable terms that *prisons are prisons*, and under no circumstances whatsoever are they to be transformed into art galleries and Chinese operas."

The whole group came to an abrupt halt. Celia Puffin let out what could have been interpreted as a low, exasperated moan. Bull Sanderson looked at Hunt's pale, shocked features and his eyebrows and lips screwed up into a sardonic grimace. The Mayor glanced back and forth, trying to gauge which way the political breeze was about to blow before committing himself to an attitude of any sort. As for Puffin Billy, he blew his stack like an over-pressured boiler.

"I find the entire concept both dangerous and absolutely preposterous," he raged. "I may be a Representative of The People—a responsibility that I shoulder with great pride and personal sacrifice—but I am also a Human Being, and as such I possess private thoughts and principles that cannot be reconciled with the whims, fancies and prejudices of the Electorate. And the one principle upon which I am absolutely *uncompromiscuous* is that if there are those who refuse to observe the laws and common decencies of Our Society, then they must be denied all decency in return."

It took (Rev) Hunt a few seconds to work that one out, then he said: "I tend to agree—up to a point. I run this jail with an iron fist, you know. No man dares to step out of line. Rigid productivity targets have been set for soft toys. Creative work is mandatory, and woe betide any man who considers it to be a leisure. The whole concept is designed to discipline and at the same time divert minds and energies from attempts to break out."

Billy gave his plump hips a little agitated twist and snorted derisively. "We have *walls* to stop them from breaking out, Mr Hunt. Enormous *impregnatible* stone walls that are there to impress upon every malefactor confined within them that they are isolated from the rest of society. Good Lord, man, why else do we lock them away?"

"And with all due respect, sir, why else do they keep trying to break out? The wall is a hated symbol, a constant reminder that they have been stripped of all basic rights and dignities. All we have done with the walls in this jail is to make them a little less hateful. We are talking about *two societies* here, Mr Minister, both of which must have certain decencies and dignities in order to survive in a civilised fashion—or else our jails will one day explode!"

"Let them explode, Mr Hunt," Billy puffed obstinately, "and then we'll teach them a lesson that they'll never ever forget."

With the group around him transfixed in various expressions of disbelief, Puffin Billy inflated to the very limit of his capacity, his face crimson with pious rage, and blew a last scalding stream of hot air. "And that, Mr Hunt, in plain, simple, no-nonsense terms, means not only is that wall to be restored forthwith to its original condition, but you can take a running jump at your arts and crafts as well! If your prisoners want to exercise their creative instincts, let them create little rocks out of big rocks or mailbags for the GPO in the time-honoured method and tradition of prison labour!"

Flushed with triumph, Billy turned to Celia and said: "I don't think My Position could be put more succinctly than that, do you, my dear?"

"I think," Celia replied very sweetly, "that I have a piece of grit in my eye. Could you come out into the sunshine with me and help me get it out? Gentlemen, would you excuse us for a moment?"

Now totally dumbfounded, (Rev) Hunt, the Mayor and Bull Sanderson watched as the Puffins moved out of earshot and Billy fussed over Celia's face with a handkerchief. Celia appeared to be chatting calmly but earnestly throughout the operation, her lips in a tight smiling position but otherwise hardly moving. All ears strained to catch what was being said, but caught nothing. Sanderson, attempting to read Celia's full, sensuous lips, could have sworn that he picked up the word *election* and an unbroken sequence of five or six others all beginning with *f*. But of course, that was bloody ridiculous. Finally the Puffins returned to the group, Celia continuing to smile graciously and Billy mopping sweat from his brow.

(Rev) Hunt, still in a state of shock, had come to the conclusion that his future in the prisons service was now well and truly down the drain.

"I trust you will be expecting my resignation at the earliest possible opportunity, Mr Minister," he said thinly.

"What? Good Lord, no, my dear Reverend," Billy exclaimed, pulling himself up to his full five-foot-four inches of limp fat and beginning to inflate once again. "We must never forget to remind ourselves, gentlemen, that Time Marches On, and we must all keep pace with it or fall by the Wayside. A nation like ours, with its Great Pioneer Heritage, cannot afford to fall back on its old outmoded ideals. It was men of Vision and Courage who made Australia what it is today, and we must continue that brave, undaunting tradition if we are to maintain our rightful place among the Great Free Nations of the Developed World and hold our heads up high as promoters of understanding and compassion for all members of the global Family of Man."

There was a short pregnant pause while Billy's words sank in, then the Mayor rattled his chain enthusiastically.

"Hear-hear. Well said. And may I say that you have the full support of myself and my fellow-aldermen, aside from the Labour faction, on the City Council."

"Do I take it," said (Rev) Hunt, "that you, Mr Minister, are in favour of my reforms after all?"

"I thought I'd made that perfectly clear from the outset, Mr Hunt," Puffin Billy blustered. "Rudimentary though they may be at this *embionic* stage. Of course, they need a hand experienced in these matters to refine them, and I was about to suggest that you and I get together with my public relations secretary at the earliest convenient date to study ways of exploiting them to their fullest—in the interests of these and other unfortunate transgressors whose only crime is that they were born into a world where privileges are handed out to a lucky few and denied the many. Oh, I say! That blue batik over there has quite a professional touch to it. Who, may I ask, er, *batiked* it?"

And so they moved on. Past the paintings in oils, watercolours, acrylics, pastels and inks and even vegetable dyes that—clashing like products in some strange supermarket of art, with impressionists alongside realists and abstracts and naturalists and allegoricals and cubists all jumbled together with primitives and some that were just plain bloody awful—all shared one thing in common: the insular, trapped, defiant yet secretly troubled faces of men behind bars.

The faces brooded with hopelessness amid a general splash of colour and inventiveness of the batiks and other arts; yet even these seemed to represent a yearning for freedom and beauty that was far beyond the creator's reach. The whole show was artistic and very professional, yet at the same time it was depressing, and it was with something of a relief that the official party finally trekked across the remaining open hearth of the quadrangle and stepped through a steel door-within-door that led them into cell-block A—where their senses immediately took flight into the soaring, cavernous, cathedral-like interior in which bright spotlights bathed the final sequence of Kevin Murphy's huge ceiling-high murals, adding to them a power and glory that might have sent the immortal Michelangelo himself into raptures, had the genius been mindless enough to reincarnate himself in a place like Parramatta.

As one, the spirits of the entire group ascended heavenward, lifting and wheeling like birds on a spiralling upcurrent of warm air— until the initial ecstacy of colour and grandeur gave way to the *subject*

of Murphy's work, and then they abruptly went haywire like badly
unbalanced kites and sput and twisted and collided and plummetted
with ungainly lack of control to the cell block's concrete floor.

"I must be seeing things," Puffin Billy gasped, gazing in horror
at the scenes that ran riot around the walls. "I can't believe this is the
work of a—a—Reverend Hunt! Is the perpetrator of this—this *nightmare* a normal man or some poor wretch who should have pleaded
insanity at his trial?"

"Murphy is as sane as you or I," said Hunt, glancing nervously at
Bull Sanderson, seeking support from his withdrawn, enigmatic features. "If one is dealing with prison art, one can't really expect pretty
pastoral scenes or two apples and a passion-fruit is still life."

"But this is not *art*, Mr Hunt. This is the inner purgatory of a
sick and malicious mind! I've never seen anything like it in my life!"

"Nor I, Mr Minister," (Rev) Hunt agreed. "Perhaps that's why I
agreed to allow Murphy to leave it there once I saw what he was up
to. It is, after all, a very personal expression of wrath and accusation
on his part, and if that is not encompassed in what we call *art* we
might just as well fill our galleries with mail-order discount prints of
white mares galloping through an angry surf in the defiant dying rays
of a storm-threatened, late-afternoon sun. Thousands of Australian
homes have one. Perhaps you're suggesting we should quit while
we're ahead." (Rev) Hunt attempted to inject a little reasoning into
the flabbergasted antagonism of the group. "But come now—it's not
all *that* shocking. I think it could possibly grow on you after a while.
What do you think, Mrs Puffin?"

For once, Celia Puffin had lost her cool, regal air. She looked
nauseated. "Quite honestly, I don't think I'd like *that* to grow anywhere near me," she confessed. "In fact, I think I'm going to be sick.
Is there something a little more wholesome that I could view while
you gentlemen continue in here?"

"I'm terribly sorry, Mrs Puffin. Of course. I believe you'll find
something more acceptable to your sensitivities in the next block—
the landing of Captain Phillip and other historic events. You may
even encounter our resident playwright, Mr Noel Chisholm, if he's
not otherwise indisposed. Would you like Mr Sanderson to escort
you?"

"That won't be necessary, Mr Hunt. I'll feel quite secure as soon
as I get away from this *ugly manifestation*."

As Celia stumbled through the main door and out into the sun's shrill glare, the Mayor, convinced by now that he was on completely safe political ground, added his two cents' worth to the outrage. "*Frightening*, Mr Hunt. Frightening and vile and a totally vindictive distortion of taste. I trust this perfidy will be erased now that we have seen it. Were a disgrace like this allowed to remain it could do great harm to this city's fine reputation."

"This *perfidy*, Mr Mayor," said (Rev) Hunt, by now a little hot under the collar, "took place within this city, or close to it. And why should we deny it, or try to conceal it? It was as much an ingredient of our heritage as was the breeding of merino wool and the brutal quest for gold. And you hardly ever hear Australians say they're ashamed of gold."

"I am ashamed," Puffin Billy declared, "that a fellow Australian, and I assume he is native-born, could have dared to even associate this *excreta* with the word art. The man deserves a good horsewhipping."

"If that is your honest and considered opinion," Hunt riposted, flushed with anger now, "then Kevin Murphy's work, however disturbing it may be, is as valid a comment on our national character as a buffoon like Ernie Sigley is on our appreciation of entertainment. And as for horsewhipping him—that opportunity is about to come your way. For here is the artist himself."

Murphy had just blown in the door on a last-minute check of arrangements for the coming jailbreak. Needless to say, he was a little surprised to find (Rev) Hunt and Sanderson there, along with a fat, short-arsed, official-looking cove who was bad-eyeing him like nobody's business, along with another joker who looked like a plonk-waiter from a posh Italian restaurant with that chain dangling around his chest. For one awful moment, Murphy thought maybe they were there to grab him secretly and without undue fuss, and haul him off to Grafton. He began backing slowly out of the door.

"Don't run away, Mr Murphy," (Rev) Hunt called out. "These gentlemen have just been studying your work. Perhaps you could explain to them what it's actually all about."

Murphy eyed the group suspiciously for a moment, undecided whether to take his chances or run like the bloody wind to where he'd stashed the detonators that Timothy Botham had assembled for him.

"Come now," said (Rev) Hunt. "Time is short and the Minister hasn't got all day."

"Move it, Murphy," Sanderson growled. "What are you waiting for, a bloody engraved invitation?"

Resigned to his fate, Murphy cautiously approached the group. Hunt introduced him to the Mayor and the Honourable William, and to both he responded with: "Gidday. Pleased to meet yer."

"So you're the man who perpetrated this *thing*," Puffin Billy said angrily. "Tell me, Mr Murphy, do you honestly call this—this whatever-it-is *art?*"

"I haven't decided what to call it yet," Murphy confessed. "Noel Chisholm wanted to call it *The Founding of Toongabbie as Performed on a Full Moon by the Inmates of Nathaniel Payten's Female Factory.* I said you'd need an IQ of a hundred and eighty just to read the bloody title. And you don't get many IQs in here." Murphy pointed up into the heart of the insane melee of tortured limbs and screaming faces. "There's still a bit of tidying up to be done on some of it," he explained blandly. "You see that sheila being whipped up there in the middle of the bunfight with the log crushing her and those two other birds tearing each other's hair out behind? I had a lot of trouble with her eyes. I can't seem to get the right expression. I wanted them to be agony with an underlying hint of peace because she knows she's just about to escape her misery through death. That one being hanged on the other wall there gave me a lot of trouble too. It's not often you can witness a good necktie job these days, so I had to go through every bloody book I could find on punishment in the Middle Ages to see exactly how their eyeballs bulge like that. Actually, I used putty to make them stand out, you know. Her body's all wrong, though. It's supposed to look like a bloody great electric shock's hitting it as the rope slowly strangles her. Still, there's some of it I'm pretty happy about. That dog tearing that old crone to pieces over there turned out quite nicely, don't you think?"

Puffin Billy's normally florid face had gone a sickly white. His blubbery lips opened and closed as he fought for words to express his deep revulsion. Finally, all he could say was: "What on earth influenced you to portray such a pageant of horrors?"

"Signorelli, mainly," Murphy explained. "His *Last Judgement* frescoes came about as close as you could get to the sort of things the convicts had to put up with. There's a bit of Bosch in there some-where, too, though I find his style's a bit abstract and airy-fairy for something like *Toongabbie*."

"I asked you a simple question," Billy snapped. "What made you do it?"

Murphy grinned cheekily. "What made Australians pick a silly drippy bloody hymn like 'Advance Australia Fair' for a national an-them when nine times out of ten the first song they get into around the keg at a party is 'Waltzing Matilda'? And doesn't it strike you as being funny that Australia's seen cruelty and suffering that'd make your bloody hair curl, yet you never see a Drysdale, Nolan or Durack that says anything about it. None of them have got the bloody guts to look back at the bloke with half his flesh flayed off his body. It doesn't look nice next to the gum trees and kookaburras and Melbourne Cup sheilas and outback pubs and jolly old Diggers and bloody two-bit, over-glamourised morons running around the countryside in iron masks."

"Some things are best forgotten, Mr Murphy," Puffin Billy pon-tificated. "No nation likes to be reminded of the darker nature of its past."

"Yeah," said Murphy savagely. "Well, it seems to me, *mate*, that if we'd all stop pulling the wool over our bloody eyes and be honest with ourselves for a change, we might not be so bloody scared about the future. Instead of saying we *believe* in it all the time."

The Honourable William naturally took this as a personal slight. And a slur on his many parliamentary speeches. "I don't see why you should be concerned about the future," he said with a prissy, sarcastic little smile. "Unless, of course, you're counting on getting out of this jail."

"I'm not counting on anything," said Murphy. "I'm in for about six counts of armed bank robbery. Plus a few more years for allegedly refusing to divulge the whereabouts of the loot from my last job. I reckon I'll see Hell freeze over before I walk the streets again."

"A bank robber, eh? Very interesting. And how is it, may I ask, that you seem to know so much about art?"

"There's an art to everything, I suppose. Even robbing banks. Anyhow, I had chronic asthma as a kid and spent a lot of time laid up in bed. I had to do something to stop from going silly in the head so I took up sketching and painting. Then I fell behind in my grades at school and failed all my exams, and then had to drop out and look for a job when I was only thirteen—"

"Come now," Puffin Billy interjected rudely, the sarcasm now dripping from his fat lips. "Surely you're not going to pull that old rabbit out of the hat about turning to crime because of socio-economic deprivation as a child."

Murphy said: "No. I turned to crime because there was a lot of money to be made robbing banks."

Momentarily floored, Billy made the mistake of trying to beat Murphy with a bit of bluster. "Well, you didn't exactly make an unmitigated success of it, did you? I trust you've now had plenty of time in which to consider the error of your ways."

"You bet," Murphy agreed. "Next time I'll pick my bank a bit more bloody carefully."

Billy made another mistake. He puffed up like a Queensland cane toad at mating time and unleashed a vitriolic wind at Murphy's head.

"You are obviously nothing more than a dangerous and incorrigible *felonial!* May you *rot* in this jail for the rest of your natural life!"

"And you," Murphy replied, very calmly, "are full of cocky-shit. And may the pores of your skin turn into little arseholes and crap all over you."

Puffin Billy directed his next blast at (Rev) Hunt and Bull Sanderson. *"This is outrageous!* I have never been so grossly affronted in all my life! I want this man placed under arrest and charged with insulting behaviour."

But (Rev) Hunt had already come to the conclusion that things had gone quite far enough. Briskly and authoritatively, he took charge of the heated situation. "Murphy, I want you to go immediately to the auditorium and make sure the men are assembled for the play. Mr. Mayor, would you be so kind as to step outside for a while and allow the Minister and me to discuss this unfortunate state of affairs in private? A departmental matter. I'm sure you understand."

"Er, well, of course," the Mayor muttered as Hunt guided him and Murphy to the cell-block door. He ushered them gently out into the sun, then closed the door, turned, clapsed his hands together in front of him, raised them slowly and thoughtfully to his chin, his interlocked fingers forming a church steeple, then stalked deliberately back to Bull Sanderson and the Honourable William Lancelot Puffin.

"*You silly little narrow-minded arrogant conceited ill-informed worthless blind and pathetic old fool,*" he said softly but with hissing, constrained rage. "No wonder your colleagues call you Puffin Billy. You possess about as much intelligence and discretion as a steam kettle whistling on the boil. With gerrymandering blowhards like you guiding this nation's affairs, is it any wonder that despite two hundred years of history we have never yet been able to graduate from the political playschool? You are not a leader, you're a demagogue screaming for retreat. You are not a legislator, you're a perambulating mixture of obstruction and absurdity. No wonder this country is facing the danger of what you would point hysterically to as a trade-union tyranny—the only protection the working masses have been able to muster against witless self-centred men like you is closed ranks and class warfare. And in a society that fools like you promote as being classless!"

The Honourable William looked as though he was about to suffer terminal apoplexy. He stood rooted to the spot, stiff as a stunned penguin, his only bodily movement being a spasmodic flapping of his hands, which were thrust so close to the middle of his fat thighs that he looked like a barrage balloon trying to gain height with sparrow's wings. His head looked as though it was about to burst. His eyes bulged with the volcanic pressure of his fury. Veins stood out like exposed plumbing on his forehead and neck. His voice, when he finally found it, was but a hoarse strangled shade of its usual timbre.

"Mr Hunt, you are relieved of all duties as from this very instance!" he gasped. "Mr Sanderson, you will assume command of this jail as acting superintendent pending Mr Hunt's official dismissal for gross insubordination and insulting behaviour towards a Minister of the Crown. As for me, I am not going to remain here a second longer and allow myself to be treated in this despicable and outrageous fashion!"

Bull Sanderson stiffened to attention and squarely addressed his stricken, still-fuming former boss. "I'm sorry Mr Hunt," he said sadly. Then he turned to Puffin Billy, loomed right over him and poked the little creep hard between his over-developed breasts with a pointed forefinger. "You're not going anywhere, shit-for-brains," he growled, "because I've got a few things to get off my bloody chest too. We had a good scene going in here before you bounced in like you owned the bloody place and got everybody upset. Everything was going along fine. The last thing we needed was a fat little fuckwit like you to start telling us how to run things. The Reverend, here, has worked like a bloody one-armed paper hanger to turn this place into something fit for human beings to live in. It hasn't been easy for him. And don't you kid yourself—these blokes in here *are* human beings. And blokes like you and me are just as bloody likely to turn into murderers and thieves like them, given the right circumstances. In fact, you're lucky I've got enough good sense and self-control to stop myself from turning into a bloody killer right now!"

Billy shrank away from Sanderson's towering anger, and his final blast of bluff emerged as little more than a frightened bleat: "As Minister for Corrective Services I herewith—"

"Dry up," said Sanderson. "From what I've been reading in the newspapers it's highly bloody unlikely that you'll be Minister for Anything this time next week. You're a dead duck, Billy. And the only bloody hope you've got left is to play along with us, or I promise you, tomorrow's headlines are going to read something like *Prisons Minister in New Storm: Jail Chiefs Quit, Tell All*. And don't forget, I've seen thirty bloody years of prison service, and that's enough to keep the newspapers crowing every day for a month. Now, what do you have to say about *that?*"

twenty-six

OUTSIDE IN THE BLAZING SUN, THE MAYOR had been getting quite nervous and agitated. Apart from the sweat that ran in streams down his broad face, the thought of being left alone, unguarded, in an open jail made him all the more uncomfortable. Especially when a crazed, cross-eyed apparition with windswept hair staggered out of an adjacent block and weaved his way towards him eyeing his Mayoral chain. The incredible figure halted in front of him, looked him up and down, and with rude familiarity gave the chain a little flip with one finger. The Mayor's legs nearly melted with fear.

"Winetaster's Club, eh? Things are looking up in here," Noel Chisholm observed. "I once had occasion to test the properties of a celebrated Schlanderheinembohm vintage burgundy, a private bin 'thirty-seven as I recall. *Eighteen* thirty-seven, that is. The wine itself was a triumph, but the bottle was something of a disappointment. The other bloke got back up and floored me with a bloody beer stein."

Chisholm looked deeply into the Mayor's confused and terrified eyes. "You don't look too good, feller," he said. "Maybe you need a drink." A silver hip-flask emerged immediately from under his attire. "Here, have a shot of this. Guaranteed to put lead in your pencil, hair on your chest and permanently scramble your brains. Don't worry about damaging those sensitive taste-buds and olfactory senses. You won't have any left after a couple of good stiff belts."

The Mayor made a weak and vain attempt to ward off the evil brew. But Chisholm wasn't having any of that. "C'mon! Get it into you, for Chrissakes. You blokes spend most of your time sucking plonk, so I'm not asking you to plunge into a life of wrack and ruin, am I?"

Trembling at the knees and still stricken mute with fright, the Mayor made the most fatal blunder of his hard-fought, up-from-nothing life. He took a deep sip of the hellish liquid—and immediately experienced what could be described as a cerebral thunderclap. His body stiffened, jerked and twisted with such violence that his chain of office spun around his neck like a hoop-la.

"Maybe you'd better sit down," Chisholm suggested. "That's better. Now relax and put your head between your knees and count to ten. And perhaps kiss your arse goodbye while you're at it."

They sat awhile in the hot sun, the Mayor making strange gagging sounds and Chisholm idly watching big bull-ants parade around them, obviously calculating the load factors involved in carrying them off. Then the Mayor managed to say his first words. "I must be going mad," he gasped.

"OK, if you must," Chisholm replied, gently forcing another draught of liquid Armageddon down the poor man's throat. "I went mad years ago. One day I took a look around me and came to the conclusion that there's no bloody hope for any of us. You see, we don't really *exist*. Nothing really *exists*. It's all simply a matter of in-dividual collections of molecules that have decided to come together in what we call human form. It's a tenuous situation, to say the least. They could just as easily separate and try something else. If we were immortal we might have something going for us. Might even learn to live together without all the bullshit and breast-beating. As it is, we're *all ultimately going to die*, and suffer a miserable, unmemorable end not unlike that of the famous Oogle Bird, which spends its lifetime flying around in diminishing, ever-concentric circles until, reaching the epicentre, it finally disappears up its own arsehole in a cloud of dust."

The Mayor burst into tears. For about ten seconds he heaved and sobbed. Chisholm tenderly offered him another belt of brain-damage and a clean handkerchief. The Mayor accepted both, under-went a short explosion of coughing and teeth-grinding and finally dried his tears. He then regarded Chisholm intently with eyes that seemed to have already separated and gone their own individual ways.

"It took me years to get where I am, and now you're saying it mean snutthing," he slurred drunkenly, rattling his chain.

"Not so much as a bullock's fart in a thunderstorm," Chisholm assured him.

The Mayor looked as though he might break down again. "I'm terribly sorry," he sighed. "It was the shock of revelation, you under-stand. What you said explains everything, particularly my confusion as to why your collection of molecules had chosen to come together in the form of a be-wigged nineteenth-century magistrate or judge in a frock coat, breeches and grey hose."

"You mean this gear?" Chisholm shook his powdered curls and neatly arranged the tails of his coat around him. "Now you see how tenuous it all really is," he said. "For the next two hours I shall be Nathaniel Payten, one of the founders of this miserable excuse for a metropolis, after which the eminent gentleman will again cease to exist and I shall take another form."

"And what form will that be?"

Chisholm closed the cap of his hip-flask and screwed it tight. Then he hauled himself up onto his feet and helped the Mayor arise.

They stood swaying for a moment, arms flung around each other's shoulders for support. "Join me. Come and see," Chisholm invited him. "You shall sit close to me and watch one of the greatest bloody disappearing tricks you've ever been privileged to see. You shall witness *The Vanishing Yahoo*. After which I sincerely hope that, as with the Oogle Bird, you will not see my arse for dust."

Both the Mayor and Chisholm had evaporated into thin air when (Rev) Hunt, Bull Sanderson and Puffin Billy emerged from cell-block A. The Honourable William had undergone indignities that might have destroyed the will of any other politician; but you had to give Billy his due—this man for all persuasions had bounced back like a beachball and was, at that very moment, puffing furiously along the track of yet another Strong Declaration of His Position.

". . . And in conclusion, gentlemen," he blared as they trudged into the hot sun, "I have always believed that Democracy is as much the Politics of Reality as it is a sounding board for Uncompromising Idealism. There are Truths that all of us must face, painful as they may be, and the fundamental truth of politics in all Free Societies is that the road to success and the ultimate welfare of the Majority winds subtley through the hills and valleys of Give-and-Take, while the alternative runs headlong into Confrontation and the legislative brick wall. In other words, you scratch my back and I'll scratch yours."

"Very aptly put," said (Rev) Hunt. "I think we see eye-to-eye at last, Mr Minister. And having achieved that, let's now enjoy the *pièce de résistance* of today's event, Mr Noel Chisholm's play, *The Vanishing Yahoo*."

"What a strange title, Reverend. Perhaps you could tell me what it's all about."

"Of course. I naturally demanded to read the script before approving its production. Mr Chisholm has drawn water from many wells to achieve a symbolic work dealing with the posthumous trial of Aaron Sherritt, the man who attempted to betray Ned Kelly and was shot dead for his pains. It is finely written and is, I believe, a strong testament to our national character. The setting is novel, to say the least, and in itself contains a number of surprises. There'll be armed guards in the auditorium to make sure the surprises do not get out of hand. Other than that, I can only say I have hopes for it outside in the legitimate theatre."

"Bravo," Billy boomed. "By the way, I wonder what has become of Mrs Puffin. Do you think she's quite safe?"

Hunt laughed. "In a prison? I should think so, Mr Minister. I should imagine she's awaiting us in the auditorium right this minute."

But Celia wasn't awaiting them in the auditorium at all. Celia had slipped into cell-block C as Hunt had suggested, anxious not only to get away from Murphy's terrible mural but also to see if she could track down that luscious young thing called Timothy Botham. Boy, she was really hot in the pants for him. Every time she recalled his sweet lips and innocent blushes she went hot and cold all over. In the quiet, deserted cell block she hunted high and low for him, but to no avail. Intrigued, and feeling a little daring because it wasn't every day she was able to peek into convict cells, she finally wandered into Noel Chisholm's lair—and found herself looking at the uniformed rear end of a prisoner bent over Chisholm's bed, his hands rummaging under the mattress.

"You there," she said curtly, a little taken aback. "Have you any idea how I can get hold of that young Botham?"

The hunched figure stiffened, his hands still lost in the folds of blanket, sheets and rough hessian. A voice said: "The usual way, dear lady. Try grabbing both cheeks."

And Henry Trembler slowly straightened up and turned to face her, his spectacles misting over with steaming, sweaty lust.

"Celia Ramsbottom, I presume," he hissed, his horrible little gnarled hands forming buzzard's talons. "What an incredible turn of events. I came here in search of vulgar materialism—namely, two thousand dollars. And here am I now, about to ravish God's gift to Australian womanhood."

"You'll do nothing of the sort!" Celia replied hotly, starting to back away towards the door.

"Now let's not waste time with silly resistance and protestations, my dear." And with the speed of a striking cobra, Henry scuttled around her, slammed the cell door and stood with his back to it, his sweaty chops forming a hideous wolf's grin.

"Let me out of here," Celia commanded imperiously. "You fucking undernourished ugly little prick!"

"*Gorgeous!* I like a bit of obscenity from my intended victims. I can see we're going to get along like a house on fire. Now, before we begin, would you prefer to be the whipper or the whippee?"

"I'll scream the place down!" Celia threatened.

"I should bloody well hope so," said Henry. "There's nothing worse than mute submission. Takes all the fun out of the game."

Incongruous as it was—this short skinny ferret challenging a female Rhode Island Red—Henry loosened his belt, ready to start the foreplay off with a good orthodox flash. Celia foolishly decided to shame him out of the scheme. Any rapist or flasher, you see, can be neutralised by simply taking advantage of his inferiority and impotence which, as any psychologist will tell you, is the root cause of his aberration.

"I hardly think a pathetic weasily little bloody runt like you," Celia said icily as Henry began opening his fly, "could possess anything that would intimidate me. Why don't you leave it where it is and . . .

"*MYYYYYY GODDDDDDDDDDDDDDD!!!*"

twenty-six

BY THIS TIME, THINGS WERE STARTING TO pop in the auditorium too. Puffin Billy, (Rev) Hunt and Bull Sanderson stepped into the large hall to be confronted by two uniformed prison guards who immediately grabbed the Minister, spun him around, threw his arms up over his head and frisked his fat bulk as though conducting a weapons search.

"What's going on here?" Billy frothed, squirming furiously. "Get your hands off me, or I'll have you thrown out of the prison service."

"You can throw me out any time you like, old mate," said Dickie King, the aboriginal terrorist, spinning the Minister around once again for good measure. As he did this, Lyle Walker, likewise clad in a warder's outfit, explained: "It's all part of the play, Mr Hunt. Just for atmosphere, like. Everybody's getting the same treatment." He patted Hunt up and down, and then turned to Bull Sanderson, who glowered threateningly at him. So he didn't pat Sanderson up and down.

"Well," said Hunt to the Minister, "I warned you that the setting for this play was full of surprises. And now that we seem to have convinced them that we're not armed and prepared to stage an act of terrorism, I'll take you to your seat."

"I don't like this, Mr Hunt," Bull Sanderson growled. "I don't like the idea of this one little bit." The hairs on the back of his neck had sprung up again.

"Oh, I don't think there's any cause for alarm," said (Rev) Hunt. "We've seen the rehearsals, and there's nothing in the play that would suggest trouble. Aaron Sherritt gets his just deserts, as did Ned Kelly. And we do have a detachment of guards in here to put down any possible disturbance."

But that didn't quell Sanderson's misgivings, and neither did it do anything to arrest Billy Puffin's nervousness as he was escorted across the hall to seats that had been reserved for the official guests in the front row of the audience.

The seating in the auditorium had been arranged so that it lay in a wide, deep semi-circle around what would have been the stage in any orthodox theatre-in-the-round production, but in the case of *The Vanishing Yahoo* was not a stage at all. It was simply a set, and the props consisted entirely of a raised courtroom bench with black drapes forming a backdrop behind it, and in front of the bench, set at a distance of about fifteen feet, two ordinary wooden office desks, each with chairs. A railing ran down one side of the set, away from the judicial bench, and behind that a dozen more chairs were neatly arranged in two rows of six. This was obviously where the jury would sit to deliberate on the fate of Aaron Sherritt, the skunk who turned police informer against the Kelly gang. One night, as he was entertaining a bunch of troopers over a log fire in his hut in the middle of a dense Victorian forest, a voice outside cried: "Sherritt! Sherritt!" Stupidly, he went to the door of the hut, threw it open, stood there silhouetted like a brick shithouse in the glare from the fireplace, and heard the words: "There you are, you fucking scum!" And a bullet smashed right through his fucking heart.

282

But then, the notorious Ned Kelly himself wasn't exactly a genius either. Bailed up later at the nearby village of Glenrowan, he staged his now-famous fighting stand against the troopers in a steel, bullet-proof helmet and breast-plate made from ploughshares—the armour allowing just a tiny slit for his eyes—and got plugged in the knee. The rest of his gang went down in an even more ignoble fashion—incinerated in the Glenrowan Hotel, which was really only a rude shanty, after one particular bright spark of a cop had set fire to it while they fought a furious gun battle from inside.

Still, Bonnie and Clyde didn't exactly go out in a blaze of glory. And Al Capone died of the clap. Which should prove something.

Anyhow, that was neither here nor there as the Honourable William was let to his seat. Billy was so nervous that it was only his mind's eye that glimpsed the packed rows of dangerous criminals pressing around him, their coarse hubbub of conversation a threatening din that filled his ears and brought a self-conscious blush to his fat features. He couldn't bring himself to look directly at them. He imagined rank upon rank of uncouth common faces leering and sneering at him, exchanging ugly jokes and obscenities—all of them ironically safe, in their outlawed status, from any reprisal on his part. Better to treat them with the contempt they deserved, he felt; and one can imagine the added blow that his feelings suffered when, upon finally reaching the official seats, he found a strange creature in a powdered wig, frock coat and breeches lurching about unsteadily with the Mayor, stuffing the distinguished personage into a bulky dark-blue, thigh-length tunic that appeared to be part of the uniform of a New South Wales policeman of the early 1800s. It also appeared that the Mayor had handed over his chain of office in exchange, for it was now dangling around Noel Chisholm's neck.

"Ah, there you all are," the Mayor bubbled gaily, flopping awkwardly into his seat as Chisholm struggled to fasten the last of the tunic buttons.

"A novelty, perhaps, but necessary," Chisholm explained to the thunderstruck (Rev) Hunt and the Minister, grunting with the effort it took to harness the Mayor into the trooper's jacket. "I demand complete authenticity in everything I do," he explained. "Also, as much audience participation as is decently possible. That, after all, is what my life has been all about—getting as many people as possible onto the dancefloor with me. Some of them have regretted it dearly, but that's simply nature's way of weeding out the weak and crippled,

283

isn't it. However, all of them, I think, would agree that their lives would have been buggered by something else if it hadn't happened to be me. Hold on now," he ordered the Mayor. "I just have to hook those two little wires there together and make a little adjustment up in here . . . And there you are—you no longer exist as the Mayor of the city, you are now a trooper in the New South Wales Constabulary, circa 1800 or thereabouts."

The Mayor jerked to his feet to adjust the fit of the tunic and nearly fell flat on his face. He was still as pissed as a newt. Chisholm, meanwhile, had picked up another jacket of the same ilk. He rounded on Puffin Billy.

"I couldn't figure out whether a Minister of the Crown outranked a City Mayor or vice-versa. So I solved the dilemma by making you both lowly constables. But as the author of this historic performance I probably outrank you both. So would you be so kind as to remove your jacket and leap into this?"

"I'll do no such thing!" Billy gasped indignantly.

"Your wallet and personal effects will be as safe as houses, I can assure you. We've arranged the seating so that the homicidal maniacs are closest to you and the pickpockets way up the back."

"I didn't come here to indulge in a crude pantomime, or to be made a spectacle of!"

(Rev) Hunt intervened with reasoning and diplomacy, aware of the growing pitch of the hubbub in the gallery around them. "Is this all really necessary, Mr Chisholm?"

"Absolutely," the celebrated playwright declared. "How can I create the authentic atmosphere of our colonial era if one amongst us is sitting here looking as though the time machine dropped him off at the wrong stop? It's important to the intrinsic mood of the play, not to mention the mood of six hundred-odd ugly bloody cons sitting around us. Many of them have laid heavy bets on the Minister's reaction. And as you can see, they're all playing the game."

The Honourable William ventured to search around him for the first time, and for a moment it was as though he'd been transported back into the rustic squalor of the nation's birth. The entire audience was dressed in ragged sheepskins, leather jerkins, ponchos made of filthy blankets, rough woollen smocks, faded and torn ex-military blouses and various other rags of an indiscernible nature, along with an assortment of headgear ranging from tassled woollen caps to wide-brimmed bush hats. To make matters all the more authentic, many of them had daubed their faces with dirt; others wore sinister black eye patches and grimy bloodstained bandages that covered God knows what sort of hideous suppurating wounds and ailments; and all of them to a man opened their mouths to leer in unison at the Minister's discomfort—revealing that they'd blacked-out several of their front teeth.

It was bizarre. It was fantastic. It was so incredibly realistic, such a vulgar, smelly, unattractive assemblage of common peasantry, that Puffin Billy began scratching at imaginary lice that ran amok under his sweating armpits.

"Amazing!" (Rev) Hunt declared, and he really was amazed. "You certainly are one for surprises, Mr Chisholm."

"Mr Payten, if you don't mind. Nathanial Payten. Now sir," he said to Puffin Billy, "do you wish to accept our invitation and join in the general spirit of things, or would you rather decline and sit amongst six hundred very disappointed men for two hours and let them call you a spoilsport and a bloody piker?"

Billy cast another glance at the humming, seething mass of horrible faces and decided it would be prudent not to stand on any principles at this *junction*.

"The coat, Mr Chis—er, Payten," he said bitterly, shrugging out of his suit jacket; and at that, a huge roar of approval rose up from the surrounding cons. Billy smiled self-consciously at the men as Nathanial Payten fastened him into the bulky costume. Then he lost his head completely and waved triumphantly to the crowd. The men went ape with excitement and derision.

Nathanial Payten handed (Rev) Hunt a frock coat like his own. Another roar went up as Hunt slipped it on.

Payten looked at Bull Sanderson and Sanderson, in return, gave him a withering, menacing stare. Payten said: "I don't think you'll need a costume, Bull. Your uniform will suffice."

"Listen, Nole," Sanderson growled, "if you pull any smart-arse tricks or start any trouble, I'll nail your bloody hide to the wall. You understand?"

The be-wigged features were absolutely mortified. "Tricks? There aren't going to be any tricks. You're about to witness the greatest moment of my literary career. Do you think I'd cheapen it with music-hall pranks?"

Right at that very moment, the lights went out. The entire auditorium was plunged into complete blackness in which a fast-rising crescendo of whistles, cat-calls, shrieks, oaths and stamping feet peaked at the decibel level of a herd of maddened elephants at stampeding time. Bull Sanderson leapt to his feet in the darkness and cannoned heavily into (Rev) Hunt as both tried to bellow above the fearful racket for the guards. Billy Puffin rocketed to such a high summit of fear that he simply jumped up and down, screaming like a fat chimpanzee.

Then, just as suddenly, the lights were back on again and the entire hall fell hushed. On the set in front of them, twelve convicts in regulation prison dress had appeared from nowhere, it seemed, to fill the jury box. Kevin Murphy, similarly attired, was sitting calmly at one of the counsel's tables. Lyle Walker sat at the other shuffling through a sheaf of papers.

"Siddown in front," a rude voice called from the back of the audience. "You're not made of bloody glass."

As Hunt, Sanderson and Billy sank warily back into their seats, Sanderson scanning the audience for signs of trouble, Arthur Hancock, the prison trusty, walked out onto the set, halted in front of the Judge's Bench and said in a loud, commanding voice: "All rise!"

The entire audience rose. And with a flourish that ended up a brief struggle as he got caught in the black drapes, Judge Nathanial Payten emerged from the backdrop behind and took his seat at the Bench. A ripple of laughter ran through the hall. Payten glared coldly around the room, then produced a drinking glass and poured what looked like iced tea into it from his hip-flask.

"Court is now in session," Arthur Hancock announced. "His Honour, Judge Nathanial Payten presiding!"

As the audience settled down again with a massed cacophony of coughs, hawking throats and a screech of chairs, the next solemn pronouncement rang out.

"Bring forth the prisoner!"

And from within the black folds of the backdrop, Willie Crewe emerged, escorted by Dickie King. Willie was wearing the same sort of bulky jacket that now garbed the Mayor and Puffin Billy. He looked out over the bizarre thicket of hushed figures in the audience, grinned smugly and raised his hands in a clenched, two-fisted salute like a prizefighter before a bout. Reaching Lyle Walker's desk, he slumped nonchalantly into a seat next to him and turned and gave the audience another cocky grin.

"Silence now for *The Vanishing Yahoo*," Arthur Hancock announced stentoriously, "a one-act drama by Noel Chisholm, performed by the inmates of Parramatta Jail!"

Another ripple of excitement ran through the audience. (Rev) Hunt shot a satisfied glance at Bull Sanderson. Arthur Hancock marched forth from the Bench and took his place shoulder-to-shoulder with Dickie King—both of them now guards standing at attention behind Willie Crewe's chair. All eyes were fixed firmly on the Judge. A ringing silence awaited his next move, which involved clearing his throat with a delicate cough and wetting it liberally with a whacking great belt of moonshine from his glass. This he then replaced carefully and with much finesse on the Bench. Staring abstractly at the audience, his face went scarlet, his fingers drummed a violent tattoo on a blotting pad in front of him and a pent-up explosion of fiery breath suddenly whistled through his teeth with a shrill "Ssssshhhhhheeeeeeeeeeessssshhhhhhh!" Judge Payten then rapped his gavel on the Bench for attention and order, and, satisfied that the outbreak of amused guffaws had been firmly quashed, turned to address the jury.

"Gentlemen of the jury," he rumbled. "You have been summoned here to pass judgement on one man—and an entire nation. The two may seem to you to have about as much in common as sugar and shit, but I urge you not to take the responsibility that confronts you lightly—and wipe those silly bloody grins off your mugs! This is serious! The issue before you is no less than betrayal. A man's life is at stake. An entire *code* is in question. Listen carefully to the evidence that is laid before you. When you make your decision, make it objectively, with your minds and not your hearts, if indeed you have any hearts and minds left after languishing for years in this bloody iron-barred loony-bin." His Honour's bony finger began poking at the transfixed jury. Winds sprang up in his hair. He was off and running.

"This nation was founded upon the principle of contempt for the law. And the law in those days was pretty contemptible—not that it's anything to poke a bloody stick at today: Cops can still indiscriminately throw their weight around and know they'll be protected if there's a complaint against them. But in the old days, a man could be transported here and subjected to brutality and abject misery for stealing a loaf of bread. Hanging was the penalty if he happened to grab any loose change that was lying around while he was at it. Convicts had the choice of bending to the whip or trying to escape and go bush. Those who managed to shoot through usually spent their freedom continually on the run. And this is the fascinating bit!—they were classed as outlaws and bushrangers because they'd had the criminal audacity to break out of what was in fact a complete penal society!

"It was out of that miserable bloody syndrome that grew one of Australia's most cherished codes: *Let no man betray another, especially to the bloody law.* Aaron Sherritt did it and got a bullet up his gumboots. Many men have done it and lived to regret it dearly. What *you* must do, members of the jury, is to ultimately decide whether in this modern complex age of plastic rubber-plants and bottled-gas barbeques the traditional codes no longer have any real place or meaning, or whether there's still life in the old yahoo yet, and a national spirit still willing to take a swift kick at anyone who *dobs somebody in!*"

There was a roar of applause from the audience, and His Honour the Judge belted the hell out of the Bench with his gavel to restore order. When the commotion had finally abated, his voice took on a bitter, scalding, hissing tone like something simmering just below the boil.

"As lies breed more lies, so do betrayals lead to more and bigger betrayals, and as each finds acceptance or passive apathy, so the next one is so much easier to accept—until the *code* is lost forever and a hatchet-faced failed Navy Minister and a man no-one in his right mind would even buy a used car from are able to join forces with a self-made, silver-haired turncoat and grab the nation's highest power in the most obscene, un-Australian fashion, and the vast majority of the people couldn't give a bloody stiff shit about it! If that great native-born Australian John Kerr had done what he did to Australia's sovereignty a few years back when Curton and Chifley and a few others like them were alive and kicking—all of them the wild yahoos of politics when you compare them with today's smooth-as-shit PR creations!—there would have been jackets and shirts off in the bloody House of Representatives and Kerr would've had his pin-striped arse booted all over the Australian Capital Territory! And we'd be a bloody republic by now instead of a nation of grown-up people trying to live down the bloody tradition of a Queen's Representative running around in an idiotic pith helmet dripping with white cockatoo feathers and waving a ceremonial sword!"

On those words another deafening cheer raised high the rafters, and the entire prison population leapt to their feet, waving their arms madly and dancing up and down in a stomping frenzy that shook the auditorium's thick timber floor.

"*YOU ARE THE YAHOOS!!*" the Judge bellowed at them. "Australia is yours! Don't fuck it like they did!"

Another tumult of hollering and whistling and stamping exploded at that point, and Billy Puffin spun on (Rev) Hunt and bawled:

"This is not a play! This is nothing but a political tirade by a rabble-rousing troublemaker—and a left-wing one at that!"

"There are left-wingers in this jail!" Hunt shouted back. "And right-wingers and moderates and Christians and Jews and atheists and Protestants and Catholics! What makes you think this place is any different to life outside!"

"But we'll have a riot on our hands if you don't put a stop to all this!"

"No we bloody well won't!" Bull Sanderson barked, and, standing up on his seat he pulled a whistle from his tunic and blew a long shrill blast. Behind the cheering audience, beyond the farthest seats, a phalanx of prison officers with guns fanned out across the rear of the hall, shouldered their carbines and then began moving in on the audience; and when the mob turned and saw them approaching, the pandemonium suddenly collapsed and died and a tense hush reigned as both forces faced each other, ready for the first move toward warfare. Judge Payten hammered the Bench with his gavel and roared: "Silence in the court! One more disturbance like that and I'll clear the whole room! This is a palace of justice, not a bloody public bar on a Saturday night!"

A rumble of tense laugher diffused the ugly confrontation, and the men gradually settled back into their seats. The guards backed off and lowered their rifles. Judge Payten took a fortifying swig from his glass and then sat still for a minute or two, preoccupied with the effect, which was such that he jerked and convulsed as though a depth charge had exploded deep down inside him. Then, with tears in his eyes, he said: "The prisoner will now rise and hear the charge that has been brought against him."

With a toss of the head and another nonchalant grin for the audience. Aaron Sherritt rose to his feet, folded his arms carelessly against his chest and slouched against the defence counsel's table. His script lay on the desk before him. For the may who was playing this role, Jesus, this acting shit wasn't such a bad screw after all, though it took a bit of doing to memorise all those bloody lines.

Gravely, the Judge read out the charge.

"William Vivian Crewe, it is charged that on the twentieth day of September in this the Year of Our Lord, you did knowingly and with intent pass certain highly confidential information to one Arnold Reginald Sanderson, Chief Prison Officer of this institution, and in doing so did cause the arrest, solitary confinement and deprivation of all rights, freedoms and liberties of a fellow-inmate, Harold Percival Pearce. How plead you?"

Willie Crewe stood blinking furiously for a few seconds as the Judge's words sank in. His face went very pale. Then it turned to white rage, and he spun around to the audience and shrieked: "You fucking cunts! What the fuck's going on here? What's this all about?"

The Judge said: "Is that a plea of guilty or not guilty?"

"Go fuck yourself!" Willie screamed.

"I take it that you're pleading not guilty," the Judge observed; and to the two custodians, Dickie King and Arthur Hancock, he snapped: "Cuff him!"

Dickie King stepped forward and cuffed Willie right across the left ear, causing him to stumble back against the table and fall forward and slightly sideways over the chair.

"Restrain him," the Judge ordered, and with the speed of greased lightning, Dickie grabbed Crewe's arms and tugged them over the back of the chair, and Arthur Hancock snapped a pair of handcuffs on him.

"You fucking bastards!" Willie screamed. "I'll kill you all for this!" The two guards grabbed him by the shoulders, dodging a couple of furious two-fisted haymakers, swung him around to face the Judge again and rammed him violently back into the chair. Dickie King then threw a nylon cord around Willie's neck and viciously tugged it tight, pulling the struggling con's head back and high over the chair-back. At the same time, Arthur Hancock had caught hold of Willie's threshing legs and slipped a set of chain-linked leg-irons on his ankles. Dickie then swiftly ran the ends of the nylon halter under the seat of the chair, looped them around the chain that ran between the leg-irons and gave a hard yank. This effectively hog-tied Willie in a neat and perfect sitting position with his head pulled slightly over the back of the chair as the rope tightened on his Adam's apple. Dickie then smartly lashed the ends of the cord to a crossbar running between the legs of the chair. And, in what had actually taken only a matter of fifteen seconds, Willie Vivian Crewe was well and truly right up shit creek in a barbed-wire canoe. Every struggle he made caused the nylon rope to bite into his windpipe, the choker fortunately strangling the horrible threats that he was attempting to utter. By contrast, a heavy expectant silence hung over the audience.

By this time, of course, (Rev) Hunt and Bull Sanderson had come to the conclusion that all was not exactly what it was supposed to be.

"Mr Chisholm!" Hunt barked, rising to his feet. "Perhaps you would be good enough to explain what exactly is going on here. I was under the distinct impression from your script that this play dealt with the trial of Aaron Sherritt, not Willie Crewe."

"And you were quite right," Chisholm assured him. "However, it's not unusual for revisions to be made right up to the time the curtain rises. And if the exact definition of a theatrical play hinged entirely on the necessity for a written script, most of our everyday social exchanges would require ghostwriters. Which isn't such a bad idea when you consider that most of the fuck-ups and malices that we commit could then be cut short at the commercial break. Or professionally choreographed so that we don't actually draw blood. As for this little charade, may I draw your attention to a certain obvious analogy between the case of Aaron Sherritt and the allegation against Willie Crewe? Why dredge up the past when we've got a real live present-day stoolie with whom to exercise our same peculiar instinct for justice?"

"*Justice!* This is not justice! The man has been tried and hanged before the trial has even begun."

"This is prison justice, Mr Hunt. And as such, Willie's lucky to have the chance to face his peers alive and in one piece in an open court. He could have been knifed in the back, or had his throat cut in his sleep, and as for his murderer—nobody would have been the wiser. As for his ultimate fate, I can promise you that he won't be hanged. And I remind you that you have enough guns on hand at the back of the room to force a halt to these proceedings if you feel they transcend the bounds of fairness and good taste. Now, do we have your permission to proceed?"

(Rev) Hunt turned to Bull Sanderson. "I'm not sure I'm willing to go along with this. But what do you think?"

Sanderson scratched his head and sighed deeply. "They're right, bugger it, on all counts. There's no getting away from the fact that Willie informed, and by rights he could've been six feet under by now. If we want this jail to stay peaceful, we may as well let them have what they want. Otherwise there'll be hostility, and they'll get the dobbing little bastard and do him in later, anyway."

But Puffin Billy wasn't going to stand for that. "I think this has gone far enough," he declared loudly. "I demand that this whole highly illegal gathering—this kangaroo court—be broken up immediately and the men returned to their cells!"

"Shut up," (Rev) Hunt replied. "You have absolutely no knowledge of real rprison life, and even less appreciation of tehe principle at stake here. Mr Chisholm! We are willing to let the trial proceed, on condition that we retain the right to intervene if there are any disturbances."

"I thank you, Mr Hunt. And as for your agitated colleague there, may I impress upon him that one more outburst like that will force me to place him in contempt of court and have him flung out on his fat arse. I now call upon the prosecuting counsel to begin his opening address."

Kevin Murphy stood up at his desk, turned to face the jury and then couldn't figure out what to do with his hands, which tried hanging at his side at first; then one climbed up to scratch his ear, then they both folded and unfolded, then shied away to hide behind his back and finally emerged to rest on their knuckles on the table. But that made him stoop awkwardly, so they went back to the folded-arm position at his chest.

"Er, yeah, well . . . I'm not much of a speaker when it comes to talking to a mob, but I guess the whole point to all this is that nobody likes a *dobber*. There isn't a bigger ratbag on earth than a bloke who puts somebody in. And it's worse when the bloody stoolie is an even bigger bastard than the bloke he snitched on. Take Willie here. Now there's a perfect little angel for you. We all know how many blokes he's belted Christ out of in this clink, and how many kids he's strong-armed into dropping their tweeds for him, and other unnatural acts of a disgusting poofta-ish nature. And the bloke he blew the whistle on, Harry Pearce, might be a bit on the tough side but his record speaks for itself—he wouldn't harm a bloody fly."

"I object," Lyle Walker interjected, rising quickly to his feet. "Murphy seems to forget that Pearce happens to be an axe-murderer!"

"Objection overruled," Chisholm retorted. "We're dealing with matters *inside* this jail. Whatever happened outside is inadmissible as evidence, and I order the jury to strike that garbage from their minds. I would also point out that this is an opening address, not a cross-examination—so pull your bloody head in and sit down."

Then it was the Honourable William Lancelot Puffin who jumped again to his feet. "This is a travesty of justice! How can you possibly disregard the fact that a man is a homicidal maniac?"

"Willie Crewe isn't doing life for shoplifting," Chisholm informed him. "There's a little matter of two murder convictions and a couple more that can't be proved because the bodies haven't surfaced. So you can stick a bloody sock in it and sit down too! Proceed, Mr Murphy."

"Well, the evidence you're about to hear proves beyond a shadow of a bloody doubt that Willie Crewe wilfully betrayed Harry Pearce to Bull—er, Mr Sanderson, because he knew that Harry was protecting Timothy Botham and he couldn't get his hands on Botham till Harry was out of the way. Timothy was going crackers over the sheila who got him sent up, and he looked like doing something stupid. So Harry fed him a cock and bull story about breaking out of jail. Timothy was roughed-up by Crewe and let the story slip and Crewe shot along like a shithouse rat to Sanderson and told him Harry was planning a break. Harry's now stuck in the Blockhouse, and the way I see it, Willie Crewe's lucky he's still there, because by the time Harry'd finished with him this'd be a bloody coroner's inquest, not a trial."

"You bet your sweet arse it would!" someone shouted in the audience, and a rumble of anger rolled through the auditorium. Chisholm rapped his gavel again to restore order.

"Counsel for the defence—if you please."

"Lyle Walker stood up, faced the jury and piously clasped his hands together over his flat, hard-muscled belly. His eyes closed for a moment, his face uplifted, as though in silent prayer or communion. "Gentlemen of the jury," he began. "Just as we, as Australians, don't like dobbers, so does The Almighty frown upon blokes who bear false witness against other blokes. And counsel for the prosecution, here, is an out-and-out bloody liar."

Kevin Murphy leapt up and rounded on the learned counsel. "Who's a bloody liar?"

"You're a bloody liar."

"Who says I'm a bloody liar?"

"I say you're a bloody liar."

"Oh you do, huh? How'd you like to back that up outside?"

"Anytime you like, feller."

"Oh yeah?"

"Oh yeah."

"Yeah?"

"Yeah."

"Think yer bloody smart, don't yer?"

"Yeah."

"You'll get yours, mate, don't worry."

"Oh yeah?"

"Yeah."

"Yeah?"

"Yeah."

Chisholm rapped the Bench and called them both to order. "If you both want to have a go at each other, may I suggest you wait until we've dispensed with the defendant. Mr Murphy, please replace your bum on that chair and button up. Mr Walker, will you please continue with your address."

With Murphy still glowering at him, Lyle went on: "As the evidence that is shortly to be given proves beyond a shadow of a bloody doubt, the defendant, Mr Crewe, said absolutely nothing about Harry Pearce planning to bust out. And we submit that it was entirely Pearce's fault, aided and abetted by Murphy, here, that led Mr Sanderson to discover that he'd quarried half the rock out of the wall of his cell. Furthermore, the defendant wishes me to point out that if the prosecution wants to push this issue any further, the Lord God has another little saying that goes something like this: *Let he who casts the first stone make it a bloody big one. And then start running.*"

"Like Christ I will," Murphy gnashed. "I don't run from anybody."

Lyle, addressing Chisholm, said: "Your Honour, I object to the prosecuting counsel's use of blasphemy in these proceedings. I will not allow the Lord's name to be taken in vain. So tell him to shut the fuck up."

A loud howl of laughter broke out in the crowd behind. Lyle turned and yelled: "Any bastard out there who wants to get smart can go a few rounds in The Pen with me when all this is over! Any takers?"

There was an immediate silence.

"Mr Murphy," said Judge Chisholm. "Would you care to call your first witness?"

"You bet. The prosecution calls Timothy Botham."

Timothy was sitting in the third row back from the front seats. When his name was called, he remained glued to his seat. His heart jumped painfully, and he felt himself suddenly fighting for breath from a rush of anxiety. He heard his name called a second time, and then again, and the cons around him were all looking at him and gesturing towards the Bench and making rude remarks and all that. Then Murphy was pushing his way along the row of seats to stand over him and roughly shake him by the shoulders.

"You gone deaf all of a sudden? You're wanted up on the witness stand. Now move your arse for Christ's sake. We haven't got all bloody day."

But all Timothy could think of was the horror of a magistrate quietly reading a slip of paper, then slowly and deliberately tearing it up into confetti. And Mrs Everingham sitting as white as a sheet next to her husband.

"I can't," he wailed at Murphy. "I don't like courts."

Murphy bent down to look into his downcast, troubled eyes. He squeezed his shoulders gently. "This isn't gonna hurt, Timothy. You're not on trial this time—Crewe is. Just tell the truth and you've got nothing in the world to worry about."

"That's what I did the last time," Timothy moaned. "And look what they did to me then."

"Yeah, but you're with your mates this time. And you wouldn't want Harry to think you piked out, would you?"

That was enough to snap Timothy, reluctant as he was, back into motion. Amid cheers and much clapping, he got up and followed Murphy onto the set. A chair had been placed below the Judge's Bench, facing the defendant, the two counsel and the entire auditorium. Timothy stood next to it, blushing deeply, and Murphy returned to his desk, picked up a sheet of notes. Noel Chisholm, perched like a buzzard over the young witness, looked down from the Bench and said: "Timothy Albert Botham, do you swear to tell the truth, the whole truth and nothing but the truth, so help you?"

"Er, yeah," Timothy pledged. "I've always like told the truth. My Mum always told me that every time like someone tells a lie an angel drops dead in Heaven."

"Christ," the Judge observed, "how many bloody angels have they got up there? Please be seated, Timothy. Mr Murphy, you may proceed."

Murphy cleared his throat with a hoarse bark and placed his wandering hands behind him in true courtroom style. "Timothy, could you tell the court what you were doing on Thursday, September the twentieth?"

"Yeah," said Timothy. "I was like doing four years for burglary."

"Yeah, we know that, Timothy. But what I mean is, what were you *doing* on the day in question? Can you give us a full account of your actions?"

"I don't know what you mean."

"For crying out bloody loud! You must have been doing *something* with yourself. Now what was it?"

Timothy blushed hotly. "I wasn't doing *anything* with myself! My Mum always told me my eyes would like fall out if I did things like that!"

A gale of obscene merriment swept through the hall. Murphy sank into his chair and put his head in his hands, and his shoulders twitched with silent laughter. Judge Chisholm, his lips jerking uncontrollably, rapped his gavel to quieten the crowd.

"What Mr Murphy is trying to do, Timothy," he explained, trying to keep a straight face, "is to establish your movements on that particular day—and he doesn't mean what time you went to the bog or anything trivial like that. Now think back very carefully and tell us, to the best of your recollection, what you did from the moment you'd performed all your ablutions, had breakfast and were ready to face another gloriously happy day."

Timothy's face screwed up with thought. "I don't think I was very happy that day, being in jail, like. I played 'Danny Boy' on my harmonica for a while and then Mr Sanderson like came in and told me he'd tread on the bloody thing and flatten it if I didn't stop making all that racket. Then he told me to get out into the fresh air and like stop mooning over Mrs—er, well, a certain problem I had on my mind."

"Mrs Everingham?"

"I don't want her name brought into this," Timothy protested, a pink blush erupting over his face again.

"OK, Timothy," said the Judge. "The jury is instructed to strike that name from their minds. For the purposes of privacy and the said lady's reputation, we'll refer to her henceforth as Madam X. What happened next, Timothy?"

"Well, I think it was like visiting day that day, and Mrs, er, Madam X didn't like come to see me and I was feeling pretty crook about that and I told Harry Pearce I had to like see her somehow or I'd go nuts. And, well, Harry said she wasn't worth a pinch of shit and that got me pretty mad, like, because she's a fine and nice lady and she told me she loved me and all that."

There was a silence, Timothy gazing at the floor and the entire gathering hanging on his last words.

"OK," Kevin Murphy demanded. "Carry on. What else?"

"Well, she said the way I fucked her it was like the greatest thing since sliced bread."

Bedlam reigned again as the entire audience fell apart. Men were doubled up with the agony of hysterical laughter. Others practically rolled on the floor between the row of seats. Judge Chisholm's gavel cracked and rattled with the rhythm of a belt-fed machinegun.

"*See what I mean?*" Timothy cried furiously in the face of the raucous din. "Every time I tell the truth everybody like takes it as a bloody joke!"

As the uproar calmed down, Judge Chisholm explained: "The last thing we want to do, Timothy, is to pry into the details of your private life. What Mr Murphy was asking was what happened to you after you'd talked with Harry Pearce."

"Well . . . Willie Crewe came to my cell and started asking me personal questions, like, about, er, well, like my relations with Madam X."

"Willie Crewe came to your cell, did he? Was there anyone else with him?"

"Hey, steady on!" Kevin Murphy protested. "Am I supposed to be the prosecuting counsel or am I just standing here to decorate the bloody place?"

"I stand corrected," Judge Chisholm apologised. "Please continue."

"Thanks a bloody million. Now, Timothy, Willie Crewe came to your cell, did he? Was there anyone else with him?"

"Henry Trembler was there too."

"That dirty little snake?" Murphy turned around to scan the audience. "By the way, where is he?"

At that same moment, as though two apparently unconnected factors had come together to make four, the Honourable William Puffin suddenly realised that, amid all this unbelievable commotion and pandemonium, he and the rest of the official party had completely forgotten about his wife. He turned to (Rev) Hunt with sudden worry and agitation. "My wife! What on earth's happened to Mrs Puffin?"

Both Hunt and Bull Sanderson looked at each other and, with fear and trepidation, put two and two together too.

"Oh my God," (Rev) Hunt breathed.

Sanderson said: "I'd better look into this myself." To Puffin Billy he said: "I wouldn't worry too much, Minister. She's probably being shown around the jail by one of the guards. I'll have her back here in two shakes."

As Sanderson rose and made his way around the courtroom setting to the auditorium's main door, evidence for the prosecution continued.

"What was the purpose of their visit to your cell, Timothy?"

"Well, at first I thought they was like trying to be friendly. And then . . ." Timothy's big brown eyes moistened and were cast with rank embarrassment to the courtroom floor.

"And then what?"

"I don't want to talk about it," he mumbled.

"May I remind you that you're under oath to tell the truth and the whole truth, Timothy. Now stop playing silly-buggers and let's hear exactly what happened . . ."

It would be completely beyond the bounds of human decency, belief and imagination to describe what was happening at that very moment in Noel Chisholm's closed cell. Suffice to say that Henry Trembler, who now saw himself as the Second Coming of Satan and was quite proud that he'd beaten the other bloke to it, was operating at the very peak of his perversity. Had the great Marquis de Sade chanced upon the horrible, bestial scene he would probably have abandoned his peculiar philosophies and instruments of pain and pleasure and turned to the Church for safety and redemption. *The Story of O* would have plummetted in literary shock-value and notoriety to the level of *Swinging Stewardesses* and *Noddy Stops at a Red Light*. So depraved were the goings-on, in fact, that with great courage and personal sacrifice this author is prepared to suppress the lurid, explicit details and, in so doing, forsake the Australian literary temptation to shock the balls off everybody and thereby invite some outraged political bush-cocky to get up in Parliament and condemn this important work as "nothing but a vile stream of filth and gutter pornography containing absolutely no literary merit whatsoever" and demand that it be banned—thereby making the author a hell of a lot of money.

And they say writers have no scruples . . .

Over in the Blockhouse, Harry Pearce was pacing slowly back and forth in his cell with worry and a number of other things weighing heavily upon him. Though he had no watch to tell him what time it was—it had been confiscated when he was committed to solitary—his own biological clock told him it must be close to exercise time, if indeed the time had not already passed. And here he was, feeling like a right bloody dill, waiting around in the costume that Bruce Greenwood had smuggled in for him.

Harry was having serious misgivings about that bloody costume. Greenwood had looked him square in the face and pledged that he wouldn't be facing any danger on this, the longest walk he would probably ever take in his life, the walk from the Blockhouse to (Rev) Hunt's office. If it was to be such a bloody piece of cake, why was he dressed up in a knee-length canvas donkey-coat and canvas strides that were supported by thick leather braces and were so long in the leg that they covered his boots—the whole get-up covered front back and both sides with close-stitched square panels containing flat slabs of steel plate? The whole attire was so heavy and cumbersome that with every step he took or bodily movement he made he felt sorry for the poor buggers who'd had to walk on the moon.

And then there was that bloody Colt pistol. With even the arms of his armoured suit chock-a-block with steel plating, he reckoned that if he had to make a fast draw from his waistband to defend himself he'd be dead, buried and forgotten before he'd even hauled the bloody thing out of his pants.

And where in bloody hell was Bruce Greenwood? The cell door clicked and swung open, and there he was.

"You ready to go?"

"Yeah," said Harry. "If you can get a bloody forklift truck in here to carry me out."

"You'll need that gear out there," said Bruce. "The whole jail's alive with armed guards. You scared?"

"Oh no, mate. I just haven't been keeping up my bloody suntan lately, that's all. I'll strangle Murphy when we get out of here—*if* we ever get out of here."

"We'll get out, Harry. Just keep cool and don't scrunch up on me, that's all."

"Christ, Bruce," Harry mused, "you used to be such a nice young lad."

"That's what comes of being exposed to criminal elements," Bruce replied wryly. "Still, from now on at least no-one's going to kick sand in my face."

"What about The Beast?"

"He doesn't go any further than the watchroom. Too risky. Besides, with his record you don't know what he might do when he gets the scent of human blood . . ."

"Blood? What blood?"

"Just a coin of phrase, Harry," Bruce sighed.

Harry breathed deeply and with a groan he straightened up in his armoured clobber. "Well, in for a penny . . . Let's get the show on the road."

They moved slowly out of the cell and into the bare passageway, Harry's tread so slow and deliberate that it was as though he was struggling along knee-deep in wet spaghetti. They halted at the door to The Beast's cell, and Greenwood took the pistol from Harry's waistband, cocked it and unlocked the door. As it swung open The Beast leapt up from his bed.

"You beauts! I knew you wouldn't leave me behind! I would've screamed the bloody place down otherwise."

"Keep your bloody voice down," Greenwood hissed. "And don't go doing anything stupid or I'll put a bullet in you. Or Harry will, anyway, because he's going to be carrying the gun."

Greenwood handed the pistol to Harry, put his hands up and clasped them together on his head. The Beast fell in next to Harry, and with Harry prodding the muzzle of the Colt at Greenwood's back, they all moved slowly along the corridor to the watchroom door. When they reached it, Greenwood touched a button that sounded a buzzer on the other side. The door was opened by a guard who had a half-eaten sandwich in one hand, two cheeks crammed with pork luncheon meat and baked beans, and a mouth that hung wide open with surprise.

Greenwood said in a squeaky, terrified voice: "Don't do anything, *please*. They've got a gun on me."

Harry prodded Greenwood into the room. "Get over against that wall," he ordered the astonished guard. "And you too," he snapped at two other officers who were sitting paralysed with shock at a table with neatly fanned poker hands poised in front of them. "Do it smartly and very carefully, or young Greenwood here gets blown apart."

When the three guards were lined up, the first one having a painful time trying to force a mouthful of sandwich down his dry, fear-constricted gullet, Harry ordered The Beast to handcuff their wrists behind their backs. This he did neatly and efficiently and without so much as a threat of atrocity. At Harry's command he then made them lie on their bellies on the floor and, yanking the laces out of their boots, tightly trussed their ankles together. He then gagged them with handtowels from an adjacent washroom.

Turning to Harry, The Beast rubbed his hands together excitedly. "Right! Let's get the hell out of here!"

"The only place you're going," Harry growled, poking the gun at him, "is right back in your bloody cell. I'm not having a maniac like you tagging along with me."

"*You lousy bastard!*" The Beast screeched. "I've been in this bloody hole for two and a half bloody years! You know what it's like.

Only an out-and-out deadshit would leave a bloke to rot in here!"

Harry raised the gun and pointed it straight at The Beast's chest. The Beast stood his ground, eyeing him defiantly. Harry said: "I'll let you come with us if you answer me one thing—truthfully and with no bloody bullshit. *What did you do out there to get slung in jail?*"

"I told you, I spat in Sand—"

"Stop fucking about! I mean *outside*, you dickhead! What was your crime?"

The Beast said: "Alimony."

Harry glared at him and then said: "All right—start moving back to your cell."

"I'm not bullshitting, I swear it! My old lady was living with some bloke and claiming half my bloody wages in alimony, so I cancelled the bloody bank draft and shot through to Queensland. Her bloody lawyer set the cops on me and I gut lumbered in Rockhampton. I got charged with defaulting and got a six-month suspended sentence. So I shot through to Darwin. Then they bloody tracked me down again, and I told the bloody magistrate he could shove his court orders up his stupid dinger because I wasn't gonna give that bitch another bloody cent, and then I hopped over the dock and thumped her bloody lawyer, and one thing sort-a led to another and . . . You can go inside for defaulting on alimony, mate! You ask some of the blokes who're stuck in bloody mines and cattle stations and drilling camps all over the bloody place where a lizard wouldn't stick its bloody nose. They're all called Bill Smith or Curly Whatsisname. I'm not a bloody crook, Harry. I just don't like taking shit from bloody lawyers, cops, magistrates and prison warders, that's all. Fair dinkum. Ridgy-didge."

Harry lowered the gun. "Jesus," was all he said. He prodded the weapon at Bruce Greenwood's back. "Let's go."

Outside the watchroom, the fiercely hot sunlight struck them with dazzling force. They stood still for a moment, their eyes gradually adjusting to the blinding glare, and slowly, amid the dizzying heat-waves, there emerged the figures of armed guards suspended surrealistically along the outer walls. A horrible thought immediately struck Harry.

"Hey! What's to stop those bastards shooting me in the bloody head? Some of those guys are expert marksmen."

"That's all going to be taken care of," Greenwood assured him.

"Now, both of you start walking around the yard as though you're doing your normal exercise. When you get level with the guardhouse at the gate, make a bee-line for it as fast as you can. By the time you get there I'll have the guard lined up so that all you have to do is to slug him with the gun."

Harry was horrified. "You mean shoot him?"

"No I don't mean shoot him," Bruce sighed. "Just belt him over the head with it. Knock him cold."

"But it might damage his bloody skull! I've heard of people tripping over their own bloody feet and croaking from a brain haemorrhage."

"Harry, just do as I tell you, *please*. You need a full swing with a ten-pound hammer to crush a bloke's skull. Now, for God's sake get going—or I'll have a bloody brain hemorrhage right now from nervous tension!"

Bull Sanderson, unable to locate Celia Puffin in the mess hall or administration section of the jail, passed by (Rev) Hunt's office, stepped out into the open courtyard which was the jail's visiting area and approached the guardroom at the main gate. Two officers stood sluggishly to attention as he stalked in.

"Either of you seen the Minister's wife?"

"No," one of them replied. "Where's it playing?"

"Don't be fucking cute," Sanderson snapped. "If it's not too much for your tiny little minds to comprehend, have you seen a lady in a pink dress and a blue hat come this way?"

"Do we look as though we have? We only just came on duty."

"Open the main gate," Sanderson ordered them curtly, and without further word he climbed through a door within the huge iron-clad double gates and, for the first time in years, since his sad sojourn in King's Cross, in fact, he stepped into the outside world. It was strange out here, like some twilight garden of the mind. Birds sang, muffled traffic noises sounded from distant streets; even the air was different, scented with flowers and trees and grass cuttings from newly mown suburban lawns where sprinklers whirled their fine mists like veils around slumbering bungalows.

The Minister's black Daimler was standing patiently a few yards from the gates, the chauffeur slumped across the front seat asleep with his peaked cap over his face. Sanderson shook him roughly into life.

"Have you seen the Minister's wife?"

The chauffeur yawned, swallowed and sucked his teeth. "Have I seen the Minister's wife? I've seen her nearly every bloody day for the past three years, mate, and it don't get any easier."

"Has she come this way in the last hour or so?"

"Not that I know of. I've been catching up on the old zeds anyway."

"Well, stay awake from now on. And if you see her, tell the blokes in the guardhouse just inside the gate to alert me immediately."

So saying, Bull Sanderson again turned his back on the world and went back into the jail to continue his search.

twenty-seven

MEANWHILE, IN THE MOCK COURTROOM, THE TRIAL of Willie Crewe had reached the stage of Timothy Botham's cross-examination. Under intense questioning by the prosecuting counsel, Timothy had related how Willie Crewe and Henry Trembler had, under the guise of friendship, first seduced him into revealing explicit details of his affair with Mrs, er Madam X, then Willie had beaten him and told him he'd just bought him from Harry Pearce for two thousand dollars, then Timothy, morally crushed and imagining he'd been betrayed, had told Willie about Pearce's plan for them both to break out of his cell block, make a dash for the main wall, knock off a few guards as they went over the top and high-tail it to freedom—in broad daylight, like, when everyone would least expect it.

That sparked off another roar of laughter in the audience, and Puffin Billy turned to (Rev) Hunt and said: "Do you condone the fact that there is obviously a vicious homosexual element in this jail?"

"I am aware of it, but I certainly don't condone it," Hunt shrugged. "But what do you expect when you deprive men of their normal sexual outlets? For some time now I've been of the strong opinion that we should allow the better behaved cases to cohabitate under certain strictly controlled conditions with their wives. At least once a month."

Billy sniffed cynically. "Why should *they* get special privileges?"

Lyle Walker was standing facing Timothy Botham and again gazing heavenward as though seeking spiritual instructions. Then he clasped his hands at his chest as though in prayer and launched his cross-examination.

"Are you certain that Willie Crewe's sole motive in coming to your cell was malice and intent to do you harm?"

"I reckon so," Timothy replied. "He belted me a couple of times and said my life wouldn't be worth living if I like didn't, er, do the right thing by him."

"*Do the right thing by him.* What exactly do you mean by that?"

"He like wanted me to, well, you know . . ."

Amid a buzz of excitement in the audience, Willie Crewe started struggling violently in his chair, kicking his shackled legs and twisting his head from side to side as the nylon choker tore at his windpipe. Dickie King stepped forward and quickly calmed him by yanking the rope from behind.

"Did he actually say in so many words that he wanted you to, well, you know?"

"No, but I like got the message pretty clearly."

"You got the message pretty clearly, eh? You know a lot about, well, you know—do you?"

A blush began to creep up Timothy's sad face.

"Well, do you?"

"Enough to like, you know, get by like."

"Yes. No doubt Madam X would testify to that."

"Don't you talk about her like that! I won't have her name like dragged into this! She's a fine and decent lady, and we are like in love with each other!"

"I object, Your Honour," Kevin Murphy objected, leaping to his feet. "The defence counsel is acting like a pure cunt."

Lyle Walker said: "Your Honour, I'll have to ask you to instruct the defence counsel to take that back—or I'll leap over there and plant him one right between the bloody eyes!"

"Your Honour," Murphy cried, "you can tell the counsel for the prosecution that if he wants to have a bloody go, I'm ready for him!"

Judge Chisholm rapped his gavel angrily. "Gentlemen! I will not tolerate this sort of behaviour in a court of law! One more display of this sort of rudeness and lack of couth and I'll hop down there and kick the shit out of both of you. Mr Walker, it would appear that you're badgering the witness about matters that have no bearing on this case. Perhaps you could choose another line of questioning."

"OK," said Lyle. "Mr Botham, isn't it in fact true that Mr Crewe and Mr Trembler came to your cell to offer advice on your relationship with this particular sheila?"

"Yeah, but they was only like stickybeaking, and they was really—"

"Just answer the bloody question. Did they out of the goodness of their hearts and as experienced men of the world come to you without malice or forethought to offer you advice?"

"Yes. No. I mean—"

"Did they offer you advice?"

"Yeah."

"What sort of advice?"

"Well, whether Mrs, er Madam X really loved me or not."

"Apart from being stuck in jail for four bloody years, did you have any reason to believe she didn't?"

Timothy's pure, innocent features knitted with pain and anguish. "No, I didn't. Least I didn't think so. She told me she loved me, like lots of times."

"When did she tell you she loved you?"

"When I was like fixing her big end."

An obscene roar of laughter drowned out Timothy's plaintive protests and Kevin Murphy's angry objections to the continuing line of cross-examination. When the howling row had exhausted itself, Murphy said: "Your Honour, do we have to allow the defence counsel to force this poor kid to divulge such personal information?"

"No, we certainly don't," Chisholm declared. He leaned over the Bench,—looking down on the boy. "Timothy, if you don't mind me asking—what was wrong with the, er, lady's big end?"

"Well, she like hadn't had it serviced for a while and it needed a good lube job, a bit of work on the nipples and a new shaft—

"NOW WHAT'S SO BLOODY FUNNY ABOUT THAT!!"

Over at the Blockhouse, Harry Pearce had just slugged a man unconscious with the butt of his pistol. It wasn't a nice thing to do, especially to a nice friendly peaceable sort of bloke with a lousy boring job and a rundown wife and three screaming kids and a stack of hire-purchase commitments who'd been chatting away about football with Bruce Greenwood one moment, his back exposed to the open door and the exercise yard, and a second later experiencing a whirling kaleidoscope of dots and stars that made funny muffled underwater sounds as they revolved in upon themselves and vanished into a pinpoint of blackness. Harry grabbed him as his legs buckled and helped him gently to the floor. Harry felt sick. The sound and physical sensation of metal on flesh and bone had aroused something awful in the armoured depths of his mind. He checked the guard's heart and put his ear close to the man's open, sagging mouth to make sure he was breathing properly.

"Don't worry. He's OK," said Bruce Greenwood. Harry watched as The Beast eased the unconscious man's heavy, lifeless arms over his back and lashed them tightly together at the wrists. He then boot-laced his ankles together and gagged him with a handkerchief taken from his breast pocket. Greenwood checked his watch. It was already two forty-five, bugger it. They were running dangerously behind time. "For Christ's sake, let's move," he exhorted them nervously.

"What about those bloody guns out there? All this fucking armour's not worth a pinch of cocky-shit if those guys decide to go for my bloody head."

"Stop panicking," Greenwood snapped tensely, "and put this on."

This turned out to be a heavy paper-wrapped affair that Greenwood hauled from its hiding place under a table at one end of the guardroom. He quickly tore and paper away to reveal a big stove-pipe-shaped cylindrical steel helmet, with a narrow slit for the eyes, and two wide plates hanging from it by leather hinges to protect the wearer's breast and the vital parts of the back.

"*You've gotta be bloody joking!*" Harry gasped.

"Like hell," said Greenwood. "It worked for Ned Kelly, didn't it?

And you've gone one better than him with that armoured suit. At least you won't go down if they aim at your legs."

"You're crazy! I'll be lucky to stand up under all this bloody weight, let alone walk right through the bloody jail. And how do I know if this stuff'll stop a bloody bullet?"

"There's only one way to find out," Greenwood said cheerily, his voice edged slightly with hysteria. "Anyway, they won't shoot if they know I'm your hostage."

"What about me?" The Beast demanded. "I haven't even got a bloody white handkerchief I can wave at them."

"You're lucky to be along for the ride," Greenwood told him. He reached into a cabinet next to the guardroom table and pulled out a portable loud-hailer. "You carry this. The moment anyone on the wall challenges us, it's your job to make it clear that I die the moment there's any shooting."

The Beast said: "Yeah. Great. And what if they shoot first?"

"Then hit the ground and play dead. It shouldn't be too difficult for you—some of those blokes can knock a beer-can off a picket fence at fifteen hundred yards."

"Now, Timothy," said Lyle Walker, turning to the jury as he spoke, "you've heard evidence given that Harry Pearce was looking out for you in here. That he was your protector. What did you do for him in return?"

Miserably, Timothy replied: "Nothing much. Except like get him mad every time I went near him."

"Didn't he expect you to do, well, you know, for him too?"

"*No!*" Timothy cried. "Harry Pearce is not that kind-a bloke! And like you know that just as much as any other bloke in here, Walker!"

"I don't know a bloody thing," Lyle retorted. "I'm the defence counsel here, and I'm supposed to be doing everything in my bloody power to make sure that ratbag there"—he pointed furiously at Willie Crewe—"gets a proper defence and a fair bloody trial! So why did Harry Pearce sell you to that bloody creep for two thousand bucks?"

"I don't know," Timothy muttered sadly. "Maybe he like reckoned we'd need money for the escape."

"What escape?"

"I told you before. We was supposed to like break out of his cell and go over the wall."

"Yeah, we know all about that, and it's about the most bloody ridiculous cock-and-bull story most of us have heard in years. Do you honestly think anyone in his right mind would try a stunt like that?"

"Well, I thought it was like a fair chance. Anyway, I reckon we might've like made it if Willie hadn't dobbed Harry in."

"Did you actually *see* or *hear* Willie Crewe dob Harry in?"

"Well, no. But like we all know it was because of Willie that Sanderson like raided Harry's cell."

"Then only Bull Sanderson knows for certain whether Willie snitched on Harry. Isn't that right?"

Kevin Murphy rose up from his desk. "The prosecution proposes to call Bull Sanderson as a witness, Your Honour . . . *Your Honour?*"

But His Honour had just suffered a complete collapse of all ambulatory, motor and intellectual faculties. It was not so much a coronary or stroke, more a massive mechanical and electrical breakdown. Like a disabled vessel, bells rang and whistles sounded from dozens of points in his diseased hull, signalling frantically for more steam, for emergency repairs, for action from the bridge. But the commander was rendered incapable of command. His foggy senses told him that after all those years steaming four-square into the face of danger and oblivion, he really *was* on a collision course with death.

But not like this. Not sitting on his arse amid a sea of ugly faces that were gradually materialising out of the mist as, miraculously, a supreme effort of sheer will weakly fired his crippled boilers and gave his stricken body enough power to answer the helm. To help things along a bit he fuelled up on a modest slug of firewater and very nearly blew his hull apart altogether, such was the sudden ferocity of his recovery.

"You OK, Nole?" It was Kevin Murphy who had rushed to the Bench and now gazed anxiously up at him.

"Never felt better in my bloody life," Chisholm croaked.

Outside the auditorium, Bull Sanderson had by now doubled back through the administration block, passed through a guarded gateway that opened onto the quadrangle and was bent on searching the cell blocks for the elusive Celia Puffin. He shuddered to think what might have become of her. By now it was clear to him that upon this fateful day, God had got out his little black book, thumbed through to the S's and decided it was time Bull Sanderson's life swung round like a compass arrow to point in a completely new direction.

At the same time, on the other side of the sprawling open quadrangle, Harry Pearce had just started out on his longest walk, his Ned Kelly armour creaking and clanking as he prodded Greenwood along in front of him with the Colt pistol. The Beast stuck close to his side, carrying the bullhorn in hands that sweated with fear as he waited for a hail of bullets to tear into his exposed back.

When Harry spoke, it sounded as though he was inside an empty forty-four-gallon oil drum. "Christ, it's like a bloody oven inside this thing," he boomed.

"If you're going to complain, give it to me," The Beast muttered. "I'll wear it."

"Like hell," Harry replied. "Just keep your eyes peeled for rocks and dips and things along the way. If I trip over anything, it's gonna take a bloody crane to get me back on my feet."

Without looking around, Bruce Greenwood said: "Any movement up on the walls?"

"I'm too shit-scared to take a look," The Beast confessed.

Up on the main prison wall, the spectacle unfolding in the wide arena below had not gone unnoticed. Three guards patrolling the top of the wall that ran along the spine of Murphy's toll-hill glanced down, saw three weird figures moving away from the Blockhouse gate, glanced at one another in wonder for a moment and then made their way in rapid Indian file directly to a covered, glass-panelled guardpost at the corner of the wall.

"I don't want to disturb you," one of the guards informed an officer who was lounging half asleep in a chair behind the butt of a fixed machinegun, "but there's a bloke in a bloody Ned Kelly outfit walking around down there."

The gunner roused himself and yawned heavily. "Probably something to do with the bloody play they're putting on."

"Yeah, well who's that long-haired bearded streak with him? Jesus Christ?"

"What?" The officer flipped his chair forward and craned his features over the breech of the machinegun to take a look. "Holy hell! That's The Beast! Now what in Christ's name is he doing out of solitary?"

Still watching the progress of the three figures, he thrust a flapping hand behind him. "Gimme the bloody field-glasses so I can take a closer look."

Down below on the opposite side of the quadrangle, Bull Sanderson had just noticed Ned Kelly too. And Bull was just as bewildered. For a moment he also thought it was something to do with Chisholm's bloody play. But then, the play wasn't exactly a play after all, was it? So what was Ned Kelly doing strolling around the bloody jail? And who was that long-haired bearded bloke . . . who only happened to be the one and only man on God's earth who had stared Bull straight in the face and *spat in his bloody eye!* Then he recognised Bruce Greenwood walking in front of The Beast and he realised there could only be one man inside that Ned Kelly suit. Harry Pearce!

Turning slightly, Sanderson yelled back at a guard at the gateway to the admin block: "Sound the bloody alarm!"

Then it occurred to him that Greenwood must be walking in front of The Beast and Pearce like that because something was threatening him from behind. Like a knife. Or a gun.

"No! Hold off!" he yelled at the guard. "Don't do anything until I give the word!"

And with that, he drew himself up to his full menacing height, flexed his massive chest and shoulders and without a moment's hesitation started out across the quadrangle toward one of the most incredible confrontations of his life.

In the courtroom, counsel for the defence was trying to establish that Timothy Botham was an unreliable witness because he was innocent and naive and everybody kept having him on. It was about as difficult as proving that sugar doesn't taste like salt.

"So what you're saying, Timothy," Lyle Walker intoned, "is that you and Harry would've made a suicidal attempt to break out of this jail if Willie Crewe hadn't *allegedly* dobbed Harry in. Now, how could that be? How could it be that you was supposed to go along with Harry if Harry had just sold you to another bloody bloke?"

Timothy's face screwed up again, and his nut-brown eyes moistened with agony. Try as he might, it was something he had never really been able to find an answer to.

"Well?"

"I dunno."

"You don't know much about bloody anything, do you? You know what I think? I think Pearce had been having you on, mate. And making a bit of money out of you, too."

"That's not true!" Timothy insisted. "He's taking me with him—you'll see!"

Kevin Murphy was suddenly on his feet: "Uh, Your Honour. . . ?"

Lyle Walker said: "Taking him with you, is he? How's he gonna do that if he's in bloody solitary?"

"Your Honour? I think . . ."

"You'll see—smartypants!" Timothy yelled. "This time it's gonna like be me and him together! *You'll see!*"

(Rev) Hunt was rising to his feet. "What's this all about?" he demanded.

Kevin Murphy said very hastily: "I think Timothy's given enough evidence, Your Honour. He's obviously been put under great strain by all this questioning and doesn't know what he's talking about."

"*You said we were all going!*" Timothy cried.

"I agree with the prosecuting counsel," Judge Chisholm said swiftly. "Timothy, you may step down. This hearing has no further use for you."

Kevin Murphy turned to Arthur Hancock. "Get him out of here, for Chrissakes."

"Hey!" Timothy yelled. "I'm not like going anywhere! I'm going with Harry and the rest of you blokes! You promised you wouldn't leave me behind!"

"Get him back to his bloody cell," Murphy snapped. (Rev) Hunt was shouting furiously at him. "What is this all about! What does he mean, he's going. . . ?" Then it all hit him with a shock that all but felled him to his knees. "My God!" he gasped, and he grabbed at Puffin Billy's fat shoulders for support. "*GUARDS!*" he bellowed.

"*GUARDS!*" Puffin Billy screeched, flapping about in his sudden panic like an overweight pelican in an alligator's jaws.

"*SOUND THE ALARM!*"

But before anyone could make another move, Dickie King swiftly galvanised into action. There was a flash of polished steel as his terrible knife emerged from inside the right leg of his trousers; and with a speed that caught everybody in various frozen states of animation he was suddenly striking his first blow for aboriginal emancipation— leaping forward and grabbing Timothy Botham from behind, locking one arm around the young man's throat and holding the quivering, sparkling, razor-sharp blade of the knife within a hair's breadth of his windpipe. Backing away to one side of the Bench, dragging Timothy with him, the knife poised to slice right through his jugular, Dickie yelled: "Don't one of you fucking guards back there move a muscle, or this kid gets his bloody head cut right off! Reverend! You'd better make sure they do what I tell 'em, or this kid s as dead as a bloody dog's dinner!"

And then, as the guards at the back of the hall began tossing their weapons to the floor, every man in the room heard at once the sudden rising howl of sirens outside and the first furious rattle and crack of gunfire.

Outside, Bull Sanderson had stridden to within twenty yards of Ned Kelly and his hostage when the officer manning the machinegun in the guardhouse up on the wall panicked and opened fire. It had been an unfortunate sequence of events that had led to the first rapid chatter of bullets. First, the officer up on the wall had homed in on the weird group with his binoculars.

"Christ," he breathed, "that character's got a bloody gun in Bruce Greenwood's back!"

He was about to flick a red emergency switch close by him to sound the alarm when one of the other guards yelled: "Hey! Bull Sanderson's on his way out there!"

Down below, Bull Sanderson was within twenty yards of the trio when The Beast raised the bullhorn to his lips and warned him: "Stay right where you are, Bull, or Greenwood gets his fucking head blown off!"

Bull put his brawny hands on his hips and laughed. "I've seen some bloody ridiculous sights in my life, but this one just about takes the cake. Where're you all off to—a fancy dress ball?"

"They're not kidding, Mr Sanderson!" Greenwood cried fearfully. "They'll kill me!"

"Not if I have anything to bloody do with it. Is that Harry Pearce inside that bloody tin can? If it is, you've got nothing to worry about.

Harry's not the type who could kill a man in cold blood—are you, Harry?"

The Beast raised the megaphone to Harry's eye slit, and Harry's strange hollow, metallic voice replied: "This is for real, Bull. We're going out of here, so stand aside or someone gets hurt."

Bull Sanderson stepped forward, and Harry lumbered out from behind Greenwood and levelled the gun shakily at Sanderson's huge bulk.

"Bull, for Christ's sake . . ." he appealed.

Up on the wall the gunner said: "He's gonna shoot Sanderson!" He hit the red switch and rammed the breech of the machinegun shut—and that's when all hell and death broke loose in a howl of sirens and a fierce spattering hail of machinegun fire that sent Sanderson diving for the ground, carrying with him a split-second blurred image of The Beast dancing and jerking about as though he were a puppet being yanked by its strings, and Greenwood screaming and convulsing and falling forward vomiting blood as the bullets aimed at Harry Pearce tore through his back and his head. From all around the prison walls, machineguns and rifles opened up on Harry Pearce, spewing a thick sheet of lead that poured down like driving rain, tearing in from all corners of the jail, hammering at Harry's Ned Kelly armour and screaming and whining as the bullets ricochetted off the thick steel. The canvas skin of the rest of his suit tore and exploded in a multitude of places as though a huge flock of invisible birds was pecking holes in it, while the hail of lead ripped through the fabric and pounded at the protective steel plates. Inside the suit, Harry felt as though an army of labourers with pneumatic drills were all trying to get at him at once. The impact of the successive waves of gunfire began telling on him—he felt himself weakening, sinking slowly, going down on his knees. Bull Sanderson was crawling away flat-bellied on the baking tarmac, heading for the watchroom near the admin block . . . Harry screamed: *"Bull, help me!"* But his scream was lost in the roar of gunfire and it didn't mean a stiff shit anyway, because Bull was on the other bloody side after all. Faint now with fear, deafened by the thunder of gunfire and weakened with each successive shock-wave of lead from the walls, Harry knew he'd had his bloody chips . . . And as he watched Bull Sanderson's retreat through the slit in his helmet, Holy Christ! Holy bloody shit! Sanderson had turned—swivelled around, still on his chest and belly, and was waving to him! Beckoning him! Exhorting him! And yelling something that Harry couldn't hear above the crash of imminent death against his armour, but by Christ he could swear that Sanderson was yelling: *"Keep up, you stupid bastard! Keep on your fucking feet! Keep coming, Harry! Keep coming!"*

Weeping with fear inside his steel drum, Harry summoned every ounce of strength he had left in him, and with a sobbing, terrified groan he heaved against the crushing, collapsing weight of his armour—and gradually, very gradually, hauled himself back to an upright position. And then, with Sanderson still hollering and waving at him, he dragged one tremendously heavy foot in front of the other and, like a crippled tank grabbing traction on a last tiny reserve of power, he moved slowly past the broken body of Bruce Greenwood. And Bull Sanderson, fucking Sanderson, one of the greatest and most half-arsed human beings alive!—Bull Sanderson crawled back to the guardroom at the gate, threw himself inside the tiny pillbox and with one swift jab of his huge fist laid cold a guard who'd been crouched at a slit-window, his rifle adding its fury to the attack on Harry's armoured suit. And Bull lay at the window screaming at Harry: *"Harry! Harry! Keep moving, you fucking little ripper!"*

And Bull broke down and cried, a grown man as tough as bloody iron-bark, he sobbed like a baby as there, out there, amid the shimmering heat-waves of the hot quadrangle, amid the roar and clatter and crash and howl and scream and whine of lead on steel, as the deathly waves swept over Harry and turned the ground around him into a dancing, shifting sea of broken asphalt and threw a rising screen of dust up around him—there, above it all, like some knight in the thick of battle, like some Black Prince, the majestic Man of Iron lumbered slowly through it all, and Sanderson had never imagined anything so unbelievably beautiful in his life. *It was Ned Kelly, you fuckers!* It was an indomitable spirit of broad grins and slouch hats and hairy tattooed arms and baking primeval landscapes and flood-swollen creeks and maniacs called Diggers baptised in fire on a Turkish headland and up to their arses in mud along the Kokoda Trail and it was "Waltzing Matilda" and wild colonial boys and Movietone News with its kookaburra laughing its arse off and it was crows picking the eyes out of dead sheep and drovers pushing mobs through a countryside that God had turned his arse on and left to blokes who had to fight and kick and bite and curse and holler and get pissed and yahoo to stop from sinking to their knees in a savage wilderness where only iron-willed madmen could survive in the most ridiculous half-arsed unbelievable fucking incredible hilarious fuckwitted downright audacious way in which Harry Pearce, the Man in the Iron Clobber, was walking through the thundering valley of death. And Bull Sanderson was now fighting for him, the rifle at his shoulder, the muzzle barking and snapping at the firing parties positioned along the top of Kevin Murphy's ridiculous colonial murals, picking the murdering buggers off, one by one, because the Man of Iron was *AUSTRALIA—YOU CHICKENSHITS! THAT WAS WHAT IT WAS ALL ABOUT! THE LAND OF THE OOGLE BIRD AND THE VALIANT YAHOOS!*

And Harry Pearce had made it all live again, brought it all back! And suddenly, there he was at Sanderson's side, and Sanderson, oblivious to the rifle fire still thudding into the tiny guardpost, leapt on him and threw his great arms around the helmet and breastplate and bloody near broke his jaw trying to kiss the fiercely hot bullet-scarred steel; and he was pounding on it joyously with his huge hands, and inside the iron drum Harry was screaming for him to get his stupid arse down on the floor before he got himself bloody killed.

"You coming with us, you ugly leather-brained old bastard!" Harry screeched.

"You bet your sweet fucking life I am!" Bull Sanderson bellowed.

"Well, let's go! We need those weapons in Hunt's office!"

twenty-eight

IF HARRY HAD KNOWN WHAT WAS GOING ON in the auditorium while he was being used for target practise outside, he might have done something violent to someone like Kevin Murphy, who'd devised the whole scheme to go for the guns in (Rev) Hunt's office.

What Harry didn't know was that there were now enough confiscated guns on hand in the courtroom to throw a whole fire-team into the battle to cover the man in the iron suit. The trouble is, they all belonged to Dickie King.

At Dickie's screeching command, his knife still quivering at Timothy Botham's throat, a guard had gathered up all the discarded rifles and brought them to where Dickie was holding his hostage. Then, amid the wail and shriek of sirens, the entire gathering stayed very still, the whole auditorium as quiet as a tomb, and listened to the long and furious gunbattle that raged outside. Kevin Murphy broke the silence to say: "Christ, Harry must be going through pure hell out there."

"Tough," said Dickie. Then, very quickly, he whipped the knife away from Timothy Botham's throat, bent down and grabbed a carbine, rammed the bolt home on a loaded breech and placed the muzzle against the back of Timothy's head. Outside, the gunfire began to die away to a sporadic flurry of firecracker sounds. The sirens began winding down. Murphy looked very pale. A telephone on the auditorium wall behind the jury suddenly burst into life with a loud ring that made everyone jump with shock, except Dickie, who swung the rifle on (Rev) Hunt and said:

"Answer it, Reverend. And tell 'em Dickie King was here. They'll know soon enough what that means."

Hunt walked over to the phone, put the receiver to his ear and listened to tinny sounds. Then he said: "There's trouble in here too. Don't do anything. Tell the men to stay at their posts, and contact Mr Sanderson and—*What?* Are you sure? Oh, my God! *No!* Don't do anything at this stage!"

He replaced the receiver and walked slowly back to his seat, his face ashen with shock. "Bruce Greenwood is dead," he announced softly and tonelessly. "So is James Dougherty, the man in solitary."

Kevin Murphy said: "What about Harry Pearce?"

"Pearce is alive and well and apparently suffering from advanced schizophrenia. He's masquerading as Ned Kelly in a bullet-proof suit."

"Bloody ripper!" Murphy yelled, and a loud cheer went up from the cons. Dickie King, feeling a little left out, fired two shots into the ceiling above them. There was instant silence.

"Mr Sanderson appears to have lost his mind, too," (Rev) Hunt said, his jaw trembling with emotion. "He and Pearce are apparently in league together."

Another great cheer erupted. And again Dickie King fired into the ceiling. A man in the second row shouted: "Hey, watch what you're doing with that thing, you black bastard! You'll bring the bloody roof down on us—"

And Dickie shot him. Just like that. Before he'd even finished what he was saying. And everybody sat very quietly, and was very very still as the man's body slumped to the floor, spraying blood from a hole in its chest.

"Anyone else wanna get racist?" Dickie bawled. Nobody in the hall had anything at all against a black man with a gun in his hands. "What about you, Reverend? Wanna try and talk me out-a this one? Blood of the lamb, and turn the other bloody cheek, an' all that? Huh?" Hunt made no reply. Dickie laughed. "You're all not so fucking quick to sling shit at us boongs when the shoe's on the other foot, are you? I'll bet not one of you honky turds has ever even given us the bloody credit of being a danger with a bloody gun in our hands. *An abo with a gun?* He'd probably sell it to buy plonk, wouldn't he? We camped out on the lawn in front of Parliament House and demanded a fair deal for the abos, an' everyone thought, leave the poor stupid buggers out there in the open for a while and they'll be back on the bloody slops in no time. *But that's all finished now!* A lot-a you blokes are gonna be given the privilege of doing something very courageous and worthwhile for the aboriginal cause . . ."

The Honourable William Lancelot Puffin, green around his fat gills with fear, rose to his feet. "We would consider it an honour, er, Mr King, to serve the cause of freedom and emancipation for all our Coloured Brothers. I myself have supported the Aboriginal Question on many occasions in Parliament, and as my Record shows, I have debated strongly on all counts. We're all behind you. You have but to tell us what we are to do."

"You're all gonna die," Dickie rasped. "And maybe that'll show the rest of the honkies out there that the abos aren't going to be fucked with anymore."

"But I'm a Minister of the Crown!"

"Great. You'll be the first to go. That'll really show people we mean business."

Puffin Billy sank back into his seat and somehow managed to muster enough courage to overcome the urge to scream like a baby.

318

(Rev) Hunt began praying silently for Dickie's soul, praying that the floor in front of him might open up right now and commit the troubled indigene as quickly as possible into God's wrathful hands. Timothy Botham, the cold muzzle of Dickie's gun pressed once again to the back of his neck, wanted to cry. But he couldn't do that, like, standing up there in front of all those blokes. Lyle Walker sat Buddha-like in his chair, not so much as blinking. Noel Chisholm, perched at the Bench, figured that if he could stall Dickie's planned massacre long enough, Harry Pearce was sooner or later going to come through the auditorium's main door, right behind them, and if he hadn't completely lost all means of perambulation in that terrible seizure he'd just suffered . . . Well, anything was worth a bloody try when the shit was hitting the fan anyway.

"Dickie," he said, "could I suggest that we finish this trial before you put us all to death? As I recall, aboriginal law is just as strict as ours. Whereas we stick offenders in jail, you blokes spear them through the bloody legs."

Dickie thought about that for a moment. Then he thought it wasn't such a bad idea after all.

"OK," he said. "But we do it *our* way." He pointed the gun at Kevin Murphy. "Untie the bastard so's he can speak."

Murphy untied the nylon choker where it was lashed to the back of the chair, and with a whistling gasp Willie Crewe straightened up, gulping and swallowing to ease the pain in his throat.

Judge Chisholm said: "Mr Walker, would you like to proceed with cross-examination?"

"Fuck cross-examination," Dickie King snarled. "We'll be farting around here all day an' all night at that rate." Pushing Timothy Botham aside, he stalked over to Willie Crewe and placed the muzzle of the rifle within an inch of Willie's sweating forehead. Then his finger tightened on the trigger.

"Did you dob Harry Pearce in to Bull Sanderson?"

Willie Crewe nodded frantically.

"Say it!"

"I dobbed Harry Pearce in to Bull Sanderson," Willie croaked.

Dickie King turned to Noel Chisholm. "There you are—instant bloody confession. Saves a lot of time and sweat. Now, I reckon that because he's such a lousy little stoolie, he should be snuffed before the Minister."

"*No!*" Willie Crewe gasped, starting to rock back and forth in his

319

chair. "No. Please don't kill me don't kill me don't kill me don't kill me please don't kill me I won't do it again I don't wanna die I didn't meant to hurt anyone don't kill me don't kill me *PLEASE DON'T KILL ME!!!*"

Dickie King grimaced with disgust. "Christ, if an abo behaved like that he'd be kicked on his arse out of the bloody tribe."

Out in the administration block, Harry Pearce and Bull Sanderson had made it safely to (Rev) Hunt's office. Their only encounter along the corridor had been with the two guards from the main gate, who rushed in with rifles raised for bloody mayhem, took one look at Ned Kelly stomping toward them like a tank on legs and dropped their weapons and ran.

Inside Hunt's office, the telephone was ringing frantically. Sanderson picked up the receiver and the voice of the city's Chief Inspector of Police babbled something about an anti-riot squad being on its way, along with half the State's police forces.

"Keep them away," Sanderson advised him. "The cons here have taken over everything, and they're armed to the bloody teeth. And they're holding the Minister for Corrective Services hostage. If any attempt's made to storm the jail—he'll die."

"Puffin Billy? Christ, we'll send in the bloody army!" the Chief Inspector.

Sanderson said: "They've got his wife too. You know, that ex-Miss Australia."

"Christ, that's different. What can we do?"

"Back off, and get prepared to negotiate," Sanderson advised him. Then he hung up. "OK, Harry," he said, "let's get that bloody cabinet open and break out those guns."

Harry was silent for a long, alarming moment. Sanderson rapped apprehensively on his steel dome. "Harry? You still in there?"

"Greenwood had the bloody duplicate keys on him," a tinny voice replied plaintively.

"That's lovely," Sanderson sighed. "And we all know where Greenwood is by now, don't we? OK, shoot the lock off."

"You do it, Bull. I don't like things that go bang."

"Let's not bugger about, Harry," Sanderson pleaded. "Just shoot the bloody thing."

With a resounding BANG! Harry fired his Colt pistol for the first time, shooting into the lock of the weapons cabinet. The padlock exploded and clattered to the floor; the steel door swung open. Harry and Sanderson began hauling out a stack of pistols, short-barreled carbines, submachineguns and wide-muzzled shotguns designed to fire ball-bearings.

"Christ, will you look at all that?" Harry's voice boomed as he marvelled at the arsenal.

"Yeah," said Sanderson. "And will you look at something else? There's no bloody ammunition!"

There was another silence inside Harry's helmet. Finally, his voice hissed like steam in a boiler. "I might have known it. Another typical Murphy cock-up. I'm gonna kill him for this!"

"Sure you are," Sanderson gnashed. "When I've finished with him."

Out on the jail wall, wounded guards were being eased down the outside face in cliff-rescue stretchers to join the dead waiting below in the ambulances. Bull Sanderson's covering fire had damaged and destroyed a lot of men. Despite his warning to the Chief Inspector, the streets around the jail were already packed with police, most of them lumbering about in flak vests and visored helmets and wielding shotguns, gas guns and automatic rifles. The sleepy bungalows around the jail were being evacuated—little old ladies in carpet slippers and brunchcoats nursing their cats and poodles as the cops single-filed them out through roadblocks and barricades. Police sirens wheeped and whooped, and radios crackled with orders and communications from all over the city.

ABC-TV and the city's three commercial networks were setting up outside-broadcast units, while newsmen stood against the dramatic backdrop of riot police and milling vehicles doing their filmed stand-ups for the main evening bulletins.

". . . And while it's not known at this stage whether the Minister is dead or alive, one thing is certain: It's going to be a long hot afternoon and night here at Parramatta Jail. Oh, just a moment . . . Here's Parramatta's Chief Inspector of Police. Chief, can you tell us what's going on in there at this moment?"

"Fuck off."

"Thank you, Chief. OK, fellers—cut it. CUT IT, FOR FUCK'S SAKE, CUT IT!"

Along the wall itself, prison guards and police lay flat on the hot stonework, guns trained on the admin block, mess hall and auditorium. In the guardpost where the conflagration had been triggered off, the same machinegunner was repeatedly trying to contact the auditorium and (Rev) Hunt's office by phone. And repeatedly he got no answer.

Then one of the cops shouted: "Hey! There's something moving down there! Over by the cell blocks!"

There certainly was. As the gunner yanked on the piston-like bolt of his weapon, cocking it for action, and a dozen rifles along the wall clicked and clattered, someone shouted: "Holy shit! Hold your fire! It's a bloody sheila!"

And it was. It was Celia Puffin's pink chiffony dress and wide powder-blue Pierre Cardin hat that had paraded out of cell block C, heading across the quadrangle towards the admin block.

"Hey, lady!" one of the cops bellowed. "Get the hell out of the way! Get down, for Chrissakes!"

The figure turned and waved casually, then continued on across the burning tarmac. The officer at the machinegun sighed very deeply and rested his confused, aching head against the cool, slightly greasy metal of the weapon's breech. "Let's see. We've had Ned Kelly, and now we've got a sheila who appears from nowhere and looks like she's on her way to a bloody cocktail party. You don't suppose we went off half-cocked over this, do you?"

"*You* went off half-cocked, mate," said one of his colleagues helpfully. "We didn't."

"That's what I like—good old Aussie mateship and solidarity."

In the auditorium, Willie Crewe was a broken, pathetic wretch of an individual. Some might consider that he deserved to be psychologically shattered into tiny pieces and then shot; others might suggest that he had never had much psychological hope in the first place, ever since his old man, a punch-drunk amateur pug, started coming home pissed out of his head and regularly punching the shit out of him. Anyway, Willie was about to die. The muzzle of Dickie King's gun was at a point right dead-centre between his glazed eyes.

Luckily, Willie had gone right over the edge of sanity and was tumbling gently somewhere in another ether, in which there was little feeling and no comprehension. *Nothing*. Maybe a glimpse or two of a puppy he'd once owned. But that was all.

Dickie was about to squeeze the trigger and blast his head off when Noel Chisholm interrupted.

"Dickie," he said gently. "If this is to be a ceremonial occasion, the beginning of the aboriginal revolution, might I suggest the whole thing would have more drama and impact if we did it right and at least sentenced everybody to death?"

Now that instantly appealed to Dickie. That was like shoving the white man's honky racist middle-class bourgeois shit right back up his own dinger.

"You got a point there," he admitted. "OK—go ahead. But make it bloody fast. I wanna start the revolution today, not this time next week!"

Harry Pearce and Bull Sanderson were in a dreadful quandary. With Harry propping up the office wall in his suit of armour, Sanderson had searched high and low for ammunition for the weapons, and all he'd ended up with was an arsenal of beautifully crafted but useless guns.

Harry's hollow voice said: "Got any suggestions, Bull?"

"Yeah," said Bull. "I suggest we pretend this is all a bloody bad dream. Anyhow, you've still got that pistol, and I've got a rifle, and those two bloody guards who shot through dropped theirs as they ran. I'll have their arses drummed right out of the service for that."

"Bull, you just drummed yourself out of the bloody service, remember?"

Bull said: "Yeah. And I still can't figure out what came over me. Anyway, I was completely cheesed off with prison life. I should've got out years ago."

Harry said: "There's no bloody guarantee that you're gonna get out now, mate. There's an army of bloody executioners lusting for our bodies out there and another bloody armed squad in the auditorium. And the blokes in there are counting on you and me to help them." Harry sighed. It sounded like steam burping in a hot-water geyser. "This is the last time I let myself get involved in any of Murphy's bloody hair-brained schemes. If he'd been one of the Great Train Robbers they'd still be picking bits of him off the bloody rails."

"Well," said Sanderson, picking up his rifle, "we've come this far. We might as well go the whole distance. You ready?"

"Help pull me away from the wall. Once I get mobile, this bloody outfit does everything on its own."

They moved cautiously out into the corridor, and as Harry stumped slowly along toward the doorway that led out into the open jail, Sanderson gathered up the carbines left by the departing guards. He then fell in behind Harry, using the massive armour as a shield as they moved out into the open air. Before them lay the abandoned guardpost where Sanderson had helped cover Harry's magnificent walk through the fires of hell. To their left, a pathway led to the main door of the auditorium.

"This is it," Harry's voice rumbled. He turned left. And at the same time a new volley of rifle-fire broke out along the distant walls, and again the bullets cracked and whined off the Ned Kelly helmet. Bull Sanderson dived for the ground, wriggling along towards the shelter of the guardpost—and then, with a shock that hit him like a mild heart seizure, he saw Celia Puffin running awkwardly on her high-heels towards him, towards the adjacent gateway.

Bull leapt out from behind the pillbox, crouching low and waving and shouting at the pink diaphanous figure: "Get down! For Christ's sake, lady, get down!" Another hail of fire swept in from the walls, tearing at the ground around him and clanging off the steel-framed gateway—and with a shrill cry, Celia Puffin stumbled and sprawled through the open gate, plunging heavily on her face in the hot dust. The back of her pink dress was a soggy, crimson, butchered mess.

Bull Sanderson, ignoring the continuing fire, crawled forward, reached the woman's body and was about to lift the wide-brimmed blue hat away from her head—until he noticed a pair of thick-lensed, wire-framed, cracked and twisted spectacles lying nearby. He didn't bother to look at Henry Trembler's face. It couldn't be any nicer to look at in death than it was when he was alive. He began crawling back behind the guardpost, ready to leap after Harry the moment Harry got that bloody auditorium door open.

Twenty-nine

". . . It was not unusual during the birth of this strange nation," Noel Chisholm was relating hoarsely, trying to keep his dry, weakening voice above the loud rattle of renewed firing outside, "for men of breeding and exceptionally high culture and education to dismiss the aboriginal race as primitive trash. As far back as 1883, the French geographist Edmond Marin la Meslée described the aborigines as repulsively filthy and degraded people doomed like other primitive races to inevitable extinction in the face of competition from the whites—"

"For Christ's sake get on with it," Dickie King snarled, poking the rifle furiously at him. "We're not here for a bloody history lesson! We're here to *die!*"

"As I was about to add," Chisholm continued coolly, inwardly praying that Harry would burst through that bloody door, "the same race is regarded much the same today, the only difference being that our modern Australian society prides itself so much on its lack of bloody culture that the aborigines would be out of their tiny brains bothering to compete at all." He drew a huge, deep breath, crossed his fingers and sombrely intoned: *"And so it is the sentence of this court that you all be taken immediately from these premises to a place outside, and thence put to death by musket squad as an example to others of your foul lawless breed. God Save the Queen! And Christ help us all!"*

"Right! Bible-basher," Dickie yelled, swinging his rifle at (Rev) Hunt, "change of plans! You're first!"

Then, with a grinding crash, Harry Pearce virtually tore the auditorium door off its hinges as he smashed his way in, the Colt pistol thrust out in front of him. "Don't anybody fucking move!" he bellowed.

Dickie spun around, jumped almost a foot off the floor with shock, then fired two rapid shots that clanged harmlessly off Harry's steel helmet. At the same time, Kevin Murphy launched himself into a running dive from his desk and footie-tackled Dickie with a cannoning impact that sent the rifle spinning from his hands and ploughed him face-down along the floor. A roar of applause and relief erupted throughout the hall, the men leaping out of their seats and scrambling in droves up onto the set where Kevin Murphy had Dickie's arms locked together right up his back and was yelling for handcuffs, and Harry Pearce was sinking slowly to his knees, going down at last, unable to bear any more the weight of the iron suit that had saved his life.

Then Bull Sanderson suddenly dived headlong through the open door behind him with yet another spatter of bullets following him like a swarm of bees, and he shouted to the crowding, rioting cons: "Get back! Get right back out of the way! There's a fucking army out there!" And as the huge mob of men wheeled and fled back over the rows of seats, (Rev) Hunt and Puffin Billy both looked at each other and let out great sighs of relief. And the Mayor, still lost somewhere in an alcoholic daze, turned to Hunt and declared in thick tones:

"If this is what they call modern theatre, Mr Hunt, I'm not sure I could cope with the strain of another act."

Dickie King had been handcuffed and was now lying on his stomach with his hands shackled behind him.

"You stupid black bastard," Murphy raged. "See what happens when you get a bit of power in your hands? You haven't got the bloody brains to use it properly. A white man would've slaughtered everybody right from square one."

So much for the aboriginal revolution.

Bull Sanderson was lifting the heavy helmet off Harry's head. Harry emerged looking like a pressure-cooked beetroot. Murphy rushed over, threw his arms around him and kissed him hard on his sweltering brow.

"You little beauty! I knew you could do it, Harry. But Jeez, it sounded like a bloody close shave from in here."

Harry said: "Do me a favour, Murph. Next time you want to break out of jail, don't tell me about it."

"But we're out now, mate! We're on our bloody way!"

"Listen, you fuckwit!" Harry rasped. "Bruce Greenwood's lying out there dead as a doornail, and so is The Beast."

"Who in bloody hell's The Beast?"

Harry sighed. "Never mind. Just a bloke I used to know. The point is, there must be a hundred-and-bloody-fifty blokes out there now, all waiting to blow us all to the shithouse. So what do you suggest we do next?"

"We get Dickie King back in the cells where he belongs—then we negotiate. By the way, where's Henry Trembler? He shouldn't be let out either."

Bull Sanderson said: "Trembler's dead too. He got caught in the cross-fire." He looked over at Puffin Billy's pale, frightened features and decided against describing the details of Trembler's flamboyant but shoddy end.

Harry said: "Who're we going to negotiate with?"

Murphy said: "The Governor, I guess. Or the State Premier. Whoever's the boss cocky in New South Wales."

"OK," said Harry. "Reverend Hunt, can you get a direct open telephone link set up with the State Governor?"

(Rev) Hunt, a pale, defeated shell of the man he had been only two hours before, shrugged and said: "I expect so."

"Well, jump to it. Tell him we've taken over the jail and we've got the Mayor and Minister as hostages, and to stand by for our list of demands."

As Hunt arose and shuffled over to the telephone, a shout went up from one of the cons in the audience: "Let's start knocking off all these fucking screws back here!"

But Bull Sanderson grabbed a rifle, jerked the bolt and fired a shot over their heads. "No-one knocks anybody off!" he bellowed. "None of these blokes have ever done anything to harm any of you, so tie 'em up if you like—but if I see one of you get violent with them, I'll make you buggers wish you'd never been born!"

Timothy Botham timidly approached Harry Pearce as Harry was hauling himself out of his armoured pants to change into a pair of prison strides. "Harry," he moaned, "I like did it again, you know. I blew the whole bloody scheme. They got me mad, like, saying you was having me on all the time, and I like just blew it."

"Don't worry, mate," said Harry, straightening up and clapping him on the shoulder. "The way Murphy had this thing organised down to the last intricate detail, it's bloody lucky you did. Otherwise we'd all be back in the bloody cells now, and they'd have a line of beasts waiting for us at Grafton."

"Hey! You mean it, Harry?"

"Yeah, you saved the whole bloody day. Now, I've got another little important job for you to do soon, so stick around."

Arthur Hancock sidled up to Harry and said: "You know me, Harry. At my age there's nothing outside that interests me. I

327

wouldn't know where to bloody go once I was out there anyway."

"You're OK, mate," said Harry. "We'll get you back in your cell snug and safe the moment Hunt gets through to the Governor."

A loud hubbub was rising again throughout the crowded hall as the rest of the prison population, having trussed up the guards, jostled about in a mob like worried cattle, ready to stampede and break up the furniture and commit other acts of a senseless, riotous nature. You've seen prison movies. They always make a mess. Harry picked up a couple of rifles and walked over to Kevin Murphy. He handed him one and said: "I don't like to do this—mainly because I don't know how to use one of these. But we're going to have to do something to calm these buggers down. A riot's the last bloody thing we need at the moment. Christ, what an ugly bunch of bastards. If we let them out on the streets, they'll frighten half of Sydney to death."

Bull Sanderson was of exactly the same opinion. Again he lifted his rifle and fired over the heads of the milling mob. As silence fell on the ugly assemblage, he and Harry and Murphy stood side by side, training their guns on them.

"OK, you lot!" Bull yelled. "You've probably got a fair idea by now that there's a breakout in progress. That doesn't mean you're allowed to go on a bloody rampage and smash everything in sight. That's one sure way of buggering the whole scheme. It shows you're nothing more than what people outside regard you as—a bunch of bloody dangerous animals. Now, you'll all get out if you calm down and leave the business side of things to us, or to Murphy here. Otherwise we'll have to shoot anyone who starts any trouble. If you all go mad and rush out there now, the cops'll have a bloody field day. It'll be like shooting fish in a bloody barrel. Now, anybody got anything to say?"

In the answering hush, the cons quietly took their seats like a theatre audience again. At the telephone on the wall, (Rev) Hunt's thin voice announced: "The Governor, apparently, is suddenly preoccupied with an important and pressing engagement. He is uncontactable. However, the Premier has called an emergency meeting of cabinet, and they are willing to open direct communication."

"OK," said Murphy. "A beaut. Now, tell them what the situation is, and we'll be in contact as soon as we've drafted our demands."

Harry Pearce added: "Tell 'em we want something immediately. We want absolute safe conduct to the cell blocks past all those guns out there for three men—Dickie King, Arthur Hancock and Timothy Botham."

"Hey!" Timothy cried, rushing up to Harry. "I thought you said I was like going along with you! I'm not going back to the bloody cells, Harry! I'm going too . . ."

"Shut up and listen," Harry snapped. "Someone's got to get Dickie King back behind bars. We can't let the bugger out of here in the mood he's in. You and Arthur are gonna escort him over and lock him up. Arthur's staying there. Then you get back here quick-smart. OK?"

Timothy said: "You wouldn't let me down, would you, Harry?"

Harry laughed. "You know me, Timothy. I'm your best mate, remember? I'll look out for you, don't worry."

(Rev) Hunt turned away from the telephone. "I don't know how to put this," he said. "But I've just been informed that there'll be no safe conduct for anyone—unless the Minister and the Mayor are released and the entire complement of inmates surrenders unconditionally. Otherwise the first man who pokes his head out into the open will be summarily shot."

There was a stunned silence. Then Bull Sanderson said: "Well, that buggers everything, doesn't it?"

An angry commotion again swept through the hall. One con with an eye patch and an ugly faked cutlass scar running down his cheek jumped onto his seat and yelled: "OK, they had their bloody chance! Now let's tear this fucking place to pieces!"

"Hold it, willya!" Kevin Murphy roared. "That's all part of the trick of bargaining. You don't expect them to cave in on the first bell, do you? I've got a few tricks of my own up my bloody sleeve, don't you worry." And with that, he reached inside his prison blouse and pulled out a little black box the size of a pocket calculator with three red buttons set into it. "Phase Two," he declared proudly.

"What the bloody hell's that thing?" Bull Sanderson demanded.

"It's a simple but very sophisticated electronic detonator," Murphy explained. "I turn it on like this, see . . ." He flicked a switch on one side of the box and the red buttons glowed like high-carat rubies. "Timothy Botham made it, so he can tell you how it works."

Timothy blushed deeply and modestly and said: "Well, it's not exactly a detonator, like. It sort of transmits radio pulses or signals to a receiver, and the receiver like detonates the explosives. This one's got different frequencies for different detonators. The detonators are set in plastic explosive. One touch of the button, like and *BOOOOOMMMMMM!!!*"

Bull Sanderson immediately remembered the putty that had been packed all over the cell blocks in Murphy's murals, and all that copper wire running through the show. Bull was astonished. "Murphy, I can't decide whether you're a natural genius or just cunning as a lavatory rodent."

Murphy beamed with undisguised pride. "If you're gonna do something, Bull, do it with *finesse*," he replied modestly. "OK, Mr Hunt, tell the Premier and his mates that there's going to be one hell of an explosion in exactly one minute if they don't start playing ball."

(Rev) Hunt spoke softly on the phone. After about twenty seconds he turned away and said: "Their reply is that if the prisoners of this jail wish to blow it up, that's just fine as far as they're concerned. It's due for demolition and redevelopment anyway. They reiterate that there will be no further dialogue until the hostages are released."

"I anticipated that," Murphy said grimly.

"OK, Murph," said Harry Pearce. "Perhaps you'd better blow up a couple of cell blocks to convince them we mean bloody business."

"Like bloody hell!" Murphy cried indignantly. "I didn't slave my guts out doing all that painting just to blow it up! That's *art*, mate— not bloody *Blue Poles*. One day that stuff there's gonna rank with Michelangelo!"

"Well, I hope he's as nutty as you are—you'll get on well together!" Harry raged. "And I'm just as bloody insane to get involved in your stupid bloody schemes. What are you gonna do now—put on a violent show of force and determination by blowing up the bloody latrines?"

But Murphy was ignoring him, watching the second hand of his watch jerk through the last fifteen seconds of the countdown.

"OK," he barked. "Everyone get down flat on the floor. And pray to Christ that I got the amount of explosives right." As everybody in the vast room dived for the floor, he walked nonchalantly around the Judge's Bench and crouched down behind it alongside Noel Chisholm.

"Three . . . Two . . . One . . . Zero . . . *BLAST OFF!*"

Murphy pressed the first of the red buttons and there was a tremendous explosion right there amongst them, right in the middle of the courtroom setting. The blast deafened everybody. The shock-wave tossed seats into the air and hurled them over the cowering, huddled, laid-out ranks of prisoners. Jagged pieces of timber flew all over the place, spinning like boomerangs and ricochetting off the walls.

Murphy, his hearing temporarily deadened by the blast, turned to Noel Chisholm, and Chisholm's mouth formed the words: "*IT WORKED!*"

Shaking like a leaf, his judge's wig blown to the shithouse by the blast, Chisholm whipped his hip-flask out of his frock-coat and took a frantic slug of amber fluid that set off another confined explosion inside him. Then he and Murphy hauled themselves up and peeked over the Bench. All over the set and the rest of the hall, from within a jungle of smashed and overturned chairs, heads were slowly raised and six hundred-odd pairs of eyes all centred their vision on one shattered, smoking spot in the auditorium's timber floor—the spot where Willie Crewe had just completely disappeared.

Noel Chisholm yelled at (Rev) Hunt: "Get back on the buzzer! Tell them the Mayor's next, and then that perambulating bloody PA system next to him, if they still think we're playing silly-buggers! They're wired up as human bombs in those jackets—just like Willie was!"

Thirty

TEN MINUTES LATER, THE WORD HAD GONE around the prison walls. All police and prison personnel were to stand down and uncock their weapons. No-one was to make any sort of move that might ignite the critical situation as, over at the distant auditorium, the door opened and Dickie King stumbled out, his hands cuffed behind him, followed by Arthur Hancock and Timothy Botham. It was late af-

ternoon by now, though time, for Timothy, had merged into a sequence of events rather than the measured tick of chronometers. Which
is as it was, anyway, before man decided to divide his life into hours,
minutes and seconds so that he could keep a close check on his approaching death. To Timothy, near-delirious with fear, that reminded
him of the old joke that if Jesus Christ had been born today, we'd all
be wearing miniature electric chairs around our necks. Ha ha ha.

Resisting the urge to get hysterical, Timothy let time measure itself by the level of the sinking sun, its rays exploding off the invisible
rim of the jail's painted non-walls, fanning through a picket fence of
black, silhouetted man-figures standing shoulder to shoulder along the
ridges and tree-tops of Murphy's great mural. Watching him, itching
for the chance to snatch up their guns and open fire as the three figures started out across the quadrangle, heading for block C.

Halfway across, Dickie King halted and screamed: "Next time
there's gonna be a fucking bloodbath, you white fascist cunts!"

"There ain't going to be a next time, Dickie," said Arthur Hancock, gently pushing him along. "There ain't enough of you blokes to
organise a decent corroboree, let alone fight a bloody war."

"We'll breed, mate. We'll *multiply*. We'll build a new race and
one day we'll slaughter the whites and take back all the land that belongs to us."

"You're welcome to it," Arthur said. "I've always been a city
bloke meself. I never did go for Ayer's Rock, anyway."

Back in the auditorium more confusion reigned. Noel Chisholm,
for one thing, had just suffered another massive breakdown of all vital
life-functions. He lay on the floor by the side of the Bench, staring
blankly at the ceiling, hardly breathing, as Kevin Murphy hung over
him trying to cajole him back to life.

"We've got 'em by the bloody balls now, Nole," he insisted.
"They're ready to give us anything. Don't give up on us now, for
Christ's sake."

Meanwhile, the Mayor was having an hysterical fit in his chair,
cold sober now and fully aware that if the delicate negotiations about
to be entered into broke down in any way whatsoever, he was to be
flung out into the quadrangle and set off like a human firecracker. He
hollered and screamed and sobbed and wrung his hands, and there

was little else he could do: Both he and the Honourable William had been warned that any attempt to tamper with the fastenings of their explosive-packed police jackets would break a battery-powered electrical circuit, trigger an auxiliary detonator and blow them to the shithouse anyway.

As for Puffin Billy, he saw his sole remaining hope resting with his talent for rhetoric, and at that moment, amid the frantic attempts to revive Noel Chisholm, (Rev) Hunt's constant chatter on the telephone and the Mayor's hysterics, he was standing on his chair and making the most critical speech of his Political Career.

"Throughout my long and uncompromising Parliametary Term," he blared, "I have devoted my efforts entirely to the critical and long-overdue need for a Complete Overhaul of the State's penal system. I shall not bore you with details of the many occasions upon which I have stood up and made My Position clear. Suffice to say that My Record speaks for itself. For instance, I would point with pride and a *modicum* of self-satisfaction to the fact that in my entire Term of Office *no new prisons have been built in New South Wales!* This compares favourably, I submit, with dozens erected during previous administrations. Also, absolutely *no* renovations or modernisations of any type have been carried out in any Penal Institution under my jurisdiction over the past three years. I need not impress upon you what all this means. It means no attempt has been made during My Term to make our prisons harder for you, the prisoners, to break out of! In fact, as you all well know, conditions generally have been allowed to deteriorate under a humane, carefully considered policy aimed at making sure that prison food and welfare compares so miserably with life outside that the urge to break out has been maintained at a constant high level.

"But one must never consider the battle won," he puffed furiously. "One must not stand upon one's laurels. And I am willing to Pledge my Political Future—nay, my very word as a Gentleman— that if I am allowed to continue in my present capacity, if I am allowed to live—if *someone* will *please* have mercy on me!—I will fight to my last breath for an age of Penal Reform unknown in the history of this Great Nation. A New Deal for all victims of incasteration! The complete abolition of all Penal Institutions! A full and unconditional pardon for all men currently committed to our penitentiaries! I shall drop my tweeds at lunchtime in Martin Place and play 'Annie Laurie' on a nose-flute stuck up my backside if need be! *I will do anything to stay alive! For the love of Christ—give me another term!*"

A thundering ovation followed Billy's last words. It was probably the best response he'd ever had to a political election speech, which normally ended with him bobbing up and down like a hot-air balloon while Labour and Liberal supporters slugged it out below him. He stepped back off the chair, grabbing the Mayor's shoulder for support, and sat down in a state of terrified exhaustion on the floor. It was quite a show they were putting on up there. Better than the bloody goggle-box any day of the week. The cons were enjoying it immensely.

Meanwhile, Kevin Murphy had managed to revive Noel Chisholm to the point where the great man at least recognised who he was.

"I'm the best fucking playwright in the world," he mumbled thickly, trying to lift his head from the floor, "and the rest of you are just a pack of cunts."

"That's the spirit, Nole," said Murphy. He lifted Chisholm's head and laid it gently in his lap.

Chisholm said: "Murph, I'm dying."

"Yeah," said Murph. "We're all dying, remember?"

"Murph," Chisholm said, "I saw something in the Pacific."

Murphy softly stroked Chisholm's windswept hair. "Yeah, well forget it, Nole."

"*No!*" It was (Rev) Hunt's voice that rang out. He was hurrying over from his vigil at the telephone. He fell to his knees at Chisholm's side. He gazed deeply into the dying man's blue eyes. Beseechingly, he asked him: "Noel—what did you see in the Pacific? Please—*I must know.*"

Chisholm coughed violently, his head twisting and bucking in Murphy's lap. A deathly, respectful hush reigned throughout the auditorium as he struggled for words.

"I saw the pathetic, shambling pygmy self that we all really are," he whispered. "For all our search for gods and a higher consciousness, it is there within us—inviolable as the chromosome. And it will inevitably triumph, as it always has, over our virtues and dreams." His voice was now so low that (Rev) Hunt had to bend an ear close to his lips to hear him. "Our fighter squadron had been sent to a large, strategic Pacific atoll which the Americans had just recaptured from the Japanese. During our first couple of days there, we could hear a constant and eerie moaning on the wind, an unearthly yet almost human groan of pain or despair. We asked the Americans what it was. They acted very strangely, at first denying the sound altogether, then laughing it off, then advising us to forget about it altogether. We demanded to know what it was—the unceasing croon and howl of it, carried by the winds, was beginning to spook us. Finally, we were taken inland into the centre of the island. There, amid the remains of a bomb-shattered jungle, was a vast barbed-wire stockade packed with hundreds of Japanese prisoners of war. All of whom were sitting on their knees, their arms clutched around their bellies, rocking to and fro and moaning and wailing with some undefinable agony. One of our mob joked that he'd probably get the shits too if a division of U.S. Marines landed on him. One of the American officers suddenly spun on him as if he was going to strike him. He checked himself, then explained to us that when the American attack was imminent, word had gone amongst the Japanese that the Marines would not only destroy them but rape and murder their families too. So, just before the first guns sounded from the sea, and the first American planes buzzed in, the Japanese themselves put their wives and children to death . . ."

For many seconds (Rev) Hunt simply gazed into Noel Chisholm's eyes. Then he slowly raised his head, and his own were wet with tears. He clutched at Murphy's shoulder, and levered himself up onto his feet. He looked back down at Chisholm. He drew breath with a deep, shuddering sigh.

"You're right," he said. "There's no bloody hope for any of us."

He turned to Murphy. "What are your demands? What do you need to get out of here?"

"We'll have them ready in a minute, Reverend," said Murphy. "Come on, Nole," he said, bending back to Chisholm. "Take a good swig of this."

The effect that this, the last remaining draught of the hip-flask, had on Chisholm was the same sort of effect that gave audiences exquisite shudders when medical dramas, losing out to cop shows and other forms of TV violence, decided to exploit the bouncing bip and electric shocks to the heart. Chisholm's whole body jerked violently and kicked, heaved and convulsed. Then he shot up into a sitting position and demanded: "Where are we?"

"Act one, scene three," Murphy informed him. "We're just about at the point where the desperate band start putting the hard word on the authorities, and the lives of two innocent hostages lie at stake. Now, Harry and Bull and me have had our heads together and we've come up with the following demands: a safe conduct out of here, a car with a police escort to take us to Bankstown Airport, a Cessna standing by to fly us to anywhere in the outback that we want to go. Plus a full and unconditional pardon for all our crimes and the release of all prisoners in all jails throughout Australia. Except the Henry Tremblers. A lot of us have got wives and kids."

"Excellent," said Chisholm. "And I'll need a Boeing 747 with a complete flight crew and cabin staff with plenty of booze and extra fuel standing by at Darwin to fly me directly to Malta and thence to Tierra del Fuego. I'll leave the Mouth-that-Walks with you and take the Mayor with me as hostage. It's about time he widened his horizons a bit."

Murphy whistled with surprise. "Shit, Nole—aren't you laying it on a bit thick? A Jumbo?"

"Why not? The first principle of bargaining is that you start at the top and they start at the bottom and you eventually meet somewhere in the middle. I'll probably end up relinquishing the hostesses. In my condition they'd be so much superfluous weight. And besides, I've never met one yet who had a sense of humour."

thirty-one

TIMOTHY BOTHAM HAD HARDLY DARED BREATHE DURING the tense, hot walk across the quadrangle. And then all of a sudden they'd made it through the door of cell-block C, and his bursting lungs deflated with a long whistling sigh of relief. The great cavern was cool and deathly quiet. With Murphy's murals emblazoning the walls, it was like the time his Mum took him on a trip to the Jenolan

Caves, then rushed him out before he could get a squizz at the drawings someone had pencilled on the walls.

"Where's your cell, Dickie?" Arthur Hancock asked quietly.

"Ground floor. Next to Nole Chisholm's."

"Sorry about this," said Arthur as they approached Dickie's cell. "I've got nothing against bloody boongs, you understand. But you can't go around shooting people. Even we're not allowed to do that."

"That's all right," said Dickie. "You name's way down on the death list anyway."

"I appreciate that, Dickie. Well, here we are. Just hop inside and I'll lock you in. And don't feel bad about it. As you say, there's always the next time."

The aboriginal question again dispensed with, Arthur locked Dickie's cell and then turned to Timothy.

"Right. You're next, sonny."

"Whaddya mean?"

"Harry told me to get you under lock and key too, mate. He doesn't want you coming to any bloody harm."

"That bastard!" Timothy cried. "That lying bloody ratbag! He was having me on, like, all the time!" Tears sprang into his big brown eyes.

"Listen to me," Arthur said sagely. "I've seen more escapes and attempted escapes than you've had baked dinners. I've planned more foolproof breakouts than you could poke a bloody stick at. And I'm *still* behind bars. It's a mug's game, Timothy. A game for mugs—you understand? You start taking it seriously, like Murphy and the rest of 'em have done, and it's not a game anymore—a lot of poor stupid bastards get hurt and killed. And Harry doesn't want that to happen to you."

Timothy looked like a man about to split in two. Half of him was about to turn and flee, the other half stay and listen to reason. Arthur said: "What Harry's doing for you is about the greatest thing a bloke could ever do for his mate, Timothy. He's saving your bloody life. And the way I see it, you'll probably come up for parole anyway very shortly, if you keep your head down until all this is over."

Arthur pushed open Noel Chisholm's cell door. "Well, what's it to be?"

Timothy sighed like a tired puppy and said: "All right. But just do one thing for me, Arthur, will you?"

"Anything, mate."

"There's a letter in my cell under my pillow, like. D'you reckon you could like get rid of it. My Mum'll have a blue fit if she ever sees it. *But promise me you won't like read it!*"

Back behind bars Timothy Botham went. As the cell door slammed and bolted, he threw himself against it, and all the tension and fear and excitement and terror and loneliness and confusion and longing poured out of him in a wrenching, sobbing grief, safe from the eyes of the grown-up blokes, like, who never cried or anything like that because men don't do that sort of thing. Only sheilas. Timothy cried and cried, his tears mapping out his grief in spidery rivulets that snaked and latticed down the cold steel door.

After a while his heaving sobs subsided, and he rubbed his swollen eyes with wet fists. And then he heard a strange sound behind him. A sound that went something like:

"Mmmmmmmmm. Mmmmmmmmm."

He turned, and his eyes swept the room and came to rest on a spectacle that made them almost pop out of his head with shock. He immediately turned crimson with embarrassment and spun back to hide his mortified face against the door. That lady who'd talked to him in the workroom! There she was! Completely in the bloody raw! The utter nutty! Tied up and gagged and spread across the bed, like. Showing everything!

"*Mmmmmmmmmmmmmmm. Mmmmmmmmmmmmmm!*"

Timothy turned and, averting his eyes so that he didn't like embarrass the lady, he awkwardly approached the bed.

"*Mmmmmmmmmmmmm. MMMMMMMMMMMMMMM!!!*"

Still trying not to look at the ravishing form laid before him, he untied a handtowel that that filthy snake Henry Trembler had lashed tightly between her beautiful jaws. As he lifted the gag away, Celia Puffin's first words were: "*Thank God you found me! You don't know what I've been through!*"

"I didn't like come stickybeaking in here on purpose," Timothy hastened to explain. "I mean, I don't make a habit, like, of walking in on ladies when they're in the, well, you—Hey! What are all those teeth-marks?"

"Never mind that!" Celia gasped. "For Christ's sake, untie me!"

Timothy untied the strips of bedsheet knotted tightly at her wrists and lovely ankles. Celia massaged her slim arms, and then, with an exhausted groan, managed to sit up, her luscious breasts tumbling and quivering tautly like ripe you-know-whats. With a sud-

338

den rush of tears to her beautiful eyes, she flung her arms around Timothy and pulled him tightly to her, burying his head between them.

"You beautiful darling young man," she breathed throatily. "I'll never forget you for this! My prince!"

Which just goes to show. Some blokes spend their whole lives looking for it and never find it. Others spend most of their time knocking it back with a bloody stick.

Back in the auditorium, the moment of truth had finally arrived. The list of demands was ready and all it needed, as Harry and Noel Chisholm and Bull Sanderson and Murphy and virtually the entire prison population waited, breath poised and hopes hanging on a prayer, was for (Rev) Hunt to read them over the phone. Murphy handed the list to Hunt and Hunt said: "I had decided not to send you to Grafton, you know."

"Then I did the right thing after all, didn't I? Because I sure as hell wasn't going to stick around here."

(Rev) Hunt glanced down the written sheet that Murphy had handed him. "Do you think you really need all this superfluous language?"

"That's just to convince them that we're tough and horrible," Murphy explained. "I'll take some of it out if it bothers you."

"No. No. Nothing can possibly bother me now."

(Rev) Hunt picked up the telephone receiver and identified himself. He then said: "These are the demands—verbatim, you understand. 'We the leaders of the Prisoners Action Committee of Parramatta Jail do hereby demand the following conditions in return for the lives and safe return of our hostages: full and unconditional safe conduct out of this fucking jail; a limousine with an unarmed fucking police escort to take us to Bankstown Aerodrome; a six-seat light aircraft, preferrably a Cessna, fuelled and ready to fly, to be provided thereat; all fucking police and other hostile forces to be kept right away from the fucking area, or the Mayor goes off like a fucking thunderflash, and the Minister gets his next; a Qantas Boeing 747 with aircrew and hostesses—and none of those fucking male stewards—to be made available at Darwin Airport for Noel Chisholm, who will be flying the fucking Cessna . . ."

And so it went on. When the entire list had been read over,

(Rev) Hunt listened on the receiver for a few moments and said: "Very well." He then hung up. He turned to the tense, waiting group. He said: "They want time to consider the matter. They'll resume contact in a few minutes."

"You beauty!" Murphy hollered triumphantly, and the whole auditorium erupted with joy, with men laughing and cheering and dancing and slapping each other on the back. "We've got the buggers, Nole," Murphy cried excitedly. "They've gone for it hook line and sinker!"

Amid the happy pandemonium, (Rev) Hunt approached Bull Sanderson, who was standing quietly to one side, detached from the celebration. "Mr Sanderson," he said, "why on earth did you, of all men, do it?"

Sanderson frowned deeply and shook his head. "I dunno, Reverend. I keep asking myself that same question. Maybe I've been too close to these buggers for too long. They get under your skin after a while. They're the only blokes I really know! And I tell you something, Reverend—when I saw bloody Harry Pearce marching through all that thunder and lightning out there in that bloody Ned Kelly suit, well, I suddenly realised what we've all lost. We've lost a lot of the old spirit."

"Pherhaps we're becoming civilized, after all," (Rev) Hunt observed. "We can't go on being a Wild West show for ever."

"True," Sanderson conceded, and he coughed self-consciously and cast his eyes to the floor and kicked an imaginary pebble with his boot. "What about you, Mr Hunt? You can't very well stick around here after all this purgatory."

"Why not? There's much work that I have to do here. More Murphys to be taught that crime doesn't pay—enough."

Sanderson said: "I don't fancy a nice well-meaning bloke like you having to carry the shit-can for all this."

(Rev) Hunt smiled. "I'll survive, Mr Sanderson. I have a strong feeling that when all this is over, the Minister and the Mayor will be indebted to me for their lives. With a little bit of political extortion on my part, they'll be promoting me as a hero. I shall no doubt decline the offer of a safe political seat and remain the superintendent of this jail. If I can keep the two idiots alive."

Sanderson said: "You're technically a hostage too, you know. We could tie you up and push you around a bit if it came to the crunch. Make it look goo, like."

"Run away? Never. That would be a betrayal of everything I now believe in."

Then the telephone rang and an expectant hush descended once again upon the huge gathering. Everyone watched as (Rev) Hunt strode solemnly to the wall and lifted the receiver.

"This is it," Murphy whispered excitedly. "Freedom, here we come!"

(Rev) Hunt was nodding and murmuring at the receiver. Whatever they were saying, they were taking their time about it. Finally, (Rev) Hunt again said: "Very well," and hung up. He looked around intently at the waiting men.

"Well?" said Murphy. "What's the score?"

"They said *GO TO BUGGERY.*"

The silence, then, was absolutely devastating. Murphy's mouth hung open with shock. His features paled to the colour of sour milk. He looked crushed.

"OK," he said weakly. "Now we launch Phase Three. The Mayor goes for a bloody Burton. Maybe that'll change their minds a bit."

"I'm afraid that won't work," said (Rev) Hunt. "They said that under absolutely no circumstances, including the death of the hostages, will they back down in the face of such violent criminal activity and terrorist demands."

Murphy licked his lips nervously and said: "All right. If they wanna play it that way we'll take old Billy Puffin outside and put on a show for the TV cameras. Show how a bloody Government Minister goes up in smoke."

"Mr Puffin? From what the Premier just said I gathered the distinct impression that his, er, *demise* would be a godsend to his party's prospects in the coming State Election. And in fact the Premier and his government are mindful of the Minister's own courageous, personal gesture of uncompromising resistance to terrorism—isn't that right, Mr Puffin?"

Poor Puffin Billy. Talk about being well and truly hung by his own short and curlies. Because that was what he had done to himself.

"Ahem," he puffed brusquely. "I do recall an Occasion upon which I stated what was *then* My Position on certain matters pertaining to crime—of a *political nature*, you understand!"

"What Mr Puffin is referring to," said (Rev) Hunt, "is that only last year he organised a covenant in State Parliament of Members who declared in writing that if they ever fell into the hands of crimi-

341

nals or terrorists of a left-wing or Communist leaning, there should be *no bargaining* for their lives—that the State should stand firm and under no circumstances yield to any blackmail or political demands. The Premier asked me to express to you his greatest admiration, and that of his party colleagues, for the ultimate sacrifice that you are undertaking in the fight against violent anti-social behaviour. He spoke in terms of a State funeral, and promised that the next election will be fought from a strong law-and-order platform in memory of the man who gave his life that others might continue to live in peace and harmony."

Puffin Billy sank back once again to the floor and proceeded to stare blankly at his Political Future.

Around him, there was a long, terribly depressed silence. Everyone was looking at Kevin Murphy.

"Well," said Murphy. "It looks like Phase Four."

"Fuck your phases!" Harry Pearce yelled savagely. "How the bloody hell d'you think we're going to get out of this one? Fight our way out?"

Murphy said: "How did you guess? I was like leaving Phase Four up my sleeve for a real emergency." He turned to (Rev) Hunt. "Get them back on the bloody blower and tell them we're willing to let the hostages go. But we do it *our* way, or there'll be a real bloodbath in here." He spun on the Honourable William Lancelot Puffin. "That black heap you turned up in, that Daimler. Is it still outside?"

"My chauffeur had strict orders to wait for me," Billy said.

"It was out there an hour ago," said Bull Sanderson.

"Right. Great. Reverend? Tell 'em to get the Minister's driver to bring the Daimler into the jail. On his own, mind you. And he's to park it in the middle of the quadrangle. We'll transfer Billy and the Mayor there, and they can drive off out, nice and neat. But no funny business, tell 'em. No shooting, or we'll fight back and there'll be a lot more blood spilled before the night's over . . ." He turned to the cons crowding throughout the auditorium. *"Won't there, boys?"*

The boys didn't exactly go wild with support. One man jumped up and yelled: "Get stuffed, Murphy!"

"Well," Murphy muttered, "they can't say they didn't have their chance. OK, Reverend—you know what to do."

(Rev) Hunt picked up the telephone receiver and the hot-line warmed again.

thirty-two

HALF AN HOUR LATER THE SCENE WAS set for the finale of *The Vanishing Yahoo*. It was an eerie, surrealistic setting, one befitting a play with a title, no script and a number of surprises. Not to mention the physical and emotional state of the principal yahoo himself, Noel Chisholm, who, on a signal from the others, cautiously pushed open the auditorium door and gazed out into what he already suspected was to be the scene of his ultimate battle with God.

A blaze of floodlights, playing from all corners of the jail wall, spotlighting a frenetic ballet of moths, bugs and mozzies in the heavy, sultry heat of the night . . . A silence. A tense expectancy, a pent-up menace—as though the harsh lights themselves were electricity, and this was a place of execution. The cell blocks towered over the quadrangle, again reminding Chisholm of wheat silos beside a lonely floodlit outback railhead. Ahead, to his right, he could see the wall of the Blockhouse, and something else that disturbed him deeply—for, close to the wall, the powerful lighting etched a stardust effect over the shadowy, sprawled forms of Bruce Greenwood and The Beast, whom no-one had yet dared to carry away. Between the Blockhouse and the outer edge of the cell blocks, a wide asphalt desert roamed right up to the main wall; and such was the lighting effect here that Murphy's toll-hill and rambling bush scenes and the landscaped domain tumbling down behind the prominent, twin-spired, holy architecture of the Church of St John came alive like a theatrical backdrop.

Not so wonderful to behold were the rows of armed guards and cops paraded along that seemingly invisible wire that ran atop Murphy's murals—their forms silhouetted in black terror, their feet set firmly apart, their guns at their hips and little slivers of light dancing off their riot helmets and visors.

"Christ," Chisholm breathed, "which spaceship did *they* drop out of?"

And right in the centre of the quadrangle, spotlighted by the main beams, looking as though it had materialised out of a midnight Checkpoint Charlie scene in a sixties spy thriller, stood the black Daimler.

A metallic voice suddenly rang out from a PA system on the wall, shattering the dreamy stillness of the scene: "You may approach the vehicle. Do not try anything smart, or we'll shoot immediately to kill."

Chisholm turned in the doorway. Bull Sanderson, Murphy, Pearce and the two terrified hostages were hovering close to him.

"I'd say this is it," he murmured. A hand gently gripped his shoulder. It was (Rev) Hunt.

"Good luck," he said. "And thank you."

"Behold the colours," Chisholm said, shaking his hand, "and keep them alive in your mind."

They moved cautiously out into the heavy glare—Puffin Billy and the Mayor at their head as they took their first steps towards the distant limousine. Harry Pearce said softly to Kevin Murphy: "All right, smart-arse. What's next?"

"You should know," Murphy whispered. "You helped me stash all that explosive stuff in the wall, didn't you? He then reached slowly into his fatigues and pulled out the second of the two detonators that Timothy had built.

"OK," he said. "I admit it's a bit of a bloody gamble, but I reckon this'll blow that fucking wall to Kingdom Come. Then we'll go through there like a bloody Bondi tram in the Daimler and lose ourselves in the suburbs."

Harry said: "It's lucky you ended up in jail, you know. Otherwise you'd be in a bloody loonie-bin." He sniffed sardonically. "Still, I suppose it's better than surrendering. I reckon we've chalked up about another two hundred years in the clink by now."

Clinging together in a tight group—the Mayor and Billy Puffin pushed well ahead of them in case of accidental explosion—they gradually reached the tall black bodywork of the Daimler. The chauffeur sat stiffly at the wheel, staring straight ahead as though this was all part of his normal everyday duties, picking up two human bombs. Murphy stuck his head through the open window and said: "When I give the word, slide out fast and stay flat on the ground. And don't give us any trouble or you'll very quickly find yourself dead."

Murphy turned to the others and said very softly: "The moment that wall goes up, leap into the car and get down on the floor. Nole? You OK to drive?"

Noel Chisholm looked as though a breathalyser bag would blow

Derek Maitland

up in his teeth. "Never felt better," he assured Murphy, and he slapped the side of the huge limousine. "I'd prefer the Hillman Imp,
though. These big buggers have about as much manoeuvre in them as
a loaded ten-ton truck with no brakes. Anybody got any booze?"

"Do you really need it?"

"Is a snake's arsehole close to the ground?"

"Here," said the chauffeur nervously. "I keep this for medicinal
purposes." It was a half-empty bottle of Johnny Walker Red Label.
The chauffeur had been dangerously ill for the past half-hour or so.
Chisholm grabbed the bottle, up-ended it and chug-a-lugged it down
in one go. The entire contents disappeared in about ten seconds flat.

"*Cher-rrrrrriiiiiiiiisssssssssssstttttttt!!!*" he gasped, staggering as
though punched in the side of the head, recovering himself and pro-
ceeding to kick the hell out of the Daimler's rear tyres. "That stuff
tastes like pure bloody gasoline!"

From up on the wall, the PA system blared again: "What's holding you up down there?"

"Sheer willpower," Chisholm choked, supporting himself against
the side of the limousine.

"You have exactly thirty seconds to complete the transfer of hostages. Or we open fire!"

"OK, you cunts," Murphy breathed. "Get a load of this!"

He pressed the electronic detonator's red button.

And nothing happened.

So he pressed it again.

And again nothing happened.

And again.

And again.

And fucking again.

"You bloody dill-brain!" Harry Pearce hissed. "Can't you do *anything* right?"

"It's not my bloody fault!" Murphy protested. "Timothy made
the damn thing. Can I help it if it doesn't bloody work?"

Harry said very nastily: "And I bet you didn't even bother to ask
for a written guarantee, did you?"

Murphy made no reply. He just shrugged self-consciously and,
along with the others, gazed at the wall.

Bull Sanderson said: "Well. That's it, isn't it."

"You're right, Bull," said Noel Chisholm, struggling to prise himself from the side of the car. "End of play. Final curtain. We've laughed at the clowns, cried with the lovers and flung shit at the man in the funny bow tie. And now it's time to go home. Vanishing time."

He reached into the Daimler and prodded the chauffeur. "Start the black bugger up. And don't bother to radio the tower for takeoff instructions. This is going to be a bloody scramble."

As the engine burbled into life, Chisholm turned to address the assembled group. His eyes were crossed for night-flying. A gallant grin was on his owlish face. A breeze had sprung up in his sandy hair. Glory lay ahead.

"It was a great play, even if I do say so myself," he said. "Every movement nothing less than poetry in motion. Every bloody word a gem. And the crowds loved it. Pity I couldn't have found a part somewhere for John Gorton. Then maybe he wouldn't have ended up selling used cars. That's the trouble with this world, you know. People don't realise we only get one grab at the bloody smorgasbord, and then there's no second helpings. I learned that flying Spits. That's why I ended up in a discipline squadron flying Ansons."

Chisholm opened the door, dragged the chauffeur out and slipped in behind the wheel. He turned and gave Bull Sanderson the thumbs-up. "So long, Bull," he said. "Throw a few rocks on a tin roof for me." To the others, he said: "There are two other important things I've learned during my little struggle through life: Australia's a great place to look back on, and there must be a God—otherwise, why do I keep creating drive-in churches for Him?"

And, with a violence that gunned the Daimler's engine into an horrific howl and spun the rear wheels to a terrible high-pitched scream, Chisholm drove the accelerator to the floor and the huge car charged forward, heading straight for the jail wall. As the black juggernaut roared towards its target, the guards above opened fire, and a hail of pink tracers poured into the nose and bodywork of the speeding vehicle. Maybe they hit the pilot; maybe he stayed alive long enough to holler and yahoo with defiance and triumph as the thundering coffin on wheels headed straight for the wide, inviting pebbled driveway that led up to the main steps of the Church of St John and the nave beyond. For one beautiful, unforgettable moment, the Daimler actually appeared to be tearing up the driveway, fish-tailing violently as its wheels spun out of control on the pebbles—and then there was a catastrophic explosion and the car, the church, the wall, the guards and Noel Chisholm, the last of the yahoos, vanished in a tremendous ball of fire.

epilogue

THEY WATCHED THE GASOLINE FIRES ROAR AND swirl amid the rubble of a huge, gaping hole in the prison wall. Through the boiling smoke and flames they could see ambulances and police cars on fire and figures running wild in a mad, shrieking pandemonium. Kevin Murphy turned to Harry Pearce and said: "I hope God knows he's on his way."

Harry said: "You reckon He'd let a bloke like Nole into heaven?"

"Not if he's got any bloody sense. He let him onto earth, didn't he? And look what happened."

"Well, wherever he goes, I reckon he'll have a good time. He took that two thousand bloody bucks of mine with him."

Murph studied the blazing catastrophe that lay before them, the huge hole in the wall. "You feel like giving it a go?"

"I don't see why not. I can't see us getting very far, though."

"You never know. What about you, Bull?"

Bull Sanderson laughed and said: "Why not? We might be able to grab a bloody cold beer before they catch up with us."

"Yeah," said Harry, checking his watch. "If the bloody pubs aren't all closed by now."

Leaving the two thunderstruck hostages, they began strolling nonchalantly towards the smashed wall, the blaze playing straight into their bland, brazen faces.

"Hey, Harry," said Murph, "we still mates?"

"Oh definitely," Harry replied with just a hint of sarcasm. "You don't think I'd let a little balls-up like today come between us, do you?"

"I wonder if they'll let me paint in Grafton."

"I dunno. I'm sure you'll be able to come up with a brilliant bloody scheme to get us out of there, anyway."

"No," said Murphy. "Not out of there. No-one gets out of there. No, I reckon the time to do it is on the way. I've heard they fly you up there in these special departmental planes. Now, I reckon if we could get hold of a couple of those little tear gas gadgets that the Yanks put out for women, you know, for when they're mugged in the street and we hit the guards on the plane with it just at the right time, like—"

"Shut up, Murph," Harry Pearce murmured. "Just do us all a favour and shut the fuck up."